SONG OF THE STORM PETREL

BOOK THREE: THE SEABIRDS TRILOGY

JESSICA GLASNER

Printed in the United States of America

First Printing: 978-1-7337629-5-3

Hope House Press

www.hopehousepress.co

www.glasnerhouse.co

Dearest Emily, Madeline, and Hope
Where would I be without sisters and cousins? The three of you have
inspired a lifetime of stories.

∾

And to Chloe
When I was ready to quit, I thought of you and kept writing.

A HISTORICAL NOTE

*P*icture this: It is 1944. Piper, Peter, and the Adleman Sisters move like phantom chess pieces among the smoldering embers of World War II. How will they resume normal lives when the war ends? Will they have a home? A place to rebuild? It is difficult to see through the dark smoke of charred dreams and memories of lost loved ones.

In Europe, Nazi Germany borders on defeat and utter collapse. It takes its last stand against the Allied Forces under U.S. General Dwight Eisenhower. The Americans, forced out of isolation by Japan's surprise attack on Pearl Harbor, lead the charge against the Germans in the Atlantic; and the aggressive and ruthless Japanese Imperial forces rapidly overtaking the Pacific.

Guadalcanal.

Okinawa.

The Coral Sea.

Iwo Jima.

Battles that will go on to live on in infamy, forever.

The war in the Pacific against the Japanese is different. Brutal.

Inhumane. American and Allied prisoners of war face torture, slave labor, disease, malnutrition, and execution. The Americans suffer total casualties of over 250,000 deaths, missing, or wounded. Close to ten times that figure for the Japanese.

Yet even after Victory Day, when the Germans surrendered to the Allies, the Japanese Imperial Government refuses to relent. Young Japanese pilots crash their fighter planes into U.S. ships. Soldiers facing insurmountable odds refuse to surrender and die holding meaningless positions. The *kamikaze* spirit drives their soldiers, sailors, and pilots to choose suicidal missions over surrender or failure in battle.

Then the United States develops a weapon of unspeakable mass destruction. The atomic bomb. Even in its early stages of development, one bomb dropped by a single plane can obliterate a major city in a poisonous firestorm hotter than one thousand suns. But is it moral to use this weapon? Will the Japanese surrender absent a show of force so violent and so extreme it forces them to relinquish prideful Imperial honor and embrace the reality of defeat and take responsibility for their people?

In the summer of 1944, no one knows the answers to these questions.

'The End' is a welcome phrase; but what comes after 'The End,' is terrifyingly mysterious.

Several characters are real, such as Hannah Senesh, Bob Hope, Myrna Loy, and General Douglas MacArthur, among others. All conversations and scenarios involving these characters are fictional unless otherwise noted. However, I have done my best to adhere to the spirit of the times and the historicity of the real persons. I've also taken some creative license with some locations, dates, and events.

With the future hanging precariously in the balance, Peter and Piper must learn to trust in the Lord with all their hearts, believing that He will not only show them the path but make it straight as well.

After the fire is over, when the destruction ceases, they, like us, must believe that God can rebuild what was torn down and that He alone can set right what was twisted and mangled by the sins of men.

FIRST MOVEMENT

"Since once I sat upon a promontory,
And I heard a mermaid on a dolphin's back
Uttering such dulcet and harmonious breath,
That the rude sea grew civil at her song,
And certain stars shot madly from their spheres
To hear the sea-maid's music."

-A Midsummer Night's Dream[1]

PREFACE

Dear Little Samuel,

I'll tell you now, I'm no writer.

I still prefer photographs over words. A face staring back at you always seems to say more than a paragraph or two... or three... ever could. I leave the romance and adventure to my aunt. She's the one who has the ability to draw out mystery and intrigue, to create characters out of words that come alive right in front of you. Not me. I wish I could. But I can't. All that said, it was Edie who told me that I had to write this one. If I didn't, no one else would.

I'll never forget her, standing on the pier, red hair wildly blowing about her face.

"You're the one missing, Piper. Only you can tell your story the way it really happened. Without your voice, it's just a collection of disjointed memories. You're as much a part of this," she pressed the manuscript into my hand, "as Horatio and I and each one of your cousins."

"But it's supposed to be a collection of the soldiers' memories! To tell about the war... " I answered.

"We were there too, Piper. Maybe not on the front, like these boys. We were on a different front, but that does not mean it is not important. Tell

7

the story, our story, right alongside theirs. Then you'll have something that matters. You'll have something true."

"But you are the writer, Edie!"

"Not this time. It's your turn, Piper." The ship's horn blasted, warning all the passengers that it was time to board. She drew me in for a final embrace, and then held me back, examining me at arm's length. "I do believe, Agatha dear, you might be my protege after all." Slightly taken aback with her use of my real name, I watched as she, Horatio, the children, and Ferguson disappeared up the gangplank.

Tell my story? How could I? I wouldn't even know where to begin! And so, I pushed the manuscript aside... hoping to forget it.

I couldn't. Neither could Peter.

For days, Samuel, I let the manuscript sit on the shelf.

Months after we'd made the move, as I lay flat on my back in bed, Peter came in from where he'd been studying and bluntly asked, "Aren't you going to do it?"

"Do what?"

"Write the story of everything that happened?"

"I can't, Peter," I floundered, looking out the window. "I'm too busy."

"Too busy?" He stepped into my line of vision with a look on his face that clearly informed me he knew as well as I that I was not too busy.

"That's too bad. I had no idea bedrest was taking up all of your mental energy."

I groaned. "That's not very funny."

"Honey, it's a story that deserves to be told." He sat down on the edge of our bed.

"I can't... I don't know how to tell it the right way." Cautiously, I voiced the fear that had kept me from the typewriter to begin with.

"Doesn't matter. Tell it the best you can. People are smart. They'll fill in the gaps." He patted my lap. "I should think a typewriter would fit right here, don't you?"

"But, Peter -" I protested, "there are so many of us!"

"Imagine how it all happened. Jump around. Go from the first person

to the second person. You don't have to write like other people. Make it easy on yourself."

"That's rather unconventional."

"So is the story. You were the one who said you wanted to put words to your photographs, remember?"

What could I say? He had me there.

"I've never known you to be scared of anything before. I think you're supposed to do this. Don't put it off any longer. Write it now, while the memories are still fresh. Write it before you forget."

"But who is going to want to read it?"

"Lots of people."

I stared, not fully believing him.

"Do it for me. Do it for little Samuel. He'll want to know how we got here."

"How do you know it's not a little girl?" I smirked slightly.

"Just a feeling." He winked.

So now that you've been duly warned, little Samuel, when the day comes, and you read this, you'll have mercy on your poor mother who is still not a writer. But that doesn't mean she didn't have a story to tell. It may not be told perfectly, but it will be told, and that's what matters.

Now... where to start? Not with 'once upon a time'... that's cliche, and it's not true. This really happened, and it happened last year. I need an opening line...

All right. I have one:

"There comes a time when the people of your past come running up behind you and collide headfirst into your present in a way that affects your future, unalterably, forever."

Not too shabby for an opening line, don't you think?

I'll love you till the day my story on earth ends,

Agatha

CHAPTER 1

MALAHINI

There comes a time when the people of your past come running up behind you and collide headfirst into your present in a way that affects your future, unalterably, forever.

For me, that time arrived in late June, 1944, on the Hawaiian island of Honolulu. And it began much less dramatically than it ended.

"So, you'll take it?" The little Hawaiian landlady looked at Peter and I questioningly. She had beautiful smooth brown skin and deep set brown eyes.

"If you bring it down $25 a month, you have a deal," Peter said, stuffing his hands in his pockets. "You think they'll be okay with it?" He glanced at me.

Shrugging, I imagined Horatio and Edie in the living room. Yes, I thought. It would do. It wouldn't be as luxurious as they were used to, but nothing was these days. Besides, we didn't have time to find anything else. Horatio was being sent with a few others in His Royal Majesty's Service to work with General MacArthur to retake the Philippines and would be here in less than a week.

The old woman shook her head and looked up at the wooden fan whirling above. "I just installed those. Brand new. And the roof is good! You will find nothing like this on the island. All the other big houses are already rented. So many officers and their wives! You don't rent it, I'll find someone else to tomorrow."

"I guess… I guess we'll have to take it," my husband sighed.

The last tenants had been, to put it lightly, hard on the place. The rattan couches were worn. A layer of grime covered the windows. I was afraid to look in the icebox in the kitchen.

"But you'll send someone to clean it, yes?" I asked hopefully, glancing about the old plantation style home.

"It is come 'as is.'" She put her hand on her hip triumphantly. She was a shrewd negotiator.

"How much to have it cleaned?" Peter looked at her.

"Ten dollars. Cash. No war bonds."[2]

"You drive a hard bargain." Peter pulled out a ten dollar bill from his wallet. The original plantation owner had no wife or children or anyone else in his life and had left it to his faithful housekeeper, now the landlady. The war had been good to her. She had made a lot of money renting out the Big House.

"By Tuesday, okay. That's when my uncle shows up. We need the house ready by then." The old woman grabbed the bill and marched out the front door, the screen slamming in her wake. She called out, "No problem."

I looked down at the dark wood floors, then up at the honey-hued paneled ceiling and the fan going around and around. The large windows opened up to the view of a green lawn, palm trees, and then, further down the hill, the Pacific Ocean. It was pleasant and tropical, and once it had a good cleaning, it would be perfect. Smiling, I glanced at Peter, "Edie will love it. She'll be inspired."

"It's overpriced," Peter huffed.

"It's the war." I answered looking about the room. The vast pineapple plantation had been broken up into plots just before the war started. The army had bought up most of them and put together hundreds of bungalows almost overnight after the attack on Pearl Harbor. Housing on the island was in high demand. There wasn't room for all the servicemen—the 'invaders.' In truth, there was barely room for anyone.

"I can't believe it's been two years since we've seen them... Two years since Scotland."

Peter looked towards the ocean through the window. The beginnings of another glorious sunset, burning orange and violet, began to dance over the waves. "Two long years." He exhaled. "We ought to dig up a record player. I don't see one."

"At least it's mostly furnished. You know how hard it is to find furniture these days." I reached out and took his hand. "How about we go home, sailor?"

He smiled, swinging my arm playfully, "Aye, aye, mon capitan!"

Home, for the last year and a half, was Peter's dream come true. A 30 ft. Broads Sailing Yacht, 'just right for two,' as the previous owner so glibly explained. Well, afterall, Peter had said, there *were* only two of us, plus Founder, who brought it to just three of us. Actually, at 85 pounds, the dog could practically count for two on her own.

I followed him outside and leaned against the wall of the porch, painted a faded light blue. "It's nice to be in a house again."

He looked back at me. "You don't like the boat?"

"I love the boat. I was just saying it's nice to be in a house again." I stopped and bit my tongue. Peter adored the *Malahini* and was content to live on the sea. I, however, was not. I'd been waiting for a house of my own for a long time. I'd almost given up believing we'd ever be anywhere permanently.

For a month after we bought it, he'd polished and shined and scraped and painted. The inside, made of dark paneled wood, was split into two rooms, the ceiling so low in both that Peter had to hunch over or risk hitting his head. The back room was just wide enough for our bed. The front room barely held the little stove and icebox and a table (which was taken up with Peter's typewriter). It didn't really matter though, the weather in Honolulu was so mild most of the time that we ate up on the deck, our feet dangling into the water of the blue lagoon where we'd docked for months.

Even though we didn't have a house, we did have quite the backyard. And for that, I was grateful.

~

"HOW'S IT GOING?" I struggled to pry the lid off a can of spam later that evening. Peter put a dime novel down and reached over to try his hand at it.

I looked at him. "Aren't you supposed to be studying?"

"Do you know how dry that stuff is?" He huffed slightly and worked on the can. "I don't think I'm cut out for business."

"I know. But still, you've got to graduate."

"Do I advise you on how to take a picture for *The Honolulu Herald*?"

I shook my head no.

"Then don't tell me how to study." He passed me the opened can and can opener.

He certainly was in a snippy mood. I raised one eyebrow and shot him a look as I began to mix the spam with some mayonnaise. "I thought you had an exam coming up?"

Peter's injury sustained in battle on the North African Front was severe. He could walk, and the limp was now almost imperceptible, but he'd been rendered physically unfit for duty. He had, as evidenced by the thick stack of books we had stuffed under our mattress, continued his education through the Harvard Extension School. Eventually, he'd have a Bachelor of Arts in Business. Not that he was enjoying it—I often found my husband looking listlessly out at sea or at the destroyers in the harbor.

"Sorry. I just..." He trailed off before locking eyes with me. "You know."

"Yeah. I know."

He opened up the small porthole, and a soft warm breeze

filtered through the cabin as I thought back to where we had been two years before. That strange morning when Amos appeared out of nowhere. When the usual radio program was interrupted to tell us that Pearl Harbor had been bombed beyond recognition. The next few days were hazy. We manned the lighthouse day and night, me, Peter, Grace, and Amos. Each of us taking turns, one by one, protecting the cold coastline of Maine.

Grace never told me what happened between her and Amos. Not really. He left for Washington DC to make his report for the RAF and we never heard from him again. She returned to Palestine a week after that. How she organized the necessary papers and flights and voyages, I'll never know. She had friends in high places.

Long story short, two weeks later, Peter and I, sleep deprived and on edge from our constant vigil against German subs lurking along our shore, were officially relieved by the Coast Guard. Edie's lighthouse was, for the duration of the war, back in service, and Peter and I were left homeless.

It was then that I got a call from *The Herald*. They needed a photographer because their man had just been drafted, and they'd heard through the grapevine, well, Horatio actually, that I was good. The job was mine. (He and Don were old friends from Horatio's glory days as president of Scottish Lobster when Horatio would run full page color ads in Don's paper, and they still stayed in touch.) All I had to do was take a train cross-country and catch a flight to Honolulu.

Of course, there was no housing on the island for business students studying through correspondence or photographers, even photographers for *The Honolulu Herald*. But there was plenty of room on the ocean. Hence, the purchase of the boat; our little paradise on water for the last year and a half.

Peter named it the "*Malahini*," which is Hawaiian for "stranger." He said he felt like a stranger on earth these days. With no clear direction or purpose he could think of for the future, I didn't blame him.

In the meantime, I took pictures of the Navy and the war effort. Peter studied when he had to. We swam in the morning and fished in the afternoon. We ate spam sandwiches and pineapple. On Fridays, we went dancing at the Tiki Bar, and on Sundays we went to the little white church nestled in the shadow of the volcano. We had friends on the boat for little sailing trips out onto the open sea, and friends had us to their military bungalows for hot dogs and Cokes. Everyone, everywhere, was Navy. Everyone except for us. Life was the war. And the war was life.

But Peter and I had our lagoon. And when we were there, you would never know there was a war. Except, you always knew. The battleships sunk by the Japanese on that fateful December day two years before were always beneath us, creating a watery grave to thousands of our best and our bravest. They hadn't had a chance in the world.

The sandwiches assembled, we crawled out of the hold, with Founder at our heels, and eased down onto the deck. Peter wore his white linen shirt rolled up over the elbow, and I wore my red polka dot swimsuit and shorts. I leaned up against him and kissed his lips before looking down at my sandwich. A year and a half in Hawaii had left us both tanned and freckled. My skin used to be the color of the inside of a slice of bread. Now, it was the shade of crust.

"And for today's news bulletin," a newscaster's voice came in clearly over the wireless we had on the deck. "US troops who took the Aleutian island of Attu from the Japanese nearly a month ago continue to make headway in the Pacific. The Pope condemns the Allies for targeting civilians in what he deems 'terror' bombings. Legendary British screen actor Leslie Howard, serving with the RAF, was shot down by Axis planes. Soviet Forces are now employing female pilots in combat. Finally, General de Gaulle insists that the French intend to win liberty for themselves from the Nazis without the help of the Allies. Thank you and good evening."

Peter threw a stick into the water, and Founder dove off the boat to fetch it.

"Grace would sure be jealous of those Soviet women fighter pilots." I took a bite.

"It's for the best she's on the ground right now. I don't think it's responsible to put her up in the sky with a couple of machine guns." He laughed, and I had to agree.

"And now," a husky female voice said, "it's time for the Zero Hour!" Some peppy jazz music started.

Founder grabbed hold of the stick and clambered to shore. Running up the little gangplank, she shook her fur wildly. "Cut it out!" Peter laughed and threw the stick again.

"What's this?" I asked.

"What?"

"The Zero Hour?'

Peter shrugged. "Skits, music. You know. Entertainment. It's broadcast from Japan. The guys think it's a laugh."

I sat up straighter.

The voice began again. "Greetings, everybody! This is your little playmate - I mean your bitter enemy - Ann, with a program of dangerous and wicked propaganda for my victims in Australia and the South Pacific. Stand by, you unlucky creatures, here I go!"[3]

With that, the show plunged into a show tune medley.

"That is bizarre." I stared at the radio, surprised.

Peter nodded. "The Japanese think this sort of thing will sap our morale. But everybody thinks it's more funny than anything else. She tells everybody that the women at home are out with other guys. There never seems to be any real propaganda."[4]

"I don't like it."

"I'll turn on something else." He finished the last bite of his sandwich and reached over to adjust the dial. Suddenly, the soft strings to a big band came on.

Peter tilted his head thoughtfully to the side and looked at me. He hummed along to the slow, sad melody, one of those songs everyone knows but no one knows the name of, just slightly off key. Abruptly, he stood up and helped me to my feet. On the tiny deck, he took me in his arms, and we shuffled more than actually danced to the music.

We stood there, swaying to the music in the fading light of the Pacific sun, the *Malahini* bobbing gently as the evening tide rolled in. Our faces were awash in a blaze of pinks and blues and purples as the clouds of an early summer rain thundered in the distance.

I didn't hear the song anymore. All I saw were his eyes and the sun reflecting in them. I leaned my head on his chest.

Whether my feelings were right or not, everyday I felt relieved he was wounded. I was relieved he limped because he slept in my arms at night. I was relieved he had nothing more important to do than study or fish because I saw him every morning when I woke up. I couldn't tell him. I could never tell him, because the fact that he was not out there with all the other boys risking their lives for our country, for the world, was killing him. Everyday it was killing him. But he was brave. He was trying. He was, he told me, trusting God even though he did not understand.

But I was relieved.

I did not want to go to bed alone. Or wake up alone.

Drops, big and fat, began to fall. In Hawaii, it seemed that rain came and left without warning.

Peter brushed my damp hair away from my face. "Maybe we ought to go inside."

"I love you, Peter."

"I know."

CHAPTER 2

'ANAKALA AND 'ANAKE

*I*t was my favorite time to be in the office.

The preparation of the Sunday edition of *The Honolulu Herald* was in full swing. There was a lot to cover. The fighting in Europe. The fighting in the Pacific. Rationing and cutbacks at home. And, of course, who'd won the fight at the Gardens. Boxing was big in those days. Every room in *The Herald*'s headquarters was buzzing.

In the radio room, a shortwave radio operator received and recorded messages from correspondents all over the world. In another room firsthand accounts from the Pacific were sent to globally syndicated papers. Today, it was all about D-Day. The Allied forces had just invaded Northern France with a heroic beach landing in Normandy. The details of the landing were still coming through days later.

Next door, a cartographer consulted a map of the war in Italy while an artist worked on a photograph of President Roosevelt that would be printed on the front page. The photograph came from the darkroom where a technician transferred every picture to a zinc plate, including those I took. There was the composing room, where the newsprint was set by hand before being carried down to the press after it was copy-read in the newsroom. And that was just the tip of the iceberg. There were the pressmen who ran the press, the writers, the editors... And somehow, in the chaos and confusion, the editor-in-chief Donald O'Leary put together a pretty solid paper. I don't say completely solid because there was no getting around it, *The Honolulu Herald* was no *New York Times*. But what we lacked in talent and professionalism, we made up for in location.

Location, location, location, Don was apt to say in his booming voice.

O'Leary was an explosive type. He had high blood pressure and three ex-wives. Nearing 65, his volatility and passion exceeded that of most 20-year-olds. He had one love. The news. But a lack of real talent had kept him out of the big leagues. He'd moved to Honolulu after he'd been fired from his fifth reporting job for not meeting deadlines, vowing to 'start his own dad-gummed paper!' and hence, *The Honolulu Herald* was born, consisting of Donald and an ancient printing press he'd bought by hawking everything he owned, which wasn't much.

Donald was among those businessmen who actually benefited from the war. With all of the action shifting to the Pacific, *The Honolulu Herald* experienced extreme and sudden growth, and with it, an inflated sense of importance from its editor-in-chief and founder. *The Herald* was the only real newspaper in the Pacific. Because of that, it boasted readers as far as the UK, which was remarkably impressive.

It currently filled the first two floors of an old bank downtown. With the onset of sudden growth, the staff of 4 had grown to 40, me included. Don O'Leary attributed all of this to his expert management, but most of his employees knew better. I could hear him shouting from down the hall, and inwardly braced myself.

His secretary, a pretty young Hawaiian woman named Julie, shot me a warning look. "He's in a mood."

"I can tell." I took my hat off and left it on her desk. "What's happening?"

"The deli sent him a turkey sandwich instead of egg salad."

I rolled my eyes and plunged in. There he was, standing behind his desk, red-faced, shouting into the receiver of his phone. "And if you don't do it right next time, I'll write a review myself! Front page!" He looked up and put his hand over the receiver, speaking in a perfectly natural tone. "Piper? What are you doing here?"

Before I could answer, his hand was off the receiver and once more he started shouting. "You better bring me a new one. And don't think the delivery boy is getting a tip!"

He slammed the phone down and looked at me. "So," he spread his hands out, "talk all ready."

"I need a day off, Don."

"What do you mean, 'a day off, Don?'" His eyes narrowed. "I don't pay you to take days off. Your whole life is a day off. You and that student husband of yours swim and traipse around the jungle all day, taking pictures with that pretty camera."

"Thursday." I continued unfazed, knowing I was the best photographer he had.

"You've got the flag ceremony at the base on Thursday."

"Give it to Vinny."

"And why should I give the Flag ceremony to Vinny?"

"Horatio is being sent with a few others in His Royal Majesty's Service to work with General MacArthur and retake the Philippines. I want to throw them a welcome party."

Donald O'Leary, rarely at a loss for words, did not speak. His jaw opened slightly, and he leaned forward in his chair, scratching his balding head. "Horatio didn't tell me he was assigned the job!"

"Consider this insider information." I turned on my heel and marched out.

"I want to be invited to that party!" he shouted after me. "Your uncle and I go way back, kiddo."

"This one is strictly family. But I'll give you the scoop, okay?

Front page feature, *Vice Admiral of His Royal Majesty's Fleet to Sail with American Fleet.*" I smiled, thinking of Horatio. Like many men of his generation, my aunt's husband never expected to witness, much less participate in, *another* world war. But the unexpected had come, and he had answered the call of duty to protect and defend his country for the second time in his life, to the end, if need be.

"You get me that story, and I'll give you a raise!"

"I'm not a writer, remember, but a picture is worth a thousand words." I laughed. We both knew a raise was out of the question.

Julie held my hat and purse out, and I grabbed both with a jovial, "See ya later, Julie."

"What are you so happy about?" She swept her long braid back behind her and swiveled her chair around.

"My aunt and uncle are arriving from Scotland."

"'Anakala and 'anake!" She smiled and explained, seeing my questioning stare, "'Uncle' and 'aunt,' in Hawaiian. You must be very fond of them."

"'Anakala and 'anake," I repeated slowly. "And yes, I am very, very fond of them!" With that, my hat in hand, I trotted back down the hall, past the desks of copy editors and writers, down the stairs and through the pressroom, clanging and sputtering, glorying in the moment.

PETER ROUNDED THE BEND, holding the steering wheel to the slightly used Ford Woody we had bought in Horatio's name the day before lightly with one hand. He glanced back at Edie and Horatio in the backseat. In the twenty minutes we'd been driving, Edie had not stopped talking.

"Isn't it just wonderful? Just wonderful!" Edie gushed, caressing the necklace made of flowers around her neck. "There were all these people at the airport, and they threw these over our necks and kissed out cheeks! Flowers behind their ears. Flowers around their necks. Flowers growing everywhere! Horatio, you have taken me to paradise!" She was beaming and fanning herself with a Japanese style paper fan. "I don't remember the last time I was this warm. How *do* you do it, Piper?"

"They are called 'lei,'" Peter said, referring to the necklace. "They give them to all newcomers on the island." He grinned and said, "If a girl is wearing a flower in her left ear, it means she's taken. On the right, she's available."

"Horatio," she commanded, "we've got to change the flowers to our left ears. We are both taken!"

"Of course, dear." He patted her shoulder and moved the orchid. I noticed her auburn hair had a few flecks of grey in it. But her face was radiant and youthful as ever.

In front of us, the pretty blue plantation house sat, nestled like a painting in the middle of the palm grove.

"Is that it?" Edie exclaimed, her pleasure obvious.

"Don't get too excited," I answered. "It needs some work. But it was the best we could come up with on such short notice."

"We won't do one solitary thing! The house is absolutely perfect exactly as it is! Why look at it!"

It was lovely, and so I nodded. But she hadn't seen the couches yet.

Peter pulled up the drive and hopped out, opening up the back door for Edie and I. Edie stepped out, wearing a lovely light cotton dress. She ran up the steps to the house like a schoolgirl, delighted and laughing. "So, what are we having for dinner, Piper?"

"You'll have to ask John."

"John?" Horatio asked.

On the porch, an elderly Japanese man appeared, waving. "John Yamaguchi," I said to Horatio, "Horatio Macleay, your new boss."

Horatio eyed me warily and extended his hand. "Nice to meet you, boss." John grinned.

"You speak English?" Horatio asked, surprised.

"Born and raised in California," he said. "But my wife's family is still in Japan. We've been back to visit a few times."

Edie was beside us now. "And how did you get to Hawaii?"

"I was a U.S. Navy cook for years. Recently retired. We both like Honolulu. Seemed like a great place to slow down. But slowing down was not exactly a great idea. I was driving my wife crazy sitting at home all the time. When I saw the want-ad for a cook, butler, and all-around-help sort of guy, I took the bait."

Horatio exhaled. "Well then, Mr. Yamaguchi, welcome aboard."

John smiled again and bowed.

"So, what's for dinner, Johnny?" Peter asked.

"I made you a real Hawaiian meal. Spam, sticky rice, and macaroni salad."

"Absolutely wonderful." Edie smiled approvingly. And then, as a second thought, she added, "No vegetables?"

"I've got pineapple for dessert."

Edie stifled a grin. I knew she was thinking that pineapple was not a vegetable.

I opened the screen door. "Vegetables for dinner aren't really the fashion. They like lots of spam and mayonnaise and fried food in Hawaii."

"I guess it could be worse." Horatio stepped into the living room. The newly installed fan was spinning around and around. "The rations in England have meant that Ferguson and your mother have figured out how to cook potatoes about a hundred different ways. I'll eat anything as long as it's not potatoes."

John followed Peter and Edie inside, bowed once more, and returned to the kitchen while Peter pointed the way to the master bedroom. Edie's sharp eyes took it in. The window, open to the view of the ocean. The slightly lumpy mattress. The little writing desk.

"Your mother is a saint, staying with children," she said, looking in the little mirror and fixing a stray hair while Peter and Horatio returned to the car to get their luggage. "She sent you something— a surprise. It's wrapped. And I've rather exciting news for you too."

I leaned in the doorframe, watching her graceful movements.

"So, how are they?" I asked.

"The baby is growing everyday. Well, she's not a baby. She's three. She walks and talks and has the most adorable dimples. And the twins and Annie are speaking English like pros. You'd be proud."

"Are you concerned about being away for a few months?"

"Of course I'm concerned. What mother wouldn't be?" She frowned. "But I insisted. I say, if Jean MacArthur can stay with her husband, I can stay with mine! Did you know she rode in a PT boat after the siege in the Philippines to escape the Japanese?"

"But the president made Jean go to Australia after all of that. He thought it was too dangerous for her..." I said.

She stopped. "But the president can't order me to do anything. I am a Brit now, remember?"

"You have dual citizenship."

"You don't have to remind Roosevelt of that. What he doesn't know won't hurt him." She sighed. "And of course, it's not safe to lug a bunch of 'kinderlach,' to quote your cousins, all over kingdom come. I'm not an idiot. They are settled in Scotland. Happy as children can be. As you know, your father has become indispensable. The local doctor was drafted, and now your dad is treating everyone." She paused and sighed quite seriously. "And besides, your mother is better at the whole children thing than I ever was or could be."

"I doubt that very much."

"I'm only saying that so I don't cry." She steadied herself on the counter. "It's just a few months... We all have to make sacrifices nowadays. Of course," she looked out the window, "it certainly is pretty." Her eyes misted over. "I may even take up painting again."

"Having a relapse of writer's block?"

She faced me, blotting her eyes. "Something like that, I guess."

Peter thrust his head through the door. "Johnny's got dinner on."

"Already?" I exclaimed. "She hasn't had a chance to freshen up or anything."

"I'll take a bath later. I want to look at you and Peter for a while. I've had a deficit of your faces that only some quality time will fill." She put a hand on my cheek. Hand in hand, we followed Peter to the small table John had set up on the porch. It was sunset, and the food smelled delicious.

"Thank you, Mr. Yamaguchi," Horatio said as the cook bowed and returned inside. Horatio bowed his head and prayed, "Bless oh Lord, these thy gifts, and us to thy service."

"Amen," we echoed.

Horatio looked up and began cutting into his spam. He motioned backwards to the house with his knife, "Mr. Yamaguchi? He is Japanese, yes?"

"American of Japanese descent," I answered.

"How do you know he's... loyal?" He was deeply serious.

Peter answered for me. "John is a strong Christian. He goes to our church. We've known him for a while. Piper posted the job notice in the church bulletin."

Horatio did not look fully convinced. "I didn't know there were any Japanese left in Hawaii."

"Only 2,000 of Hawaii's Japanese population were put into internment camps," Peter answered. "For the record, there are nearly 160,000 Japanese on the island."

"So many?" Edie asked.

"A lot of the Japanese are Christians who left Japan because of persecution. Like John's grandparents." He paused before continuing, "On the mainland, a lot more were taken into custody."

"What do you mean," Edie put a spoonful of macaroni salad in her mouth, "*custody?*"

"Hawaii has officially been under martial law ever since Pearl Harbor was attacked. The whole island is practically an army base. There are a lot of people of Japanese descent on the islands. American citizens and otherwise. We really aren't terribly far from Japan, all things considered. It gets tricky knowing who is loyal and who is not."[5]

"But custody?" She looked at me.

"Many of the Japanese on the mainland have been put into internment camps," I answered.

"You mean, like *concentration* camps?"

"Well... yes. But they aren't like those in Europe. Everyone is afraid because of Pearl Harbor," I tried to explain. "The Japanese pilots at Pearl Harbor flew their planes into our ships, remember? 'Kamikazes,' they call them. They don't fight fair, and they practically sunk our entire fleet."

Her eyebrows raised. "Are there camps here in Hawaii?"

"There is a camp or two. But they've only sent a few away, like I said," Peter answered. "Hawaii's different."

"Most of the people here are just like John. They don't speak Japanese. They are loyal Americans. Why, his son is serving in the 442nd Infantry Regimental Combat Team. It's a new all-Japanese American unit."

"So, they are keeping some locked up and sending others to war." Horatio shook his head, slowly understanding the complexity of the situation.

"Some want to prove their loyalty, even in the midst of racial persecution." Peter sniffed. "Welcome to the Pacific."

It was a strange business. Many times I had wondered why only the Japanese had been singled out. Why not the German Americans? Or the Italian Americans? But then, as Peter reminded me, it was not the Germans or Italians who had bombed Pearl Harbor or who had come close to destroying our entire Pacific Fleet, not to mention the hundreds of planes that were parked on the nearby airfields. It was not the Germans or Italians who, nine hours after Pearl Harbor, attacked, invaded, and overran the Philippines, a commonwealth under American control.

After a horrendous siege, no medicine, no food, and no ammunition left, the American soldiers left on the Bataan Peninsula, starving and sick with awful tropical diseases, were captured as prisoners of war and forced to march for days without food or water. Thousands died. Conditions in the camps were too terrible to speak of. And all this was not at the hands of the Germans or Italians but the Japanese.

"I'm not so biased to not recognize that ethnicity doesn't implicate political sympathies. And he's a great cook." Edie sighed sadly. "Well, I like him, and I'm glad you've hired him. I haven't had macaroni salad in years. Not since moving to Scotland, actually." She looked out across the lawn to the ocean, deep blue and purple in the fading light. "I can't believe anyone would want to fight in a place as beautiful as this."

John came out and refilled the cups with water before setting down an elaborately carved pineapple proudly in the center, asking Edie if he should put on a pot of coffee.

"Most definitely, Mr. Yamaguchi. And make it strong, will you?"

"Ah," he nodded, "long night ahead? E'ōlelo nui, yes?"

She looked up. "E ōlelo nui?"

"It means, 'make much talk' in Hawaii. I've picked up a little Hawaiian here and there."

Nodding, her eyes twinkled. "Indeed! And how beautifully, beautifully spoken. I am going to learn Hawaiian. And you will have to teach me!"

He bowed again and chuckled kindly. "I like you, Mrs. Macleay. I think we are going to get on just fine."

After John had left, Edie turned her attention to me and Peter, folded her hands on the table, and leaned forward as if she was preparing to share a great secret. It was so subtle a shift, we almost missed it.

Pausing for dramatic effect, she inhaled and then exhaled. "Guess who is coming!"

"Coming where?" Peter shot me a look.

"Here, of course!" Edie smiled, enjoying the moment.

I looked at Peter and could tell he had no idea what was up. We waited, expectantly.

"Your cousins are coming. All three of them!"

"They are what!" I was completely taken unawares. "How? Why?"

"Any chance you've heard the song, 'Chick, Chick, Chick, Chick Chicken!' on the radio?" Horatio asked, an amused expression on his lips.

"Of course," Peter answered. "It's on every time you turn on the radio. Has been for the past month."

"The trio who recorded it," I thought for a second, "what is their name again? The Macleay Sisters! Of course." I chuckled. "How could I forget a name like that. It's your last name." I put two and two together. "You don't mean?"

"Indeed, I do," Edie grinned from ear to ear. "It's our own Katrine, Lorelei, and Grace. They are the hippest young swingers of the season. They arrive tomorrow morning to join the USO show leaving from Honolulu."

I leaned back in my chair, letting it all sink in. It had been nearly two years since I'd seen Grace at the lighthouse. And it had been three years since I'd been with Katrine and Lorelei in Scotland.

It had been a long few years, for all of us. I wondered if we would find each other much changed.

Horatio took the last bit of pineapple and leaned back in his chair. Mr. Yamaguchi put a record on the new record player inside the house and the warm voices of a Hawaiian men's quartet accompanied by a soft strumming guitar came through the open window onto the porch.

Over the last eighteen months, it had become one of my favorite sorts of music, almost like the western ballads in Texas. But then, there were still big cattle ranches on the islands. Hawaii had its fair share of cowboys. It only made sense that the music would be similar.

29

Edie exclaimed, "We'll need to fix up the guest rooms for them! They'll be here for two weeks before they join the USO show."

"When will they arrive?" Peter looked at Horatio.

"Tomorrow morning."

"How are the girls?" I asked, still not quite believing they were practically in Hawaii.

Edie's face grew serious. "Harry was recently declared missing in action. We don't know more, but Lorelei wrote that Katrine did not take the news well at all. I think this trip will be good for her. Help her get her mind off of things, you know?"

I wish I could agree, but I couldn't. I knew from experience what it was like not to know where your love was or if he was alive or dead.

CHAPTER 3

SONG OF THE ISLANDS

he day of the Adleman sisters' arrival came, and we found ourselves at the airport standing in the partitioned-off space next to the runway. Peter insisted we bring Founder for Grace, and she was trying very, very hard to be good, but with all the other people waiting for the plane's arrival, it was difficult. Edie, like the dog, could barely contain her excitement and shifted her weight from one foot to another nervously. Her light gauzy skirt gently blew in the wind.

"You want to hear something crazy?" Peter folded his arms.

Keeping his eye on the horizon, Horatio answered, "What?"

"During Pearl Harbor, one of these planes had just taken off carrying 24 passengers. It got caught in the Japanese fire, and the engine burst into flames."

"I don't like where this is going." Edie frowned.

Peter smiled. "But a stray bullet set off the fire extinguisher. It put the fire right out."

Now Horatio looked at him. "You're kidding."

"Not at all," Peter protested. "It made it into *Ripley's Believe it or Not*."[6]

"Well," I said. "I'm not sure I believe it, but I'm grateful that we didn't have any Japanese fire to deal with today. Or since Pearl Harbor, for that matter."

"Regardless, I prefer boats to planes any day." Peter said smugly.

"Indeed." Horatio nodded seriously, agreeing with his nephew. "Only trustworthy mode of transportation."

The plane, a Hawaiian Airlines DC-3, came into view. We watched in silence as it made its final descent. "Right on time," Edie said, checking her wristwatch as the wheels touched down and the plane began to screech to a halt.

A few minutes later, a smart-looking stewardess, with a large flower in her hair, opened the door while the ground crew pushed the portable stairs to the base of the plane. A businessman descended and then a young mother with two children.

"There they are!" Edie said pointing to a window.

We began to wave and shout, for what reason I've no idea. It just seemed the thing to do after a long absence from loved ones. The girls made their way down the stairs, trailed by Frank carrying his accordion case, and rushed into our open arms. Edie and I put flower leis around their necks, and there were tears and laughter, awkward pauses and starts and stops, and all the usual little moments in such meetings.

"Katrine," I said, taking her hands in my own and kissing her cheek, "I heard about Harry. I'm so, so sorry."

Before she could reply, Founder practically jumped into Grace's arms, and it took all my strength to pull her back.

"Do you think she remembers me?" she asked, surprised.

"Who knows?" I shrugged. "You did save her life."

"But she was just a baby. How could a dog remember?"

Peter patted Grace's shoulder. "If I was a dog, I would remember."

Clapping his hands together, Horatio got our attention and signaled that it was time to move towards the baggage claim.

Johnny was preparing a great big dinner for all of us, and he didn't want us to be late.

Once we had their bags packed into the back of the Woody, and we'd all crammed inside, Horatio at the wheel and me crammed between him and Edie, the girls in the middle with Founder at their feet, and Frank and Peter thrown into the back with suitcases and hat boxes stacked on their laps, Edie began to pepper the girls with questions about the trip. How were they? How did Frank - a ruggedly handsome sailor with a thick Brooklyn accent formerly under Horatio's employ - become a member of my cousins' musical ensemble? Why had the girls brought the group back together after they'd been retired for so long? Why had they changed their names from Adleman to Macleay? How had they all managed to get from Cairo to Hawaii in just 10 days? The only question that was answered was the last one. "A mixture of planes, trains, and auto-mobiles, not in that order," Grace said dryly.

"Same for our journey." Edie looked back at Grace and undid the window, letting the warm afternoon air in. Katrine's face was glued to the window. She looked older than I remembered, still beautiful, but something in her eyes was gone. A brightness was missing. And she seemed nervous, as though sitting still was difficult.

Grace seemed different too. She didn't really look at Peter or me, and I wondered if it had something to do with the fact that the last time we had all been together, Amos had been with us too. She seemed only to want to talk to Founder, who was, we all agreed, her puppy as much as ours.

Lorelei was, of the three, the only one who seemed able to connect. She kept smiling and pointing out the beauty of the cliffs, the banyan and eucalyptus trees, the smell of the cool air.

"So, what's the schedule for today," she asked as we pulled up to the house.

"No schedule at all," I answered. "We thought you would want to rest up tomorrow too." I paused and then asked, "If you don't mind,

I told my editor earlier today that you would sit for a photograph and an interview. He wants to put it on the front page."

"The front page?" Grace pulled her aviator sunglasses up on her head.

"I don't think you girls realize how famous you are. Your song, that one about the chickens," Horatio put the Woody into 'park' and took the key out of the ignition, "all the boys in uniform are singing it. It even has its own dance. A swing number they call 'The Cluck.'

"I think I am going to die from shame," Katrine said, her cheeks burning red.

Equally embarrassed but trying to keep face, Lorelei croaked, "A hit's a hit, right? People like it, and that's all that counts."

Grace smirked and said, "Der oylem iz a goylem."

"What's that mean, dear?" Edie asked politely.

"People are idiots." She pushed her sunglasses up on her nose. "Its Yiddish."

"The Cluck, huh?" Frank pushed the boxes and suitcases off his lap and crawled out of the car behind Peter. "Looks like me and Lorelei are going to have to start practicing." His wavy brown hair was longer than I remembered, and he had a new tattoo on his wrist. It looked like a ship.

Lorelei didn't answer. She stood with her back to the house and faced the ocean. She inhaled and exhaled as the Pacific crashed against the island's shore.

"Come on." I pulled her towards the house. "I'll take you all to the beach tomorrow after the photo shoot, and we'll do nothing but lie on our backs and get sunburned, and you can tell me everything you've been up to. I heard you may have a friend in the corner?" I teased.

"Oh, Piper," she laughed nervously, "If only it was that simple!"

"Isn't it?"

She stopped and shook her head as though deciding whether to talk and then, choosing against it, followed me inside. Already, Edie was showing Katrine and Grace photographs of little Agatha, my namesake. Peter and Frank were pouring lemonades and talking like long-lost brothers about baseball stats and 'the good ol' days' in His Royal Majesty's Navy and on Horatio's ship, the *Grey Goose*, before the war.

All were introduced to Mr. Yamaguchi, who smiled and bowed and told the girls how much he loved their song on the radio and how, in their honor, he was making Hawaiian-style chicken and rice. This dish served in a carved-out pineapple, caused quite the ripple of excitement among the sisters. It was all very new and exotic. So unlike Europe or the Middle East. The flavors were bold and sweet and strange. It sort of reminded Katrine of the Egg Foo Young that Harry had made for her once. But then, this wasn't like that either.

The thought of Harry, the taste of something similar - soy sauce - along with over a week of travel across a war-torn world and the mortifying fact that she was sort of famous for a song about chickens and a dance called "The Cluck" was too much for Katrine, and she had to excuse herself, disappearing into the back of the house.

"Don't worry about her," Frank said, serving himself an extra large portion before passing the pineapple to me. "She's been doing that lately."

"Frank!" Lorelei glared at him.

"Sorry, I'm just saying the truth." With that, Frank took a very large bite of the chicken and rice. He had a heart of gold but sensitivity had never been one of his strengths.

Edie leaned to Lorelei and plunged right in. "So, Lorelei, I vaguely remember Katrine vowing never to set foot on a stage again. I thought the three of you were finished performing forever. Something very special must have happened to get an ace pilot, an archeologist in the middle of uncovering ancient palaces, and a field nurse on the front of the biggest war in history, to up and quit their jobs for a few pairs of tap shoes and a microphone."

"It wasn't quite so drastic as all that." Grace laughed joylessly and shrugged. "My term of service ended with the RAF, and my unit was disbanded after everything that happened in Europe. Not enough of us survived to continue the program... That's when I started working for the Palmach in Jerusalem. But it's not like they had any planes for me to fly. And the British practically have us on lockdown. All our activities are heavily restricted. We haven't been able to accomplish anything of substance." Her voice was flat and emotionless. "I honestly had nothing better to do than volunteer for the good ol' US of A."

This monologue seemed so out of character for Grace. Out of all my cousins, she was the most focused, the most passionate. She always knew what she wanted, and she knew how to get it. But ever since Amos left for Russia, and Hannah had died, Grace had lost all sense of direction. Life had turned a dismal grey and nothing seemed to matter the way it used to for the beautiful, strong young woman. This USO show was a welcome escape from her heartache, whether she admitted it or not.

Lorelei took over. "It was all Joe's idea. He thought it was time to put the act on the road - for the sake of the troops."

"Joe?" My ears perked up. "Joe... Miller? But how does he know anybody with the USO show?"

"You know Joe. It seems like he has a spoon in every pot in the kitchen. For a lower-level diplomat in Cairo, he certainly gets around." She sighed and shook her head. "I guess I ought to tell you the whole story."

Lorelei took a deep breath. I could tell she was trying to figure out where to start.

She tilted her head back slightly and glanced at the wooden slats of the porch cover and began. "Well... it all started in March 1943. March 14, to be precise, just over a year ago..."

March 14, 1943

Cairo, Egypt

JOE MILLER STOOD on a table and shouted above the rowdy din of merrymakers in the dim, smoky nightclub in Cairo he had commandeered for the night. "Thank you all so much for coming."

This was met with cheers and whoops.

"And thanks so much for kicking the Germans and Italians off the African continent!" He grinned. "You all know that yesterday, Old Montgomery pommeled Romel and Arnim right into the sea, where the Royal Navy was waiting to catch them. Africa is safely in our hands, thanks to all of you."[7] He bowed magnanimously. "Drinks on the house!"

The band plowed in, and the nurses, soldiers, and bureaucrats were off and running. They had much to celebrate. The war wasn't over, certainly, but yesterday had seen the victory they had been working towards for years. The losses were immense on both sides. The Axis lost 620,000 men. The Allies—the United States, the United Kingdom, and France—220,000 men. The battlefields of Tunisia were thick with blood. But now Africa was safely in the hands of the Allies.

The victors were tired, exhausted even. But with victory came a surge of energy. They wanted to dance. They could dance all night.

"Hey, Lorelei!" Frank pushed through the crowd with a glass of punch in his hand. "I got you a drink." No longer able to serve because of wounds sustained in battle, he had hung around Cairo, working as a hospital orderly and vaguely wondering what to do next with his life while keeping a watchful eye on Lorelei—a friend who, if he was honest, he hoped might one day be more than a friend.

"Thanks." She took the punch and sipped it.

"Here, give me your jacket. It's too warm in here for you."

"Frank, I'm perfectly comfortable, but thanks for thinking of me."

"None of that now." He helped her take off her jacket. "Horatio and Edie gave me strict instructions to look out for you. And don't think I won't. I haven't seen you in a month."

He took Lorelei's bolero and disappeared to the coatroom. When he came back, they stood side by side. Neither really felt like dancing unlike the rest of the room.

"Was it very bad out there?"

"It's a war, Frank." She kept her eyes on the dancers, trying for a moment to forget the brutalities of battle she had seen on the field. Her German accent was very slight.

He sighed slightly and then groaned. Joe Miller was making his way towards them. "Here comes your boyfriend," he muttered.

Lorelei frowned.

Joe was a special assistant to the American Ambassador to Egypt. He was someone she could fall in love with. Or rather, she would think wistfully on their drives through the streets of Cairo in his convertible with the top down that he was the sort of man she *should* fall in love with. He was handsome. He was smart, quick, and brave. Why, he risked his career to help show the world what the Nazis were doing to the Jews in Europe. And he was a Christian. Just like her. It all added up.

Except that it didn't.

Oh, she had tried. Certainly. They looked great together. It could even be said they were a steady couple. She enjoyed his company and considered him a good friend. And everyone seemed to think that she and Joe would get engaged any day now.

But the spark wasn't there. Not for Lorelei. And she suspected it wasn't there for Joe either.

All these thoughts quickly passed through Lorelei's mind as Joe slapped Frank on the back and took Lorelei in his arms and began dancing gracefully into the center of the floor.

Suddenly, the band stopped playing, and a short Australian soldier jumped on top of the piano. He put his hands to his mouth and shouted for the party to quiet down.

"Okay, ladies and gents. We are now going to play us a little party game!"

He rubbed his hands together. "Now, I say a word, and whoever starts singing a song with that word first scores a point. Do you understand?"

Lorelei looked at Joe. "This will be a piece of cake."

The man on the piano struck a pose. "All right, first word: 'Rookies.'"

Immediately, Lorelei sang out the lines to the Irving Berlin song, *"This is the Army, Mr. Jones."*[8]

The crowd looked at her. "Wow," one young man said, "that girl's fast!"

"How about 'weather?'" The man on piano looked at Lorelei.

She sang out to the familiar ballad made famous by Lena Horne, *Stormy Weather."*[9]

"'Fence?'" There was no way she could come up with a song with the word 'fence' in it, certainly. He was sure he had her this time.

She laughed. *"Don't Fence Me In."*[10]

A pretty nurse with curly red hair near the bass player said loudly, "This game's too easy for her. You need to make it harder."

The Australian winked at Lorelei and hopped off the piano. He went straight forward. "Here's an idea," he said conspiratorially. "I give you a word, and you have to *make up* a lyric."

"Make her play the piano too, Tommy boy!" Frank called out from the back of the room. "She plays the piano real good."

"Frank!" Lorelei was blushing from all the attention. But then, she chided herself, she had asked for it, calling out the answers so quickly like that. Joe, still by her side, whispered, "I didn't know you played the piano!"

She was sitting down at the instrument now, a crowd of friendly faces, some familiar, some not, all happy with the glow victory, huddled about the instrument, ready for a good laugh.

The Australian sat beside her. "Okay little lady. Here's your word, 'ocean liner.'"

JESSICA GLASNER

"Ocean liner?" she asked archly.

Hesitantly, she stretched out her fingers on the keys. Well… if they wanted a song, she thought to herself, she'd give them a song. She could come up with a song on the spot, certainly! She was an Adleman. An Adleman always delivered. They were competitive that way. She played a nice full C Major chord. And then a G. She threw in a dissonant jazzy tone and tried the first line that popped into her head. "I could fly to North Carolina… Hop aboard an ocean liner… Oh, oh, oh." She brought out a peppy little bass rhythm, swaying back and forth on the piano bench. The violinist caught on and began to accompany her, and then, the drummer took off.

"If the final day of the war came,
I would take a train to Brisbane,

Just to see my pretty baby's smile again

I could fly to North Carolina
Hop aboard an ocean liner

Just to see my pretty baby's face again…"

Everyone was singing now, swaying to the chorus. "Just to see my pretty baby's face again. Oh, oh, oh." Lorelei's clear, low voice carried them along. With a flourish, she lifted her hands off the keys, and the party erupted into applause and cheers.

The Australian put his hands up. "Now, who votes Miss Adleman here does a little encore!"

More clapping, more cheers.

"Oh no!" Lorelei protested. "I couldn't!"

"Just one more." The Australian wouldn't take no for an answer. "Here's your word."

"Make it a doozy!" An officer winked at her.

"Oh really!" She answered, but still, she was enjoying herself.

40

The Australian puffed out his chest. "'Chicken.'"

She stopped... It came to her instantly, the melody and the lyrics. Without warning, she plunged in, her fingers floating over the keys effortlessly.

"Oh, I like you in the morn morn morn morn morning
And when the day day day day day ends

If you'll be my roo roo roo roo rooster
I'll be your chick chick chick chick chicken!"

The room burst out into laughter, and once more the band took off. Now, everyone was dancing and singing, and the party was in full swing. Joe smiled at Lorelei and pulled her to her feet and back to the dance floor. "You didn't tell me you had secret talents."

"You knew that my sisters and I were in a trio in Germany."

"Yeah, but I didn't know you could play the piano like that."

She shrugged. "I guess we've never been in the same room with a piano before."

Joe laughed out loud. "How did you get so good with coming up with those clever little ditties?"

"My sisters and I used to make up silly little songs all the time."

"But I bet you were the brains of the operation."

"I'm not going to answer that." She smiled.

"Always the lady." He exhaled, and then, looked quickly back at Lorelei, he said, "Hey, I've got an idea. Something to spice up your life a little."

She looked at him questioningly. It was a full moon shining straight down on them. A pit formed in her stomach. She hoped this wasn't the moment - the moment he would ask her to marry him. She geared up, squaring her shoulders. No matter what, she promised herself, she would tell him the truth, even though she couldn't bear the thought of hurting him.

"How would you like to hear that song on the radio?"

JESSICA GLASNER

Her head jerked towards him. "What?"

He began to whistle to the melody of the chicken song.

Lorelei laughed out loud. "Oh, Joe Miller. Don't be ridiculous. Whatever for?"

"I can't tell you why Ms. Adleman. Not yet, but it would really help me out."

❧

"AND WITH THAT," Lorelei, turning back to me, finished, "he pecked me on the cheek leaving me quite relieved not to be engaged and rather suspect of what he had in mind."

"But why in the world would recording a silly song like that help Joe Miller out?" I asked.

"Not just one song," she corrected. "Over the next year, he asked me to write several. He said that my lyrics lit up the room with happiness. And it *was* nice to do something with music again." Lorelei smiled softly.

"But how did all three of you wind up on the radio?" Peter asked. "I thought Grace was still working as a pilot, and Katrine was digging up old pots in the desert of Palestine or something."

"They were." Lorelei nodded. "And we didn't record any of my songs together until a couple of months ago," she paused, "when they came to Cairo (where I was) rather unexpectedly."

"Why?'

"Paulina finally turned 18 and graduated from secretarial school —" Lorelei began.

"So she and Yosef could finally get married!" Edie clapped her hands together, finishing Lorelei's sentence.

"Exactly." Lorelei shot Grace a look. "And Katrine wasn't holding up so well…"

Grace stood up. "I think I am going to take a walk."

"But what about the rest of the story, dear?" Edie, concerned, looked up.

"Lorelei can finish it without me. I've been sitting for a week. I've got to keep moving."

I watched her walk down the stairs and take off jogging towards the beach. Grace, her light brown hair cut shorter than before, just under her ears, had changed into khaki pants, rolled up to her knees, and a men's shirt she had tied about her belly button and rolled up over her elbows. Unlike Katrine, the years had not aged her. But they had hardened her.

"Grace!" I called out after my cousin, running after her. "Wait, I'll go with you!"

CHAPTER 4

I GAMBLED, AND I LOST

I reached out and touched Grace's arm after we'd walked in silence for at least 10 minutes on the beach. "It's been a long time."

"Yes," she agreed, barely opening her mouth. She gazed out over the Pacific Ocean, the diminishing daylight casting her face in shadow. I could tell she was somewhere else completely.

"Where are you Grace?" I asked, cautiously.

"Somewhere far away from here." Her smile was joyless.

"How is Amos?" I asked tenuously. "We never heard anything after you..."

She swallowed and looked out at the sea, muttering the lines to a poem I didn't know. "'The waves come in, and the waves come out. Washing away dreams like so many grains of sand...'" She paused. "You heard about Hannah, didn't you?"

"Your paratrooping friend?" I wondered why she spoke of Hannah instead of Amos.

"She's dead. The Nazis shot her." She exhaled. "Very few of my unit survived."

Grace sat down on the sand and looked straight ahead. "And

Amos is gone. I don't know Lorelei anymore, and Katrine's had a breakdown."

I hesitated. "Do you want to tell me about it?"

"It would be nice to tell someone." Her eyes welled up. "But I barely know where to start."

"How about you start with Hannah?"

She frowned. "Hannah was caught by the Hungarian police working with the Nazis almost immediately after she had parachuted down. She was thrown into a prison where they did who knows what to her. They said she never told them anything. Not one word about the mission. Even when they told her that they'd arrested her mother, she refused to talk."

I said nothing.

"She was executed by a firing squad. She was only 23 years old."

"Just your age now," I offered.

"So many of my friends from the Jewish paratrooping unit are dead, murdered by the Nazis... Everything we worked to build, gone, like that." She snapped her fingers. "So few of us made it back, they disbanded our unit. The RAF did offer me another position, but I chose not to accept. I couldn't imagine going on without everyone... Sometimes I wonder why I am still alive." She struggled for a moment as though the pain of remembering was too much. And then, the words began to flow freely, and I listened as Grace tried to make sense of her life and her uncertain future. As she spoke, the scenes of her life played out in front of me. It was as though I was there. I could see her, standing on a shore far away. I could hear the waves. I could feel the breeze.

~

April 1, 1944
Mandatory Palestine

OF THE 32 Jewish paratroopers sent out with Grace by the RAF, only a handful had returned to Palestine. Some remained in Europe, hidden. Twelve had been captured almost immediately after their arrival. Seven of these were executed within days. Hannah was one of them.

In Grace's hands, she held Hannah's last poem gently, a tragic poem about gambling and losing. A poem written with death knocking on her door.

Grace sat perched on top of the ruins of the crumbling Roman aqueduct, looking out to the glorious aquamarine sea. The remains of a life gone by littered the coastline. The city erected by Herod had a harbor that once boasted to be as large as the one at Athens. Now, only half the city still stood in the form of crumbling towers and scattered pillars. The other half had disintegrated into the sand and the sea. She'd walked through the old hippodrome where horses had raced neck-in-neck, their charioteers steering them around the sharp corners as 13,000 spectators watched, cheering loudly. There was no audience now. The only sound was the crash of the waves and the occasional cry of a gull.

It was here where, during the 2nd Century CE, the ten greatest rabbis in Judea were publicly tortured to death for entertainment, for refusing to give up teaching the Torah, as well as many, many others.

It was a shore filled with ghosts of people and times long gone. And some, not so long gone.

Hannah, the beautiful poet had lived on the kibbutz just a stone's throw away. She hadn't made their date, the one where they had promised that once they returned from their missions in Europe, they would meet right there on that very beach and drink lemonade and eat Hannah's mother's famous cookies.

Grace whispered, "I gambled like you did Hannah. I risked everything. And I lost..."[1] Her words echoed those that brought Hannah's life to a close.

It was her poem as much as Hannah's. And while she had not

died at the end of a firing squad, a part of her *had* died. And now, she didn't understand how to keep on living.

Why had she made it out of Europe alive, only to go and lose the one thing that mattered most? She knew that now—what mattered most. Loving and being loved. But she had gambled, and she had lost.

Grace carefully stood up for a moment on the top of the aqueduct. Out of her pocket, she pulled out two dice. These she placed within the folds of the paper of Hannah's poem. And then, Grace clambered down the arch and jogged towards the surf. In a swift motion, she threw the dice and the poem into the sea and watched as the receding water carried it out a few feet before it disappeared under the surface.

"I'm done, Hannah," she said softly. "I won't gamble again. Never."

Not that it mattered. She had nothing left to gamble with. Her life felt very meaningless without Amos. Nothing mattered anymore.

Behind the crash of the waves, she heard someone calling her name, again and again.

Grace turned and saw Morris and Cecilia coming up the beach, hand in hand. They'd been engaged for a month and were still in the throes of their young romance. Cecilia had filled out a bit, no longer a gawky teenager. She was healthy and strong and happy, wearing a bright yellow cotton dress, her hair in a simple bun. Morris had changed too. He was taller, and his shoulders were broadening. He had the beginnings of a thick beard. He now taught in a Yeshiva in Jerusalem. Once they married, Cecilia would move from Kibbutz Kinneret to the little flat he'd found for them. His teacher's salary afforded just one room with a shared bathroom down the hall, but to them, it was a palace.

They were nearing Grace now. She could hear their laughter, carried on the wind. A gull cried out in the distance. It would be a young marriage, she thought. Morris was 18. Cecilia nearly 20. But how old were they really? Their souls were as old as the ruined stones littering the beach, given everything they had seen and done. Yes, they belonged here, Grace thought, among such old, old, stones.

"Grace!" Morris called. "The truck is here. We've got to get back to the kibbutz before dark!"

Reluctantly, Grace tore herself apart from the sea and walked towards her friends. She knew Morris was right. Between British curfews and angry Arab rebels, three Jews traveling through the countryside with night approaching was a recipe for disaster.

Mrs. Herring tried to be kind to Grace, she really did. But it was difficult. She'd never gotten the full story of what had happened between Grace and her son, her golden child, Amos, before he had abruptly returned from Washington DC and taken up an extra risky posting on the Russian Front. All he'd said was, "She... Oh, what's the use. She didn't want me."

Dafna couldn't understand. She was sure that there had been some mistake, she had been positive that Grace was in love with her brother, and she was the one who had encouraged Amos to make the big jump and follow Grace to America. But Amos had shot his sister a look that clearly said, no, there had been no mistake. No mistake at all. Grace did not love him. Perhaps she had never loved him.

He had left. And now, a year and a half later, Grace had returned.

Dr. Herring knew nothing of what had transpired between Grace and his son. And for that, Grace was grateful.

They all sat at their old table in the communal dining room, pretending everything was as it had been. But among the women at least, it was a facade, it was quite tense. Cecilia, feeling Grace's pain, gave her compassionate, feeling looks throughout the dinner as they spoke of how Lorelei and Katrine fared and of what Uri (Dafna's husband) had been up to on the RAF base in Tel Aviv. They chuckled at old memories and discussed plans for the upcoming wedding of Cecilia and Morris.

By the time Mrs. Herring had brought over the plate of her coconut macaroons, the table had lapsed into an awkward silence.

Dr. Herring leaned back in his chair. "So, Morris. How is it going at the Yeshiva?"

"I've 12 unruly 11-year-olds all studying for their bar mitzvahs." He chuckled. "They are a bunch of hoodlums more stuck on playing jokes on the teacher instead of studying their Torah."

Dr. Herring nodded understandingly. "And the apartment for you and Cecilia?"

Grace spoke up. "It's very nice. Though, it needs a woman's touch."

Mrs. Herring said nothing and looked at her daughter, Dafna.

Dr. Herring sighed. "So, you are staying in Jerusalem?"

"With Becky, Lorelei's old roommate, the nurse." Grace sipped her tea.

"You are still welcome at the kibbutz, you know that, don't you?" Dr. Herring asked kindly.

Honestly, Grace knew that she was not welcome. But she smiled and answered, "I'm closer to the Palmach headquarters. I'm a captain now, remember." She paused for a minute before continuing, "You know, we are working on training pilots for when we have an airforce of our own. I could only get down here for the night." It wasn't a total lie. There were lots of things she needed to do back in Jerusalem. But the truth was, she couldn't bear being at the kibbutz one moment more than necessary. It brought memories of what had been, and what could have been, too close.

Cecilia looked at Dafna. "She's agreed to be my maid of honor."

"Amos would be very excited to hear that!" Dr. Herring bit into a cookie.

"He would?" Morris asked, surprised.

"No." Dr. Herring cleared his throat. "I meant that part about an airforce of our own."

Mrs. Herring tried to keep her face placid. "I'm sure he would, dear. But he's on the Russian Front. But, I'm sure you know all about that." The old woman's gentle face was touched by stress.

Grace swallowed.

Nodding grimly, Dr. Herring continued, "He's been smack dab in the middle of the Rzhev-Vyazma Offensive. There have been terrible losses on both sides."

Ever since Hitler had violated his pact with the Russians, turning on his Soviet ally and invading the Soviet Union, the face of the war had changed. The Russians now fought alongside the British and the Americans. It seemed that there was fighting everywhere, the West, the East, the Middle East, the Pacific, Africa... Was there anywhere left untouched by the bloodshed? The United States, almost. Canada? South America... Well, Grace sighed, perhaps it wasn't as dark as it seemed. They could always live in Bolivia if it came to that.

"I hope he's alright," she murmured, looking down.

"I'm sure that Amos will come out just fine," Morris said. "He's a great man. And smart too."

"I know that," Mrs. Herring said proudly. "Any girl would be proud to have him."

Dafna rolled her eyes. But Grace understood Mrs. Herring's meaning and felt sick to her stomach.

"But we have a bridegroom right here!" Dr. Herring slapped Morris on the back. "We are very proud of you children." He chuckled as he continued, "One, two, three, four. Marry your girl at the early score! Do not philander, do not delay, or somebody else will snatch her away!"[12]

Cecilia beamed. "What a sweet little ditty."

"Bialik, my dear. One of our greatest poets." Dr. Herring's eyes twinkled.

Grace bit her lip. She'd philandered. She'd delayed. And someone else had torn him away. She had just never expected it to be the Eastern Front.

"Do you have a wedding dress yet, Cecilia?" Dafna asked.

"Oh yes. Grace and I found one that will be perfect." Cecilia had been staying with Grace over the last weekend in Jerusalem to shop for the wedding and to clean Cecilia's new apartment so she wouldn't have to after the wedding. She giggled. "I can't believe the wedding is only three weeks away."

With that, Morris stood up and helped Cecilia out of her chair. "If it's all right with you, Mrs. Herring, we'd like to look around the courtyard before it gets dark. We want to see how many people will fit. I think the whole Yeshiva wants to come out for the weekend. Do you mind if we set up tents for them all under the date palms?"

Mrs. Herring shook her head. "Of course not. You can set up tents on the roof for all I care. Your friends are welcome here anytime."

"Thanks, Mrs. Herring." Cecilia leaned down and kissed her cheek.

"Dafna, would you like to come?"

"Oh no. You three go ahead. I'm on kitchen duty." The young redhead began to stack the dishes and left for the kitchen without looking at Grace.

Grace tried to compose herself as she followed Morris and Cecilia out into the courtyard.

As they wandered from one corner to another, Cecilia took Grace's hand and held back as Morris waved down an old friend. "Are you all right? It was pretty rough in there."

"I don't think they'll ever forgive me."

"You didn't have to marry Amos, you know."

Grace shook her head. "I... It was complicated, Cecilia."

"Is love so complicated?"

She nodded, not speaking to Cecilia in particular. "I liked him. I flirted with him. I ignored him. I caught him. And then, for some reason I'll never fully understand, I told him 'no.' I told him I had to go and fight a battle alone that, to be honest, we could have fought just as well or better together. I think I broke his heart."

"Did you love him?"

"I didn't know back then."

"Do you know now?"

"Oh yes. I love him."

"Then tell him! Write to him!" Cecilia urged her friend.

Grace pushed a tear out of her eye and willed herself to be strong. "I did." She swallowed. "But it was too late. He said… he said he wanted a woman who knew what she wanted. Don't you see, Cecilia, he doesn't love me anymore. I hurt him too much."

"But dear, maybe you're wrong, maybe it's—"

Grace looked steadily at Cecilia. "It was all very clear. He stopped writing."

"Oh," Cecilia said quietly. "I see." She wrapped her arms around Grace, so tall and strong. "I'm so sorry, dear."

"Me too." Grace pulled the young girl's arms down firmly. "But we are not going to talk about me anymore. I'm here to help you plan your wedding. We should be laughing and dreaming not crying."

Cecilia tilted her head sadly, but Grace pressed on. "I think we should put the huppa right there—like we did for Uri and Dafna's wedding, don't you think?"

Morris jogged back to where they were. "Did I miss anything?"

"Not a thing, Morris, not a thing," Grace said, looking out on the courtyard. She could hear some teenagers coming in from the fields. How happy those days had been. How simple. Once more, she fought back tears.

That night, in her old bed in the women's dormitory, many of the old gang surrounded her, peppering her with questions. What was it like in America? Was it very frightening jumping from a plane? What about her secret mission? Tell us everything, they said, eyes wide, girlish figures folded on the floor and crammed on the bunks nearest to the one Grace was borrowing.

"Secret missions are secrets, Sadie!" she said playfully, proceeding to tell them how exactly one flies a plane in the dark. She told stories of great storms and horrifying landing conditions, of hiding in a cave in Germany for a month so she would not be caught. She told of the lighthouse in Maine and her cousins, Peter and Piper, and how she'd found a puppy on the side of the road. She told them about almost everything, everything except for Amos. And thankfully, no one remembered to ask.

Long after the girls had fallen asleep, Grace lay awake. Being back where she had first fallen for Amos kept memories fresh in her mind and worries deep in her soul. She thought of him fighting on the frigid front in Russia. Though she tried, nothing she did could seem to push him out of her mind. Of course Dafna and Mrs. Herring were angry with her! She was angry at herself! Her indecisiveness had broken more than Amos's heart. It had broken theirs and hers as well…

What did it matter? Nothing mattered. Nothing at all. At least, that's what she tried to convince herself. And with such a dim view of her future spread out before her, Grace finally fell asleep.

CHAPTER 5

NEVER AGAIN

*B*ack on the beach, Grace took a deep breath. Her expression barely changed through the telling of her story. The flat, monotone voice continued, "Cecilia and Morris are probably married now."

"You missed the wedding?"

"Oh yes." She looked at me. By now, it was completely dark, and only the light of the moon illuminated our faces. "It was the day after that day on Kibbutz Kinneret that I returned to Jerusalem, and there was a telegram waiting for Katrine—about Harry."

"She wasn't there to receive it?"

"No. She had been out at a dig site for months in the desert. At first, I didn't think anything of it, and I went ahead and opened it. I'll never forget what it said. She closed her eyes and repeated the horrifying message one word at a time.

THE SECRETARY OF WAR DESIRES ME TO EXPRESS
HIS DEEP REGRET THAT YOUR HUSBAND
HARRISON STENETSKY HAS BEEN REPORTED
MISSING IN ACTION SINCE JANUARY IN

GUADALCANAL IN THE SOUTH PACIFIC IF
FURTHER DETAILS OR OTHER INFORMATION
ARE RECEIVED YOU WILL BE PROMPTLY
NOTIFIED
T.A. FURTHING THE ADJUTANT GENERAL

"Twenty minutes later, I had a small overnight bag packed and caught the first bus that came by and rode it to the central bus station at the end of Jaffa Road. From there, much to my relief, I caught the only bus that drove to the Judean Desert within minutes of its departure. There aren't any phones on Masada. I had to find her and tell her the awful news myself..."

~

April 2, 1944
Mandatory Palestine

IT WAS ONLY when the bus left the city and began the steep descent through the white stone canyon that Grace's thoughts caught up with her. A lonely Arab herding several camels stopped and stared as the bus whirred by.

It was always startling how quickly the city gave way to the barren wasteland. All was white and gold and gleaming. She pulled out her aviator sunglasses and slipped them on to reduce the glare.

Masada is really a large mesa-like plateau that abruptly ends in steep cliffs. Remarkably difficult to navigate, it made an ideal natural fortress. And that is exactly what Hasmonean ruler Alexander Jannaeus built on the top of it in the first century. Herod the Great captured the fortress and improved upon it. He thought of everything. A palace, barracks, armory, cisterns, a Roman-style bath...

It was there, overlooking the Dead Sea, that a group of Jewish rebels overcame the Roman garrison stationed on the top and

55

barricaded themselves. They had enough food for years. The cisterns were filled with plenty of water.

There, the Roman governor Lucius Flavius Silva led the Roman legion X Fretensis in a siege against the Jewish rebels who had so boldly thrown off the bonds of their oppressors. The siege lasted three months, during which the Romans built an enormous rock ramp to reach the plateau and breach the wall of the fortress with a giant battering ram.

When they arrived, the Romans found no rebels. Only two women and a handful of children. The rest, 960 men and women, had chosen to die by their own hands rather than enter Roman slavery or execution.

All of this was recorded by the Jewish historian, Josephus, who encountered two of the survivors and wrote down their story. Not long after, the fortress was abandoned to the passage of time and the sands of the desert.

No one except for a few Byzantine monks attempted the climb in the ensuing decades. And even they abandoned the tragic mountain after life in such a harsh climate proved too hostile, too lonely. It remained solitary and forgotten—until 1838, when an American missionary and a painter climbed the mountain on a whim, stunned to discover the remains of what many thought was a myth.

For some strange reason, no archeologist took an interest in the site for *another* hundred years. And only in the last few months had the mountain taken on the importance of a significant archeological find. It was all very exciting, the exact sort of work Katrine liked.

The road through the desert was bumpy and dusty. As the plateau with the fortress rose up in front of them, Grace carefully stood up and moved to the front of the bus. "Let me out here, will you?" she asked.

The bus driver looked confused, "We are in the middle of nowhere. I can't let you out here!"

"I'll be just fine. I've got friends at the basecamp at Masada." She pointed at a hand-painted sign on a wooden post on the side of the road with an arrow that said *Masada.*

He frowned and then slowed the bus down. He glanced at the other passengers, two old Arab women on their way to Jordan.

"You may have friends, but I am not going to let a young woman wander around in the desert alone."

Grace held on as the bus hit a bump, and he turned down the dirt road. This would shave off some time at least. The driver wound his way up for about half a mile before the road abruptly ended. He looked at her suspiciously. "Are you sure about this young lady?"

"Quite sure." She pointed up the hill. They could barely make out the outlines of a few canvas tents.

"Have it your way then." He sighed. "You are staying here overnight?"

She nodded.

He opened the door, and she stepped out into the heat and the wind.

Grace told herself, *steady on girl, steady on. One foot in front of the other.* The rocks crunched under her feet as she approached the campsite. A young man of medium build, wearing what could best be described as a safari outfit, scrubbed dishes in a metal bucket. Noticing her, he looked up and smiled. He had a nice boyish smile, a sunburned nose, and light brown hair.

"Shalom! We weren't expecting any new students today, were we?" he asked pleasantly.

Grace looked around. Under an open tent were some makeshift tables piled high with pottery shards and other old things she could not place. All the signs of a true dig. Notebooks. Pencils. Crates. A camera...

An old woman cooked flatbread over a hot stone oven nearby.

"Shalom," Grace answered. "I'm looking for Katrine Adleman?"

"Adleman?"

Grace stopped herself. "I mean, Mrs. Stenetsky." She wondered if that name would ever roll off the tongue. Try as she might, she could not get used to calling her sister by her married name. "I have to speak to her immediately. It's urgent."

"Oh! *That* Katrine." The man dried his hands on his pants and frowned. He had a slight English accent, the product of a good English public school before he and his parents had left for the Holy Land a decade and a half before. "She's up on top. Won't be back down until tomorrow morning. They spend a few days up top and then come down to replenish supplies."

Grace looked up the steep cliff face. "Is there a trail up?"

"Well, yeah. But-"

"Where is it?"

Before he could answer, Grace had already begun racing towards the steep climb to the mountain's top.

AN HOUR AND A HALF LATER, huffing and puffing, Grace made it. In the interim, the day had gone from late afternoon to sunset. After she caught her breath, she gasped. She was on the top of an enormous precipice. She could see the Dead Sea. She could see for miles and miles. It was a vast emptiness that sent a chill through her heart.

A great wind swept over the mesa. So strong, she feared she would be blown off the mountain, but she was not.

"Katrine!" she shouted, scanning the various ruins. The wind drowned out her voice. It seemed totally deserted. "Katrine!" she shouted again.

"Hello!"

Grace tried to place where the sound had come from. "Katrine!"

"Hello!" the voice repeated.

A head covered in dark curly hair popped out from the entrance to the building right in front of her, eyes immediately widening in surprise.

"Why, Grace!" Katrine crawled out of the space and stood up.

She was dressed in a similar safari suit to the one the man below wore. She brushed her hands off and jogged towards her sister. "I didn't expect to see you up here! You didn't tell me you were coming." She hugged her close. "What a lovely surprise!"

The wind picked up again, howling mournfully as the sun sank lower and lower.

"Where is everyone?" Grace asked, looking around the site. It seemed very harsh and lonely. She tried to shake off the dread of the place.

"There's only five of us at the site." Katrine smiled. "Dr. Hildesheimer is over there in the bathhouse." She pointed towards the east. "I'm working on the hanging palace with Helen—she's another Ph.D. student. There's another palace on the north side, but it is nothing to the hanging palace."

"And the other two?"

"Down below. Dr. Hildesheimer's son is helping out while on leave from the British Army. You know that Dr. Hildesheimer's wife is from London, don't you? He met her when he was at Cambridge."

"I think I met the son." Grace shivered as a cool breeze swept across the desert.

"And there is an old Bedouin woman who lives at the basecamp and cooks for us." Katrine pulled Grace towards the palace. "You just have to see this place! Herod built three terraces connected with staircases, a semi-circular balcony... and the whole thing is paved with mosaics. Just stunning! And so well preserved. It's so dry, some parts of the palace seem so fresh and bright, you would think it was built yesterday! Untouched for nearly thirteen centuries! Except of course, for when the Byzantines came. They built a monastery over there," she glanced over her shoulder, "but abandoned it not long after. Too difficult a terrain, you know." Katrine was beaming, her face bright with excitement. "Imagine the Jewish revolt! It's like what we are doing again, you know, with the Jewish resistance against the Nazis? And even the Haganah against the British! They work with the British with their right hand and work against them with their left because they know from history not to rely on outside powers to establish our homeland."

"That's an awful thought, Katrine!" Grace knew the tragic ending of Masada and prayed they would not meet the same end. Grace knew it was true that the Jews in Palestine were prepared for the worst when it came to British involvement with the formation of their nation. Although the British were fighting against the Nazis, and the Jews in Palestine were serving under the British in His Royal Majesty's armed forces, in reality, the British attempted to 'safely' maintain loyalty to both sides; the Jews *and* Arabs.

Even in the face of British promises, everyone knew that after the war ended, the Jews had no guarantee of a country of their own.

For many of the Jews in Palestine, the British Mandate was just as bad as the rule of the Roman Empire. This time though, they were determined to stay. Never again would they be forced from their homes.

"I don't mean that," Katrine said. "*That* will never happen again. Never again," she repeated softly. "That's why we are here, isn't it? To build homes so solid that no one can steal from us. To create a safe place where our children can grow up without fear of being beaten for being born a Jew or killed for it."

"Katrine," Grace stopped her. "We have to talk. I have something to tell you—"

"What is it?"

They were standing outside the entrance of the palace. "Let's get out of this wind," Grace said. It was so loud, it was driving her to distraction.

"All right," Katrine said slowly.

The two sisters crawled into the palace, and Grace's eyes took it in. Beautiful columns, lovely frescos. Here, in the safety of the ancient stone walls, they were protected from the wind.

A woman, in her early thirties by the looks of it, was brushing dust away from the face of a girl painted on the wall. Turning her head, she smiled and asked, "Who's this?" The wrinkles on her forehead were creased with a grey film. It covered her light brown hair as though she were wearing a powdered wig.

"Helen, this is my sister." Katrine smiled.

Helen's eyes darted from Katrine to Grace and back again as Grace took the telegram out of her pocket and passed it to Katrine.

Pushing a stray curl out of her eyes, she quickly read the words. She read them again. And then once more all the way through. A roar filled her ears. At first, Katrine thought it was the wind. But then, a wave of nausea rose up in her stomach, and she felt the earth give way beneath her. That was the last thing she remembered.

CHAPTER 6

BASECAMP

My cousin stared out at the dark horizon beyond the ocean. She talked and talked, the words flowing more easily and freely with every passing moment. I had the distinct feeling she had not truly talked with anyone in a long time. And still, she kept talking, her words painting a frightening and lonely image.

I could see her in the desert of Palestine, bearing the terrible news about Harry and wondering what in the world to do next.

I could hear the roar of the desert wind mingled with the real waves crashing on my Hawaii shore.

And I wondered how much more Grace had locked up inside that she needed to share.

~

April 3, 1944
Mandatory Palestine

WHEN KATRINE AWOKE, she saw Grace. Her big blue eyes were open very wide and looking down at her with a terrified expression. Carefully, Katrine pushed herself up on her elbow and tried to remember what had happened, but she was coming up blank. Then, she felt her fingers grasping a thin paper, the telegram informing her that Harry had been lost somewhere in the Pacific. She felt sick again but was determined not to pass out.

"Helen ran to find Dr. Hildeshimer. Are you—are you all right?" Grace's voice cracked a little.

Katrine groaned and rubbed her head. It was throbbing.

"You haven't passed out like that in years." Grace took her big sister's hand and helped her sit up straight. "Put your head between your knees, remember?"

"I remember!" Katrine was annoyed and embarrassed. "You didn't need to call Dr. Hildeshimer. I'm quite all right."

"Oh, shut up. You went white as a sheet and crumpled to the ground like a rag doll. You were out cold for a few minutes."

"I was?" The dizziness began to diminish, and she carefully looked up. Grace was beginning to calm down, slowly.

The sound of footsteps outside the entrance, crunching on the hardened stone and sand, approached and then stopped quickly as Dr. Hildesheimer and Helen stooped through the entrance.

"Why, Mrs. Stenetsky!" The tall, distinguished professor was breathing heavily from jogging across the mesa.

Helen had found him hunched over a pot in the storeroom. "Katrine fell and hit her head! She won't wake up!" she'd exclaimed.

At first, the old man had pictured a hundred terrible scenarios. She had fallen off the cliff! She had tripped into a collapsed cistern! And he had promised Harry that he would take care of his wife while he was away. This was terrible, just terrible!

With such awful thoughts racing through his mind, he'd crossed over the fortress to the palace, Helen on his heels. Upon seeing Katrine sitting up, pale, yes, but with the obvious use of all her faculties, he breathed a heavy sigh of relief.

Katrine turned her face up towards him. She looked ashen.

"Are you okay?" Helen brushed past him and knelt down. "You ate lunch, didn't you?" She put her hand on Katrine's forehead. "Are you ill?"

Katrine didn't answer. She wasn't listening to a word anyone was saying. All she could think was that Harry was gone. Harry was... No one knew where Harry was. Anger, resentment, fear—a wave of emotions settled on her shoulders so heavily she almost felt numb with the weight of them all.

"Katrine?" Grace asked nervously.

Katrine shook her head. "I... I..."

Dr. Hildesheimer took over. "We are going to get you down the mountain right now. You are going to sleep in your tent, a good solid sleep. That's what you need." He looked at Grace. "What happened?"

"Harry's been reported missing in action. Possibly taken as a POW."

"Oh." The professor let this sink in before he took Katrine's arm. "As I said, Mrs. Stenetsky, let's get you off the mountain and back down to the base camp before it gets dark. You are well enough to hike down, yes?"

Katrine pushed her hair back off her face. "Oh, Dr. Hildesheimer," she tried to steady her voice. "I am perfectly all right. Harry will be just fine. You know Harry! He can get himself out of any scrape." She looked out the frame of the entrance. "There must be a good 45 minutes left of light. We all ought to get back to work."

"Are you quite sure, my dear?" He looked at Grace.

"There's nothing we can do." Katrine continued, "Nothing I can do at all. The most sensible thing is to carry on."

He looked hesitatingly from Katrine to the fresco.

She was kneeling down now, her small shovel and brush back in her hands. She ignored the three people looking over her shoulder. And once more, she began the small, careful movements removing the sands of time from the wall.

Dr. Hildesheimer patted Grace's shoulder and sighed sadly before leaving. "It is bad business in the Pacific. Very bad."

Grace sat down. "I guess I'll just wait here then." She shivered. It was starting to get cold. The temperature in the desert could drop quite low at night, even if it was sweltering at noon.

Katrine worked methodically, almost oblivious to Grace's presence. The light grew dimmer. Helen left, saying she was done for the day. But still, Katrine worked on.

"Katrine," Grace finally spoke, "it's so dark, you can't see what you are doing."

"I'm not done yet." She didn't turn around. "I've got a torch around here somewhere, don't I?" she asked herself.

She felt Grace's hand on her arm. "I think you are done for tonight," Grace said softly.

"I can't be done yet! I can't!" Katrine violently turned back to the wall, brushing it without rhyme or reason. The room was now almost completely dark. Grace had never seen her big sister like this. She had no idea what to do at all.

If possible, it seemed that the wind began to howl even louder. Grace tried to reason with her. "Let's go back down to the basecamp. You should eat something hot... not sardines and crackers."

"I'm not leaving until I'm finished! There are two lamps over there." Katrine motioned over her shoulder.

Grace swallowed and stepped back. Against the wall, she saw two oil lamps and a lighter. Carefully, she lit both and stepped outside, carrying the smaller one. She could make out a campfire and the two figures of Helen and Dr. Hildesheimer huddled around it, and she quickly made her way towards them.

"She won't stop working."

Helen looked up. "What?"

"I said she won't stop. I can't make her stop."

Dr. Hildesheimer exhaled. "I will talk to her."

∽

"KATRINE?"

"I'm not tired Dr. Hildesheimer, really. I told you not to worry." Katrine didn't turn around.

"Your sister came a very long way to be with you. I don't think you are being a good host." Dr. Hildesheimer waited.

"What do you mean?"

"Take her down the hill."

Katrine knew exactly what Dr. Hildesheimer was doing.

"Work is the best thing for me right now."

"No, Katrine, it is *not*." He looked at the wall. "You may be doing more damage right now to that wall than anything else."

She grimaced. "Are you ordering me to go back to the camp?"

"I am. In fact, we are all going."

Before she could protest further, he took her arm and steered her out of the palace. By the time they reached Grace and Helen, the girls had already put out the campfire and each held a lamp for the steep hike back down the mountain.

Katrine did not open her mouth the entire way.

It was much faster going down than going up, Grace noted. Why, they were almost there. She could smell the sweet smoke from the campfire, and it sounded as though Dr. Hildesheimer's son had the radio on. Or was it only her imagination filling in the sound of the wind with horns and strings?

"Thomas!" Dr. Hildesheimer called out. "Thomas!"

From out of a tent, the young man appeared.

"What happened?" he asked, worriedly. "Is everything okay?"

Before he could answer, Jameela, the old Bedouin woman, emerged from her own tent at the sound of voices.

She nodded quickly and stared at Katrine with a discerning eye. In a low, husky voice, she asked Thomas, "Hal alshshabat murida?"

"What did she say?" Grace asked.

"She asked if Mrs. Stenetsky is ill."

"I'm perfectly all right, Thomas. I'm perfectly fine - all of you!"

Katrine exclaimed. The old woman looked at Thomas and pulled her shawl closer, her eyebrow raised.

"I'll be in my tent." Katrine ran past them to a tent on the far side of the camp.

Grace, Helen, Dr. Hildesheimer, Thomas, and Jameela stared at one another in silence.

The old woman, her face lit by the fire embers still glowing from when she had made Thomas his supper, looked towards Katrine's tent. "'Anaha tahtaj 'iilaa 'ana takul shayyanaan."

"It looks like Jameela is going to make Katrine something special. Perhaps," Thomas looked at the newcomer and his father, "you are hungry as well?" Then, suddenly remembering himself, he extended his hand. "I'm Thomas Hildesheimer."

"Your father told me."

"You don't look anything like your sister." He smiled.

"Oh." Grace said, taken aback.

Dr. Hildesheimer was walking to his tent and overheard the comment. "I taught you better than that, Tom! Be a gentleman! When I come back, bathed and shaved, I expect you to have behaved yourself!"

"I didn't mean, uh—" Thomas blushed. "I mean you are very pretty. But you are a lot taller than Katrine. And your hair is lighter."

"So what?"

Thomas shrugged. "Sorry."

Helen chuckled, "He hasn't seen a girl his age in a while. He's either on the field or stuck out here in the desert with your married sister and me, the old maid."

Grace had too much on her mind to flirt. But she did not want to be unkind to the young man.

Jameela was bustling about the fire, stoking it and preparing to heat up a pot of stewed vegetables of some kind. It smelled spicy and sweet at the same time. "Can you ask her to make some tea as well? I think that is what Katrine really needs."

"Alshshay jdty jiddaan," he said, and Jameela looked up and nodded.

Grace waited, not knowing if she should follow Katrine or let her alone for a while. She opted to let her alone and sat down on a rock. Helen had disappeared, she assumed, back to her own tent. It was just her, Thomas, and the old woman.

"Do you have a radio here?" she asked after a second.

"No. I wish I did!" he exclaimed, sitting down on the ground. He was obviously happy for the fresh company.

"A record player?"

"Nope."

Grace looked up at the sky. It was remarkably clear. She felt like she could see every star for miles. It was the sort of sky that was heaven to fly in. It had been a long time since she had been in a cockpit. Too long... Looking back at Thomas, she said, "I was so sure I heard music on the way down the mountain. I thought it had to come from the camp."

"The desert will do that to you. You hear things out here." He shivered.

Grace drew closer to the fire. She didn't like this place. She didn't like it one bit.

Jameela poured a tin mug full to the brim with hot water and brought it over to Grace. She stood up and nodded at Thomas. "I'll take this to Katrine now."

Katrine was lying on her cot, staring straight up at the tent's roof.

"Sit up, Katrine," Grace said. "Drink this."

Katrine sat up and took it, but she didn't drink it.

The two sisters looked at one another. The wind whipped the canvas of the tent, and Grace noticed the heavy stakes holding it on the ground.

"I'm sorry, Grace." Katrine was trying very hard to control herself.

"You have nothing to be sorry for."

"I shouldn't have behaved in such a manner." Katrine put the tea on the ground. Grace waited patiently, seeing that Katrine still held the letter in her fist. She wondered if it had been clenched like that the whole time since she'd given it to her. "Please," she said, "I just need some time alone."

"You want me to go?"

"Just a few minutes more. By the time you come back from Jameela's supper, I'll be myself again."

But by the time Grace came back, she was not herself. She was crying uncontrollably. She pushed Grace off, telling her she just needed a moment to gather herself. But a moment stretched into an hour and then two hours. Grace, who was borrowing a sleeping bag, grew distraught and ran to the nearest tent, which happened to be Thomas's.

"She won't stop crying," the young girl said, looking up into the soldier's face.

He frowned. "You go back to your sister. Don't leave her alone. I'll send Jameela over with something."

Grace went back to the tent and sat by her sister until Jameela appeared. She pressed a steaming mug into Grace's hands and motioned towards Katrine.

"I don't need anything!" Katrine protested between hiccups and sobs.

"Oh yes, you do," Grace said, holding the cup up to Katrine's lips. The hot liquid burned down her throat.

"What did you just give me?" she sputtered.

Grace shrugged. "What's it taste like?"

Katrine shook her head. It tastes like mint, but with a strange, almost metallic aftertaste."

"Is it helping?"

Katrine shook her head no, but she was slowly starting to calm down.

"What is it, Katrine?" Grace took her hand and gently brushed tears of her sister's face.

"Harry and I were together only eight weeks before he was drafted. Eight weeks," she repeated.

"You haven't seen him since?"

Violently, she shook her head no. "He promised we'd never be apart again."

Grace said nothing.

"It's like a dream, you know? Sometimes I have to tell myself I'm married. I feel the ring on my finger and tell myself it's all real. But sometimes it doesn't feel real. Oh, Grace." she looked down. "What if it was only real for a little while? What if it was all a dream? What if he's dead?"

"Katrine, you are not making any sense." Grace bit her lip.

By now, Katrine was standing up and pacing inside the tiny tent. "I've got to get out of this place!" she burst out. "This godforsaken desert where dreams come to die! I hate it!" She covered her ears. "Make the wind stop, Grace! Make it stop!" Then, she fell to her knees. "Oh God," she pled, "What if he's dead? What will I do? What will I do?"

Not knowing what else to do, Grace pulled Katrine up and made her drink what was left in the cup.

"I've got to lie down," Katrine said suddenly, feeling woozy. Grace helped her into the bed. A moment later, Katrine was snoring.

Thomas and Jameela's faces appeared in the opening to the tent.

"What is in that stuff?" Grace passed them the empty mug.

"Two of my sleeping pills dissolved in some of Jameela's mint tea."

Grace's eyes bugged out of her head. "Two! She has a very sensitive system."

Thomas shook his head. "If there is anything I know about hysterical women, it's that sleep is the best cure. Trust me. I had a mother."

"Has anyone told you that you need to work on your diplomacy skills?" Grace groaned and then turned back towards Katrine. "I need to speak with your father. I'm taking Katrine back to Jerusalem with me."

CHAPTER 7

TOGETHER AGAIN

The temperature on the beach dropped and I shivered. So much had happened since I'd last seen Grace. She was remarkably unhappy—a deep, lingering sadness had settled into her voice, into her eyes.

"Grace! Piper!" Peter shouted from further up shore. "It's after curfew . . . You want to come on in?"

"Oh my," Grace said, surprised. "I can't believe I talked so much. You must be worn out listening."

Kindly, I shook my head no. "Of course not. Sometimes you just need to talk." Helping each other up, we brushed the sand off our clothes and began to walk back to the house.

"Katrine certainly seems more stable now." I tried to smile.

"Yes." Grace sighed. "I suppose she is. It was frightening though. I had no idea what I'd do once we got her back to Jerusalem, but I knew it was a bad idea to leave her up on the mesa with no one for company but the memories of Roman soldiers and Jewish zealots long since dead and buried." She exhaled. "She needed to be around people, around friends. Her Ph.D. could wait. So she moved in with Becky and me for a few days. Becky and Paulina were already going to Cairo for Paulina and Yosef's wedding. Becky thought it would be best if Katrine had both her sisters nearby, especially considering that Lorelei is a trained nurse... All I wanted to do though was go home."

"But you had no home to go to?"

"Yes." She faced me. "Exactly." I could barely see her face.

I understood what she meant, more than she knew.

"It was on the journey that we first heard one of Lorelei's songs. Of course, we didn't know it was hers at the time."

We stopped on the lawn outside the house. I could see Peter on the porch, sitting with Frank and Horatio, their dim outlines on rocking chairs, the glow of Horatio's pipe barely visible.

In the distance, I heard Peter whistle for Founder to come inside. The whistle, shrill and high, seemed to reach the exact same pitch as that of a train.

"When we heard it, we thought it was just, oh you know, just some silly song. But boy, if you'd told me it would shortly change my life, I would have listened more closely!"

~

April 10, 1944
Mandatory Palestine

PALESTINE RAILWAYS
RAPID AND COMFORTABLE TRAVELING FACILITIES TO
ALL PARTS OF PALESTINE WITH CONNECTIONS TO
EGYPT, SYRIA, TRANSJORDANIA.
EQUIPPED WITH MODERN PASSENGER COACHES, SLEEPING AND DINING
CARS, DAY AND NIGHT SALOONS, LUXURIOUS TOURIST TRAINS
SPECIALLY ARRANGED.
REGULAR DAILY SERVICE TO AND FROM EGYPT AND THE SUDAN.
DIRECT AND QUICKEST ROUTE TO DAMASCUS, BEIRUT, BAALBEK,
ALEPPO, AND TRANSJORDANIA, FOR AMMAN AND PETRA.

For All Particulars (Time Tables, Rates, &C.) Apply To:
Superintendent Of The Line, Haifa Station, Or The Leading
Tourist Agencies.
1922, Haifa[13]

"You know," Paulina said looking at the poster, "this is my first trip since I was a very small child. Will we really sleep on this train tonight?" she inquired.

Since the taxi had picked Paulina up after her final secretarial exam and taken the whole group of girls straight to the Jerusalem train depot, she had been giddy with the excitement of seeing her fiancé. From the depot, they had caught the three-hour connecting train to Haifa, where they now prepared to board the direct train to Cairo leaving promptly at 6:00 pm.

"Well, it *is* an overnight journey. But whether you are able to sleep or not is another thing. I've never been able to sleep on trains very well," Katrine answered, looking over her shoulder at the poster. She peered closer. "This poster is over 20 years old."

She wore her brown traveling suit and in her hand was a little suitcase with two changes of clothes, a swimsuit, a nightgown, and an evening dress. Similar ensembles were found in the suitcases belonging to Becky, Paulina, and Grace. Katrine was paler than usual. She completely refused to crack a smile. But she had pulled herself together enough to leave the apartment and go on this 'vacation,' as Becky kept calling it. The thought of going back to Cairo was a strange one. She never thought she would ever go back... Maybe this time she would get to see the Pyramids after all, she thought bitterly.

The platform was crowded with British soldiers. There were very few tourists these days. Everyone going anywhere was always going on war business. But not these four lovely ladies. They sat there like a breeze from the past as tourists on holiday. But they would have to squeeze in among the privates and sergeants the whole way there.

Becky pushed through the crowd, waving four tickets triumphantly. "I've got them!" She gave one to each of her companions. "Do you think we can take a Nile cruise?"

"We'll talk to Lorelei," Grace said holding her ticket. "She's been living there a few years now. I'm sure she knows all the wonderful things to do."

"And she knows we are coming?" Katrine asked.

"Oh, yes. I sent her a telegram yesterday, and she'll be at the station tomorrow morning to pick us up," Grace answered, following Becky to their car after giving their suitcases to a valet.

Paulina's face took it all in as they climbed the short steps from the platform into the train and made their way through the cars looking for their seats. The rough wooden floor, hard wooden benches, windows nailed shut, and smell of stale cigarettes illuminated the reality of war—even for 'fun-seeking' adventurers. "Oh dear," she murmured. "What happened to 'luxurious tourist train?'"

"This is us." Becky pointed to two rows. She and Paulina slid into one, Katrine and Grace, the other.

Katrine turned around to face her. "The railway is used so often by the army these days, they've combined forces. They are able to fit more troops inside with the benches like this."

A quiet 'oh' was all Paulina said as a stream of soldiers began to fill the cabin.

"As long as the Germans don't bomb the tracks or blow up a bridge, we'll be just fine," Grace said loudly, realizing how completely un-assuring such a statement sounded as it came out of her mouth.

"Oh, stop your worrying." Becky took her gloves off and dabbed at her lipstick with her handkerchief. "Nothing bad is going to happen. We are going to have a wonderful time and a change of scenery. A wedding! And when the rest of us come back, we are going to be able to focus and work and..." She didn't finish. There were so many soldiers in the car, it was almost unbelievable.

It was going to be a long and, by the sounds of it, loud journey.

"Do we have sleeping berths?" Katrine looked at Becky.

"Between my nurse's salary and your stipend..."

Katrine nodded and turned back around. She should have guessed.

The conductor, a middle-aged man with dark eyes and thick, black hair made his way up the aisle, collecting tickets. He stopped by the girls and informed them that the dining car had been replaced with another passenger car to accommodate the troops. "But don't fear!" He smiled at Paulina. "We've got plenty of sandwiches and Coca-Cola to go round."

"Sandwiches and Coca-Cola?" Paulina was getting increasingly upset. "If I'd known, I would have packed us some real food!"

Katrine put her head against the window and shut her eyes. She didn't really care. She wasn't very hungry.

With that, the engine gave out a burst of steam and a long whistle and lurched forward. The wheels went around, faster and faster, and soon the train was whizzing along the tracks headed out.

Katrine braced herself as the men clad in khaki broke out into song. It was a rollicking melody, sung in time with the rhythm of the tracks.

"Oh, I like you in the morn morn morn morn morning
And when the day day day day day ends
If you'll be my roo roo roo roo rooster
I'll be your chick chick chick chick chicken!"

She opened one eye and then the other. It was a catchy melody, in a silly sort of way. The men were all obviously enjoying it, swaying and clapping. Everyone knew it.

Grace beside her was looking up at all the soldiers, suppressing a smile.

Becky and Paulina were both laughing at the words, and Katrine could hear Paulina's soft voice start to sing along. It went on for a while, and then the men broke out into another, the newly popular, 'Stalin wasn't Stallin.'[14]

By the time the men reached the 6th verse, and the Fuhrer was melodiously hightailing it from the brave and noble Yankees, several porters with baskets of sandwiches began to make their way down the corridor. The singing broke up, and the men settled back into their seats, more than one sending a longing look or an impertinent wink in the direction of the girls, which all four ignored.

"Butter and cheese, tomato and horseradish, or aspic jelly?" the porter looked down at the women.

The young soldier across the aisle put out his chin and frowned. "No meat?"

"There's meat stock in the aspic."

"What's an aspic?" Paulina whispered.

Katrine turned around and answered, "It's gelatin."

Paulina's face showed her disgust, and she asked for butter and cheese while the soldier took his aspic sandwich and opened it cautiously. He shook his head. "This is nothing like my mother's aspic."

Both Paulina and Becky were in a talkative mood, much more so than the sisters. They hadn't been out of Jerusalem for several years. The feeling of a great adventure was upon them. They could have been riding in a car fit for the king as far as they were concerned. They were on their way to an exotic location to see close friends and a fiancé. It was all so exciting, they almost forgot there was a war on.

"Your mother's aspic?" Paulina turned towards the soldier.

"Oh, yeah," he replied, revealing a row of crooked teeth and a cockney accent. "Her aspic is real nice."

Paulina shook her head politely, wondering how meat in gelatin spread on brown bread could ever be 'nice.'

"Young man," Becky leaned over, "that song everyone was singing--"

"'Stalin wasn't Stallin?'" He laughed. "Clever don't you think?"

"No, the other one," Becky clarified, "about the chickens—"

"Oh! That one? It's a newer one. It's been on all the entertainment programs for the last month. You can't turn on the radio without hearing it."

"You're kidding." Becky was genuinely surprised.

"You mean, you haven't heard it?"

She shook her head no.

The soldier sitting beside the one with the aspic sandwich butted in, "I know who wrote it too." All eyes focused on him, and he blushed. "I mean, my cousin knows her. He was at this party in Cairo last year, and there's this nurse see? And she gets up and just makes it up, on the spot. He snapped his fingers. "Like that, see?"

All of this Katrine listened to, or rather, half listened to. All she really seemed to hear was the thump of her own heart and the thump, thump, thump of the tracks. Outside, as the barren desert landscape blurred past, and the sun lowered, and the men once more began to sing, she fell asleep with her head resting against the window.

THE FOUR WOMEN, rumpled and bleary-eyed from a night spent sitting up in a train car of singing soldiers, thought they must be dreaming. This was no 'apartment,' as Lorelei had said on the drive over. This was palatial.

The door swung open, revealing the gorgeous, modern, sleek foyer of Joe's apartment in the poshest neighborhood in Cairo. Lorelei moved aside for Katrine, Grace, Becky, and Paulina, followed by Yosef and Frank, the happy luggage bearers.

There was a grand staircase leading to what they assumed were several bedrooms. From where they stood, they could see a large dining room with a table that sat twelve, at least. Directly in front, a formal study. And to their left, a sort of sitting room or office that opened out onto an enormous balcony with views of downtown

Cairo. The girls could make out the outline of the Pyramids on the horizon, and they were so near the Nile that an intoxicatingly cool breeze filtered through the gauzy curtains.

Katrine glanced at Lorelei. "I thought Joe Miller was a government worker? How can he afford this?"

"His father is in oil or something. His mother sent a decorator from New York to finish it," Lorelei said disinterestedly. She turned to Frank and Yosef. "Will you boys take those upstairs to the guest rooms? Katrine and I will share the blue room. Give Grace the yellow one and Paulina and Becky the green room."

"It's real nice seeing you girls together again," Frank said, pecking Grace and Katrine on the cheek before following Yosef upstairs.

"It's nice to see you too, Frank." Grace smiled at the sailor. "You look quite a bit better than the last time I saw you." She thought back to that day in the hospital, with Frank flat on his back, an arm and a leg in traction.

Paulina's eyes followed Yosef up the stairs. The tension between them was palpable ever since their initial meeting on the train platform an hour and a half ago. They hadn't seen each other in two years, and regardless of her family's disapproval, they were going to be married.

They were all each other had in the world. And yet, it was as though they had forgotten how to speak at all. Every time they looked at one another, they blushed like children.

Katrine stepped into the living room and glanced around. The inlaid wood floor shone with layer upon layer of shellac. The furniture was minimal, an architectural leather couch, two chairs that seemed to float on the ground, suspended by spindly curves of metal and bent wood. Everything was black and white, except for a canvas leaning up against the wall, nearly six-feet tall, filled with rough blocks of orange, blue, and yellow. She looked at the signature—*Hans Hoffman*.[15] "

"Are you sure Joe doesn't mind us staying here?" Katrine asked, eyes still on the painting. Strangely beautiful, it reminded her of a canvas she had seen at the Vienna Secession building years ago and could only be described by the German word, 'kunstwollen,' or 'art that expresses a fundamental spirit of an age.' This was such a painting. It was bold and invasive. Just like the present.

These moments, where only a German word would fit, always left Katrine conflicted. She refused to speak in her mother tongue, and yet, there were some feelings inside of Katrine that only German could fully express. It was a problem all three Adleman girls ran into on occasion.

"Of course not," Lorelei said. "Joe was adamant. Besides, there is plenty of room at Frank's place for him and Yosef. He understands my housing limitations, with me living the nurse's dormitory, and he loves to host. Honestly, he does it all the time."

Noticing Katrine staring at the painting, Lorelei came up behind her. "Joe is into art," she explained. "Neo-Impressionism, cubism. He has a Picasso. It's hanging in Grace's room."

"Joe or his mother?" Grace asked from the dining room.

"Don't be impertinent!" Lorelei shouted back.

Paulina had never seen anything like the apartment. "Where is this Joe?" she asked, gazing out the paned glass doors to the balcony where Becky stood.

"He's at work." Lorelei looked at her watch. "But he's planning to meet us in a half hour... I heard a rumor that someone wanted to take a Nile River cruise?" She looked at Becky and winked.

"We have time to change, don't we?" Becky asked, looking at her wrinkled suit. She felt slightly uncomfortable in the midst of such wealth.

"Ten minutes enough?" Lorelei replied.

Nodding yes, Becky and Paulina bounded up the stairs and found the green room, named for the walls lined with silk paper in sage and matching sage bedspreads on the two twin beds.

Frank and Lorelei refused to allow Katrine to stay home, despite her protestations that she was simply not up for a pleasure cruise.

And so, she too changed into a thin summer dress and platform sandals, threw her hair back into a ponytail and marched down the stairs. She looked ready for the beach but acted like she was going to a funeral.

Finally, the pleasure-seeking party of young women chaperoned by the rough sailor and the shy Palestinian mechanical engineer, hailed a cab and drove to the banks of the River Nile, where a dahabiya, or a river going sailboat, had been secured and was waiting.

CHAPTER 8

THE RETURN OF THE ADLEMAN SISTERS

I'd worked in the newsroom for a while now—I could tell when I wasn't getting the full story. While Grace spoke in a hushed, restrained whisper, I wondered if she was telling me the entire truth. She seemed to be holding something back. There was something missing. I couldn't put my finger on it, but I knew that this part Grace's tale was heavily edited.

And as Grace told me of how the three Adleman sisters, Becky, Yosef, Paulina, Joe, and Frank boarded the boat tethered to the banks of the river, and how in silence, they watched as the small father and son crew steered the boat out onto the Nile, I knew this was one of those times. There was a *lot* missing to her story. I didn't know *what*, but I was determined to find out.

"We passed the sandstone Temple of Khnum and the double temple of Kom Ombo, once serving Sobek and Horus, the crocodile god and the falcon-headed god." She paused. "And I thought that was rather nice because all that time I was in Egypt training with the RAF, I never once took a cruise and saw those things."

She bit her lip. "At the front of the bow, Paulina and Yosef awkwardly stood side by side."

"I'm sure it was difficult, seeing one another after so long apart," I prodded gently.

Grace lifted her shoulders nonchalantly.

"I wouldn't know..." And as the slight breeze swept over the lawn from the sea, I listened as she continued to share the memories that somehow seemed to haunt her present.

~

April 12, 1944
Cairo, Egypt

"THEY'VE WAITED a long time for this moment." Becky sighed and turned to Joe. He had a pair of binoculars and passed them to her. "Look in the reeds there." He pointed, enjoying his role as a tour guide to the spunky Irish nurse. Her enthusiasm and ready smile were a welcome break from the embassy. Truth be told, he was having a better time than he had had in a long time.

She took them and gasped. "Is that what I think it is?"

"Certainly. We are in Egypt. This is crocodile territory."

"They don't have crocodiles in Ireland or Palestine for that matter." She gave the American the binoculars back, glancing up at his face. Her sparkling eyes betrayed she liked the young diplomat. He was honest, kind, and earnest. She hadn't met a man like that in a while.

Closer to the shore, women worked among the reeds. The river, the one source of life in the barren landscape, provided everything for those living in the tight-knit small communities lining the ancient waterway.

"Aren't these boats something?" Frank stood up and reached out, touching one of the two sails of the unusual vessel, shaped like a barge but powered by two elongated sails, one at the front and one at the back. A large portico covered the middle, shading the various small tables and chairs and couches.

"It is all so untouched by modernity." Becky sighed. "Why, I can almost see Moses's mother putting him in the reeds in a basket! Can't you, Katrine?"

Katrine looked out over the water to the small village where the sound of music wafted across the water. She shut her eyes against the glare.

"You need some coffee, Mrs. Stenetsky?" Joe offered politely. "I can get the steward to serve our lunch now."

Opening her eyes slowly, she said, "I honestly never thought I'd see you again, Joe Miller."

He coughed slightly. "An old Egyptian proverb says that once you drink from the Nile, you are destined to return.'"

She smiled softly.

"I was sorry to hear about your husband."

No one spoke for a moment, and the wind picked up, carrying the boat faster down the river.

"This certainly is a humdrum little group," Frank said, frowning. "What's the matter with everybody?"

"I'm having a good time," Becky, always cheerful, answered, trying to ignore the overall depressing atmosphere of the rest of the group, except for always charming Joe, that is.

"You know what we need?" Frank stood up and reached into the duffel bag he had brought on board. Pulling out his little accordion, he looked up and said decisively, "Music."

Before anyone could protest, he began playing the distinctive notes of Lorelei's *"If you'll be my roo roo roo roo rooster, I'll be your chick chick chick chick chicken..."*

Lorelei turned beet red. "Oh, Frank! Don't! It's too embarrassing for words. We can hear the music from the village! It is much more pleasant than that..."

Frank shook his head no. "Who wants to listen to those sad songs anyway? We can't understand a word those women are singing about!" He looked to the banks where women were cutting reeds to make into sandals and baskets.

"I know this song," Becky said. "We heard it on the train, remember?"

"I bet you didn't know that Lorelei wrote it!" Frank said.

"You did?" Katrine was suddenly feeling much more awake. She looked at Lorelei, surprise written all over her face.

"She's been writing lots of little ditties recently," Joe answered simply.

Lorelei shot him a look. "Yes... Mr. Calhoun sings them on the BBC Cairo Entertainment Hour..."

"Why?" Becky asked bluntly.

Lorelei faltered for a moment before answering, "It's pretty good money."

"Everyone needs a side hustle these days." Joe smiled. "Another one of her songs is going out tonight."

Katrine was taken aback. "Do they really pay you so little as a nurse that you need to write songs on the side for the radio?"

Lorelei shrugged.

"Sing it for us, will you, Lorelei?" Becky pleaded.

"But I don't have a piano or anything!"

"I'll accompany you on the accordion." Frank grinned.

Lorelei looked from Katrine to Grace. "Well, only if my sisters sing with me."

"But we don't know it." Grace's lips turned down.

"You'll catch on. It's really not that hard at all." She nodded at Frank. "Give me a G over B7."

The accordion blared out the desired note, and Lorelei plunged in, her singular voice carrying over the river and onto the banks, the sun glaring down upon them.

> "Big daddy promised me he'd always stay and never leave,
> Said he was locked away forever and in my love,
> But he broke his little promise, and he gone and broke my heart.
> Big daddy gone an' left home.
> Big daddy gone and left me all alone."

She looked at her sisters, beckoning them to join in.

"Big daddy said he'd finished looking round for other mammas.
Said he'd never leave the castle of my love.
But they told me he jumped the train west,
With his best green suit and brown vest
Big daddy gone an' left home.
Big daddy gone and left me all alone."

Once more, Frank struck the G, and the Katrine and Grace began to sing along. Their voices melded and flowed over the sad, sad words. At that moment, they forgot the war. They forgot the cruise. They forgot their loneliness, and they were back. The Adleman Sisters were back. They swayed together to the rhythm.

With their friends as their audience, the troubled girls (now all smiles) instantly transformed into the great entertainers they had once been, the entertainers they had almost forgotten ever existed.

"Big daddy gone and left home,
Big daddy gone an' left me all alone..."

The group sat in astonishment, struck by the discovery of the sister's secret showmanship.

"Wow," Joe said after they'd finished. He and Becky looked at one another. Paulina and Yosef had made their way from the bow of the boat to where the rest were sitting.

"Wow!" he repeated.

"The accordion was not a bad touch if I do say so myself," Frank added.

"I had no idea you girls were so talented." Becky smiled.

"We were professionals once... I guess." Katrine looked out at the water.

"You really ought to record that song," Paulina said wistfully. "It's the sort of thing I want to dance to. Maybe you can play it at the wedding?"

"Oh no." Lorelei shook her head from side to side. "The days of the Adleman Sisters are long gone. We've all moved on, you know."

With that, Frank took up the melody once more, and the boat drifted down the river...

BACK IN HONOLULU ONCE AGAIN, Grace turned her big blue eyes on my face and said, "Nothing would have come of the whole thing at all if Mr. Calhoun, the 'Crooner to the Troops of Cairo,' who was scheduled to sing live that evening, had not come down with a terrible head cold that very day. But he did, and that was how we found ourselves at the broadcasting studio, performing live, much to the satisfaction of Joe who schemed up the whole idea of our recording one song, accompanied by Frank's accordion, to replace poor sick Mr. Calhoun—all without any rehearsal at all. There wasn't any time." Grace stared listlessly out at the lawn bathed in velvety darkness.

"How peculiar." I exhaled.

"You have no idea," she agreed.

"Piper," Peter stuck his head out the front door and looked down where Grace and I sat. "We ought to head home. Frank's coming with us. I told him he could sleep on the deck."

"I'll just be a minute." I shooed him away. When the screen door shut once more, I pressed Grace to continue. "No rehearsal or anything?"

"Nothing. The producer told us the idea was to get the song good enough, not perfect by any means." She stood up and hummed, "*Big daddy gone and left home, Big daddy gone an' left me all alone...*"

"And?"

"And what?"

"So the song just 'became a hit,' and now you are a part of the USO show?"

"Give or take a little."

"Give or take a little?"

"You know how it goes. The broadcast was more popular with us than Mr. Calhoun. We were asked to do a few more live broadcasts. The station started getting calls requesting our songs. We did a live show at a club in Cairo. We recorded Lorelei's chicken number for ourselves, along with a couple of others. It played on all the radio stations in North Africa and the Middle East. Then it got put on the European and American stations." She exhaled, finishing with, "And *then* came the call from the USO show. "

"In a matter of weeks?" I shook my head incredulously. "And why Macleay? Not Adleman?"

"We want our privacy. Lot's of celebrities use fake names." Without responding further, Grace turned to go back inside the house.

Peter and Frank were both waiting by the door. "Where's Edie and Horatio?" I asked.

"They went to bed. I think the trip caught up with them." Frank grinned.

At that moment, Lorelei passed by us, car keys in hand. "I forgot a bag in the car and am going to grab it. Are you leaving?"

I nodded yes and pecked her cheek. "It's late. And I'm sure you are all exhausted."

"I'll help you with the bag, Lorelei." Frank followed Lorelei off the porch and towards the back of the house.

Reaching out to touch Peter's arm, I said, "I'll be ready in just a minute. I want to say goodnight to Katrine."

"I'll be waiting." Peter smiled at me as I braced myself for whatever state Katrine might be in.

Standing outside her door for a minute, I knocked, and then, when there was no answer, I pushed the door open. I found her methodically unpacking her suitcase—in the dark. I switched on the lamp. Her eyes met mine.

"Thanks," she said after a moment. "I guess I didn't realize it was dark."

"It's been dark for hours."

She sat on the edge of the bed. "You'll have to forgive me. I haven't been myself lately."

"You don't need to apologize, Katrine." I sat next to her. "I'm married too, remember?"

Before she could answer, a voice from outside the open window drew our attention. Simultaneously, we began to listen.

"Lorelei! Wait a second!"

It was Frank's voice. He had been waiting outside to catch Lorelei alone for a moment and obviously had no idea anyone could hear them.

"Yes?" she responded. We could hear the sound of her feet crunch on the gravel outside towards the place beneath the window where Frank stood. "What is it?"

"I've..." He faltered for a moment, obviously grappling for the right words. "I've been meaning to talk to you ever since we left Cairo. But there's always been other people around."

Katrine looked at me, putting her finger to her lips for me to be quiet. We both waited, listening.

"All right," she answered slowly.

I glanced at Katrine, wondering if we should be eavesdropping. Her eyes were riveted on the window.

"Lorelei Adleman, I... I have to tell you how much I like you."

"I know that, Frank."

"And if that Joe fellow has been leading you along—" He stopped. "I know you and him were thinking about getting married. You were always together in Cairo. And I know you don't have a ring on your finger, and he let you come here to Hawaii without him, and I got to thinking—"

"Frank—" Lorelei tried to stop him.

"Let me finish, Lorelei. What I mean to say is, if he won't marry you, I will."

Neither spoke for what seemed an eternity. Katrine shot me a nervous look.

"Oh, Frank." After a moment passed, she continued, "I like you too, but you know we shouldn't be married."

"Because you are a Christian? I've thought all about that. It doesn't bother me one bit. We'll work through it!"

"Work through it? Frank," she sounded very sad, "you know that it isn't like that."

"I could become a Christian if that's what you want."

"No, Frank. Though that is sweet, no."

"Why not?"

"Because it wouldn't be honest, that's why. It would be missing the whole point! You have to want to know Yeshua for yourself, not for me." Neither spoke for what seemed to be a long time but was really just seconds. Finally, Lorelei said, "My faith is the most important thing in my life. It's something I have to share with whoever I marry. It wouldn't be fair to you or to me otherwise."

"I knew you would say that." Frank let out a wistful sigh. "And you are right. To put it bluntly, religion is not my thing."

"It's not about religion—" Lorelei stopped in a way that made me think they had talked about her relationship with Yeshua many times before, and it was not worth talking about again. She continued, "But I won't say your offer wasn't the nicest I've ever received. Only a true friend would offer to marry me in light of someone else *not* marrying me. But don't worry. I'm not in love with Joe Miller."

"Then, he didn't break your heart?"

"My heart is safe and sound."

"Good." He exhaled as though a great weight was off his chest. "Are you going to marry Joe if he asks?"

"I don't know. We just... aren't there yet."

"If that guy doesn't know by *now*, you need to move on." He began to speak faster. "You, Lorelei, are a great gal. And you deserve someone who makes you smile and laugh. And I know you don't love me the way I love you. And that's okay. But don't think I'm going to just let any guy marry you. He's got to be special."

Katrine and I looked at each other, struck by the intensity of what we were overhearing. She inhaled sharply, and I bit my lip, shaking my head slowly. Poor Frank! Poor Lorelei! My heart ached for them both. By the look on Katrine's face, she felt the exact same way as me.

I could hear Founder barking, and then Peter called out, "We've got to go, Piper! Frank!"

"That's my cue," Frank said, seemingly unfazed. "I guess I ought to go."

I turned to Katrine and whispered, "Sounds like it's my cue too."

Wiping a stray tear from her eye (whether for Harry or Lorelei, I didn't know) she reached out hugged me.

"I'll see you in the morning, okay? Promise me you'll try to sleep."

"I promise," Katrine answered.

~

"YOU SURE THERE'S room for me?" Frank looked at the Malahini doubtfully. "Looks like there's barely space for both of you and the dog!"

"We'll set up a little tarp so you don't get rained on," Peter said. "I still can't believe you're going into show biz. What a riot."

"I'm an *integral* part of the act," Frank said importantly.

Poor Frank. What he must be working through! Of course, he had no idea of what I'd heard.

I had to speak to Lorelei. So much had happened. She had been forced to navigate so much on her own. Sometime tomorrow, I determined, we *would* talk.

I crawled into the hold and found the sleeping bag we'd brought along for emergencies and our one extra pillow. I passed these to

Frank who laid them out on the flat deck, barely wide enough for the sleeping bag. "Maybe," he said to Peter, "Founder can sleep up here with me?"

"I'm sure Founder wouldn't mind one bit."

From below, I heard Peter and Frank sit down and then saw their feet hanging over the edge of the boat through the porthole. "So, Frank, when are you going to settle down? It's about time you know. You aren't getting any younger!"

Oh, Peter! I thought, willing him to be quiet. How could my husband ask such an insensitive question! But then, how could he possibly know what I knew?

"You know me, Peter, the quintessential bachelor. I'm too set in my ways to change now." He sighed with what I imagined to be great pain. "But there is something about this tropical air. Makes one feel pretty romantic. You never know."

"Piper's got some real nice friends. We could introduce you to a few..."

"Maybe," Frank answered after a second, and then repeated, quieter, "Maybe."

CHAPTER 9

LORELEI GETS CAUGHT

I looked at the placement of my cousins for the picture that would grace the cover of *The Honolulu Herald* the next morning. The famous Macleay Sisters were in Hawaii, and my editor wanted the world to know it. They stood before a fake sunset made of special lights with blue and pink filters. Peter held a fan to make it look like a light island breeze was blowing through their hair. And behind them was a crude backdrop that almost looked like a beach, if you squinted.

"Now, a little to the left," I said, motioning to Katrine. "And adjust the flower, won't you?"

I had protested that we had a great beach, hundreds of them, right outside the office! But Don didn't want reality. He wanted the Macleay Sisters on a fake beach doing the hula in the paper's photography studio. Ever since Pearl Harbor, it was illegal to take pictures at the beach in case the Japanese got a hold of the picture and discovered an entry point to the island.

"This way?" She pushed the red plumeria further up behind her ear.

I shook my head no and looked to Edie, who stood off to the side, for help. "Would you, Edie? Please?"

"Of course, dear," Edie stepped over the set dramatically. With a quick motion, she artfully placed the flower back behind Katrine's dark locks.

Once she was out of the frame, I frowned and took the shot. The flash exploded. It wasn't the sort of picture I liked to take at all. Oh, Katrine, Lorelei, and Grace all looked fabulous. They wore matching sarongs, red with pink flowers, and heaps of leis. Each had assumed the quintessential 'hula' position. At their feet sat Frank, his accordion posed 'just so,' muscles bulging, and gazing straight into the sunset. He wore a black and white striped T-shirt, black sailor's pants, and a red bandana tied around his neck.

Grace put her arms down and sighed. "Can we please be finished now?"

"One more." I got down on my knees and tried a new angle. "Pretend you are having fun. Not a care in the world!"

She glared at no one in particular and put her hands back up. Once more, I shot a photograph and put the camera down.

"All right." I stood back up. "We are done."

At that moment, Don and Horatio burst into the studio. "You can't believe how enthralled I am, *enthralled*," Don emphasized, "that the Macleay Sisters are the daughters of my old pal Horatio here. Who would have thunk." He tapped his bald noggin.

"Who indeed." Edie looked at me. I could tell she wasn't a fan of Don.

"Your girls are going to make quite the cover. Quite the cover. Biggest news on the island since Pearl Harbor." Don frowned. "Upstairs in my office, your husband's been giving me quite the exclusive. What a harrowing adventure! What pathos! Finding the girls shipwrecked on a Grecian island as babies, abandoned by the parents, whoever they were! This is the sort of thing my readers will eat up. And imagine, the talent in those vocal cords!"

Frank pushed the accordion together, letting loose a discordant strain.

I gave Lorelei a questioning look, wondering why she wasn't correcting him. In response, she leaned in and whispered, "I told Horatio what to say. It's best if we have a cover story. Better for publicity."

Edie looked at Horatio. "No embellishment, huh?" She winked at me. "And I thought I could tell a story!"

She then looked at Don, "Any chance you can get your printers to do another full-size color version of the last one? I want it of the girls."

"Anything for Mrs. Macleay." He smiled a tight smile and looked back up to Horatio. "I want you and Edie to come to my place for a little luau I'm having tonight. It will be just like the good ol' days. All the mucky mucks on the island are coming. You kids are invited too." He looked at me. "And you'll be on duty, missy. No more days off."

I tried to smile. Don's parties were not my favorite way to spend the evening.

"Good. Come hungry. I've ordered the fatted-calf. Or rather, the roasted pig." With that, he swept out of the photography studio like a hurricane and raced back to his office upstairs.

"So, boys," Horatio clapped his hands together, "let's get going before we lose the day. I've been looking forward to this tropical fishing adventure since we arrived."

Peter put the fan down and grabbed his poles that leaned against the wall. "We've already lost the day. It's nearly ten o'clock in the morning." To a fisherman, it might as well have been midnight.

"It's the principle of the thing," Horatio rumbled. "I've not had a pole in my hands in months, and who knows when I'll have another chance to spend the afternoon with my favorite nephew and my old shipmate. This could be my last day off for some time."

Frank chuckled. "Sounds good to me."

"The fishing here is good. Butterfish. Snapper. Shark—which

makes pretty good steaks, actually." Peter passed a pole to Horatio and another to Frank. "So, we'll be off then." He turned back towards me. "You sure you girls don't want to go? I was going to take the boat out off the coast. It's a nice day for a sail."

"Not us!" Edie answered quickly. "We are going to lie out on the sand and burn and talk until we're hoarse. I need some girl time and a taste of the true Hawaii. Piper," she commanded, "lead the way to Malaekahana beach!"

~

MALAEKAHANA WAS a secluded stretch of white sand that sloped gently towards crystalline blue waters. It backed up to emerald green trees that provided shade from the bright sun. Enormous, fluffy white clouds, just enough to provide interest, filled the sky.

"It's simply our favorite beach on the island," I explained as my sandaled feet plodded down the trail. "That out there," I stopped and pointed towards an island not far from the beach, "is Goat Island. The locals call it Moku'auia. It's got some beautiful tropical birds, Edie."

"I did bring my travel paint-set!" She shifted the basket from one hand to another. "I do wonder what is in this basket. I think Johnny outdid himself."

Katrine and Grace took both sides of the quilt we'd brought and stretched it out on the ground. We all sat, and Lorelei began to help Edie set out the basket's contents: Cokes all around, little ham and cheese sandwiches on sweet rolls, deviled eggs, and traditional Japanese butter cookies called Hatu Sabure in the traditional dove shape for all.

Edie held two of them up. "Have you ever seen anything so precious! Wherever did he get these?"

I passed out the napkins. "Johnny makes them for every church potluck. He's practically famous for them." Out of the corner of my eye, I noticed Katrine take two of the little sandwiches and pick them apart, eating only the roll and throwing the ham filling into the bushes.

Edie smiled contentedly and threw her head up to the sky. The breeze blew through her hair, and she looked very young and very happy. "Look at us, girls! Can you believe this moment? Take it in. Breathe it in!" She inhaled and looked back at us.

"It's a nice beach," Lorelei said, looking out towards Goat Island. "Different than Palestine. Different from any beach I've ever been to, actually. The air is different. It almost smells sweet."

"That was quite a story Horatio told your editor." Grace kicked off her sandals and dug her feet into the soft sand.

"What?" I looked up.

"All that about us being Greek orphans." She laughed. "By the time all this is over, I'm not going to remember who I am! A Macleay, an Adleman, a pilot, a singer. How am I going to keep my stories straight."

"Technically, I am a Stenetsky," Katrine said bluntly. "And trust me, it's easier than you think. I've had *plenty* of practice."

"Anybody who's interesting has to have a story," Edie said with an air of authority. "You just have to play a character. And your character now is that of a famous singer."

"It makes me feel silly." Grace stood up and began to stomp away.

Edie called after her, "Don't you want your lunch?"

"Not hungry!" she called over her shoulder. "I'm going to take a walk."

"She's always getting up and walking away," Lorelei groaned.

We all watched her walk down to the water's edge. Her long, strong legs carried her into the surf, and then back out.

"All right, Lorelei," Edie finally said after a moment. "When are you going to tell us?"

"When am I going to tell you what?"

"About Joe Miller. My future son-in-law?"

Lorelei turned red. "Who told you that?"

"Well…" Edie faltered. "I just assumed…"

"Why is everyone assuming?" Lorelei stopped herself. "I'm sorry. It's just that… Joe Miller has not asked me to marry him. And even if he was to ask, I wouldn't accept."

"Is that so?" Edie lowered her chin.

"It is."

Katrine listened in silence. I couldn't read her expression.

"What happened?" Edie asked quietly. "If you don't mind me asking."

I saw Lorelei swallow. She was trying to decide how much to say, and then, she seemed to throw off any concerns and plunged in. "I'll be honest. I went to Cairo expecting God to lead me to the love of my life. My heart was open, which was a miracle after everything that happened with Rolf. You know all about that…" She twirled her Coke lid in her fingers. "But everything went wrong. My life in that area feels all mixed up right now, and I would love to find a way out of it all! The man I thought I would love, I don't. Or I should but can't. And the man who loves me… Well, it's all wrong. I love him back, dearly, but I could never love him the way he wants me to."

Katrine and I looked at one another. We both knew she meant Frank.

"Why not?" Katrine asked, looking at Lorelei sideways.

Pain filled Lorelei's eyes. "I don't know if you would understand, Katrine. But it has to do with my faith in Yeshua. I've made a commitment to only marry someone who shares my faith."

Edie reached out and patted Lorelei's face. "Good girl."

"So, here I am," Lorelei shrugged, "single as ever. Perhaps God never wanted me to go to Cairo. I don't know what he's saying anymore. I wonder if I heard him right."

"My dear," Edie looked at her straight on, "if I've learned anything in my life, it is to doubt what I doubt and believe what I know to be true. If you truly believe God has called you to marriage, it will come. Trust him for the timing. Perhaps he brought you to

Cairo for some other, different purpose." Edie looked past her and towards me with a knowing expression. "Life is like a bouquet of wildflowers, dear, some tall and fragrant, some dark with thorny stems, but when you see them all together, it's a beautiful thing."

"I suppose so. But at this point, I've concluded I may be meant to be single after all."

"Tut tut tut!" Edie chided. "For all you know, your man may be out there," she waved vaguely to the ocean, "swimming around!"

I laughed out loud.

"None of that now, Piper!" she silenced me. "Stranger things can happen."

"Not for me." Lorelei frowned.

"I absolutely refuse to agree with you." Edie smiled and broke a dove cookie in half, taking a methodical bite. "Things do happen. And I believe they are going to happen to you, sooner than you expect!"

Lorelei laughed. "If you say so, Edie. Regardless, I think it's better to be single than make a mistake and marry the wrong man. I am determined to be sure about whoever I marry. Life's too short to be desperate."

"Well, that's true, dear." Edie sighed. "But falling in love is not about being sure, Lorelei!"

"Then what is it about?" Lorelei asked. "I was one-hundred percent sure about Rolf."

"And Rolf, God rest his soul, was your first love. You were young. Too young to see his flaws, I take it. But he had them. All men do." She sighed and looked at the sky. "No, no. Love is about trust and choice. No one is one hundred percent perfect. You have to trust God to lead you and then choose the one he leads you to. No doubt, whoever God leads you to will make mistakes, and you will too, and you'll have to choose each other in spite of them. Being sure means you risk." Her eyes lowered to Lorelei's, and she stared deeply into them. "And risking love is exactly what you chose to do when you gave Rolf's bracelet to Paulina."

Lorelei frowned and dug her feet into the sand. I could tell she didn't particularly like what Edie had said. Lorelei liked being sure. She hated mistakes. She'd had enough unknown for the past four years. Though she may have been ready to risk once, long ago, the years hence had not been kind. Things had not turned out as she had expected.

Risk had once sounded exciting and hopeful. Now? It was a word filled with pain and unfulfilled dreams.

"Well, on that note," I stood up, "I'm going for a swim." I dug into the bottom of the basket and pulled out two sets of snorkel gear and held them up. "Anyone with me?"

"I'm going to join you," Lorelei said.

"I'm going to stay here," Katrine replied laying down on her back.

"You two have a good time." Edie followed suit. "Be careful of sharks."

As we neared the water, Lorelei, in her dark red swimsuit, looked at me worriedly. "Are there really sharks?"

"There are, but we'll keep an eye out," I said playfully as the sun reflected off my own perfectly white crisscrossed back suit.

Unafraid, I waded into the water and dove into an oncoming wave and swam out beyond the surf, with Lorelei several strokes behind me. Once we were out into the calm beyond the waves, Lorelei motioned towards the island. "Is it too far to swim to?" she asked.

"Not at all!" I took off towards the island.

By now, we were very far from the beach and nearing the island. I wondered if this would be a good time to bring up my suspicions. "Lorelei," I began, slowing my stroke to talk, "I wanted to ask you, this whole USO show business, is it for real?"

"Of course it's for real," she said.

"That's not what I mean. I know you girls. I didn't think you ever wanted to perform again," I answered, looking back. She had stopped swimming and was treading water.

"I have a cramp," Lorelei called as I swam back towards her.

"Lie on your back and float!"

"I can't!" she shouted. She was thrashing around. I wracked my brain trying to figure out what to do. "You have to calm down. Relax!"

At that exact moment, out of the water, to my horror, I saw a grey fin coming towards us. And then another and another. The fins were everywhere and getting closer. Sharks! This had never happened before the whole time I'd been in Hawaii!

"Lorelei!" I screamed. "Don't move." I had heard that sharks can smell fear.

"Are those what I think they are?" Lorelei sputtered, terrified.

In my panic, I began to pray out loud. "Jesus, help us!"

And then, like a voice from heaven, my prayers were answered. Over the waves, the sound of a robust, gallant voice reached my ears. "Having some trouble?" I spun around in the water. There, round the island, came an outrigger canoe rowing towards us steadily—roughly 30 feet away.

"We need some help!" I shouted. "We're surrounded!"

"Help is on the way!" he shouted back strongly, paddling faster.

"Hurry! There are sharks, and she has a cramp!"

"Not to worry," the man said in a relieved tone. "Those aren't sharks. Just a dolphin pod!"

"How do you know?" I shot a nervous glance to the fins.

Without any warning, one of them jumped out of the water, making the telltale 'eep!' of a dolphin. The man maneuvered the boat to where Lorelei and I were splashing about. He reached out with a strong arm and pulled her up into the boat.

Lorelei sat there, gulping air down and trembling slightly.

The man smiled at Lorelei and then down at me, revealing a row of perfectly white, straight teeth.

As I recovered from the moment and gathered myself, I got a look at him. He was handsome. Excessively so. His thick blonde hair with a slight natural curl was parted on the side and swept back to create a wave. His eyes were a cross between blue and green, with flecks of gold, or perhaps it was just the sun reflecting off his pupils. I couldn't tell. He wore a t-shirt and swim trunks.

"I guess I'm a little out of practice." Lorelei managed a slight laugh.

The man reached down again and helped me into the boat as well. I noticed he had a guitar in the back of the canoe.

"I don't often find mermaids on this side of the island," he said playfully as he passed Lorelei a towel. It struck me that Lorelei was nervous. More nervous than I'd ever seen her in my life.

"I've never seen a boat like this," Lorelei said, taking off her goggles and trying to regain her composure.

"My husband would love it," I replied, thinking of Peter.

"Traditional Hawaiian outrigger. Made it myself." He patted it proudly. "Well… I fixed it up, to be more precise."

"And you are?" Lorelei asked.

"Paul Sinclair."

"More like Lorelei's knight in shining armor." I smiled and patted Lorelei's shoulder. "Are you okay, Lorelei?"

She nodded. "I'm feeling better. Much better." She looked at Paul and then hiccuped loudly. "What *are* you fishing for, if not women?" She flushed slightly, hiccuped, and put her hand to her throat, embarrassed.

The man shook his head no. "Actually, I don't fish. I just like to get on the water when I've got time off. I spent the morning on the other side of Goat Island. You two should check it out." He kept his eyes firmly on Lorelei. From the moment he paddled up and helped us, it was as though I wasn't even there.

"That's what we were trying to do!" she attempted.

I noticed a pair of binoculars around his neck. "Are you, by chance," I asked, "a bird watcher?"

He glanced at Lorelei and nodded sharply. For a split second, I thought I saw a faint blush creep up his neck. Why he almost seemed as nervous talking to Lorelei as she seemed to be talking to him. I settled back into the boat. This was getting interesting.

"There's a lot to see around here. Like dolphins or struggling mermaids." He took the oars and rowed a swift, strong stroke.

Lorelei looked up at him and another hiccup escaped her lips. "Oh dear." She tried to stop, "Excuse me!"

He continued, "Actually, there *was* a lovely Hawaiian Petrel I was observing when I heard your SOS." Looking up at the sky, he pointed to a white and black bird circling over us. "It's an 'Ua'u' in Hawaiian. Endangered species actually. There are only 50 or 60 breeding pairs left on the island. They're a special bird. The male and female both take turns keeping the egg warm till it's time to hatch."

Lorelei looked at him out of the corner of her eye. "You obviously have done your research."

"Just interested, I guess."

"What else are you interested in?" I asked.

He kept rowing, throwing Lorelei another look. "Languages, history, politics...These days I'm into physical fitness." He rowed harder, obviously trying to impress her. "I like to keep fit, you know." He looked at Lorelei, "Do you like to keep fit?"

"No. I mean—yes. I mean..." Lorelei looked at me and shrugged. "Not more than any normal girl."

"You should, you know?" Paul lifted his right hand off the oar and flexed his bicep. "Healthy body, healthy mind." He paused and then added, "Could help with your swim stroke. Endurance training and all that."

"My swim stroke?" Lorelei stopped hiccuping, observing him, suddenly suspicious.

He shrugged. "If you ask me, you are pretty stiff in the water. You need to even out your breath, and not thrash around so much. Then, you won't get cramps." He examined her. "Forty pushups a day, I should say, for a girl your size."

"A girl my size?" She stared at him, not blinking.

"Yeah, or fifty if you're strong. You look like a strong girl. Twice a day."

She raised one eyebrow and sat up very straight. "For the record, I was only thrashing around like that because I had just eaten and gotten a cramp."

"You know the cardinal rule of swimming—don't try it after eating."

"Where I come from," her eyes flashed slightly, "men don't tell women what they should or shouldn't do."

An awkward silence filled the canoe.

The sound of someone shouting on the shore drew all of our attention. It was a young boy, waving and calling.

"Oh, that's Timmy." Paul quickly looked to the shore and frowned. "I told him to stay at the campsite until I came back. We spent the weekend camping... I better get back. I need to make sure everything is okay." Paul Sinclair picked up speed. Neither he nor Lorelei looked at one another.

The boat caught a wave and surged towards the sand, riding along with it like a surfboard.

Once we were in the shallows, we hopped out and helped Paul drag the canoe to the shore. Standing up, I noticed that he was quite tall, probably 6'4". It struck me again how attractive he was.

The boy met us, his hand on his hip. He appeared around 11 years old and wore an impish grin.

"You lost track of time," the boy called Timmy chided Paul.

"I guess I did. An unexpected lifeguarding job came up." Paul turned towards us, "I've got to get Timmy back home before an event tonight. It's going to take us some time to pack up the campsite . . . You two can make your way up the beach all right, can't you?"

The current had carried us about a quarter of a mile from where my aunt sat with Katrine. He was looking at Lorelei with genuine concern.

"Oh yes." She nodded. "I am perfectly fine now."

As we walked down the beach, Lorelei turned around and stared for a second at the man and the boy.

"What are you thinking?" I asked.

She paused. "He's handsome, I'll give him that. His son is cute."

I shrugged. "He *might* be single."

She didn't answer.

"So...?"

"So?" She looked at me. "So, I have a rule, that's what."

"A rule?"

"Yes. I don't trust men who are that good looking. If he's single... Besides, he's more brawn than brain anyways. And pushy. Telling me to do push-ups!"

"I think he was nervous and trying to impress you." I stopped and looked back in Paul's direction.

"Piper," she sighed, "you obviously know nothing about men."

"Lorelei, have you forgotten I've been married for several years now?"

It was as though she hadn't heard me. "Besides," she started walking again, "he's got a kid. He's probably married."

"You don't *know* he's married. In fact, if you ask me, he was acting pretty single." I thought back to the way he had been looking at her. He didn't strike me as a player. If anything, he had appeared honest, kind, and, quite honestly, struck by Lorelei. And he had obviously been trying to flirt with her. He had to be single... at least, I hoped he was single.

"Oh *really*, Piper! How could a man that handsome not be married? It's completely absurd. Why it's almost wrong to talk about it like this! Besides," she repeated, "he's so pushy."

"You may be right." I paused before adding, "But you didn't exactly win an award for politeness yourself. 'Where I come from, men don't tell women what to do...'" I imitated her soft German accent. Sometimes, Lorelei could come across as a snob. And this had been one of those moments. "You didn't even say 'thank you.'"

She groaned. "He seemed quite self-absorbed. Let's not talk about this anymore."

"We could talk about something else," I started.

"Like what?"

"Like the trio."

"What about it?"

I put my hand on my hip, "I think there is something you aren't telling me."

"Whatever do you mean?"

"The Macleay Sisters, overnight sensations traveling from Egypt to Hawaii? Seriously?" I put my hand on my hip. "You and I both know that Katrine hates performing. And Grace would never leave the Palmach for anyone, including the USO." I steadied my gaze on her. "And you? I can't imagine you trading in nursing for a musical gig."

"Everyone else seems to appreciate the sacrifices we are making for the war effort."

"I'm not everyone else. How is this better than your other hands-on work? Besides that, I'm a tough newspaperwoman now, remember? "

"Photographer," she corrected. "*Photographers* aren't supposed to ask the hard-hitting questions, remember? Journalists are."

"But I can spot a fake a mile away." Frowning, I exhaled. "Are you girls in a jam?"

"Of course not." Lorelei put a reassuring hand on my arm. "We are just doing our job for the war effort. And I needed a tropical vacation."

I looked at her, completely unconvinced.

She shook her head, "There are some things I *can't* tell you. Please don't ask me to, Piper." Then, looking up at the sun, she squinted and took my hand. "We ought to head back and get ready for the party, don't you think?"

CHAPTER 10

HARRY

*E*die gushed,"Oh, Piper! You look very, *very* professional. What a lovely suit!"

I smoothed out the light pink linen skirt and matching blazer. I could see Horatio's outline in the bathroom mirror, carefully trimming his full beard. He was humming loudly, completely oblivious to our presence. Edie's auburn hair was up in curlers, and she was in the process of ironing her dress. She held it up. "Gorgeous, don't you think?"

"Very fancy." I looked closer. "Is that silk?"

"You won't believe where I got it." She lowered her voice before saying, "You know how hard it has been to find anything nice in Scotland these days. Clothing was one of the first things to be rationed, and it's only gotten worse since you left. It's been a complete nightmare."

Nodding, I fingered the soft fabric. I hadn't seen silk this lovely in a long time. Since the war, all the silk had gone towards making parachutes, maps, and gunpowder bags.

"You know how many ration coupons you need for a jacket? A

full 13! And you only get 66 coupons a year. We've had to become very resourceful."

"I didn't know you could iron silk?"

"You just have to do it carefully. You must make sure the iron isn't too hot. If it's dupioni silk, which this is not, just put a cotton cloth on top of it and iron both. It works like a dream. Never steam silk," she looked up, "the water droplets can stain the fabric."

"So…" I prodded, knowing how much Edie appreciated quality, fashionable garments. "Where'd you get it?"

"An old nightie your mother and I found when we were cleaning out the attic. Probably belonged to Horatio's grandmother. Fabulous, don't you think!" She held it up for a moment, admiringly.

It was definitely no longer an old nightie. It was the height of fashion. Anyone would think it was out of one of the major fashion houses in Europe—that is if they were still making dresses as they had before the war.

She went back to ironing. "Are your cousins coming along? We've not much time."

"They'll be ready."

"What about Peter and Frank?"

"Dressed and waiting on the porch."

Edie propped the iron up and went to the dresser, pulling out a red scarf. "Give this to Katrine, will you? She said she needed something extra with the navy dress she's wearing tonight." She paused and then looked up at me, "Have you noticed anything odd about your cousins?"

I thought about my own hesitations surrounding my cousins' backstory. As noble as it was to drop everything and entertain the troops in the Pacific, the truth was, they weren't 'show' people. Katrine was an academic who preferred books and research to society. Lorelei was a dedicated nurse who practiced the piano in private to clear her mind. And Grace would rather spend all day jumping out of planes than rehearsing high-kicks.

"You mean, like there is something more than meets the eye about their joining the USO show?"

She looked relieved. "I was worried I was making it up. I've been sleuthing around, but they are as tightlipped as a safe at the national bank."

"What?" I asked, grinning at her odd metaphor.

"Mark my words, I am an expert safe cracker!" she remarked confidently, dabbing her lipstick with a handkerchief.

"Lorelei said... Well, she asked me not to ask questions."

"I'm the wife of an admiral. I'll ask as many questions as I very well please."

Scarf in hand, I turned and backed out of the room and closed the door behind me. Johnny was vacuuming the living room. Lorelei and Grace were both in the guest bathroom putting the finishing touches on their makeup.

Johnny stopped vacuuming and looked at me. "Who are you looking for, Piper?"

"Have you seen Katrine?"

"The little one with dark hair?"

I nodded and took my camera bag from where'd I'd left it on the table, slinging it over my shoulder.

"She went down to the beach 20 minutes ago."

Frowning, I thanked Johnny and took up a small trot out of the house and down the small winding path towards the beach. I found her a few minutes later sitting on the sand and looking out over the ocean. She turned her head around and looked at me a moment before facing the ocean once more. Her hair blew slightly in the breeze, and the sun sat low in the sky, casting a pink glow on her pale skin.

"Katrine?" I asked carefully.

"Is it almost time to go?" She didn't turn back around.

"In a few minutes." I slipped my heels off and walked through the sand, sitting beside her. She stared straight ahead.

Then, barely above a whisper, she said, "Where do you think he is out there?"

"You know," I put my hand on her shoulder, "I understand, a little bit anyway. When Peter was wounded off the coast of Africa, they sent me a telegram telling me he was missing in action. In all the confusion of the battle... it took time to get everyone organized. Peter was sent to a hospital in Cyprus. Frank was sent to Cairo. No one knew where anyone was. For all I knew, Peter had died and sunk to the bottom of the ocean. But he hadn't. He was alive. I believe that Harry is alive."

"You do?" She looked at me, her eyes brimming over with tears.

"I do. And I am going to keep believing he is alive."

"Lorelei said something similar to me." Katrine inhaled deeply. "You know, Piper, it's almost as if she is a different person than before. Lorelei, the one who used to be the most afraid of the dark, the most sensitive, the least ready to try new things, now she is the strong one. She told me that whenever she prays for Harry and me, she feels peace."

"What did you say?"

"I told her she would have to have faith for both of us. I'm a woman who believes in cold hard facts. Right now, the facts aren't looking so great. I get this awful sinking feeling that I'm never going to see him again. Waiting like this, it feels like I'm dying or something."

Out of my mouth came words that I had said a million times when Peter had been wounded. "May the God of hope fill you with all joy and peace as you trust in him, so that you may overflow with hope by the power of the Holy Spirit."[17]

"Christian scriptures?" Katrine tilted her head.

"The words of a Jewish rabbi, Katrine, who met Yeshua as his Messiah. They've carried me through. Carried Lorelei through too." I paused. "Look, Katrine. You will not get through this waiting on your own. You have to trust someone while you wait."

"I do. I trust myself. I trusted Harry. But then he had to go and disappear in battle." She laughed joylessly. "Where is he, Piper? Where is my husband?"

She shut her eyes, imagining Harry suffering and alone. Only later would we learn that what she imagined was, in fact, the truth.

~

Luzon

The Philippines

June 30, 1944

"IT'S NOT A BED," the kid next to Harry said, completely distraught. "It's a shelf."

"It's better than the floor." Harry patted the young man's back and squinted. In reality, he wasn't so sure. His glasses, lost somewhere in the craziness of the last few days, were gone. He couldn't really see the bed clearly. Regardless, the truth was that he and several hundred other men who had survived what would later be dubbed the Bataan Death March were expected to sleep stacked up eight men high on rough wooden slats.

Harry couldn't remember the last time he'd laid down at all. Sitting down on the shelf next to the younger soldier, Harry extended his hand. "What's your name kid?"

"Claude." He looked like he was about to cry. "Claude Simons."

"So, Claude Simons," Harry reached into his pocket, "how old are you?"

"Eighteen last February."

Eighteen last February… Wow. Harry shook his head. He had been 18 over two decades ago. This kid could be his son. He pulled Katrine's photograph out of his pocket and unfolded it for the millionth time. It was the only personal item that had escaped the Japanese's notice.

"Who's that?" Claude asked, looking at the picture admiringly.

"My wife." Harry's voice was proud.

"What's she doing?"

Harry swatted a mosquito on the back of his neck. "She's riding a camel."

"Where'd you ever do a crazy thing like that? Circus come to town?"

Harry chuckled. "Nah. It was on our honeymoon. We went out into the desert with the Bedouins."

"The who?"

Harry, realizing again how young the boy beside him was, was about to explain but was instantly cut short by the arrival of several Japanese guards demanding quiet.

Warily, Harry stuffed the photograph back into his grimy pocket and stood up with the rest of the captured soldiers. He could tell that Claude was shaking. Harry shot the boy a firm look, silently willing the boy to buck up. Any sign of cowardice or fear was giving in to the enemy and could make you a target for their animalistic cruelty.

"I am Commander Yoko," spoke the leader in a halting, labored English. "You will call me Taichou-sama, Most-Venerable Commander."

He was overweight with an ugly sneering face that looked down at the POWs as though they were dogs or even lower than dogs. Harry hated his guts.

"Welcome to my camp." He looked from face to face. "I do not feed idle workers. You don't work, you don't eat. Those who do not work hard will be punished. Officers will work as well as common soldiers."[16]

Harry had seen enough on the march to the camp to know that Commander Yoko was telling the truth.

"Escape is impossible," Most-Venerable Commander Yoko continued. "We are on an island. Not to mention the barbed wire and the guards. You escape, you die."

Major Canning, the highest-ranking American officer among the POWs, stepped forward. "Commander," he held his chin out, "we are prisoners of war. Under the Geneva Convention of 1929, you are not permitted to force us to work on any war-related project."

Commander Yoko's bushy eyebrows went up. The guard nearest him took the butt of his rifle and thrust it into Major Canning's kidneys. He doubled over in agony as the guards began to laugh, and the rest of the barracks instantly grew silent.

"An honorable soldier dies in battle. It is your shame and dishonor that brought you here. Be grateful that you have useful labor to do!" Commander Yoko sneered at Major Canning and then turned on his heel and left as quickly as he had come.

"Major!" A young man called Danny rushed over and helped the major to a sitting position on one of the wooden shelf-beds. "Are you okay, sir?"

Shakily, Canning shook his head. No one moved. Then, as he regained control, he motioned for all to step in closer.

"As you all know, the Japanese have appointed me as POW liaison. I'm in charge, but they are in control. But, I think it is obvious, this is not a prisoner of war situation that we have been prepared for."

"How so, sir?" someone asked.

"We've all seen what our enemy is capable of." He rubbed his back. "We are not in a nice German POW camp where they give men baseballs and playing cards and garden plots. The Japanese are going to use us for slave labor. They will, no doubt, unflinchingly kill us off like flies if we ruffle their feathers. Maybe even if we don't. To them, we are less than human."

Everyone nodded. The Germans generally treated American prisoners of war humanely. Eventually, 99% of prisoners would live to tell of their long "wait to win" behind barbed wire in Bavaria and Austria and Czechoslovakia. The odds for prisoners taken by the Japanese were not nearly so optimistic. Only four out of ten would return home alive.[18]

Major Canning's eyes narrowed. "Nevertheless, boys, we may be under Japanese control, but we are still soldiers. It is our sworn duty to escape. It is our sworn duty to throw as many wrenches into their plans as we can. We are not going to let them take our dignity. You understand?"

Again, everyone nodded. Major Canning was the true authority in the camp.

"Remember, they can take everything from you, except for your feelings, your thoughts, and your convictions." He pointed to his head. "No one can take your personality or your attitude or what you believe in unless you let them."

The men looked at one another. For the moment, they were strengthened.

"Good. Now, you are dismissed."

An hour later, Harry and Claude joined a long line of POWs for one of two meals offered daily: a half cup of boiled rice and a cup of water. In the tropical heat of Luzon, the island they all were trapped on, Harry knew dehydration was going to be an issue—and that was before the work had even begun. This was going to be bad. He knew it. Major Canning knew it. And so did every other American, British, and Australian soldier on the island.

As he stood in line, out of the corner of his eye, he saw a soldier making his way towards the latrines. They had all discovered that they were not sufficient for the number of men in the camp. There were also no showers. There was no way to bathe. No escape from the rancid smell of unwashed bodies that had been so for weeks. As he watched, the soldier began to whistle cheerfully. Harry had no idea why. Maybe to relieve the stress? Maybe he was a nervous whistler? Who could say... The point was that as the soldier passed by the chain metal fence, a Japanese guard in the tower shouted for him to be silent—in Japanese. The young man, unhearing, kept whistling. The guard lifted and aimed his Arisaka Type 99 rifle with the bayonet mounted at the young man and pulled the trigger.

Miraculously, the bullet missed the mark. The young man fell to his knees, his entire body shaking. The message was received. No whistling in the camp. No whistling on the job either. Silent, strict obedience... or else!

The next day, stomach rumbling, throat burning for water, Harry found himself stripped to the waist, a pickax in hand, hewing solid rock for what he assumed would become a landing strip. Japanese guards, bored on their lunch break, hurled rocks and laughed at the POWs who were powerless to respond.

Two men were executed on the spot for trying to escape when the guards weren't looking.

For perhaps the first time in Harry's life, he was truly afraid.

"Hey, Harry," Claude whispered late that night.

"What's the matter, kid? Can't sleep?"

"Me and some other guys—" He nervously lowered his voice even more, "We are planning an escape."

Harry was instantly wide awake. "Claude, you can't escape now. You've seen what these guys do!"

"Are you afraid?"

"Yeah, I'm afraid. And I'm also not stupid. You want to survive this? Wait. Escapes, ones that work, take a lot of planning."

"I'm not staying here a minute longer than I have to," the young man said impetuously.

"How are you going to escape?"

"A friend of mine found a pair of wire cutters. We are going to cut through the fence tomorrow morning and get out of here."

Harry frowned. "And what exactly are you going to do on the other side of the fence?"

"We'll find a boat and sail to another island."

"You do realize that all the surrounding islands are under the control of the Japs, right?" He turned his head on the rough slat and stared incredulously at the side of the boy's face. "You escape, and they catch you, they *will* kill you. They won't bring you back here and punish you."

"But they can't kill us for trying to escape. I know about the Geneva Convention!"

"Something the Japs would spit on." Harry's voice took on a new urgency. "You know those two guys were killed today for making a run for it."

Claude was panicked and not thinking rationally. "I'm not going to stay here and starve to death. I'm hungry!"

"Claude, the idea of getting out is making you crazy." His voice sunk lower. "I'm a few years older than you. Believe it or not, I've made it out of some pretty tough scrapes. If we are going to try to escape, it is going to take a *real* plan. Not a pair of wire cutters and nowhere to go afterward."

Claude blinked. "You mean, we *are* going to try to escape."

"Yeah. Of course. We are going to try." Harry emphasized the word 'try.' "You heard Major Canning. It is our sworn duty to try to escape. But not with those idiots tomorrow. Mark my words. They aren't making it anywhere but six feet under the sand. You get me?"

Wordlessly, Claude nodded. Somehow, he knew to trust Harry. It was something in his calm, self-assured demeanor. It commanded confidence. "Sure," he said. "A real plan… A real plan."

The next morning, Harry's prediction came true. Claude's friends were caught and shot within two minutes of sliding under the barbed wire fence. Claude was convinced that Harry had saved his life and stuck as close to him as a lost puppy.

That evening, as Harry ate his half-cup of rice, looking out at the ocean through the chain-link fence, he concluded that the world was a crazy place. He couldn't decide who was worse, the Nazis or the Japanese. He imagined he was back in Palestine with Katrine. He tried to ignore the terrible sunburn on his shoulders. He tried to ignore the drunken laughter of the Japanese soldiers coming from their barracks several feet away. He pictured Katrine and felt relieved that she was far away, safe and sound in the desert where he had left her.

～

As HARRY LOOKED out onto the Pacific, he would have been shocked to learn that Katrine was not in Palestine as he thought. He would have been shocked that, in fact, she and I were on the shores of Hawaii. And he would have been shocked to know that at that moment, we were looking out onto the same ocean, towards the same horizon as him. It was incredible but true.

Katrine, as broken in spirit as he was in body, leaned heavily on my arm, desperate for comfort, longing for hope, but terrified she would be dreadfully disappointed.

Inwardly, I plead with God to give me the right words to speak, knowing of Katrine's fragility but believing he could give her strength to press on even now, just as he had given me the strength to press on in my time without Peter.

"I don't know if I can go on, Piper, not knowing! I don't trust myself anymore. And I don't know who to trust! Life is so... difficult." She looked down. "Piper, would you - would you pray for me?"

"I didn't know you prayed, Katrine?"

"I don't. Not really. But Lorelei does. And when she prays for me, I'm able to think. It makes me feel... peaceful."

"I would be honored to pray for, you Katrine, but you do know you can pray for yourself."

She shook her head. "Oh, no. I'm not that sort of person. I'm not even sure I really believe in God. Certainly not in the way you and Lorelei do."

I sat there thinking for a moment of her contradiction. Katrine liked it when Lorelei prayed for her. She couldn't deny she felt peace. And though she acknowledged a certain power over her emotions was involved, she was hesitant to say she believed in God at all.

Struck by an idea, I quickly unclasped my necklace and secured it around Katrine's neck instead.

"What are you doing?"

"When you begin to have that sinking, despairing feeling, reach for God, Katrine. You need it now, more than me."

"Your necklace?"

"Indeed. My mother gave it to me… years ago."

"Ha Tikvah." Her eyes glistened reading the Hebrew inscribed on the front piece of gold. "The Hope? But," she faltered, "I don't have hope the way you do."

"Hope is found in a person, Katrine. Not a thing."

"A person?"

"Hope is found in the Messiah. I'll pray for you, Katrine, and Lorelei will too. But I think it would be better if you go to him on your own. He'll give you peace, I promise."

Katrine tilted her head, considering my words. I wondered if she was going to take the necklace off, but she did not.

Suddenly, Peter began to call for us while Horatio honked the horn of the Woody.

"Looks like it is time to go to the Luau," I said as I stood up.

Katrine followed suit. We both dusted the sand from our feet and slipped our shoes back on once we reached the packed earth of the path back to the house.

"Oh," I felt the scarf still in my hand, "here." I gave it to her. "Edie said this is for you."

Katrine took it and held it a second before tying it around her neck in a fashionable little knot. "What do you think? Do I look like a famous Scottish-American singer from Greece, by way of Egypt?"

"Most certainly," I agreed. "In fact," I took my camera and adjusted the new 50mm Leitz Elmar lens, positioning her head towards the sun, "I think you look so lovely we need to remember it forever."

CHAPTER 11

LOVE AT THE LUAU

I made my way through the crowd in the Tiki Room, a restaurant and bar that Don had rented out for the party to see the USO show off. He thought it would be good publicity for the paper. And so, I spent the evening snapping pictures of starlets and officers, their faces lit by an abundance of fake tiki torches. Everyone was fascinated by the new kids on the block, the overnight sensations, the Macleay Sisters.

The actress Myrna Loy and comedian Bob Hope, among others, laughed and drank volcanoes, a mixture of grapefruit and lime juice.[19] Myrna was even prettier in person than on the silver screen. She wore a dark blue satin dress that was cut on a bias. The deep 'V' neck was held up by two thickly beaded straps. Her light, airy laugh carried over the crowd, as glittery as the straps to her dress. All the men, including Bob, wore their military dress uniforms.

Everyone had already eaten the heaps of Kalua pig, Lomilomi salmon, and Hawaiian sweet potato.

I took pictures of all of them, smiling, drinking, dancing. I took pictures of the entertainers Don had hired, a troupe of Hawaiian men and women in grass skirts who danced and chanted to the songs of the hula, each carefully orchestrated move telling the stories and myths of the islands.

"It would have been a much nicer party on the beach instead of this crowded restaurant." I felt Peter come up behind me. He looked uncomfortable, the way he always did at these sorts of events. "You about done?"

"I've got one more shot." Then I added as I looked at the blackout curtains lining the restaurant's windows. "You know beach parties are out, pet. No lights at night."

He took the camera out of my hand and quickly snapped one of a very surprised looking me.

"There. Now you're done." He laughed. "You are always behind the camera. I need more pictures of the photographer."

I grinned and felt myself blush as he handed my camera to Julie as she passed by. "That's for safe-keeping. You can tell Don she's done for the night, Jules." He winked and led me to the dance floor.

"PETER!" I exclaimed, looking over his shoulder. It was our fourth song.

"Did I step on your foot again?"

"No, no," I assured. "It's that guy!"

"What guy?"

"It's that lifeguard!"

"What lifeguard?" He twisted his neck around so he could see what I was looking at.

"The guy who helped me and Lorelei earlier this afternoon when we were swimming to Goat Island. He's not a lifeguard at all! He's an officer!"

Peter looked down at me curiously. "Who's an officer?"

Paul caught my eye and pushed through the crowd. He tapped Peter's shoulder, and we both stopped dancing.

"*He* is Peter!" I answered as the three of us stood for a moment.

It was true. Paul's dress uniform insignia - a golden oak leaf - marked him as a Major.

"You look familiar," Paul said with a chuckle.

"Paul Sinclair, meet my husband Peter." Then, to Peter, I said again, "This is the man who rescued us this afternoon."

Peter slapped Paul's back and laughed. "It's a pleasure to meet you."

"How about we go sit at one of the tables?" I asked. The music was getting louder, and more couples were pressing onto the dance floor. We were all in the way. Paul nodded, and Peter grabbed my hand, pulling me towards an empty table on the edge of the floor.

"So," Peter looked at Paul as he helped me into a chair, "when you're not lifeguarding, what do you do?"

Paul paused distractedly, scoping out the room as though he were waiting for someone. "Uh, actually, I am a fisher of men, of sorts. In my spare time, I volunteer as a chaplain here at Pearl."

A chaplain? That meant Paul was a Christian. My ears perked up, and I suddenly grew more invested in the conversation than I had expected to be.

Paul continued, "But my day job is with the Signal Corps. I'm pretty good at languages and work in cryptology."

Interesting. Paul was a coder.

Nodding, Peter smiled. "Then I am doubly glad to know you."

"Looking for someone?" I asked the distracted young man.

"No. I mean, well… That uppity mermaid wouldn't happen to be here, would she?" He smiled. "I thought because you were here… she might be here too."

"Lorelei is here." I looked around as well. "I don't know where she is though. And hey, what do you mean by 'uppity?'"

"You know, she seems a little snooty," Paul said, still looking around. "No offense intended."

Finally, he gave up and turned back around.

"Lorelei isn't a snob," I said, coming to my cousin's defense. "She is actually very sensitive. She and her sisters have been through a lot, and she doesn't always communicate her feelings very accurately."

"Could have fooled me." He crossed his arms and looked at Peter. "So, what do you do?"

Peter hemmed and hawed a moment before answering, "I'm finishing up my degree through correspondence. I'm studying business."

Paul leaned forward excitedly.

"I love school! Before the war, I was a professional student of sorts," he said, speaking wistfully. "I was working on my second PhD. What made you decide to study business?"

Well, Lorelei, I thought. You're wrong there. He's definitely more brain than brawn. Or at least, I took a look at his substantial chest, equal brain and brawn.

Peter looked at Horatio across the room and then at me, at a loss for words.

As he began to answer, my cousins took their place on the stage and prepared to perform. The small band began to play the opening notes of 'Big Daddy,' and out of Lorelei's mouth came the sad, sweet melody, her sisters humming in perfect harmony behind her.

Paul, whose back was turned to the platform, cocked his head to the side, listening intently. "What a voice," he said, facing me, completely enraptured. "You don't hear a voice like that very often."

"A voice like what?" I asked.

"So *real*. You can hear everything in that voice. Pain. Sweat. Tears. But not just sadness. Oh no, there's hope there too. It's a voice I could listen to all night long." He shook his head. "Where in the world did Don find a singer like that?"

He turned around in his chair, straining to see the singer. "Why!" he slowly exclaimed, "it's the mermaid!"

"Her name is Lorelei, remember?" I said, grinning.

In response, I was loudly shushed as Paul kept his eyes glued on my cousin. "Music like that," he said solemnly, "must be respected."

Peter smirked and laughed into his napkin, pretending he was coughing.

At the end of the song, the crowd burst into applause. Grace and Katrine immediately stepped off the stage as Lorelei bowed. The first two returned to Edie and Horatio's table, but Lorelei, on her way up from the bow, caught my eye, got off the stage, and moved towards us with a gentle smile as the band took off with the next number, a samba. As she neared our table, she stopped short. She saw Paul.

"Mr. Sinclair?" she uttered slowly. The sequins on her mint green evening dress sparkled.

"Hello." He stood up quickly and offered her his chair. Then, pulling up another for himself, he added, "It's Major Sinclair, actually. Fancy meeting you here!"

She swallowed, shot me a glance, and sat down with an awkward thud.

I waited for her to assume her usual charm, but she didn't. Normally, in interactions with anyone, she was confident and in control. Instead, a deep shyness swept over her, silencing her sharp conversational skills.

She looked at his face and then down at the floor. "Yeah," she offered lamely after a second. Being around Major Paul Sinclair turned her into a tense wreck. I'd never seen Lorelei so awkward before. It was as though she had morphed into a gawky schoolgirl.

After what seemed like the longest minute ever, Paul pulled a pen out of his pocket, sat down, and began tapping it nervously on the table. "I can't tell you what a shock I got pulling you out of the Pacific like that." (At that moment, he became, possibly, more awkward than she was. But it was a toss-up.)

"Me too." Lorelei looked at me again, as though pleading for help. She exhaled deeply, obviously having forgotten to breathe for a while. "I mean, I'm so glad you caught me." She stopped.

"They say I'm the 'catching type.'" He smiled. One tooth seemed to sparkle blindingly.

Peter squirmed in his seat, and I struggled not to laugh out of embarrassment. The interaction was cringe-worthy.

"I meant to say," Lorelei's vision cleared for a moment, and she stared at him, stunned, "I'm glad you saved me from drowning."

"It's what I do..."

"What?"

"Save people."

Peter stifled a chuckle at the joke, and I kicked him under the table.

"That's very interesting." Lorelei looked away, appearing disinterested. At that moment, his overconfidence must have confirmed her concerns that his beauty was only skin deep. After that, every attempt Paul made to connect seemed to make her walls go higher and thicker.

After a few more horribly awkward minutes, Paul stopped, suddenly at a loss for words. He tried to catch her eyes once more, then, defeated, checked his watch. "I've need to get home. I've got Timmy tonight."

He stood up and excited abruptly, leaving his pen on the table.

Lorelei's eyes rested on the pen and she exclaimed, "I ought to go and give it to him. It's a very nice pen." She ran off in the direction Paul had gone, once more her normal conscientious self.

Peter folded his hands together and glanced at me. "Was it just me or was that painfully uncomfortable?"

I nodded as Edie, notebook in hand, crept up behind us and sat down. She scribbled furiously, mumbling under her breath, "While Katrine sat mournfully looking at the couples on the dance floor, Lorelei desperately chased after the handsome officer. Frank, pale with jealousy, fumed in his seat while Grace danced with every single man on the dance floor, though none could capture her attention."

"How do you know Frank is jealous?" I looked at my aunt sideways and then at Frank, whose eyes were rooted on Lorelei working her way through the crowd. He was obviously not hearing a word that Bob Hope was saying to him. The comedian's animated face made me wish I could hear what he was saying for myself.

"Whoops!" Edie blushed. "I didn't realize I was talking out loud. But, to answer your question, I wasn't born yesterday. It's obvious that Frank's been in love with Lorelei since the day he first laid eyes on her. Problem is, and I'm saying this as a writer, two characters like them never, ever end up together. It's like the princess and the barber. It's bound to end tragically or comically. Only time will tell which."

"That is a load of hogwash." Peter looked disapprovingly at Edie. "Things are going to turn out just fine for Frank. He's a swell sort of fellow." He looked at her notebook and pencil. "What are you doing, Edie?"

"Taking notes." Her eyes did not leave the dance floor where Grace danced with an officer who was boring her with a very long story. Across the dance floor, Katrine sat at a table with Myrna Loy and the producer of the USO show, a small, thin man who had been a choreographer on Broadway for years. Ansel Thornton was never without a cigarette in his fingers or hop in his step.

"On what?" Peter pressed.

"Why, the girls of course!" She looked at me with a shocked expression. "For my novel."

"There she is," I said as Lorelei made her way back to the table, a faint trace of disappointment on her face.

Edie shook her head. "Cupid's arrow has struck."

"What are you talking about?" Peter looked at Edie.

"That officer is, shall we say, romantically interested in your cousin-in-law." She folded the notebook and drummed her fingers on the table. She made a motion like he was casting a fishing line and began to reel it in. "If he plays his cards right, I'd say Lorelei's a goner. How could she not fall in love with a man like that!"

"His name is Paul Sinclair," I said smugly. "And she seems to be doing a pretty good job."

"You know his name?" Edie asked, genuinely pleased.

"He's the one who rescued us today!" I stopped her before she could say anything more. "But he may be married. He has a son."

"How do you know?" She leaned forward, enthralled by the story. "Was he wearing a ring?"

I shrugged. "He's a chaplain."

"A priest!" Edie blurted out.

"Okay," Peter put his hands up, "this has got to stop right now. A priest who is married and has a son? He is totally not eligible! What are you two? Nuts?"

"He could be Anglican," Edie offered after a second. "Anglican priests get married. Oh, I do hope he's widowed."

Peter was horrified. "Edie!"

"You're right. That was an awful thing to say. I meant to say, I hope he's available, for Lorelei's sake. She's had enough heartbreak."

"You are assuming a whole lot! Plus, if that interaction was at all telling, I'd definitely say she is not interested. People don't fall in love at first sight."

"Frank did," Edie said in a know-it-all tone.

"I can't believe I'm having this conversation." Peter shook his head slowly like we had betrayed someone.

Lorelei arrived and sat down in the last free chair, putting her hands under her chin.

"So...?" I asked as we all looked at her expectantly.

"I missed him. He's gone."

"You should have asked him out," Edie stated bluntly.

Lorelei blinked in shock. "I don't ask arrogant jocks out."

"He's not a jock," Peter said. "He's got two PhD's, almost."

Lorelei fell silent, hiccuped once, and then stuttered, "I... I'm about to leave on a USO tour. It's not exactly a stellar time to get t-t-to know someone."

"Oh sure." Edie nodded solemnly. "That's what all great heroines say before they fall madly head over heels for the hero."

Lorelei held the pen up and pointed it in her adoptive mother's direction, about to respond when Edie took it and said assuredly,

"There's no doubt in my mind that that young man will want this back. I certainly would. It's a fine specimen of a pen." Then, to herself, she added, "I wonder if he writes?"

"How will I do that?" Lorelei asked, slightly concerned.

"You know his name, and you have his pen."

For good measure, I threw in: "He works at Pearl in cryptology with codes and such. And he volunteers as a chaplain. You can find him."

Edie patted Lorelei's hand. "I'm sure he'd appreciate it. It *is* a nice pen. And who better to return it than you."

"For the record," Lorelei stated, "I'm only returning this pen because it's the right thing to do. Not because I'm interested, understood?"

We nodded.

"That is," Lorelei's eyes darted back to the direction where Paul had left, "not... much."

"You just need to send him a message," Edie said.

"What?"

"You know, through code," Edie answered.

"What in heaven's name would ever make you say a thing like that!" Lorelei knocked an empty glass over in surprise. "I'm sorry," Lorelei said, gathering herself. "I, uh... I don't know why I'm so jumpy."

Edie's eyes narrowed suspiciously for a split second and met mine. Then, looking past me, she smiled and said, "Oh, look who's come to join the fun!"

In the chair where Paul had just sat, Frank took a seat.

"Swell party, huh?" he asked.

No one said anything, and a troupe of Hawaiian dancers ran into the middle of the dance floor. A drummer on the bongo started to pound it like he was going to war. The show was starting. Across the floor, behind the line of performers, I saw Ansel Thornton - the USO show's director - trotting in our direction. "Frank? Frank the accordion player?" He was practically shouting over the drums.

Frank looked up. "Yeah. That's me."

"We need to talk." His voice was syrupy smooth. "There's been some changes in the show."

"What sort of changes?"

"You are no longer needed, to put it bluntly."

The drumming abruptly stopped, and the dancers ran back to wherever they'd come from. The room erupted into applause.

"What do you mean?" Frank protested over the loud audience. "I am an integral part of the act!"

"Not anymore. Budget cuts."

"Budget cuts?"

Frank was incredulous.

"Well," Ansel sighed without conviction, "it was nice to meet you. And thanks for coming all the way from Cairo." He trotted back to the table.

Edie patted Frank on the shoulder. "Tough break, kid. But that's show-biz."

"That's show-biz," Frank repeated, looking down and then back up. "But it's not show-biz! I was supposed to go to help with—"

"Help with what?" Peter asked.

Frank caught himself. "Oh… nothing."

At that moment, Don emerged from the fray and pulled up a chair, the metal legs scraping uncomfortably against the cement. "Piper, I need you to clear your schedule for the next few months. I'm sending you on the USO show."

"What?" I exclaimed, nearly spilling my volcano.

"I need you to go on the USO show to take pictures."

"You mean," Frank looked from me to Don, "she's going, and I'm staying?"

"I don't know what you are talking about." Don looked blankly at Frank.

"What am I supposed to do?" Peter's face immediately fell.

"You're a big boy, you'll figure it out." Don patted his shoulder.

"Certainly you can let your wife go on the tour for a couple weeks for the sake of the war effort?"

Edie's head popped up from her notebook. "I know! How about Frank stays with Peter at the plantation house?"

"You'll be gone too!" Peter sounded very distressed.

It was true. Horatio and Edie would start their tour of the fleet right after the USO show was set to depart—literally, their boat left the same day. It looked as though Peter and Frank would be bachelors for the summer. The two men looked at one another. "I guess it could be fun," Peter said without conviction. "We can fish."

"Yeah," Frank said, equally flat, "It could be real fun. Everybody out there, doing their part for the troops. Singing and dancing and fighting. And we'll be fishing."

"I don't have to go, Peter," I said quietly, putting my hand on his arm. "I'm not even sure I want to go. It may not be safe."

"It's not like you'll be a full-on war correspondent." I could tell Peter was carefully thinking through his words. "You'll be with the show. They only send the troupe to places where the fighting is over. Trust me, I know about these things."

"I know, but..."

"There's not a single good reason for you to stay in Hawaii when you get an opportunity like this." Peter shook his head knowingly. "I'll be waiting for you right here. I won't say I'm going to like waiting, but it would be very selfish of me to ask you to stay."

"If you asked, I would."

He was determined not to hold me back. Smiling softly, he looked into my eyes. "No, you have to go. It's like—it's like you've been drafted." He stood up and held his hand out for me to take.

"What are you doing?" I looked up questioningly.

"I'm going to dance with my wife while I still have a chance."

SECOND MOVEMENT

HERMIA
I frown upon him, yet he loves me still.

HELENA
O that your frowns would teach my smiles such skill!

HERMIA
I give him curses, yet he gives me love.

HELENA
O that my prayers could such affection move!

-A Midsummer Night's Dream[1]

CHAPTER 12

SHIPS IN THE NIGHT

$\mathcal{A}$ ll the drive from the plantation house to the strip downtown to meet the gang for lunch, Lorelei and I barely said a word. Edie, however, had not stopped talking.

"General MacArthur is all anyone talks about anymore," Edie said. "What a character! Larger than life, that's what Horatio says. You either love him or you hate him. Horatio hasn't decided what he thinks yet. But I've an inkling he admires him a good deal, a very good deal. They've been discussing the Pacific Campaign. It's all very, very interesting. How to retake the Philippines after the Japanese stole it—"

She paused. "'Philippines' is plural, so I suppose it would be more accurate to say, 'them.'"

Cranking the Woody's front window down, she inhaled the sweet island morning air. "Now that the Americans have Guadalcanal and Papua New Guinea, we are pushing through to invade the islands that the Japanese have forgotten about, the isolated ones without much defense.[2] Horatio says MacArthur is a real genius. We are going to cut off their 'chow lines' so they can't get fuel or food."

"So, once we get these islands, we'll be able to essentially leapfrog across the Pacific to Japan?" I asked, accelerating slightly down the highway.

"I suppose so." Edie sighed. "We'll be going to the Marshall Islands," she extended her right arm, "and you girls will be going to the Solomon Islands." She extended her left arm. Then, she circled her arms together until her fingers touched on the dashboard. "And that is Japan. MacArthur is drawing a big circle, a two-pronged offensive they call it..."

"And we have to take all the islands in the middle?" I kept my eyes on the road, thinking more about Katrine and Grace. Frank and Peter had driven them into town hours earlier to see the main strip of shops and hotels between the beach at Waikiki and the high-rises a few miles inland. He thought they might enjoy some real Kona coffee and maybe a frozen ice. Somehow, I doubted they were having any fun. The girls were not in a touring mood, and that was putting it lightly.

"Not all. Just the isolated, undefended ones." Edie looked back at Lorelei. "Remember? With help from the Allies, of course. Which is why Horatio and I are here, after all."

"One prong of the offense will be singing and dancing, and the other," I looked at Edie quizzically, "will be whatever you'll be doing?" I imagined Edie leading the charge at the helm of a battleship. "The Japanese are probably quaking in their boots with Edie and the Macleay Sisters after them."

"Do they wear boots?" Lorelei asked innocently. She thought back to all the soldiers she had seen in Germany, in Palestine, and in North Africa. Boots had been the norm, but here in the tropics, the weather was so humid, she couldn't imagine anyone wearing something as heavy and hot on their feet as chunky army-issue boots. It would be remarkably uncomfortable and seemed a recipe for blisters. She looked down at her own foot shod in a trendy white buffalo sandal with a two-inch heel; they were the epitome of

American fashion. At that moment, she'd never felt so far away from Germany in her whole life.

"I've no idea what the Japanese wear on their feet." Edie frowned. "I still can't believe I'm going. I hope this wasn't a big mistake... leaving the children behind."

"I still can't believe I'm leaving Peter behind. *In one week!* And on my birthday of all things. What a strange way to turn 21. But that director was clear there was no room on the boat for husbands. Especially when they are humble students and not admirals. I don't know why Don chose me!"

"It's because you are the best photographer he's got, and he wants some real photographs from the front. At least, the USO show front. I would think this would be every photojournalist's dream! Why, you'll practically be where all the action is. Who knows?" Edie looked excited. "You might take some incredible shot of a torpedo just before it hits a destroyer. And then, boom! Pulitzer Prize."

"Only if the torpedo doesn't hit the boat and blow up right after she takes the shot," Lorelei said.

"Besides, I'm assured they are very, very careful with the USO people. They won't put us in the line of fire or anything... I think."

"Well, I for one am ready to get this show on the road," Edie intoned. "The sooner we all leave, the sooner we can go home. Funny, isn't it? That we are all leaving the same day?"

Everyone... except for Peter and Frank, I thought to myself.

At that moment, the blinking lights of 'Benson Smith Drug Store' flashed on the corner of the busy downtown. "Here's where we are meeting everyone," I said as a parking spot opened up right in front, and I pulled in. "Peter and I go here once a week or so for lunch. It's a social hotspot downtown. You'll both love it. And after lunch, we'll run by Paul's house and deliver the pen."

Lorelei looked uncomfortable.

"You have it with you, don't you?" Edie asked.

"Yes." She patted her purse and looked out the window.

Inside the drugstore, Grace, Katrine, Horatio, Peter, and Frank were already there and waved at us through the front window. Thankfully, they had managed to save the three of us seats at the counter. All the other seats were taken with servicemen in uniform, more of whom filled the booths lining the window by one of the side streets. They had no parcels or bags, and I correctly assumed they had not found anything of interest to buy. Not that there was much to choose from, beyond little funny dolls for the dashboard of your car and bright floral sarongs.

There was an empty stool in between Peter and Frank, and I carefully hoisted myself up and pecked Peter on the cheek while glancing at the menu written in chalk above the soft serve machines and grill. Bacon and Tomato...35 cents. Baked Ham and Cheese... 35 cents. Ham Salad... 40 cents. Banana and Pineapple Split... 29 cents. Malted Milk... 20 cents. Soda Syrups: Lemon, Peach, Orange, Ginger, Raspberry, Pineapple, Chocolate, Vanilla... 5 cents.

"Hey, Rich!" Peter called down to the soda jerk who was leaning over the counter across from Grace.

"Nah, nah." The red-faced teenager smacked on his gum loudly. "I wasn't old enough to enlist yet. Only 16... But you better believe me, the day I turn—"

"Rich!" Peter shouted louder. "You can talk to my cousin later. We want to order."

Winking at Grace, he stepped closer to Peter and whipped out his notebook. "What'll you have?" He looked at me. "Usual?"

I nodded.

"Got it." He scribbled quickly, "BLT, no L extra T. And leave out the mayo. And a peach soda?"

"I'll take the same!" Edie pounded on the counter. "Exactly like my niece, thanks."

Rich looked at me. "Your aunt?"

"And my uncle, my cousins." I pointed them out. "And an old friend, Frank."

135

"Nice to meet all of ya." The boy blew an enormous bubble. "What'll the rest of ya have?"

"Does everything here have ham in it?" Katrine looked down from the menu.

The kid blinked.

Katrine shrugged. "I guess I'll have a banana and pineapple split."

Grace and Lorelei stared at her, stunned. "Ice cream for lunch?"

"Don't they eat anything but ham in Hawaii?"

"But you'll get sick," Lorelei said.

Frank nodded. "I'll take the ice cream too. But leave the pineapple off mine."

Horatio scratched his beard. "I'll take the pimento cheese and ham salad combo." Then, he added, "What's pimento cheese?"

"You're not from around here are you?"

Horatio shook his head no. "I'm from Scotland."

"That would explain the strange accent." The boy smiled. "It's cheddar cheese, cream cheese, mayonnaise, and jalapeños."

"Sounds all right." Horatio looked at Edie.

Rich's pencil scratched on the pad and then looked up at Peter.

"What'll you have, Pete? Grilled peanut butter?"

Before Peter could answer, Rich had turned to the grill to quickly whip out the sandwiches and fill tall soda glasses with syrup and cream and who knows what else.

"Piper," Lorelei stood behind me, a small coin purse in her hand, "I need some new shampoo. I'm going to purchase some. I'll be back before the food comes."

She waited, and I spun around on the stool. "What's the matter?" I asked.

"Can you help me? I'm not used to American brands."

"Oh!" Edie interjected, listening to us over the buzz of the counter. "I know just the thing, Power's Shampoo Glamour-Bathe. It has an olive oil base."

Lorelei nodded, and we began to meander down the aisle towards the shampoo. A few feet ahead, she stopped, looking quite distraught. With her hand, she motioned for Edie, who nonchalantly got off her stool, looking concerned. "What's the matter? Are they out? Because if they are you can try Drene Shampoo. It's a close second."

Shaking her head, Lorelei pulled us down the aisle past boxes of home permanent solutions and bars of soap. She suddenly stopped short and furtively held up a box. Edie took it and examined it. A photograph of a man with a dashing expression and a full head of hair gazed into the future. "My dear," she shook her head sadly, "this is not a shampoo. It's a balding cream. You don't need this. You aren't going bald. Besides, this stuff doesn't work."

"How would you know that?" I asked.

She clapped her hand over her mouth. "I promised Horatio I would never tell!"

"Horatio?" My jaw dropped as I turned and looked at the back of his head. It certainly looked like his own hair. "It doesn't look like a pomade."

"That's because it's a toupee." Edie bit her lip. "Oh no! But you didn't hear it from me!"

"Who cares about Horatio's hair!" Lorelei rolled her eyes and pointed to the model. "Look at the model."

"Oh my goodness." Edie gasped loudly. "It's Paul Sinclair!"

It was true. By all appearances, Paul was the full-hair-headed model on the cover 'Dr. Boulder's Bountiful Bald-No-More Balm' box.

Stunned, we looked at the photograph. "His hair *was* beautiful," Edie said, thinking back.

"Do you think it was really his?" Lorelei spoke just above a whisper, still shaking her head. "What did I tell you? Men that handsome are never trustworthy. That's not his real hair!"

"Quite the contrary, my dear, Horatio is completely trustworthy." Edie stood up straighter. "He just is self-conscious."

Lorelei tapped the box angrily. "But this is different! This is false advertising! It's dishonest."

137

Edie and I glanced at one another uncomfortably.

"Well, I guess it's just as well." Lorelei seemed to only be talking to herself. "I'm happy to know about this. It's always better to know sooner rather than later the true character of a person."

"If that makes you feel better, dear." Edie patted her arm.

"Between us, it does. Now that I know who he really is, I won't be so nervous around him. He made me so nervous I couldn't speak like an adult."

"It was probably his smile. It's the type that makes a woman go weak in the knees." Edie looked off into the distance.

"You're no help." Lorelei huffed, putting the box of pomade down. "A hair-growth model? Really? I bet he models for dentures too. Maybe we ought to go down the toothpaste aisle and find out?"

Gently, I pulled her back to the counter. "Come on. Looks like our lunch has arrived."

WHEN WE RETURNED to the counter, Frank and Katrine had just received dishes filled precariously high with the frozen cream and fresh fruit. Katrine delicately put her spoon in and tentatively took a bite while Frank plunged in with gusto.

"Everything okay?" Peter asked.

"I'll tell you later," I whispered.

Grace boldly reached behind the counter and grabbed another spoon. Taking a bite of Katrine's ice cream, she asked, "What I want to know is why we are fighting in the Pacific to begin with! I've been turning this over in my mind since we got to Hawaii, but I still can't grasp how Japan got mixed up with the Germans."

Rich turned on his heel and held his spatula up dramatically, his white apron spotted with bits of ketchup and unidentified brown patches.

"Power, plain and simple."

Grace rolled her eyes. This kid was impertinent.

"No, he's right," Horatio said, putting his hands on the counter and unbuttoning the top button of his new Hawaiian shirt. "The Japanese had been having economic problems for a long time. It's one of the reasons they kept on invading China. They thought they could solve their money issues by expanding their territory and taking over the Chinese import market. You remember the Nanking Massacre a couple of years ago?" He slurped some of Edie's soda. "America didn't like how the Japanese treated the Chinese. Their behavior was pretty reprehensible, and I won't say some of the things that went on—it's not lunch talk. To punish the Japanese, America slapped them with some pretty heavy economic sanctions, trade embargoes and such... specifically regarding oil."[3]

"Why?" Lorelei asked, growing interested, thankful for a distraction from balding potions and dentures and handsome (but dishonest) models.

"The general thought was that without supplies, the Japanese would be forced to stop trying to expand their territory. But the opposite occurred. They just became more determined to become an imperial power. Looking back, it's really no surprise that war broke out."

"And yet," I said, "we sure were surprised when they attacked Pearl Harbor."

"Well sure, of course you were!" Horatio slammed his fist down with more force than he intended. "American Intelligence was sure the Japanese would aim for Singapore or Indochina - European colonies closer to Japan. Hawaii is nearly 4,000 miles away! Believe me, if the Americans had known what Japan was planning, no one would have left the entire Pacific Fleet practically undefended, sitting in Pearl Harbor like a bunch of lame ducks."

Frank was shaking his head. "But it was pretty brilliant going after Pearl. By taking out our fleet, how could we fight back?" He scooped some pineapple bits to the side. Rich had forgotten to leave them off.

"But why the alliance with the Nazis?" Lorelei asked.

"When the fighting stepped up in Europe, America's economic sanctions cut off Japan's supply to oil imports drastically because they needed it for themselves. By aligning with the Germans, who the Japanese have long thought to be the model of a modern monarchy, they were only doing the natural thing," Horatio explained quite satisfied with himself and enjoying his role of a lecturer. He cleared his throat and continued, "The Japanese military is indoctrinated to be unquestioningly loyal to the Emperor. It's what their state is based on. Why they are almost religious about it. It is a different sort of war for them." He looked down. "They don't surrender. And goodness knows what they do to those who do."

Katrine paled and pushed her sundae away. Edie glared at Horatio, whispering, "You shouldn't have said that!"

"What should I have said?"

"Oh, I don't know. Anything but that!" Eddie took a bite of her sandwich and put it down.

No one spoke for a few moments. I don't think anyone ate either.

Finally, I turned to Peter. "Do you need anything before we leave? Maybe we need to buy you some more t-shirts so you don't have to manage the laundry so often."

"Piper." He laughed good-naturedly. "Don't worry about me and Frank. I survived just fine before we were married. Besides, we are going to be staying with Johnny up at the plantation house, not the boat. He'll take very good care of us."

Rich placed his grilled peanut butter in front of him. "You going somewhere, Ms. Piper?"

"She's going with the USO show, to report for *The Herald*."

"For how long?"

"Just under two months," I answered... Then I added, "If you see these two getting skinny, help me out, huh?"

"Deal." He shook my hand heartily and waved as two sailors came in the front door.

"Are you sure you are going to be fine?" I leaned in, meaning the words for Peter only.

"No. I can't imagine being fine without you," he said, equally quiet. "But I know this is something you have to do. It's something *we* have to do. At least one of us should be helping with the war effort." He added, with a kiss to my cheek, "And it is just for a few weeks. Barely two months."

"Barely." I nodded, not able to imagine being any more in love with Peter than I felt at that moment.

I saw the turnoff for Paul Sinclair's neighborhood. It was one of several military communities quickly constructed in the madness after Pearl Harbor. Little row houses, each identical, for the soldiers and their families. My eyes searched the house numbers. "Oh, there it is." I pulled up to the curb. "Number twenty. That's Paul's house."

I looked back at Lorelei. "Do you want me to go with you?"

She nodded quickly, and I took the key out of the ignition.

Edie and I followed behind Lorelei, making our way up the short walk to the front door.

Lorelei quickly rang the bell and turned around, showing a nervous smile.

Almost instantly, the boy called Timmy opened it. He wore overalls without a shirt underneath, and his thin youthful arms held a beautiful model plane. The boy squinted up at Lorelei and me, suddenly remembering us from the beach.

"Hello," he said without smiling.

"Hello, Timmy," Lorelei said.

"What do you guys want?"

"We have something that belongs to your father."

The boy's eyes widened and then he called loudly, "Mother! Mother!"

From out of the back of the house, a beautiful young woman

with very curly dark chestnut hair braided down her back, wearing a gingham apron with pretty lacy frills, appeared.

"I'm so sorry," she said apologetically. "I didn't hear the door." Her large dark eyes looked curiously from Lorelei, to me, to Edie.

Timmy looked up at her. "Mom, these guys say they have something that belongs to dad."

Her eyes widened and she paled. "You have something that belonged to my husband?" She stepped aside for us to come in. "Please, please come inside. I'm Constance Gentry, by the way. And this is my son Timmy."

"Timmy and I have already met." Lorelei smiled at the boy and took the pen out of her purse and handed it to the woman. She took it in her hands and examined it. "How did you get this?" She put the pen on the side table.

"Last night at the party. We were talking, and he left it on the table."

Shaking her head sadly, she replied, "This does not belong to my husband."

"What do you mean?" Edie asked.

"This is my brother's—Paul's." She stopped and looked up. "My husband died at Pearl Harbor. Paul has lived with me and Timmy ever since."

"I see," Lorelei said slowly.

"Wait," she looked at Timmy, "is this the girl Paul fished out of the water yesterday?"

Timmy nodded. "Yep."

Constance leaned against the wall and crossed her arms more closely, examining the group, "Interesting. Paul mentioned something about meeting you again last night."

"He did? Again?" Lorelei spoke quickly.

"He thought you had a nice voice." Timmy looked straight at Lorelei.

"He did!" Edie spoke too loudly and we all looked at her. She coughed slightly and clarified, "That's not the sort of thing I would think a priest would say, I mean."

"Priest?" Constance laughed out loud.

"Well…" she coughed again. "If he's single and a chaplain… I was just putting two and two together."

Shaking her head, Constance smiled. "He's a minister, not a priest. He has a PhD in philosophy from Yale Theological Seminary."

"And the other one?" I asked.

"Linguistics. Also Yale. Though, that one he's still technically working on. He taught there after he graduated. When my husband died, Paul felt called to leave everything and help his family and his country."

On the wall behind Constance, I noticed a photograph of a much younger Paul in a football uniform. It hung beside a photograph of Constance and her late husband at their wedding, standing behind an elaborate cake, her hand poised to cut the first slice. Constance followed my gaze and nodded. "Yes, that's him. He was a kicker in high school."

"My, my, my," Edie gushed. "Brilliant, athletic, and so handsome! And so sensitive. Is there anything Paul doesn't do well?"

Constance inhaled. "Well… just between us, sensitive is not the word I would use to describe my brother."

"What word would you use?"

She bit her lip. "Don't take me wrong, but Paul can occasionally be a bit self-assured and presumptuous."

"From what I've seen of him," Edie shook her head knowingly, "understandable faults indeed."

"But faults nevertheless." Constance was on a role. "Once Paul gets something in his head, no one can talk him out of it. He does things his way, on his time. It's why he just dropped everything and joined up. But it's all just as well I guess. He would have been drafted anyway."

"You stayed in Hawaii?" I asked the pretty young woman.

"I teach at the high school. English Lit. I didn't want to leave my job and all of Timmy's friends... Our life was, *is*, here."

Edie caught sight of the clock on the wall. It was nearly two. "Oh dear, Mrs. Gentry. We've taken up too much of your time. You will tell Paul that we *all* stopped by, won't you?"

"I only wish I could."

"What do you mean?" Lorelei asked.

"He was shipped out this morning. Who knows where he is or when he'll be back for that matter. That's why he and Timmy were camping all weekend. Kind of a goodbye trip."

"He seems like a very special young man," Edie said.

"He is."

Lorelei listened closely not saying a word.

Back in the car, Edie sighed dramatically and put her hand over her heart. "Like ships that pass in the night. I am so, so, so sorry my dear. To have loved and lost so quickly."

"Oh, Aunt Edie, I don't love him!" Lorelei chided with a smile. "Anyway, I could never love someone dishonest or who lives a lie. As I said, you can't trust men *that* handsome."

CHAPTER 13

ABOARD THE TROOPSHIP

The night before we were due to ship out, Peter and I crawled into our little berth for our last night together for nearly two months.

"Too bad I'm going to miss your birthday."

"It's just a birthday." I squeezed his hand. "Besides, you won't really be missing it. We'll have breakfast together in the morning before we all ship out."

Reaching out to switch off the lamp, his voice dropped. "If I could get you anything, what would you get. Money is no object."

"No object?"

I closed my eyes and listened to the water lap up against the sides of the *Malahini*. "I'd like a house to come home to. A real, honest to goodness home. On solid land. I'd like the war to end. I'd like to know what is going to happen after the war... I want to know what God's plan is."

Peter sighed. "You and me both."

"You mean, you still don't feel him leading you one way or the other?"

He shook his head no, and I could tell he was as disappointed as

I was. "Though it delays," he kissed my cheek, "wait for it. He won't leave us out in the cold. He has a plan... he just hasn't let us in on it."

"But I feel like we aren't really doing anything."

"You are about to go on a grand adventure with your song and dance team cousins. I'm the one who isn't really doing anything."

"About that," I rolled over, "we need to talk."

"We are talking."

"No... about something else." I could hear Frank walking around on the deck, and I leaned in close to Peter's ear, whispering, "I think the girls are up to something."

"Something more than singing?"

"Yeah." I tried to find the words for what I suspected. I thought back to the suspicions Edie had shared while ironing her dress before Don's party. "Edie thinks so too, but she doesn't know what."

"You don't think it might just be the product of Edie's crazy imagination, do you? She can think up some pretty wild stories."

I waited a moment before answering. "If you had asked me at any other time, I would have said yes. But I can't deny that the girls have been acting unusual. I know they haven't told me the whole story. And with Katrine's background working for the Jewish Agency and Grace's history with the RAF... they are worth a lot more than just singers."

Peter looked to the side. "Well, if I'm honest, Frank's been a little cagey too." He paused and then continued, "I wish I was going with you. It sounds like it could be dangerous..."

"It's too late to back out now."

"You better keep your wits about you." He exhaled. "Seriously, promise me you'll be careful."

"I'll try. I'll also try to keep those girls out of trouble!" Then, rolling back over, I added, "A house, Peter. When I come back, I want a house."

"Name the place."

"I don't know. Let's pray we know by the time I get back."

~

AS OUR BOAT left the harbor headed towards the Solomon Islands, and Edie and Horatio's destroyer left in the opposite direction, I turned 21. It was a strange way to start a new year, surrounded by marines off to war.

The H.M.S. *Americus* was not like the *Queen Mary* or the *Aquitania* or any of the other enormous ocean liners converted to become a carrier for troops or a hospital ship. For one thing, it could only carry 400 or 500 men, rather than the 10,000 troops that the larger ships could carry. The *Americus* was a modified Liberty. Bunks were stacked five deep. Generators kept the power going. Two automatic cannons guarded the precious cargo against the enemy.

Thankfully, they had made a makeshift partition for the show people. One room for the boys and one for the girls. It was in this partition, filled with four sets of bunk beds and suitcases crammed with dresses for the show, that Grace, Katrine, Lorelei, and I lay on our backs and pondered what lay before us.

Dinner sat heavily in my stomach. It reminded me of a cattle drive, and all the men (us included) were the cattle. We had to wait in line for two hours for the mess hall. Food was dumped on a tray, and we ate standing at a chest-high table that ran the width of the room.

"What do you think the boys are doing right now?" I asked, drumming my fingers together. I thought of Peter. Usually, every night about this time, we were curled up in our little berth in the sailboat. He would read aloud sometimes. It was funny, I already missed the sound of his voice.

The girls didn't answer.

"I almost forgot." Katrine sat up and searched through her purse, finally pulling out a small little box wrapped in red paper. "From Peter, for your birthday."

My heart warmed slightly. "He already gave me flowers this

morning when we left! He shouldn't have bought me anything." I thought back to that morning. Edie and Johnny had prepared an elaborate birthday breakfast. A large poster, crepe paper in green and yellow strung all over the place. Steak and eggs (don't ask me where she got the rations for it!) and a coffee cake with 21 candles stuck all over the top. Edie and Horatio had brought a gift from my parents along, a new novel called *The Robe*, along with a long inscription inside the front cover. Edie, Horatio, and my parents had taken turns reading the book aloud not long before they'd left. The story of the Roman soldier who won Jesus's robe as a gambling prize had shot to the top of the best-seller list.

"Aren't you going to open your present?" Grace sat up too.

My fingers tore at the paper, revealing a rather fancy looking longish box. I pulled open the lid. There, lying on a bed of creamy velvet, was a beautiful fountain pen.

"Oh dear." I sighed. "Peter knows I'm not a writer."

Katrine tossed a small little notebook, the kind reporters use, over the side of her bunk to where I lay below. "And that's from us."

"You had all this planned, didn't you?" I smiled up at her as I flipped through the tiny black book. "Now I'll look like a real war correspondent."

"Even if you don't write every little detail down, you can at least get the bullet points. You can pass them off to Edie by and by, and she will turn it into some sort of fairy tale. Trust us, we know from personal experience." Lorelei inhaled and was about to say something else when she was interrupted by a rap on the partition door, and Ansel Thornton poked his head inside.

"I've got something for you, Lorelei."

Lorelei swung her feet over the side of the bunk and hopped down. "What is it?"

"A message," Ansel did a little jig followed by a playful bow, "compliments of the captain."

"Thank you." Lorelei stopped, her eyes narrowed. "But I'm supposed to get the messages from the captain. *Personally.*"

I looked quizzically at my cousin, unsure of what she meant. Why would it matter if Thornton delivered a message?

His lip curled almost imperceptibly. "He was busy. I thought I would save him some time."

I turned my head on the pillow. Ansel Thornton was, for some reason, inherently unlikable. He was talented to be sure. I'd seen him in rehearsal. He knew what he was doing, that was clear. It was something else. Just being near him made my skin crawl.

"Aren't you going to read it?" he asked.

"I like to read my letters in private," Lorelei said quietly. "You understand, of course."

"Of course," he repeated.

"Well, you girls better get your beauty rest!" He gave Lorelei a half-smile, slapped the partition wall, and winked at me before leaving.

Once he was out of earshot, I sat up and shuddered. "Does that guy give any of you the creeps?"

"It's his voice." Grace was sitting up now too, watching as Lorelei tore open the note. "It's too smooth."

Lorelei sat down beside me on the bunk and scanned the message.

"Well, this is going to be difficult without a piano. How am I supposed to write a song without a piano? And listen to these words — Moasi, Lah Cha Eh, Dzeh, Tkin... A-Keh-Di-Glini? Total gibberish!"

"You're supposed to write a song with that?" Katrine asked.

I could sense something fishy. The girls were obviously leaving vital bits of information out of the conversation. I could feel it.

Lorelei's eyes were glued to the message, and she ran her fingers through her hair. "I wish Bob Hope was on this boat. He would be inspired by this!"

It was true. Myrna Loy, Bob Hope, and all the other A-listers were on a different route. There were three USO shows traveling through the Pacific. We were, with the exception of a small group of acrobats and pantomimes (the boys next door) and two tap dancing twin sisters, who were taking their turn in the saltwater showers at this very moment, quite on our own in the talent department. Ansel planned on pulling in a soldier or two who knew his way around a guitar at the various stops along the tour to serve as backup, but as far as real musicians went, Lorelei was on her own.

She moaned slightly. "I have to come up with something. It has to be ready when we get to Alu Island. I am completely unfamiliar with Native American culture, besides the few Western Movies I've seen. Lots of drums and... I don't even know where to start."

"I wish I was more musical." I patted her back and tried to figure out what was going on. "If that would help."

She smiled a small smile.

"You could just do one of your old numbers? You know, from the underground jazz club in Germany."

"No," Lorelei sighed, "only new numbers."

I shrugged. It seemed like a lot of extra work for nothing. The girls had 20 songs they could easily pull out of their back pockets that everyone would enjoy.

"Right now, the only thing that would help is some peace and quiet." She looked at the partition wall. It was paper thin. We could hear the voices of 450 young men talking, whistling, eating, laughing, and doing whatever it is young men off to war do. She looked very serious. "I have to get this right."

"Maybe you should try to get some sleep," Katrine said. "It's been a big day. We're all tired. In the morning, you'll be fresh and feel more creative."

Lorelei looked up at Katrine, leaning over her bunk. "I guess so. I'm going to go brush my teeth."

"I'll go with you." I stood up and rummaged through my little suitcase for my toiletries bag. "As nice as all the boys are, I don't like walking through the ship alone."

"Too many lonely soldiers." Lorelei winked and smiled.

"Let's all go together." Katrine carefully crawled off her bunk.

On a whim, I grabbed my camera and took off after the girls. Carefully, we wound our way through the underbelly of the transport ship, in search of the showers and sinks. All the while, I replayed the scene with the USO show's director. Why did it feel so off?

Row after row of bunks, each one filled with a fresh-faced kid. Their haircuts were identical. Very, very short. They wore white t-shirts and tennis shoes. A tangle of duffel bags, packs with bedrolls, rifles, steel helmets hung from hooks and poles and posts. It was a jungle of gear, a maze of men, some asleep and some awake, mostly playing cards or dice. "Hiya, toots!" and "Where are you going, kiddo?" and other various renditions of the classic cat-call were tossed back and forth, not unkindly. They *were* lonely. But they were scared too.

I took out my camera and shot a picture of the girls in front of me. Three little songbirds in a sea of sailors.

One kid caught my eye. He smiled kindly. "Hey, take a picture of me!" He sat up and stuck out his chest. I snapped the shot and put the camera down.

"What's your name, sailor?" I extended my hand.

"Alexander Fletcher." He shook it firmly. "And I'm a marine, ma'am. We are all Marines."

"First deployment?"

"Oh no. I was at Guadalcanal."

At that word, Katrine stopped short and took two steps back, standing by me. "You were?" she asked.

"Sure I was."

"Would you—" She paused. "My husband was there. Would you, uh, tell me—" She stopped, not even knowing what she was asking.

"Well, ma'am..." The young man looked at Katrine. It had been such a long battle, in such extreme conditions, that it was difficult to know where to start. "It was last August. Right where this ship is headed, 2,500 square miles of jungle in the Solomon Islands. We had to get possession of the Guadalcanal airbase from the Japanese, you see, in order to control communication between America and Australia. It was quite the battle. If we hadn't had won, who knows where we'd be right now."[5]

"You didn't," Katrine held her breath, "know a man named Harry. Harry Stenetsky. He's about this high," she held her hand up, "with beautiful blue eyes and curly dark hair?"

"I'm afraid not, ma'am." He looked down sadly.

She tried to smile. "Well, thank you. You're the first soldier I've met who was there. I just thought that maybe you might... have known him."

"I understand, ma'am." He looked from me to Katrine and then at Grace and Lorelei, who were both talking with a few of the boys further up ahead.

"He was captured."

His face darkened. "That's too bad. Rumor has it that things are pretty grim in those camps."

"Come on, Katrine," I pushed her forward, "we ought to get moving."

"Yes," Lorelei said. "I have to get to work on that song."

Frowning, I pushed onwards, still wondering why they couldn't just use an old standby.

ALEXANDER FLETCHER WAS CORRECT. In the POW camp where Harry was being held, the situation *was* grim. In fact, grim was putting it lightly.

"At this point, I'm sorry to say that we cannot risk another escape," Major Canning addressed Harry and a handful of other officers in the barracks. "At least not from the camp. We've simply no chance. I have a responsibility to keep the boys here alive. We've dug four tunnels. We've risked going through the wires a handful of times. Not once have we been successful. That is, we've not been successful in escaping. We've been plenty successful at getting shot for trying to escape. We've been successful at being put on half rations for 'impudence.' And we've been successful at being put in The Hole."

The Hole. The 4-foot by 4-foot tin box that men were stuffed into as punishment. Temperatures soared. When the man inside came out, he was half alive. That is if he lived to stay half alive.

"If we keep on the way we've been keeping on, not one of us will survive to tell the tale." He wiped his brow.

"Then we try to escape on the work crews while we are out in the jungle," Harry suggested, unwilling to accept defeat.

No one spoke. It wasn't a new idea. It was simply very difficult to accomplish. They were guarded like hawks. And while they may have been able to run and hide a month or two before, each one by now had lost a fair amount of weight. They were weakened by hunger and the rampant illnesses that swept through the camp. Escape from the camp had proved impossible and foolhardy, but at this point, it was their last resort.

"Roy," Major Canning, suddenly regaining courage, turned to a small man on his left, "you said you know where they keep the dynamite?"

"Yeah. I'm on the blasting crew. I think I can... *borrow* some," Roy said.

"Good." Major Canning smiled. "I think that is an amicable start."

"And what are we going to do with this dynamite?" Another officer—Jordan Simpson—asked.

"Blow something up," Major Canning said. "Obviously."

CHAPTER 14

MEANWHILE, BACK IN HONOLULU

I looked at my empty bunk repugnantly.

"I've never slept without Peter beside me, not once since we got married. We have never spent a night apart. Can you believe it? I hope I can remember how to sleep."

"It might take a few nights… or months," Katrine said, climbing up to her own bunk. "But you'll get used to it. Not that I ever did. But you might."

Grace shook out her army issued blanket and began to brush her hair. "I have no problem sleeping alone at all. I probably will have to for the rest of my life."

Lorelei stopped buttoning up the top to her pajamas and stared at Grace. "That's a dismal thing to say."

"I vaguely remember you telling me that sleeping alone was the only thing you were scared of." Katrine looked at her younger sister knowingly.

"You're one to talk," Grace responded quickly. Her voice had an edge to it.

"Grace," Lorelei fluffed her pillow, "you are young and pretty. There's someone out there for you." Lorelei knew next to nothing of how serious Amos and Grace had once been. She had no idea that Amos had asked Grace to marry him while she'd jumped out of a plane. She also did not know that later Grace had told Amos she wanted to wait to marry him until the war was over and hadn't heard from him since.

"I don't want 'someone.' I don't want anyone anymore. I'm very happy alone, and I want to stay that way," Grace spat.

"Don't be so melodramatic." Lorelei laughed and crawled into bed. "Maybe it didn't work out with that Herring boy, but there is the right man for you out there somewhere."

"Sure, just like there's a nice guy for you? If that's true, why aren't you and Joe Miller married? Or even Frank for that matter!"

"I said the *right* man, not a 'nice' man. I'm not going to just go and marry someone because he is a 'nice' guy. Marriage is a lot more than that!"

"My sentiments exactly." Grace angrily crawled up into her own bunk and slammed her head down onto the pillow. After a minute she said, "We are pathetic. I mean, look at us. You don't take what you *can* get and are in love with a man you barely know! And I—I couldn't see the forest for the trees." She trailed off, unable to speak of what had happened with Amos. It hurt too much.

"What are you talking about?" Katrine asked.

Grace didn't answer.

Lorelei, meanwhile, was stuck on what Grace had said to her. "I am absolutely *not* in love with Paul Sinclair! I do not even trust him!"

"Yeah. Sure. Then how come when anyone says his name you turn purple and get the hiccups?"

"I didn't say he wasn't attractive!" Lorelei exclaimed. Then, more seriously, she said, "I'm looking for something more than attraction. As the Proverbs say, beauty fades. The truth is, I could never fall in love with someone so..." She struggled to come up with the right word.

"Handsome?" I offered.

Lorelei looked down. "I don't know. But I know someone who does know exactly who is right for me. And he is *completely* trustworthy."

"Who?" Grace protested.

"Yeshua."

"Let me tell you something." Grace's voice rose angrily. "Your silly faith isn't going to get you far this round."

"Grace!" Katrine chided. "You need to calm down. Everyone can hear you. It's not good for morale."

"I'm not being unkind. I'm just realistic. You three could use a dose of it, if you ask me," Grace replied.

"A dose of what?" I asked.

"*Reality.*"

At that moment, the twin tap dancers tiptoed into the room, both smelling of soap, their wet hair, dyed orangish red, was up in curlers.

"How were the showers?" I asked.

"Cold," they both whispered in unison.

With that, they switched off the swinging bulb and crawled into their bunks.

The creak of the boat and the sound of the water against the hull mingled with the steady murmur of voices from the troops. I had to try to sleep. But it was difficult.

I thought of what Grace had said and how unhappy she must be. I thought of Katrine, of Harry… of Lorelei and Paul and Frank and Joe… and Peter. Oh yes, I thought of Peter.

As I TRIED to sleep that first night alone, Peter and Frank were wide awake. It was a few hours after Horatio and Edie had shipped out, going in the opposite direction as our transport ship. Both of them laughed about old times on Horatio's yacht and told battle stories through lunch and dinner. And still, they talked on and on.

"Frank," Peter eased down into the chair beside his old friend and leaned back, putting his long legs up on the porch rail, "have you thought about what you want to do once all this is over?"

Frank didn't answer right away. In one hand, he held a cup of coffee, the other dangled over the rocking chair and caressed Founder's head as the sweet dog lay sleeping. Slowly, he shook his head. "I've thought about going to Palestine."

"What will you do there?"

"They've got a port or two. I could go back to sailing. Maybe even help out with the navy."

"What navy?" Peter shifted his shoulders so he could see Frank's face.

"The Jews in Palestine have been working on building a military for a few years now. I know the region still belongs to the British... And I know the Arabs want it just as bad as the Zionists do."

"I never imagined you leaving the States for good." Peter looked back at the beach.

"I never imagined my people being wiped off the face of the planet. And you know how it is, being forced out of the game. I want to get back in there, get my hands dirty. Fight the good fight, you know?"

"Yeah, I know," Peter answered slowly.

"But you seem all right with it. I mean, your wife is out with the boys, and look at us, we are drinking coffee, looking out on the beach. There is something wrong about this picture."

Peter laughed. "Oh, Frank. It was hard at first. And I won't say there aren't days when I see guys in uniform and feel left out or guilty. But I know the truth. I can't run anymore. I can walk. Thank God, I can walk. But I would do more harm back on a battleship than any good. And you too, for that matter. Your hand has never been the same. You can't make a fist, much less tie a taut-line-hitch. And I also know that God has a plan, even in this." Peter looked straight ahead. His fight was coming. God hadn't told him where yet, or even what yet, but he would.

"Even in *this?*" Frank was cynical. Shaking his head, he said, "You sound just like Lorelei. I know you are a Christian. You think the Messiah already came, and that gives you hope and a bunch of other nice fluffy feelings. Here's the truth. I'm not sure I even believe in God anymore. How can I after all that is going on in Europe?"

"The fool says in his heart, 'there is no God.'"[6] Peter looked at Frank straight on. "But you are right to be angry. This madness, it is pure evil. It violates the very law of God, the moral law that he wrote before time. That's why it is so outrageous, and we don't know how to respond. But it's because of God's existence, even his love, that we are able to even recognize how wrong it is."

"That is a very nice sentiment... Very nice sentiment. So tell me this, college boy, if God is so loving, why are the Nazis and the Japanese allowed to be doing what they are doing?"

"He gave us free will. We can choose right and wrong. You know your Bible enough to know we live in a fallen world, hence, people choose wrong. But with Jesus," Peter put his hand on Frank's arm, "with Jesus there is redemption and healing and life, even in all of this death and pain."

"I see it this way, the world has gone down the tubes. Everybody has an angle. And if you see something good, you better grab for what you can before somebody else does."

"Wow." Peter whistled. "What happened to you? You didn't use to be this cynical."

"A boy's gotta grow up someday. But I will say this, right now," he started lowering his defenses, "it almost feels like there isn't a war. It's so peaceful and quiet."

Immediately, a squadron of B-17s roared overhead.

Frank's voice hardened. "Never mind. Spoke too soon."

The screen door slammed shut, and Johnny stepped out onto the porch and looked at the boys. "I'm headed home. You kids need anything else?"

"No, Johnny." Peter smiled at the gentle man. "We are just fine.

And thanks for supper. You certainly know how to make spam taste like beef."

Johnny laughed out loud and then suddenly remembered something. "Oh, Peter, I forgot. While you two saw the girls off on the *Americus*, a telegram came." He pulled an envelope out of his pocket. "This one's for you Frank."

Frank's eyes opened in surprise. "I can't imagine who would send me a telegram."

"You have a good night, Johnny. Say hello to the wife for me."

"For sure. You boys sleep well. You have my number if you need anything. I'm less than a mile away, remember that." Johnny spoke like a concerned father.

"We'll be just fine." Peter smiled.

Frank had already torn open the telegram and was now absorbed in the text. He mumbled, "Yeah... just fine."

Satisfied, Johnny stepped down off the porch. He raised his hand without looking behind him and wished the boys a goodnight once more.

"Peter," Frank's voice dropped very low, "we have a Class A problem."

"What's the matter?" Peter took his feet off the railing and sat up a little straighter. Frank looked like he was ready to punch someone or something. "Who's that from?"

"It's from Joe. Joe Miller... I'm not supposed to tell, but *now*... This whole 'Macleay Sisters' thing was *his* idea." The way he said it showed Frank's obvious dislike of the American bureaucrat. "He's still in Cairo. Look, what I'm about to show you is top-secret, okay?" With that, he passed the telegram to Peter and waited on edge as Peter's eyes scanned the words in the dimming light.

FRANK. RAT ON BOARD. DO NOT REPEAT. DO NOT TAKE
PILLS FROM ANYONE OTHER THAN DOCTOR BROWN.
WIRES CROSSED. STAY WITH BIRDS AT ALL COST.

A cold feeling shot up Peter's back. "I'm not a decoder, but I can guess what this means. Frank," Peter faced his friend, "is this what I think it is?"

Frank hung his head. "I should have known something was up. I should have known! How could I be such an idiot!"

"What's this about, Frank? What's going on?"

"The girls are transmitters. The 'pills' are messages that must be 'administered' via live broadcasts of the USO shows. By writing songs with these encrypted codes and then having them broadcast on the radio, we can get vital information regarding location coordinates, battle plans, and the numbers of enemy soldiers to our men without the Japanese catching on. You know the drill, Peter."

"Lorelei has a gift that Joe discovered during a party game. She can turn any silly little phrase or group of words into a catchy song. With her sisters, the act seemed legit. In fact, with me playing accordion behind them," he smiled smugly, "it was legit. We were a hit." He paused. "And Katrine and Grace's harmonies didn't hurt."

"But they cut you out of the act?" Peter swallowed.

"Probably because whoever the rat is was worried I'd figure it out. No doubt he noticed my sharp reflexes and brilliant powers of observation."

Peter was up on his feet. "My wife is out there," he gestured towards the ocean, "on some boat with a traitor?" He shook Frank. "We've got to do something! We've got to warn them!"

"And how are we going to do that? We can't risk sending them a message. I assume that is what the 'wires crossed' refers to." Frank felt sick. "I failed them. I failed the girls! Joe told me to protect them! I assumed he meant... Well, it never occurred to me that something like this might happen." His voice was a mixture of anger, remorse, and urgency.

"Maybe we need to tell somebody here about Joe's message?"

Frank shook his head violently. "Absolutely not! If the rat has an accomplice here, it could put the girls in danger! We have to catch the show and rat the rat out. It's the only way! And remember, Joe said to keep mum. We can't tell anyone about this. Anyone, and I mean *anyone*, could be the traitor."

Both boys were swept up in the moment. Their nearest and dearest were caught in some sort of trap. They had to rescue them.

Two hours later, Frank and Peter were pouring over a nautical map. "Okay," Peter put his pencil on Alu Island in the Western Province, "Alu Island is where the girls are scheduled for their first show. They'll be there a couple of days and then, according to the show schedule, be at Santa Isabel next in the central province. Given that we are roughly 3,555 miles away," he scratched down the number on a notepad, "and if we make an average speed of 30 knots an hour..." he thought a moment and then looked up, "...it will take us about 105 hours to get there."

"About four and a half days, give or take."

"Yeah. And the girls are a day ahead of us, but those troopships aren't very zippy. They cruise along at about the same speed as us. So we should aim for Alu Island. Who knows, we could even get there on the same day if we get a good wind."

"When's the next tide?"

"Should be around three this morning."

"Can we be ready to go by then?" Frank ran his fingers through his light brown hair. He poured himself another cup of coffee from the small percolator. He was already pretty jumpy and more caffeine certainly wouldn't help, but he gulped it down anyway.

"Here's what I say we do," Peter was also jittery, "we get whatever supplies we need. A couple of cans of pineapples and coffee and such. Then, we set sail with the next tide under the cover of darkness. No lights. Nothing. We are two professionals. We can sail around any patrol, right?"

"Definitely. Not only were we officers on a yacht once, but we were both members of His Royal Majesty's Navy—decorated veterans, both of us. We'll not use the radio, and we are too small a vessel to get picked up by radar. We may move slower than we used to, but we can still handle a tiny sailboat on the open sea, right?" He paused and then added, "You'll need to help me with the ropes though."

Peter nodded in agreement. "Yeah. Of course!"

They stood there, steadfast in their purpose, confident in their ability, but unsure of how to proceed.

"We can drive back to the *Malahini* without any headlights. God willing, we won't run into a patrol. It's long past curfew." Peter looked at his watch. "Are you ready?"

"I was born ready." Frank rubbed his hands together.

And so, under the cover of darkness, with the heavy shades drawn over the windows, they made stacks of peanut butter sandwiches and gathered every can of food Johnny had in the pantry. There was ample tomato juice, golden corn, green beans, and mayonnaise. Of course, there was spam and tuna and processed cheese. Frank filled two big drums full of drinking water and few extra bed sheets because he knew from experience that bedsheets could come in very handy as bandages or even a makeshift sail.

"We could last for weeks," Peter whispered loudly as they hoisted the water drums into the back of the Woody.

Peter returned to the house and made sure that Founder's leash was secured to the porch. Johnny would find her in the morning, along with a note asking him to care for the dog until they returned.

Frank nodded. "Anything else you think we might want from the house?"

Peter shook his head no. "We've got soap. Rain gear. Extra underwear. And a first aid kit."

"No guns though." Frank frowned. "That could be a problem. You know, for when we find the rat."

"We'll cross that bridge when we come to it." Peter quietly shut the trunk of the Woody, and the two men shook hands before getting into the front and turning on the engine.

Neither man spoke on the drive back down to the *Malahini*. Wordlessly, by the light of the moon, they carried the crates of food down the beach and up the gangplank to the sailboat as the tide rose higher and higher.

At three o'clock on the dot, they set out for the open sea. The tight knots of nervous anxiety in their stomachs and excitement kept them more awake than the absurd amounts of coffee they had consumed all night. They worked as one, adjusting the sails and setting their course with ease. It was almost like the old days.

As the outline of Honolulu grew smaller and smaller, Frank turned to Peter, his good hand on the wheel and exhaled. "It feels good to be back. Real good."

Peter glanced at his school books, shoved to the corner of the table to make room for the nautical maps. "You have no idea."

CHAPTER 15

OPENING NIGHT

*K*atrine limped off the makeshift stage and sat down on a folding chair beside me under a palm tree.

"You need to be relaxed and happy! Don't tense up like that! Smile!" Ansel Thornton bellowed. "You look like you are in pain, Kathy!"

"Katrine! It's Katrine!" she corrected the director loudly. "That's because I *am* in pain, Ansel." She rubbed her calf. "I like dancing as much as anybody, but those high kicks are simply too much. I'm not a 16-year-old."

Lorelei and Grace watched from the stage, wiping the sweat off their brows. They had been rehearsing for hours.

Ansel looked up at the heavens and extended his arms pleadingly. "This is who they send me! I get a 30-year-old with the flexibility of a table and who looks like a sheeny! We've got a show to put on, Kathy!"

"My legs won't go on." Katrine blanched and refused to move off her chair. "And my name is *Katrine*, not Kathy!"

The use of the anti-Semitic slur 'sheeny' was not unusual with Ansel. Of course, he didn't know Katrine was Jewish. He thought

164

she was Greek, along with everyone else. But the longer we were on the island, the more he said about his political views. He didn't like Jews, throwing about old stereotypes about 'commie-Jews controlling Broadway and Hollywood and everything in-between.' He blamed 'Jews' for his failure to ever make it to the top. Of course, the girls kept quiet about their true identity.

He turned his attention to Lorelei, who still stood by Grace on the stage. "I remember back when I was in New Mexico," Ansel Thornton groaned, "I was asked to do research for a show set in the American West; *Chief Puhuskaw's Last Stand*. Never made it to Broadway, but it had a pretty good run." He coughed awkwardly. "Six long months on the reservation studying language and dance and music. Count them, six." He poked his finger at Lorelei. "And this 'song' of yours is NOTHING LIKE THE REAL THING!"

Lorelei stared at him, taken aback. A strong breeze blew across the stage, whipping her skirt between her legs.

His voice lowered once more to a normal decibel. "You really should sing it in a minor key."

"It's too late to change it now," Lorelei responded firmly.

"Temperamental artists are a thorn in my side!" He marched off the stage, throwing in, "Well, if you insist on doing things your way, that's that. You just better not mess up the lines. This is a live broadcast, you know. No outtakes."

Ansel glared at her before throwing his hands up as though he was giving up.

"All right." He looked at Grace and Lorelei and the tap dancing twins waiting on the side of the stage to rehearse their number (who we'd learned were named Mopsy and Popsy). "Take 10 minutes. I need a drink."

With that, he stormed off the stage to his tent muttering, "As soon as I am off this island I am going straight back to New York where I belong and people appreciate my talent. They give me this!"

Grace looked at me questioningly. "Do you think he has opening night jitters?"

I shrugged. "Your guess is as good as mine."

"Well," Lorelei said looking at the sky, "I think we might have a storm blowing in. I hope we won't have a problem with the show tonight."

Even as she spoke, the wind picked up speed, and the palm trees began to bend slightly in the wind. The water, a brilliant emerald green, lapped gently at the shore.

"No clouds," I answered. "It's just windy."

"I was up early this morning. It was a red sky."

"So what?" I shrugged.

"You're married to a sailor, Piper. You know the saying 'red sky in morning, sailor's take warning?'"

"Sailors take warning?" I glanced out to the horizon beyond the sea. Not a cloud in sight. Not a speck of a cloud.

"More like showgirls take warning." Grace motioned towards the road leading to the base where 1,000 marines waited to be entertained. An armed guard kept them from taking their seats 5 hours early so the girls could rehearse. "Oh boy, look at them!" She laughed out loud.

There were probably 50 marines marching towards them, laughing, cheering, waving. Some of them were singing the chick, chick, chick, chicken song. It was too hot for full uniforms. They all wore t-shirts and shorts. Some were barefoot.

The armed guard, a paunchy guy from the Midwest who was rather proud of being assigned guard duty over the show, tried to hold them back. But the leader of the troop pushed right past him. "We won a bet with the captain. We get to watch rehearsal." This was met with more cheers and jeers from the boys following behind.

"Those boys sure are starved for entertainment," Katrine whispered in my ear, coming up beside me.

The leader stepped up to us and bowed. "You three the Macleay Sisters?"

"Not me." I stepped back, blushing a little and pointing at my cousins. "*Them.*"

"We have come to get your autographs, ma'ams, and to tell you how happy we are that you came."

"Thanks." Lorelei blushed.

"We've been singing that chicken song since the first time we heard it." He looked back at the other men. "Isn't that right, boys?"

They nodded and agreed and cheered and whistled some more.

"So... we thought, uh, as long as you are rehearsing, we could, you know, help out."

"Help out how?" Lorelei chuckled.

"Allow me." He put his hands up and motioned for the guys to be quiet. Then, he said, "And a one and a two and a one, two, three!" And they were off. Somehow, these fellows, in between morning exercises and sleeping in their hammocks and marching and waiting and waiting some more, had managed to dissect Lorelei's one hit wonder into a men's choral masterpiece. Some of them sang the parts of the base and the trumpet, another few played the percussion with various claps and slaps, and the majority sang the lyrics with more intricate harmony than Lorelei had ever intended for the little ditty.

She looked in amazement from her sisters to the twins and then at me.

The song ended, and the boys looked at us, waiting. Of course, we broke out into applause, and Lorelei gave the leader a solid handshake. "I think you boys ought to be up there tonight, not us."

"But we," he blushed, "do not have beautiful green eyes."

"Oh sheesh." Grace rolled her eyes.

He turned to her. "Or such beautiful blue eyes." He winked. "Want to be my chicken?" He made an annoying clucking noise.

"I have to go put on my costume." Grace groaned and grabbed Lorelei's hand. "Come on, ladies!"

"Sorry, boys," I said apologetically. "The show must go on. But you are all pretty good. You could go on the road. Really. I can see it now, 'The Clucking Marines.'"

"'The Clucking Marines.'" He nodded. "I like it."

"See you tonight." I turned and ran after my cousins.

"I'll be here, front row and center!"

~

"I CAN'T WEAR THIS." Katrine threw the costume back on her hammock. "Absolutely not! What in the world is that Ansel Thornton thinking? That I'm some chorus girl?"

"I think that's exactly what he is thinking," Grace answered, holding her own set of coconuts and a grass skirt up. "I'm not wearing this unless I've got long johns underneath. Which I didn't happen to pack because we are in the South Pacific in the middle of the summer!"

"It's too hot to wear the evening dresses you brought, isn't it?" I asked quietly, trying to think of some other solution. "Why don't you wear your swimsuits under them? At least your stomachs would be covered."

"And we can wear our nylons. No bare legs, that's something." Grace visibly cringed. "I sure hope this really helps the war effort."

"It better!" Katrine tried to get into her hammock, swung over too quickly, and landed firmly on her bottom.

"Oh my goodness!" I rushed to her side. "Are you okay?"

She stood up, rubbing her backside. "Yeah... the bruise won't show through the grass skirt." She sighed. "I hope."

She imitated the director earlier that afternoon during rehearsal. "And a one, two, three, four, one, two, three, four. Kick-ball-change, kick-ball-change, and big kick, big kick, big kick! GIVE ME MORE DRAMA. Smile! Smile!" She shook her head. "He still doesn't know that my name is Katrine... I'm going to request cots for us. I can't sleep in that thing. I can't even sit in it."

I nodded. It was an excellent suggestion.

"My eyelashes won't stay on." Mopsy stuck her head into our tent. "The glue won't work in this humidity. Any chance you have some mascara?"

It was very hot and humid. So hot and so humid that with every breath I felt like I was inhaling bath water. I was sweating. The girls were sweating. Even my camera was sweating.

Lorelei nodded and dug through her makeup bag, passing the small tube to the young woman. As she took it, she moaned, "Oh no! My eye!"

"What's the matter with it?" I turned my head and saw that her left eye was sealed shut, the false eyelash hanging at a bizarre angle.

"It's glued my eye together, dang blast it!" She ran out of the tent, calling loudly for her sister.

Katrine began to pull her hair back into a tight bun. "Well, I'll say this, it certainly is going to be a show that the boys are not going to forget, that's for sure."

I began to rummage through my suitcase for something presentable and cool but found nothing. I decided to stay in my shorts and a light cotton blouse. I wasn't going to be on stage anyway... and the nurses at the base wore the same thing. I'd be in good company.

"I want to try it one more time, okay?" Lorelei rubbed her eyes. "I'm just not confident about the chorus."

"Oh, stop your worrying." Grace was adjusting the tie of the skirt over her swimsuit, a dark navy one with white sailor buttons. "We all know exactly how it goes. We've been singing it non-stop since you wrote it." She paused and then belted out, "All my tushka chipotas, wait for paaki paaki, don't need no wakaree'e, just more tushka chipotas on a paaki paaki..." All the while, she danced and stomped her feet, imitating the very few movies about cowboys and Indians she had seen in her young life.

Lorelei frowned. "Not exactly what I had in mind... But I guess it's good enough, given that we don't know what we are singing about." Her fingers ran through the grass of her skirt. "I feel really stupid about all this. Pretending to be a Greek, dressed up as a Hawaiian with a modesty complex, and singing a song in a native language I don't know. Well..." she looked up, "maybe dishonest is the right word."

"You are just doing your duty." I patted her shoulder.

"Right."

The wind began to whip the sides of tent ominously, and we all grew silent.

"I guess we ought to finish getting ready." Lorelei sighed after a second.

"I'll see you guys at the show, okay?" I grabbed my camera. "I'm going to go get my seat. You three break a leg." I closed the tent's opening and began to walk back towards the open space by the beach where the soldiers had set up the platform. The space in front of the stage was filled with hundreds and hundreds of boys. I stopped and took a picture. They were so happy. Their excitement at a little music, a little fun, was barely containable. Some of them had experienced the most brutal fighting the war had seen yet. They'd spent months in holes in the ground, hiding. Some had crawled through bodies of fallen men to land a beach. Others hadn't seen any action yet. All were waiting. And waiting. A day felt like a week. A week felt like a month. But their time would come. Or come again. It always did.

"Can you see him?"

I looked behind me. It was Katrine. She was dressed in her swimsuit topped with the coconuts and grass skirt over her nylon stockings. On her feet were block heels. She had opted out of both false eyelashes and mascara, knowing it would melt down her face anyway.

"See who?"

"Harry."

I reached out and took her hand.

"I see him everywhere around here. Every dark curly head, I

want to call out. I did to one. You never know. There could have been some mistake," she said hopefully, though without conviction.

"I guess so..."

At that point, Mopsy and Popsy called from behind us, urging Katrine to get behind the backdrop, a rough canvas strung up behind the platform, before the boys saw her costume. With a raised eyebrow, she shrugged, knowing fully well that they wouldn't care if they saw her now or later.

A moment later, I found my seat next to the chief nurse, a stern-looking matron who frowned on such activities but still somehow found time to get away from the clinic. In the corner, I saw the radio transmitter setting up his equipment to broadcast the show live.

Ansel got up on the stage and motioned for quiet amidst the shouts of the crowd. He told a joke about the food. Another one about the Japanese. Both of which were met with riotous laughter. And then, he said, "Without further ado, the Marvelous Macleay Sisters!"

The amateur band of marines struck up the opening notes to the new song, and right on the beat, Grace, Lorelei, and Katrine marched out onto the stage, belting out into the microphone the song that was then being broadcast all over the Solomon Islands. *"All my tushka chipotas, wait for paaki paaki, don't need no wakaree'e, just more tushka chipotas on a paaki paaki..."*

It didn't matter what my cousins looked like or sounded like or even how they danced (which wasn't half bad, even if the kicks were not as high as Ansel's standards). The boys were happy and entertained, swaying away to *"All my tushka chipotas, wait for paaki paaki, don't need no wakaree'e, just more tushka chipotas on a paaki paaki..."*

It was on the second stanza that the wind really started to pick up. Dark clouds began to form over the stage, and big fat raindrops began to fall, or rather, plummet, to earth. They tried to continue for a while, but the weather simply grew too intense. I'd never seen a storm come up so fast. The girls' voices were drowned out by the howl of the wind.

Lorelei looked at the radio broadcaster and yelled, "What do we do?"

"Can't keep going! Can't pick up your voices! Wind's too loud!" he shouted.

"But the show has to be broadcast! Or, at least this song! The whole thing!"

"Nothing I can do about it, lady!" he answered, quickly packing up the equipment.

"You have to try!" Lorelei exclaimed. "There's two more verses!"

Lorelei was acting crazy. It was much too dangerous to be out in this storm. Why was she so stubborn? I watched her and Grace and Katrine whispering on the stage.

A flash of lightning struck a nearby tree, sending sparks flying. But still, the girls didn't move off the stage - even when another flash of lightning cracked above us.

Edie had to be right. The girls were up to something. This was not a normal song. It was *something* else. I could feel it. There was a reason they had to get that song on the radio. An important reason.

"Get back to your tent, ladies," the radio transmitter shouted firmly as his hands deftly wound up his cords and equipment and prepared to make a dash back to shelter. "Now!"

Much to the dismay of the boys, the show was instantly cut short as the 'Marvelous Macleay Sisters' ran off the stage, their grass skirts clinging precariously to their nylons.

CHAPTER 16

RED SKY IN MORNING

*K*atrine held up a few leaves to her disintegrating skirt. "I think we are going to need new costumes."

Wiping my wet hair away from my forehead and cheeks, I stared at my cousins seriously and went straight for the jugular. "Why were you so obsessed with getting that song broadcasted, ladies?"

They looked at one another, not speaking.

"We're just singers," Katrine said unconvincingly.

"And I'm in the 2nd grade." I shot her a look. "I know what you girls are up to."

"I told you not to ask, Piper!" Lorelei had an odd expression on her face.

"I'm practically your fourth sister," I protested. "I've known something was up almost from the moment you got off the plane. You are coders!"

Katrine grimaced. "No… we're not."

I raised one eyebrow. "So what are you?"

No one moved.

Grace bit her lip. "Honestly, we *aren't* coders."

I wasn't satisfied with that answer. Not one bit. But my cousins were stone-faced. I wasn't going to get any information out of them, no matter how hard I tried.

"Do you think they were able to broadcast any of the song?" Lorelei asked after a minute.

"I don't know," Grace answered. "I certainly hope so."

The wind picked up and blew the flap of the tent wildly about. I jumped out of my hammock and secured the ties, keeping the wind at bay. I thought of Peter, wishing very much that he was there. I wanted to talk to him about… well, I didn't know what exactly. The girls wouldn't tell me! It was remarkably frustrating. It also made me feel left out. And feeling left out made me feel lonely, which made me miss my husband even more.

I felt Lorelei put her hand on my shoulder. "Piper, if I could tell you, I would."

Trying to smile, I nodded. Though I didn't like it, I knew she was telling me the truth. If she could tell me, she would.

Swallowing, I looked out the small opening in the tent flap that served as a window and graciously changed the subject. "I sure hope Peter secured the *Malahini*. Who knows what might happen to the boat in a storm like this?"

"You don't need to worry. We're thousands of miles from Hawaii. There's no way the storm is anywhere near your sailboat." Grace adjusted her hammock and moved it closer towards the center of the tent where it was slightly dryer.

If the *Malahini* was still in Hawaii, Grace would have been correct. But the *Malahini* was not in Hawaii. At that moment, Peter and Frank were steering her right into the eye of the storm.

~

"WHERE ARE the tiny storm trysail and storm jibs?" Frank asked, referring to the storm sails. Both helped balance the boat in the case of a major force of wind. He looked up at the sky. Dark, nearly black clouds were forming and churning above, nearly as wild as the rough sea below.

Peter was hunched over the chart of the Solomon Islands. They were too far from any of the islands on the outer periphery to make a run for cover. But then again, on second thought, it might be better to be out on an open sea in a gale like this—or hurricane or cyclone or whatever it was. Far from land, they would be safe from being blown ashore or onto a reef.

He glanced at Frank and pointed to a little cubby above the icebox where they kept the flares and extra sails. Quickly, Frank retrieved them, and Peter stood up to help him.

"We've gotta get out of the path of the storm, Peter," Frank said as they moved towards the deck.

Peter nodded. "I don't like our location either."

Out from the hold, he felt the wind on his face. They were on the right side of the storm which meant that they were in the storm's 'dangerous semicircle,' a position that had sent many sailors to an early end. He frowned and tied the storm jib into place. "I'll deploy the sea anchor," he said, looking at the white foam cresting the growing waves. "It will help keep the bow up in these breakers."

"Aren't you worried about the load on the rudder?"

"It's a risk we have to take."

Frank grasped a line with his good hand as the boat tossed forward. "It's getting nasty out there. We better get below. We've secured everything on the deck that we can, right skipper?"

"Right." Peter looked once more at the deck. Satisfied that they had indeed stripped it of all excess gear, he followed Frank back inside.

It was, simply put, the worst storm of 1943 to hit that part of the South Pacific. An unrelenting northeast wind bore down at 60 knots. Then, the wind slackened and turned around in the opposite direction.

The *Malahini* was blown ridiculously off course. The boys tried to drink hot coffee until the tossing and pitching of the ocean became too much to light the stove safely.

Three hours in, at nearly six in the evening, they opened the hatch to check on the deck. Surprisingly warm water gushed through the hold, soaking them through. The boat slanted precariously to the side, and together, they shut the hatch and secured it against the pounding waves. It was too risky to venture out. They could both be swept overboard in a second as one enormous wave after another threatened to break the mast or capsize the little sailboat.

"Do you think this is the way Jonah felt?" Frank said, laughing tensely. He noticed Peter's lips moving slowly.

"Are you praying?"

Peter looked up. He was indeed. Managing a small smile, he said quietly, "When my soul fainted within me, I remembered the Lord. And my prayer came in unto thee, into thine holy temple."[7]

"What's that?"

An enormous clap of thunder punctuated the moment while a flash of lightning lit the dark interior of the *Malahini*.

"The prayer of Jonah. Chapter two, verse seven. I thought every sailor knew it. Especially Jewish sailors."

Frank shrugged. "Yeah, well… You go ahead and pray if it makes you feel better."

Even as they spoke, the storm began to spiral into a tropical cyclone, i.e., strong winds spinning about in a circle and sending out rings of thunderstorms and heavy rain in all directions. The rain seemed to be flying horizontally.

As the boat lurched to the side, Frank grasped the wall and tried to stay upright. He was white with fear. "Never thought I'd live to see the day when I met a storm I couldn't brave."

"You'll brave this one," Peter said confidently.

"How can you be so sure?"

Peter didn't answer.

Cynically, Frank sneered slightly before adding, "Well, I'm

looking on the bright side. Odds are, if we go down, the storm will take down the whole Japanese fleet too."

"I'll make you a bet," Peter said after Frank managed to get back in his seat. "If you shut up, I'll pray for you too."

Frank chuckled. "Deal."

FOR HOURS, it only grew worse, and the boys, unable to do anything, waited.

And waited.

And waited.

Until exhausted, both fell asleep.

It was Frank who opened his eyes first. One eye and then the other. At first, he wondered what had woken him up, and then he realized what it was—it was quiet. The wind had stilled. It was also light outside. "Hey." He poked Peter in the ribs. "It's tomorrow."

Carefully, he stood up. The cabin was a wreck. Everything in every cabinet seemed to have spilled out. Peter's books were strewn about the floor.

"And we are alive," Peter said in a triumphant but sleepy tone.

By then, Frank had opened up the door and was halfway up onto the deck. He was met by a burst of sunshine, a calm, sweet breeze, and the still, deep blue water of the Pacific rolling gently as though there had never been a storm at all.

"The question is, where do we happen to be alive at?"

Directly ahead was a thin shoreline. Frank frowned and put his hands on his hips. It seemed too dangerous to attempt to go on shore without knowing if it belonged to the Japanese or the Allies.

Peter and Frank both stood on the deck and looked around, not really knowing what to do. "Well," Frank stepped over some rope, "I don't know how we did it, but there doesn't appear to be any real damage. What a solid little boat!" He lovingly patted the mast of the *Malahini*.

"Prayer, Frank... Prayer."

Frank waved him off. "Yeah, yeah, yeah..."

"So," Peter ran his hand through his hair, suddenly growing serious, "Frank, we can't turn on the radio. Anybody could be in these waters. The Japanese or the Americans. Both scenarios won't look good for us. Our guys will probably think we are spies. The Japanese will say we are spies. We'll wind up in a POW camp or in the brig."

Frank licked his dry lips. "Come to think of it, I don't even know the best way to reach Joe."

Peter swallowed. "You know, Frank, I don't think we thought this through very well."

"Neither of which will help us get to the girls in time." Frank looked down. "That is if we aren't too late already."

"We've got to figure out where we are and then get to Alu Island as soon as we can."

"If the girls are even still on Alu Island."

"We can wait for tonight. If it stays clear, we'll be able to plot our location and figure out a new course using the stars." Peter bent down and examined the drinking water barrels, lashed down to the deck. "Oh no." He groaned.

"What's the matter?" Frank kneeled beside him.

"We didn't seal them properly." He moved aside. "Look!"

Frank saw that the plugs had fallen out during the storm. Their drinking water was, no doubt, tainted with saltwater. "How much water is below? Enough to get us to Alu?"

"Who knows?" Peter stood up. "We don't even know where we are. We've got enough for two days, max. But for all we know, we could be a week's sail to the island."

The boys looked at one another, both thinking the same thing: they would be forced to sail to the island on the horizon and look for freshwater. They couldn't go forward, or even back to Hawaii, without it.

"Do we wait for nightfall or risk a day landing?" Frank asked.

"I, uh…" Peter pursed his lips. "Wait a second," he disappeared below and returned with a pair of binoculars. Peering through them, he smiled and nodded, "Look, over to the left."

Frank took the binoculars.

"You think that's an inlet?" Peter asked.

"Could be. It's impossible to tell from out here," Frank answered.

"My gut tells me it is. And if it is, we'll be able to hide the *Malahini* in there. We'll be invisible, and it will buy us enough time to refill the kegs with water."

"If there's water on the island." Frank shot him a look.

"There's water on the island. All these islands have freshwater. Look how green it is!"

"Okay," Frank sighed, "so we wait until dark, and then we sail into the supposed inlet."

CHAPTER 17

THE ISLAND DWELLERS

The *Malahini* sailed carefully around the rocks that jutted out from the coast as the first star rose in the sky.

"What'd I tell you, an inlet!" Peter whispered triumphantly.

"It's perfect," Frank agreed.

"We've been watching the coast like hawks all day. I think this island is deserted."

Frank didn't answer. The coast did appear to be clear, and the naturally protected harbor they'd discovered seemed equally void of humans. It was quiet, with only the sound of seagulls and other jungle creatures reverberating through the brush that came up nearly to the water's edge.

Peter steered the boat to the far end of the lagoon and lowered the anchor. Working quietly and in unison, they untied the water kegs and swam ashore, pushing the kegs in front of them. "There's got to be a river or a stream somewhere around here," Peter whispered as they pulled the kegs up into the jungle.

Frank didn't answer. He was looking past Peter, his face frozen.

"Peter," he said slowly," don't make any sudden moves." As he spoke, Frank raised his arms in surrender.

Peter turned his head towards Frank's gaze. There, illuminated by the light of the moon, was a young native. He was very muscular and wore khaki pants, army issue, roughly torn at the knees. He had thick, curly black hair, with an equally thick and curly beard, and smooth dark skin. Dark eyes, unable to read in the dim light, several necklaces made of bone or shell seemed to glow in the darkness. In his hands was a bow and arrow poised in their direction. Several dead birds hung limp, attached to a string wound about his torso. The man had obviously been hunting.

The hunter did not speak nor move. Peter and Frank followed suit.

Finally, the man lowered his head and stepped closer to the boys. By now, Peter's hands were also raised in surrender. With a slight movement, the man tilted his head, studying them closely. Then, he lowered his bow and put the arrow back into the small case that hung on his back.

The hunter put a finger to his lips, signaling quiet. With his other hand, he motioned them to follow him.

Frank and Peter looked at each other and shrugged. What choice did they have?

The man led them along a path through thick jungle. In silence, they tread through the brush, listening to the sounds of the exotic birds and the rumblings of large wild animals. It was beautiful and would have been almost peaceful if the hunter had not been so tense. Every few steps, he seemed to turn and motion for the boys to keep quiet. They were, unlike him, unaccustomed to moving through the jungle undetected.

After at least a couple of miles, the hunter stopped suddenly and crouched down. Frank and Peter ducked behind him, wondering what on earth was going on. They heard it first before they saw it. The crunch of boots. The ominous stomp, stomp, stomp of a patrol. Then, the shouts of something in Japanese. The very unknowing of what was being said caused tremors of fear to run down their spines.

The patrol passed by within feet of their hiding spot.

Hidden so, the hunter waited for what seemed an eternity before carefully standing up and motioning for the boys follow again. Frank held back. "What if he's leading us into a trap?" he whispered fiercely.

"We can't get out of it now. Besides, why wouldn't he have just turned us in to the patrol?"

Frank's brow furrowed, and he seemed about to turn back.

"Frank, you have to come now. We've been zigzagging every which way. There's no going back."

The hunter glared at them, and once more made the motion to be quiet.

Begrudgingly, Frank began to follow Peter and the hunter, slowly picking up speed. Now climbing uphill, the jungle cleared slightly, and the path became more discernible and rocky. In the moonlight, Peter could tell they were at the base of a large mountain or volcano. A few minutes more, and they were climbing, nearly vertically, up the side of the mountain. One hand at a time, every foothold sharp. They were breathing heavily and sweating buckets. Finally, the hunter disappeared into the mountain. His dark hand reached out and helped Peter onto a precipice jutting off the side of the rock. Frank was the last to reach the top.

From the precipice, the opening to a cave was barely visible. The hunter smiled, revealing two perfect rows of white, even teeth.

"I guess he wants us to go in there." Frank grimaced. "I hope this is not going to end ugly."

"If he wanted to kill us, he would already have done so, don't you think?" Peter said, completely unconcerned, following the hunter into the cave. The pitch darkness immediately shifted to the soft glow of hot coals on the cave's floor as they rounded one corner and then another.

Over the fire, a beautiful young woman, as dark as the hunter and with equally curly hair that hung down to her waist, with a baby strapped to her back, was busy cooking something. She looked up, obviously surprised by the guests. Suspicious of the newcomers, she spewed out what they could only assume meant, "And who have you brought home for dinner, darling?" in an incomprehensible language.

Before he could respond, Peter and Frank noticed two other figures in the cave, their faces cast in the eerie orange glow of the coals. One sat with his back to the cave's wall. He wore the uniform of a marine. Peter immediately recognized the regal high cheek-bones and almond eyes—a handsome dark brown—all characteristics of a Native American.

The young marine broke out into an enormous smile at the sight of Frank and Peter. Immediately, he was up on his feet and moving towards them. "Who are you guys? What happened!?"

"What happened?" Peter repeated, looking past the young man to the other figure in the cave. This one was stretched out on a grass mat. He too wore a uniform. But his was bloodied. It looked like he had been shot.

"Paul!" The marine turned back to his wounded comrade. "Help is finally here. They must have decided to send back-up after all!"

"We weren't sent," Frank said slowly. "The storm destroyed our freshwater, so we slipped into the lagoon here to resupply."

The marine's eyes darkened. "What?"

All eyes turned to the figure on the mat who struggled to sit up. His arm was in a sling, cradled close to his body. He had beads of sweat on his forehead as though he was feverish. "No matter," the man said pleasantly. "We are happy to see you all the same."

Peter looked closer. He knew that face. Where had he seen this guy? Then it hit him. It was the priest!

"Paul?" He knelt down. "Major Sinclair?"

"Yes?" Paul answered, confused.

"You saved my wife and her cousin two weeks ago from a fleet of killer dolphins." Peter shook his hand.

"You're the mermaid's cousin's husband!" Paul's eyes widened in both recognition and shock.

"What are you doing here?"

"We," Paul looked at the other soldier, "were sent to set up a communication station. The Japanese are planning to build an airfield on the other side of the island. I'm certainly glad to see you!"

Peter looked back at the marine. "What's your name?"

"I am Chito Chochokpi."

"Cherokee?"

"No." He shook his head. "Choctaw."

"You a code talker?" Peter asked.

"Yes." Chito pointed to a transistor radio set up in the corner. "Not that it's doing much good. We've run into some trouble, obviously."

"We know," Frank said.

"How bad are you hurt, Paul?" Peter asked.

Chito answered for him. "Real bad. The woman's been giving him something to keep the fever down. It seems to be working —sometimes."

Peter looked at the blood soaking through the bandage. "You have a first aid kit?"

Paul shook his head. "We used it up already. No more bandages, iodine... nothing."

Peter didn't like the look of the wound. It had a funny smell coming from it. "We've got one on the *Malahini*. I want to get you back to the boat as soon as possible."

The hunter stepped between the men. A stream of words poured forth from his lips. Paul nodded and translated. "He says we will talk after we eat. It's a local custom. He also says we won't be able to move for several hours. There are extra patrols out tonight."

"YOU HAVE TO EAT," Chito explained discreetly as the woman served them 'poi,' a traditional meal made of boiled taro, a starchy vegetable not unlike a potato but sweeter and nuttier. "It's considered an insult to your host around here if you refuse."

"No problem here." Frank received his portion of taro from the woman. "I'm hungry." Frank held the hollowed out coconut shell and a tin spoon and tried it. "Can you tell her I think it's good?"

Paul translated, and the woman smiled and nodded. Then, she busied herself with the baby while her husband eyed them warily, sharpening a small crude knife.

"What are they doing here? The man and woman?" Peter glanced at Chito. "Why are they helping us?"

"He's one of us." Chito took a large bite of taro. "There are a lot of islanders who are 'loyal helpers,' as they call themselves, to the Americans. They do scouting work. Watch the coast. That's how he found you guys."

"But why are they loyal to us and not the Japanese?" Frank eyed the hunter who met his stare with a greater strength, forcing Frank to look away.

"The British were here a long time. When the Japanese showed up, they painted themselves as the 'great liberators' of the Islanders. But the locals didn't buy it. They saw what the Japanese were doing. Forced labor. Worse. The Japanese were the true foreign invaders. The British and Americans were more trusted. They also are protecting their home from the enemy."[8]

"Where's the rest of the tribe?" Peter asked as the flicker of the fire cast shadows that danced on the cave wall.

"The Japanese deported most of them. Mike here," he paused and explained, "I call him Mike. He hid out in the cave. He told us the Japanese were pretty brutal."

No one spoke.

"What about you two?" Peter put his bowl down. "How did you wind up here?" He looked over at Paul. The young man had his eyes closed. He was, by all appearances, asleep. "We've *got* to get him to a doctor. Did you get separated from your troop?"

Chito shook his head no. "We parachuted in a week or so ago.

Paul speaks Japanese and is learning Mike's lingo. They assigned him with me."

Frank moved his hand along, as though he wanted Chito to keep talking. "So you parachuted in a week ago."

"We were tasked with setting up the radio and keeping tabs on the Japanese. General MacArthur wanted intel on the island. It's got an airfield and some other things we sure could use, on the other side. We were supposed to do surveillance and report back."

Peter still looked at Paul.

Chito continued, "But we were spotted. A patrol chased us down for miles, Paul caught some of the fire. We wouldn't have made it without Mike here. We ran and hid out in the jungle. He found us and got us up here. We've been waiting ever since. I was able to send out an SOS," he glanced towards a small radio in the corner, "but the message we received said we are too far out to get help for a while." He paused. "I thought we were going to have to hole up here until the end of the war." He glanced at the newcomers curiously. "Which begs the question, how in the world did you boys get here!"

Frank and Peter looked at one another. "We were actually on our way to Alu Island."

"Alu?" Chitu shrugged. "You're *way* off course."

"We got caught in the storm. Pushed us right to your doorstep."

"No uniforms?" Chito asked.

"We aren't in the service." Peter stretched his legs out straight on the floor of the cave. His knees were beginning to hurt. "Not anymore. We both volunteered in the British Navy and were honorably discharged for injuries sustained in battle before America got in on the war."

"And you were just sailing around the Pacific on vacation?" Chito raised an eyebrow. "I don't buy that for a minute. Why, there are mines all around this island. Heaven knows how you avoided them."

Peter and Frank shared a glance.

"No," Frank answered. "I, uh..." He scratched his head, wondering how to explain. "We discovered some highly sensitive intelligence. So sensitive, we can't risk transmitting it via the radio."

"I'm pretty good at codes," Chito said. "What do you need to say?"

"You trust us," Frank looked at Chito, "enough to send a message?"

"I know good men when I see them." He smiled at them steadily.

Peter's mind raced. They couldn't transmit that there was a traitor in the show. It might be intercepted, and then they were back at square one. The thing to do would be to send a message telling the USO show that they couldn't transmit the shows live all over the islands. "Say that the USO show is suspended. All shows must be canceled until further notice."

An amused expression crossed Chito's face. "Cancel the show? That's not going to go over well with the boys."

"It will go over a lot better when they find out there's a rat in the show sending messages to the enemy about the location of the troops, among other things, via the broadcasts from the show," Frank said seriously.

Understanding registered on Chito's face. "Wow." He shook his head. "Oh, wow. This is bad."

Immediately, Chito stood up and went to the radio. A flick of a switch, and it turned on, powered by a small generator. A stream of words, a mix of Choctaw and Navajo came out in a rush. He repeated it again for good measure. He looked up, satisfied. "Okay. I told them that the USO shows, all of them, must be stopped until further notice."

He smiled. "I spent my childhood in a government-run school where they forced me to speak English and punished me for speaking Choctaw. And now they pay me for it."

Frank chuckled. "Life is ironic like that."

"We need a plan. Men like you and Paul are prime targets. The Japanese know you are here, obviously. They know you got away."

Peter was in deep thought. "And now that we are here, the risk is even higher. Our presence is putting them in danger." He smiled sadly at the hunter and his wife. The baby was sleeping soundly in her arms.

"Frank," Peter took charge, "we've got to get Paul and Chito to the *Malahini*. We can sail out the way we came in. We'll try to get to Alu again. We've got to try to find out who's intercepting the USO codes and stop him—or her, for that matter—for good. And we've got to get Paul here fixed up fast."

He nodded a slow yes. It would be difficult, managing to get Paul out of the cave, down the mountain, and through the jungle, even more so in the dark. Attempting to do it and avoid the Japanese patrols presented a nearly impossible task. But both men knew more lives were at stake than their own.

CHAPTER 18

THE EYE OF THE STORM

*C*hito gently shook Paul awake as he struggled to grasp onto consciousness. "Hey, Paul, can you sit up?" Even in the dim light of the coals, it was obvious he'd lost all color.

"These guys have a boat. They found a lagoon, and it's hidden. If we can get to the boat, well, we can make a run for it."

"A sailboat?" Paul's voice cracked, astonished. "How will we get past the enemy?"

"We got here safe enough, didn't we?" Peter said. "And besides, you are a God-fearing man. Oh ye of little faith."

At that, Paul managed a weak smile and then coughed several times. "What can I say to that?"

"What about them?" Frank motioned towards the native couple. "Tell them they can come too. We'll take them to Alu."

With his last measures of strength, Paul explained their offer in the Native's island tongue. But the hunter began to shake his head no vigorously, and he spoke for a long time with much animation. When he finished, Paul nodded in understanding. "He says they must stay here. It's their home." He looked at the radio. "And he says that we still need someone here to keep watch."

"There won't be any way for him to transmit messages." Chito frowned.

"Can you give him a quick lesson in working the radio?" Paul asked

Chito became stressed. "Are you kidding? It took me months to learn how to code, transmit, and receive. And he doesn't even speak English, much less anything else."

"Teach him three codes," Paul spoke slowly. "'Come.' 'Do not come.' And 'wait.' It's better than nothing, and it gets the point across. 'Come' for if it's safe for a landing, 'do not come' if the Japanese increase their forces, and 'wait' if something is strange."

"I guess I can do that. I'll have to teach him how to use the generator and the radio too."

"He'll learn. He's got a wife and a baby to protect."

"We have one more problem," Frank spoke up. "We don't have enough fresh water on board to get us three miles, much less all the way to Alu Island. That's why we came ashore—to get water."

Paul translated this to the couple, and the wife spoke up, her voice low and serious.

"She said she will lead the two of you to a spring. You can fill up the barrels there. By the time you are done, Chito here should have had enough time to teach the fundamentals of sending secret messages." Without thinking, he bent his arm and cried out in pain. Then, gathering his strength, Paul said firmly, "Get moving. The sooner we are out of here the better."

THE HUNTER'S WIFE, the baby still on her back, led Peter and Frank through the jungle as silently as her husband had. But this time, they did not run into any patrols. The water kegs were right where they left them at the beach, and the spring, nearly a mile inland, flowed quietly down a smooth creek bed into the lagoon where the *Malahini* was anchored. The three worked in quiet unity, filling one keg at a time. Finally, Peter and Frank swam with the kegs to the sailboat and hoisted them on board, tying them down and, this time, making sure they were properly sealed.

It took a few hours from start to finish, but once they returned to the cave, Chito had completed the tutorial and packed up their gear. Now, the question was, how to help Paul down the steep incline from the cave to the boat. His fever was so high, he could only walk a few feet before getting dizzy and blacking out. In the end, Paul was strapped down to a very light piece of driftwood, which was then lowered carefully down the mountain by a rope. It was almost like sledding.

The journey through the jungle was slow going. But once again, they did not run into a patrol. They reached the lagoon undetected, each person relieved beyond words.

The hunter and his wife watched from the shore as Peter, Frank, and Chito pulled Paul to the *Malahini* and lifted him on board. After Paul was secured below the deck, Frank and Peter cranked up the anchor and unfurled the sail. A small breeze carried them out of the lagoon. Both the hunter and his wife raised their hands in farewell. A silent, heartfelt parting.

Chito watched them until he could see them no more, which did not take long. The wind was growing in strength, and the night was dark. He touched his neck and fingered a strange necklace, a sort of hemp with a tooth of some sort hanging on it.

"From your tribe?" Peter asked.

Chito shook his head no. "From Mike. A dolphin tooth. He said his people used to hunt for dolphins." He looked out to the sea. "My people are not seafaring anymore. We used to be, before my time. But we were pushed to the plains of Oklahoma. Now, we are land people."

"Not a fan of sailing, I take it." Frank looked over at the nervous young marine.

"No. But tonight I am."

Silence once more descended on the band, and they sailed away from the island, their eyes searching the black waters for mines or enemy ships. No lamps were lit. They, of course, kept complete radio silence.

Down in the hold, Peter extricated the first aid kit from under the sink. Paul's skin had a strange, waxy pallor to it.

"Sinclair?"

"Yeah?" His eyes opened.

"I want to get some antiseptic on that wound."

Paul grimaced and nodded. Peter unwound the bandage.

"It's a miracle you boys showed up. I prayed help would come, but to be honest, I was starting to prepare myself for the worst."

Peter poured something out of a vial onto a clean handful of cotton. "God works in mysterious ways."

"Are you a Christian, Peter?"

"Most certainly."

Paul smiled. "Then you'll understand that I wasn't afraid to die or get caught. But I was disappointed…"

"Disappointed about what?" Skillfully, Peter went to work cleaning the wound. Paul barely winced, though it must have hurt something fierce.

"I felt I wasn't done with life yet. Actually, in some ways, I felt I hadn't even started yet. I always dreamed of a family… a chance to serve God in my life with someone else."

"You did?"

"Well sure! Don't you?"

"I'm married already, so the obvious answer is yes," Peter answered, not taking his eyes off of the wound. It was very red around the edges, but as best as he could tell, there wasn't gangrene. That was positive. "Do you have a girlfriend?"

Paul shrugged. Peter imagined that Paul could have his choice of dates any night of the week.

"I've dated here and there. Haven't met that special someone yet." He stopped talking suddenly and looked away. "I think I haven't met that special someone yet, that is."

"Well, I wouldn't worry too much. There are plenty of fish in the sea." Peter looked up. "I think Chito was wrong. Doesn't look like it went through the bone. You're a lucky man."

"Piper seems like a sweet girl." Paul shut his eyes in pain. "But whoa, that Lorelei. She's a real lady. Probably her European upbringing. Where I'm from in California, we're more laid back."

"Piper's from California too." Peter began to wrap the fresh bandage around Paul's arm. "Lorelei's not a snob, Paul. She just gets sort of stiff sometimes."

"All my usual tactics weren't working."

Peter looked at up the handsome man's face and then back to the work at hand.

"Is it infected?" The *Malahini* creaked as it swayed from side to side.

"Yes. Probably why you have a fever. By the looks of it, you have lost a lot of blood too."

"Were you a medic?"

"No," he ripped the bandage with his teeth and secured it, "but I've studied first aid here and there. And a good sailor knows his way around some pretty bad bang-ups. Everyone should know how to treat a burn or poison ivy or whatever. It's a rough world." He laughed.

"You have a gift."

"What?" Peter blinked.

"Ever thought of going to medical school?"

"Just between us, Paul, I've never enjoyed school that much." Peter looked back at the wound. The truth was, he saw so much wrong with the world. Nothing seemed right. Studying business to sell lobster to rich people seemed rather meaningless these days. He believed God wanted him to help fix whatever it was that had gone wrong, but he had no idea where to start. The idea of being in medical school for another ten years before starting to help fix it seemed like an eternity.

Smiling good-naturedly, he replied, "Maybe it's just because you haven't found something you are interested in yet."

Peter brushed off Paul's comment and began putting away the kit.

"Now me?" Paul continued. "My problem is that I'm interested in too many things. My dad always used to make fun of me that I would turn into a career student. I guess I was for a while. Even after I went to seminary, I kept studying. I would have kept on racking up the degrees if it wasn't for this war. And then there's Timmy. After my brother-in-law died, I knew I had to be there. Boys need fathers."

"You know," Peter started, "never underestimate the influence of what you are doing. My uncle is like a father to me. Don't know what I'd do without him." Peter shut his eyes and thought of Horatio. What would he say if he knew what his only nephew was doing at this moment?

THE NIGHT DRIFTED ON. One pot of coffee turned into two. The remaining peanut butter sandwiches disappeared.

It was as dawn approached that they saw it.

Paul, asleep in the hold, was awakened by the fear-filled voice of Frank calling for Peter to look through the binoculars.

"It could be a whale, right?"

"I don't think so. Too angular." Peter's eyes were as sharp as ever. He'd been spotting subs on the horizon for years.

This was followed by, "Could it be the enemy?"

Peter's voice, tense and focused, responded, "Impossible to know. The question is, have we been spotted?"

Paul pulled himself up off the bed and carefully poked his head out. "What is it?"

Chito's eyes were glued to the horizon. "A ship of some sort. I … I think it's actually a sub."

"He's right," Peter said.

"That means it's got to be close, right?" Paul asked.

No one answered. They didn't need to. They were so close to the sub that they could see the water running off the sides. With every second, it grew bigger as it surfaced.

"Maybe we should put up a flag of surrender," Frank said, "if it's the Japs."

"Oh no. We will fight them to the end," Chito said firmly. "Never surrender!"

"Chito," Peter placed his arm on his shoulder, "we are in a sailboat named the *Malahini*. We have your pistol, Paul's pistol, and my flare gun. We will not stand a chance against a sub. Besides, maybe they won't see us. If they don't up the periscope, we are practically invisible."

Even as he spoke, the periscope was raised.

"Never mind." Peter frowned. "Let's put up the surrender flag."

Just as Frank was about to go and get the flag, a loud voice boomed out of a speaker on the sub's tower. "THIS IS THE U.S.S. *SWORDFISH*. DO NOT MOVE. REPEAT. DO NOT MOVE."

Immediately, the hatch to the tower opened, and several sailors armed with assault rifles stepped out onto the tower. They were so close, no bullhorn was needed.

"Hey, sailor!" Frank shouted with thankfulness at the sight of Americans. "You are a sight for sore eyes!"

Several of the sailors smiled, relieved. "Looks like you fellows got lost!"

"You have no idea. The *Malahini*, and its passengers are in distress. Request permission to board, sir?" Peter asked in his most official sounding tone.

Over the speaker, another voice spoke, this time with a strong Scottish accent, "Peter! Peter, my boy! What in the world are you doing out here?"

CHAPTER 19

ISLAND FEVER

The base on Alu was small and unassuming. No troopships heading back to Hawaii were scheduled for another two months. And because the show was, for all intents and purposes, canceled due to the strange and sudden message sent out canceling all USO shows for the time being, the higher-ups thought it best if we just wait it out. We were stuck in a weird sort of limbo, unable to go home and unable to go forward with the show schedule because the show didn't really exist anymore. And so, day after day, we waited on the little rock in the middle of the sea.

July turned to August, and there was no hope for escape until the end of September. It was, to put it bluntly, mind-numbingly dull. All thoughts of a riveting adventure with my cousins went out the window with the reality of the exceptionally boring day-to-day life on the island that came with the show's hiatus. It was the longest few weeks of my life.

"I know what's the matter with all of us," Katrine said knowingly. "One of the boys was telling me about it. It's a disease."

"Oh, be quiet," Grace retorted and shifted on her cot.

(All of our hammocks had been replaced, as per Katrine's request, though it had been met with a snide, "What do you think this is, lady? Some sort of hotel?")

"That's one of the symptoms." Katrine was using her 'know it all' tone in full force. It came with the territory of being the eldest, and Katrine slipped into the role more often than she, or anyone else for that matter, liked.

"What's the disease?" I asked, growing worried.

The small hairs not in my ponytail were stuck to the back of my neck with sweat.

"Island Fever."

"That's ridiculous." Lorelei sat up. "I'm a nurse. There's no such thing!"

Katrine was on a roll. "The first stage is when you feel slightly peevish." She looked at Grace. "That develops into severe impatience."

Grace rolled her eyes dramatically.

"The second stage is growing restlessness, a feeling that there is nowhere to go."

"There *is* nowhere to go!" Grace exclaimed. "It's 10 miles from one end to the other of this island. And it's even less if you go across it the short way!"

Katrine spread her hands out. "Like I said, a feeling that there is nowhere to go."

Grace exploded and threw her little pillow at Katrine, hitting her squarely on the face.

"Stage three — sudden attacks of rage directed at nothing in particular." Katrine threw the pillow back.

"And the last stage?" Lorelei asked, her eyebrows raised.

"Complete claustrophobia."

Grace sat down with a huff. "Then I guess I've got it bad. What's the cure?"

"In the later stages of the disease, there's nothing you can do to cure it except for a change of scenery." Katrine looked glum. "Which we cannot do because there are ocean mines inbetween us and the other islands. And there are no boats going to the mainland, or planes for that matter, until further notice, at least not for a mediocre troop of USO show people."

"We could swim," Grace said flatly.

No one answered. The truth was, none of us wanted to do anything except get off the island. But in the meantime, we would just have to wait. Just like we had been waiting for weeks.

Power on the island was sketchy at best. So we didn't get 'A' rations or those that incorporated foods needing refrigeration. We were stuck with 'B' rations. It was all canned, packaged, or preserved... supplemented by some fresh island produce. We were eating a lot of Vienna sausages and pancakes with a syrup made of sugar and water. There were also chocolate bars, so hard you couldn't break them with a brick, and dehydrated mashed potatoes.

Freshwater on the island was limited, so we washed in the ocean... which meant we never really felt clean because the salt seemed to stick to our skin. We rubbed lard into our hair to keep it from drying out, a trick one of the nurses told us about early on.

And then there were the Atabrine pills. Big, ugly horse pills we choked down every day to keep malaria at bay. Some of the men refused to take the pill after a while, complaining it turned their skin yellow. Personally, I would choose yellow skin over the debilitating, raging fevers of the disease that Lorelei saw at the clinic where she volunteered her nursing skills. The 'powers that be' did everything they could to make sure everyone took their daily Atabrine along with their breakfast. They knew that we had to win against malaria first if we were ever going to defeat the Japanese. Thankfully, the Japanese had an equal, if not more difficult, battle against the fever. Rumor had it, they didn't have enough Atabrine or good enough supply lines to get it to their troops.[9]

Ultimately, apart from the climate and monotony, the worst part was the feeling of utter uselessness and separation from the outside.

No letters came from the mainland. At least, no letters for us. We had heard nothing from anyone.

What made it worse was the heat wave. Usually, in August the weather hovered at a balmy 84 degrees Fahrenheit. But for the last week, it hadn't dropped below 90.

I *had* to do something somewhat productive or go crazy. So, every other afternoon or so, I commandeered a marine, took a few notes on his adventures in the Pacific with my birthday pen, and snapped a photograph. What I would do with these photographs was up in the air, but the possibilities were endless, and in my gut, I knew it was important to document the personal stories of such wonderful heroes.

Lorelei, in contrast, didn't have to make up anything interesting to do. She was recruited by the small band of nurses at the clinic and spent most mornings treating tropical rashes and dishing out aspirin.

Grace and Katrine spent most of their time in our tent trying to stay cool. And when they weren't in the tent, they were on the stage rehearsing along with Lorelei and the rest of the show.

Yes. Rehearsing. Ansel insisted the girls keep up with the act which irked everyone—even Mopsy and Popsy. What was the point of rehearsing for a show that didn't have a performance date in sight?

So, unbeknownst to us, as Peter, Paul, Frank, and Chito set sail with Horatio and Edie, I followed the girls out of the tent and sat in the shade of a palm near the stage, watching them all shuffle-ball-change for the millionth time, growing more annoyed by each futile ball-change.

"THAT'S A WRAP!" Ansel called. "You girls can call it quits for the day! And Katie—" Katrine rolled her eyes, "I'm still not satisfied with those kicks!"

When Ansel was out of earshot, Popsy muttered angrily, "If I'd known what a dummy show this was going to turn out to be and how hot it is, I would have made us sign up for the Donut Dollies instead. I've heard it's a lot cooler in France."

"What's a 'Donut Dolly?" Lorelei asked, looking through the stack of records on the side of the stage.

"They drive these big busses through Great Britain and Europe with a phonograph and cigarettes and gum, and, of course, lots of donuts and coffee. They give the boys on the front a good time and clean conversation. Helps with the homesickness."

"Oh? Why didn't you do it?" I asked.

"Are you kidding? No colored nail polish. No earrings. No bright makeup. I'm a showgirl. I feel naked without my lipstick."

"Is that so?" I asked, suddenly feeling quite conscious of my own naked face. I never wore makeup, at least, not on normal days.

"Popsy, I says to myself, I am a talent. Why not use my talent where it will do the boys the most good? So we signed up for the show. I thought it would be better than the half-rate theaters we were playing in New York."

"And we couldn't make donuts if you paid us," Mopsy added after a second. "What I would do for a donut right now."

The two girls walked off the stage, leaving Lorelei, Katrine, and I alone. In the distance, a faint rumbling disturbed the stillness.

"Did you hear that?" I asked, perking up.

We all listened intently. It was silent. The sirens didn't sound.

"False alarm." I exhaled.

So far, five enemy planes had flown overhead doing surveillance. When this happened, a loud siren broke out, giving us exactly 90 seconds to dash from wherever we were into holes in the ground dug for just such an event. They never dropped any bombs, though they had shot at us. Thankfully, we had not seen any casualties or even any major injuries from these incidents. The worst was when Mopsy twisted her ankle falling into one of these pits in the dark.

What she was doing wandering around on the beach in the dark was another question, one answered by the fact that she was with a handsome sergeant at the time, even though we were under strict orders not to fraternize with the men.

The only way Mopsy or Popsy could escape for a romantic interlude was under the cover of darkness and away from the camp. These moments were few and far between and had ended with the ankle incident. The majority of our extensive free time was spent walking up and down the coast or in our tent simmering in the heat, reading *The Robe*, and counting down to... nothing (or Ansel's next rehearsal).

"All right," Katrine clasped her hands behind her head. "Let's go back to the tent. I need a break." She glanced at me, "Any chance you could read more?"

I shrugged. "Why not?" There wasn't anything else to do.

"You girl's go ahead," Lorelei said. "I told one of the nurses I'd take her shift this afternoon so she could perm her hair."

And so, Katrine, Grace, and I returned to our steamy tent completely unaware that the monotony we'd almost grown used to was about to be abruptly shattered.

"KEEP READING." Katrine turned over on her back and swatted a fly away.

I cleared my throat and turned the page. "*'No, Your Majesty; we did not send Marcellus to Athens to consult the diviners. We urged him to go away for a time, so that he might not be embarrassed by meeting friends in his unhappy state of mind.'*"[10]

I turned on my Tiberius voice and said, "...*'The Jews are a queer people; very religious; believe in one god. Evidently this Galilean was a religious fanatic, if he got himself into trouble with the Temple; had some new kind of religion, maybe.'*"[11]

"'Did Your Majesty ever hear of the Messiah?' inquired Gallio. The Emperor's jaw slowly dropped and his rheumy eyes widened. 'Yes,' he answered, in a hoarse whisper. 'He that is to come. They're always looking for him, Telemarchus says. They've been expecting him for a thousand years, Telemarchus says. He that is to come—and set up a kingdom... a kingdom that shall have no end; and the government shall be upon his shoulders."[12]

Grace stretched her lanky legs up off her cot and stood up. "I feel like I can't breathe!" She gasped. "This book is... silly."

"No, it's not!" Katrine chided her.

The story intrigued Katrine. Though she would never admit it out loud, secretly, Marcellus' spiritual longing was awakening something inside of her she had never felt before. And as Marcellus journeyed along the path that Yeshua had traveled before his execution, meeting those who Yeshua knew, she felt like she was right there with him, wondering the same things, asking the same questions. But she would never say this to her sisters.

Rather, she said how well-researched the book was. How historically accurate it was. That's why she enjoyed it, from a purely academic point of view.

Grace, in contrast, tolerated it because it was the only book we had.

"Stop complaining." Lorelei said as she lifted the tent flap and threw herself down on the cot.

Before I had a chance to ask her how her shift went, a cheery male voice called out, "Hiya, ladies!" at the entrance to our tent.

Lorelei wearily got back up and went over to the flap and opened it. A young marine stood there with a sack of what looked to be mail.

"What's this?"

"Mail plane came through today. There's a letter here for Lorelei Macleay." The Mail plane came without fail twice a week.

"That's me." She smiled. "We haven't had mail since we arrived!" She read the various markings on the letter. It had been forwarded from the USO office in Hawaii. "Looks like it's from Becky in Cairo! Thanks for bringing it."

The young man nodded. "My pleasure. I know Ansel usually hands out the mail for the USO folks, but I couldn't find him today."

Lorelei shot me a worried look. "What do you mean, Ansel likes to hand out the mail?"

The courier looked confused. "You kids have gotten a few letters, and Ansel said he'd give them to you to save me time."

"That's odd," I stated. "We haven't gotten any letters."

"What?" He scratched his forehead. "You mean, he didn't give you your mail? That's a federal offense!"

"Maybe he forgot?" Katrine said, unconvinced.

"I can talk to him about it if you like." He shuffled his feet, embarrassed, as though it was his fault somehow.

"No," I answered quickly. "Don't bother. It's USO business..."

"Well," he frowned, "if you say so."

He stood there a moment more, not moving. Finally, I pushed him forward. "You go on and deliver the mail. I'm sure there are a lot of young men wanting to know what's going on back on the farm and to know that their fiancés still love them."

"Well, if you say so," he repeated and reluctantly went on his way.

Once he was out of earshot, we huddled together, whispering fiercely. After nothing happening for months, we had a mystery on our hands. A *real* mystery.

"What could it mean? Ansel not delivering our mail?" Grace looked worried.

By now, Lorelei had ripped the letter open and begun to read out loud.

"Dearest Lorelei," she began....

I pictured Becky in Cairo, just as my cousins had described her to me. The lilting Irish accent, her golden hair, her beautiful, youthful face, and bright blue eyes the color of cornflowers.

"Dearest Lorelei,

I've been staring at this page for a solid 20 minutes, not knowing how to begin...

You are constantly in my prayers. Your bravery in following the Lord wherever he leads you inspires me, my friend. From the first day I met you to the day you left Jerusalem for Egypt, I have known you to be a woman of courage. As you have embarked on your new journey, I must tell you some more of mine.

Paulina and Yosef finally tied the knot. It took some time, but after the awkwardness wore off, they remembered how much they loved one another, and that was that.

Lorelei, I realize you must be hurt and angry regarding the contents of my last letter, but I humbly ask as your sister in Christ for your forbearance.

Joe has asked me to stay on in Cairo indefinitely... as his wife."

"Oh my goodness." I looked worriedly at Lorelei who inhaled sharply before continuing.

"His family is endowing a children's home, not unlike the Spafford Baby Home. They'll need a full-time medical staff, and he wants me to head the whole thing up. We are looking for a proper building now. There are some very nice old mansions just along the banks of the river. I've just about narrowed in on one I like very much. It's got a great courtyard and good ventilation. There's plenty of space for lots of little ones. So many have been displaced, I barely know where to begin to help.

We didn't know how to tell you or if to tell you! You are out there on the front. But we've always been honest - I honestly love him. Can you believe it? And I have such peace about the whole thing, I've determined it's God's will for me to go for it."

"You have got to be kidding me," Grace spat. "You've been gone for less than two months!"

Katrine looked steadily at Lorelei. "Are you," she said hesitantly, "all right?"

"Just between us, I feel pure relief. I didn't want to have to write a letter to Joe first."

"You mean, you are okay with this?" I asked, motioning to the letter in her hand.

She looked as though a great weight had lifted off her shoulders. "I began a letter to him to break it off at least a dozen times but kept putting it off, which only made me feel worse. To be honest, I've barely given Joe Miller a thought this whole trip. I'm happy he's happy. I'm happy Becky's happy. And... I'm happy I'm free!"

Grace, Katrine, and I shared a slightly bewildered look.

"Well," Katrine exhaled, "I'm happy you're happy. I was worried I was going to spend all night consoling you."

Lorelei shrugged. "Every time I told you I don't love Joe that way you didn't believe me. I was telling the truth." Her eyes turned back to the letter, continuing to read, her tone light, "*I pray for you every day, Lorelei. For your safety especially.*"

I saw Grace roll her eyes.

Lorelei's tone completely changed. "Oh my." She exhaled.

"What is it?" Katrine leaned in.

"There is a postscript from Joe!" She pointed to the letter. "See, this is his hand."

"What does he say?" I asked.

"*P.S. Lorelei, I realize you must be very angry, or you would've responded long ago to my letter.*"

She looked up. "He must mean a letter I never got."

We nodded for her to continue.

Eyes back on the page, she kept reading, "*I'm sorrier than words can ever say. I never thought I'd hurt you like that or write a 'Dear John' for that matter. I thought only the ladies did that. However, it is of the utmost importance that you put it aside for now.*"

Lorelei's voice manifested a fresh urgency mixed with a growing confusion we all felt as soon as we heard Joe's next words. "*You must let me know if you received my last several messages. Be careful, do not take pills from anyone other than the doctor. Someone is prescribing over-the-counter meds under the table. Protect the boys from cheap goods!*"

Instantly, all thoughts of Joe and Becky's upcoming nuptials were forgotten. There were more serious things afoot.

"Read that last part again," Katrine commanded.

"*Protect the boys from the cheap goods?*" Lorelei bit her lip, her eyes opening wide. "How many messages have we *not* gotten?"

Grace shook her head as an ominous silence filled the air. "You don't think there is a traitor among us, do you?" She whispered.

CHAPTER 20

THE SINGING SPIES

*M*y mind was working overtime, trying to figure out what Joe was talking about and what my cousins had to do with 'protecting the boys.'

A cryptic message from Joe hinting at something sinister. The canceled show? And now, missing mail? I'd had enough of my cousin's keeping mum. I needed to know what was going on. And I needed to know *now*.

"A traitor?" I asked, slowly standing up.

My cousins stared up at me.

"I get that you've all been sworn to secrecy or something, but I've had enough of this. You better tell me what is going on!"

No one spoke. Joe's letter hung limply in Lorelei's hand.

"You *are* coders after all, aren't you?" I thought hard. "Is that what the 'cheap goods' are?"

"You're half-right," Grace answered. "But we aren't coders."

"So," I prodded, "what are you?"

Lorelei struggled a moment and frowned. "You can't tell anybody."

I held up my right hand. "Scout's honor."

"I guess you could call us couriers." She inhaled nervously.

"We carry the messages through the songs and hope the radio waves carry them where they should go," Katrine explained quickly. "The Germans and the Japanese have been catching on to our codes. It's quickly turning into a war of information." Her eyes were still on the letter in Lorelei's hand.

All of Lorelei's strange lyrics began to make sense, along with the trio's bizarrely fast rise to fame.

"That's rather clever," I said slowly. A shiver ran down my spine. I was a part of something much more important than I knew I had signed up for. Peter was right. It could be dangerous. In fact, by all shapes and appearances, it was already.

Grace shrugged. "It wasn't our idea, it was Joe Miller's."

"Keep your voice down!" Katrine hissed

Slowly, I sat back down. "So, how does it work?"

Lorelei tucked her feet up underneath her on the cot. "The captain of the base, whatever base we'll be performing at, will pass me a coded message. I'll quickly come up with a song that will be sung at the show—which is broadcast all over the Pacific. Sometimes, the code is in the actual notes, and I only write the words," Lorelei whispered. "Like every third note is a letter spelling a word or standing for something. But we never fully know what the code is for or what it's saying. It's safer that way... you know, in case we're caught by the enemy."

She paused briefly before continuing. "Other times, it's the rhythm. But the last message was in the words. Joe said a lot of men from the Native American tribes were drafted for the purpose of coding because their languages are so complex, and most Japanese don't speak Navajo or Comanche or Hopi... hence the last song. I assume we'll be doing many more Native American numbers in the future. You would be shocked at how many Navajo and Cherokee kids are holed up in caves all over these islands who are waiting to hear our songs that will tell them when supplies are going to be parachuted in or where the Japanese are planning to build another airfield or when to expect reinforcements or who knows what."

I looked at Lorelei. It was all coming together. "And between Katrine's clandestine Jewish Agency experience and Grace's military training, and your quick wit, they thought you were a perfect fit for the assignment."

They nodded.

"The Palmach thought it was an excellent idea," Grace said.

"The opportunity to help this war end made my university work seem a lot less interesting," Katrine added. "I thought, perhaps, though I swore I would never spy again, I might somehow help Harry. What if one of these messages helps him escape? Anything would be worth that."

"What about Frank?" I asked, suddenly suspicious. "What was his part in all of this?"

"Oh, Joe just wanted us to have a bodyguard on hand just in case —" Lorelei stopped before continuing a second later. "In case something went wrong."

"I think something's gone wrong," Grace said bluntly.

"Don't you find it strange he wasn't allowed to come?" Lorelei looked at Katrine, trying to control the fear quickly rising in her throat.

Katrine shook her head. "I certainly find it strange now!" Her voice trembled slightly. "It was *Ansel* who made the decision not to allow Frank to come."

"And it was *Ansel* who stole our mail," I added.

"If there is a traitor in our midst," Grace spoke solemnly, "and I think we can all agree that's what Joe's code was trying to communicate, Ansel Thornton certainly fits the casting call."

Lorelei groaned and said with a hint of cynicism, "The question is, why would our dedicated USO show director, Ansel Thornton, betray us and his country?"

"I have no idea," I answered. "But I have to agree. He certainly *feels* like a traitor. He called Katrine a sheeny and a lot of other names I won't repeat!"

"We can't accuse a man on feelings alone," Lorelei faltered, though she obviously agreed. "Or name-calling, as much as I don't like that sort of thing."

"But you *can* accuse a man of stealing your mail!" Grace's voice trembled.

"And message tampering," Katrine added. "It's too bad that Captain Brown is long gone, and we've no way to reach him to see if his original message is the one we sang out on the radio. Do you remember on the troopship when Ansel brought us the message from Captain Brown? The one Lorelei wrote the Navajo song to?"

"What about it?" Grace asked.

"We were supposed to communicate *only* with the captain. Ansel brought us the message!"

It hit me like a load of bricks. "With Ansel making himself the intermediary, he could change the codes. Why, he could have sent messages to the enemy through you!"

"Should we go to the base commander?" Lorelei shook her head gravely.

"I don't think so," Katrine answered. "Not yet. We need proof or else he could turn around and implicate us. We were the ones who wrote and sang the song, remember? I have experience in the spying department. I've seen similar situations like this go south. It can easily turn into a game of 'he-said-she-said.'"

Grace looked furtively around the tent. "Well, at least we have something to do! A real mission! We have a target and a plan... sort of. This is the first time we've had a purpose being here in weeks! Maybe not the purpose we set out with, but catching a traitor is nearly as good!"

I glanced out the tent flap. As if on cue, Ansel Thornton sashayed out of his tent, did a bright little jump and a kick, and disappeared into the jungle.

"I'm going to go search his tent. Right now!" I exclaimed. "There could be a clue in there, something that might implicate him."

"I'm going with you," Grace said. Then, she turned to Katrine and Lorelei. "Lorelei, you watch the jungle from here. The moment you see him, distract him long enough for us to get out of his tent."

"How?" she asked, bewildered.

"Tell him you are working on a new song, and you need his feedback. Tell him, well, tell him anything at all!"

She frowned with concern. "All right."

"And Katrine, the minute she has Ansel pulled aside, come and get me and Piper." She grabbed my hand. "Hurry! We don't have much time!"

"No, wait!" Katrine put her arm out. "You stay here, Grace. Let me go. I know what to look for."

KATRINE MOVED SLOWLY about Ansel's small tent, her trained eyes narrowed. "Nothing should seem unusual, Piper. That's the point. We have to think creatively. We have to think like spies... or traitors... for the moment."

She picked up a pencil and held it up, examining it closely before putting it back on the desk. "It's just a pencil. Never-mind."

"What did you think it was?"

"Oh, they've got pencil pistols and sometimes even tiny little knives hidden inside. But not this one. It's just a normal pencil."

"You learned a lot when you worked with the Jewish Agency, didn't you?"

She smiled and continued to scan the desk, honing in on a small tin bowl with a gaudy men's ring, some cigarettes, and a lighter in it. Immediately, she grabbed the ring. Deftly, her fingers felt the rounded blank onyx stone that was suspended in gold. "Probably costume jewelry," she said quietly. "It feels cheap, certainly not solid gold."

At that, as though struck by some unusual inspiration, her fingers began to twist the stone. Stunned, we watched as it began to unscrew, opening up to reveal a miniature compass.

"What's it for?" I asked.

She shrugged. "Escape or evasion… or who knows what. Sadly, it's not illegal to have a compass."

"It's a *concealed* compass though. That seems like it should be illegal." I took the ring out of her hand and turned both pieces over, gasping at what I saw under the stone 'lid' to the compass.

"Katrine! Look!"

We both stared at my palm. Under the stone was nothing less than a tiny engraved Swastika. Not only was Ansel anti-Semitic, he was a full-fledged Nazi.

"This has to be enough proof!" I was nearly shouting. "I knew it! I just knew there was something wrong with that guy."

"Keep your voice down." Katrine was tense, her eyes wide. "I only wish it were. Technically, we are still in the same boat. He could say we planted it here. I wish Harry was here! He would know what to do!" She put the ring down. "Come on, keep looking."

Frustrated with the whole situation, I groaned and moved towards the cot. Carefully, I lifted up the thin mattress. Nothing. Then, I knelt down and swept the ground under the cot with my hand. Just dirt. Aside from the swastika ring, it appeared that Ansel's tent was clean.

When I got back up, Katrine was still rifling through the contents of Ansel's desk. She glanced at me. "Just notes for the show." Katrine swallowed and picked up a deck of cards laying on his chair. Nervously, she slung them from hand to hand. They were unusual. Instead of the usual Bicycle design on the back, these cards had images of sleeping kittens and puppies.

A shrill whistle shot through the tent. It was Grace's signal. Ansel must be on his way back. Panicked, Katrine and I made a mad dash out of the tent and dove behind a nearby shrub. A few seconds later, Ansel jauntily sashayed past. We watched him enter his tent and close the flap behind him.

"That was close." I exhaled with relief.

"He looks rather pleased with himself," Katrine whispered. Standing up slowly, she held out the deck of cards. "Oh no! I forgot to put them back! He'll know someone was messing with his stuff."

Grace and Lorelei waved at us from our own tent, and we jogged over. Hurriedly, we relayed what we'd found while Lorelei had cornered him, begging him to show her how to do a bogo-pogo step without a partner.

"Okay, so he's got a Nazi ring." Lorelei crossed her eyes. "Now what do we do?"

We all looked down at Ansel's playing cards. Katrine opened the box and took the cards out. "We'll have to get them back into his tent before he knows they're missing." She shuffled them nervously and held one up for all of us to see.

Before we could move, Ansel pushed our tent flap open and stood there, staring at us—his cards in our hands. There wasn't any time to hide them. We were caught red-handed. Katrine opened her mouth and shut it.

He looked at the cards and then at Lorelei. "I just wanted to run that bogo-pogo with you one more time. I wasn't sure you really had it."

Lorelei tried to smile but failed. This was going downhill fast.

What would Edie do? What would Edie do? I frantically racked my brain. Then, it hit me. I would gamble just the way she would.

I grabbed the cards out of Katrine's hand and smiled. "I hope you don't mind. We've been so bored, I suggested a round of poker. But we gave our deck to some boys who never returned it. Your tent was nearby, and I thought certainly you would have a deck lying around..."

"Strange choice of cards." Grace shot a look at Ansel.

"That's because they were custom made. A gift from my dear mother." It was impossible to read his expression. "You know, it's considered impolite to take things from people's tents without asking."

His eyes narrowed suspiciously. On his hand, I noticed the ring. In the short span of time since we'd left his tent, he had returned and put it on.

"We were sure you wouldn't mind," Katrine faltered, playing along.

"Up for a game?" I asked innocently, sitting down on the ground and looking up at Ansel.

The moment was thick with tension. Finally, he exhaled and seemed to relax. I was pretty sure he bought my little story. "What are we playing?"

"The correct question," I swallowed, "is, what are we playing for? And it can't be for money. I never play for money."

"How about matchsticks?" Katrine asked.

"Poker, huh?" He sat down across from me. "I have to warn you, I am a pretty good poker player."

"Not matchsticks. It has to be something of value." I swallowed again. "Like my camera and your... ring?"

"My ring?" He paused. "What would you want that for?"

"A souvenir for my husband."

"I don't think so, kid. It's got sentimental value."

"So does my camera." I smiled. "And besides, I'm sure you are a much better poker player than me."

"Certainly you don't think you will lose against a girl, do you?" Grace said.

"Of course not," Ansel answered quickly. His enormous ego was wounded. "It's just that this ring has sentimental value," he repeated.

"Oh no." Grace tried to sound sad as she looked at her RAF pilot's watch. "It's already four o'clock. We'll be late."

"Late for what?" Ansel looked up.

I put my cards down. "I have permission from the base commander to interview a few soldiers on their firsthand battle experience..."

He smiled thinly. "Who are you interviewing today?"

"Robert Benson," I answered.

"How… industrious of you."

I stood up, accidentally scattering the cards with my foot.

Lorelei nodded. "Yes, indeed." Kneeling down, she quickly scooped up the deck and pressed it into Ansel's palm. "Sorry we borrowed them without asking. Come along, ladies. We all ought to be going! Robert's waiting."

"Another one from Guadalcanal?" Katrine asked, trying to play it cool.

"Yeah." I stood up and grabbed my little black notebook and the camera.

"Then I'm coming too," she said.

With that, the four of us dashed out of the tent, leaving a very confused Ansel behind.

"That was close," Lorelei whispered fiercely as we marched towards the table where Robert waited. "But you know," she turned back and waved at the director. "I think he bought it."

CHAPTER 21

TOGETHER AGAIN

*R*obert Benson, the farm boy from Iowa, paused and explained, "We'd held up for four months against the Japanese on the Bataan Peninsula. This was in '42. The Japanese blockaded Bataan and Corregidor—that's another island close to Bataan—and we ran out of everything. Food. Ammunition. But we fought back. Oh yes, ma'am, we fought back and were pushed back until all we had was a tiny strip of beach up the coast. We dug out fox holes and lived in them, in the sand, for weeks. I lost nearly 30 pounds." Robert sighed. "I was always kind of plump to begin with," he blushed slightly, "so it didn't worry me as much as some of the others. Not yet anyway. After a while, I learned that I had no idea what it meant to be hungry. Every time I closed my eyes, I saw a banana split."

He trailed off, and I looked at my cousins and then back to Robert. I was having an absolutely terrible time concentrating. I saw his lips moving and heard words coming out, but the truth was, all I could think about was the Nazi in our midst, Ansel. Even if he wasn't the traitor Joe warned us of, it was enough to know that he was for sure our enemy.

I tried to steady my thoughts. We *had* to move slowly and carefully... or the whole thing might blow up in our faces. I didn't want to deal with Ansel accusing the girls of changing Captain Brown's message. If that were to happen... it could mean prison... or worse! Death at the end of a firing squad! My thoughts ran wild, and it took nearly all my strength to reign in my panic over our predicament and focus on Robert's testimony.

"General King finally surrendered to Homma's army." He stopped and looked me in the eye. "Now you must understand he is an honorable man. He had to surrender. He didn't want more of us to die." His eyes filled with tears. "Homma wanted to clear the peninsula for another battle, so all of us, 70,000 if you counted all the Americans and all the Filipinos, were marched to Camp O'Donnell in the Tarlac province. Nearly 65 miles." He eyes took on a far-off look and filled with tears. He looked down. "What they did, I... I still can't talk about it. You are ladies."

He shut his eyes, remembering the awful things he'd seen. The Japanese did not subscribe to the Geneva Convention, an international treaty that protected soldiers captured in war from torture or worse. Because the Americans had surrendered, they considered them cowards and deserving of torture and death. Stragglers, suffering from dysentery and starvation, were killed on the spot. Others, tortured for sport.

"As our troops got closer to the Philippines, the Japanese started evacuating the healthy ones, shipping them to Japan as slave laborers for the coal mines. Most won't make it back alive. I've never seen anything so brutal," his eyebrows twitched, "than what those Japanese did to us soldiers. It..." his voice cracked, "wasn't human."

"You never happened to meet a man named Harry Stenetsky during all of this, did you?" Katrine asked, her voice shaking slightly.

"No ma'am, can't say that I did."

She swallowed and nodded. She would keep asking. She would

probably keep asking for as long as she lived. Then, she shot a furtive glance towards Ansel's tent. He had left once more and traipsed into the jungle. "I wonder what he's doing in there," Katrine whispered.

"I'm sorry, ma'am, what was that?"

"Oh, I apologize Robert. Just... talking to myself. Do go on." She coughed delicately.

He took a swig of his water. "Anyway, I was in the jungle a few months, and we found a local fisherman willing to get us to the next island—still under Japanese control, mind you. And from there, we were able to get another boat. It ran into an American battleship. They sent me here to gain some weight. I, uh... I'll be going home on the next carrier."

Grace looked at my list of questions, asking the next one for me. "How'd you escape?" She had a 'let's get this show on the road' attitude.

"God made a way for me to escape. Not many did. Those trying to make a run for it were shot. Most weren't healthy enough to manage it. There was a band of guerrillas we joined made up of other Americans and some Filipinos. We would stage raids on the Japanese. Never give up!" he said triumphantly. "You mark my words, General MacArthur is coming back. He'll recapture Bataan, and he'll liberate Manila. We'll get our boys back. We'll get your husband back." He smiled pityingly at Katrine and then lifted his eyes to mine. "Do you need more for your story?"

Shaking my head, I shut the notebook and raised my camera to snap the shot. Robert stopped me. "Wait," he turned a little to the left, "I want you to get my good side."

"You've been a good sport, Robert," I said, slipping both the camera and my notebook into my camera bag. "One day, your kids will read this and be real proud. Not everybody can say their dad fought at Guadalcanal and Bataan."

We all stood up from the table as he smiled. "I'm just grateful I'll get to see my kids."

"You have children?" Katrine looked from Lorelei and back to the soldier, surprised. "You are so young!"

He quickly pulled out his wallet and opened it, revealing a photograph of a happy young family by the side of a lake.

Katrine stared at the photograph and then back up at the soldier. Grace pointed to her watch and anxiously tapped the table. She and I were both ready to move, but Katrine seemed stuck.

"My wife Jennie and I got married when we were both 18. Just out of high school... I've got two boys. Bobby Junior, here." He pointed to the older of the boys in the photograph. "He's my oldest. He's almost five now. And his brother Jake. He's 11 months younger."

"I'm sorry, Robert." Grace stood up and took Katrine's arm. "We've got another appointment. Like Piper said, you've been a good sport."

"Strange isn't it? How different two people's lives can be," Katrine spoke quietly as we quickly returned to our tent. "Harry and I... we got started so late." She glanced up. "I never used to think it was late until I realized how little time we'd have together. And there's a 24-year-old kid with two little ones and a home and a wife. And I'm floating around on the Pacific on a mission that's been compromised."

I looked at her and she smiled sadly.

"I'm envious of him."

"I didn't know you wanted kids," Grace said, speeding up towards our tent.

"I didn't know I wanted them either."

Lorelei bit her lip. "What is he doing in the jungle?"

We all knew she spoke of Ansel.

"I could have won that ring if he had agreed to play poker." I huffed quietly and sat on my cot. "If he had bet the ring, that is..."

"And then what?" Lorelei looked at me.

"We could have proven it was his and then proven he's a Nazi. Simple. Case solved."

She blinked and sat down beside me.

"Do you think he suspects us of snooping?" Grace got down on her hands and knees and crawled under the cot we were sitting on, lifting up the edge of the canvas slightly so she could see out.

"What are you doing down there?" I asked.

"Keeping watch. I can see the jungle and his tent from here. It's less obvious than keeping our tent open." She adjusted slightly and exhaled tiredly. Then, a second later, she exclaimed, "Hey, look!"

Grace's hand reached out beside my calf and tapped it with something. I leaned over to look.

"One of Ansel's silly cards!" I turned it over; a Queen of Hearts. "Maybe it wasn't a complete loss after all. I'll give it to Peter as a souvenir."

Katrine groaned. "I have to be honest. I have absolutely no idea what to do now."

"We'll just have to do what we've been doing our whole time on Alu," Lorelei answered thoughtfully.

"And what's that?"

"Wait, watch," she paused, "and pray."

The chow triangle rang out. In a few moments, a line going the length of the camp would form of hungry men waiting for their dinner. Tonight's supper was the same thing that had been on the menu for the last two weeks: Corned pork loaf with carrots and apple flakes. It tasted as strange as it sounded, but it had lots of vitamins and minerals, etc. that the war department deemed necessary to keep the army healthy and happy.

Grace's voice was slightly muffled under the cot. "How about you girls go get dinner, and I'll keep watching."

"All right." Sighing, I got up. I sincerely hoped we would not have to wait much longer. "Coming, ladies?"

Katrine and Lorelei nodded and followed me out.

"Don't be gone too long," Grace said as we left. "I don't like the idea of being caught alone by that man."

"Maybe I'll stay here with you, Grace," Katrine replied, hanging back. "Bring us something back, would you two?"

~

IT WAS on our way back from dinner, an extra pork loaf in hand, that we saw them. Roughly 200 yards away, I could make out a small group of men walking near the water's edge.

Lorelei paused and then spoke. "I've been wracking my brain to figure out some way to expose Ansel, but I can't think of anything. At least, nothing that won't leave us vulnerable. I'll give it to the man, he's created quite the act. He has the upper hand."

"What makes you say that?"

"He's the loyal American. We aren't Americans. We are the ones singing the messages. He's just the director." She shook her head sadly. "Oh, Piper, I think we need a miracle."

I squinted my eyes in the glare of the setting sun. "Then let's pray for one."

She chuckled after a second. "I don't know why we didn't think of that before."

Lorelei put one hand behind my back and bowed her head. "Dear Father in Heaven, we need a miracle. Deliver us from Ansel. Show us how to reveal his true character!"

I shifted the pork loaf to my other hand and offered a hearty, "Amen."

A soft breeze swept across the beach, and slowly, I watched as Lorelei lifted her head. Suddenly, her chin jutted forward and she rubbed her eyes. "Call me crazy, but I think my eyes are playing tricks on me."

"What do you think you see?" I asked, not seeing anything unusual on the beach.

Lorelei squinted. "I know it's impossible. It's almost too silly to say it!"

"Just say it," I squinted in the men's direction.

"Well, doesn't that one look like Paul Sinclair?"

I blinked several times. Believe it or not, one looked uncannily like Peter. Same height. Same build. I shook my head. I wondered if the longing for my husband and the heat and humidity could cause such a realistic mirage. "Could it be?" I asked.

"Certainly, we are just imagining things," she said.

As far as silhouettes go, it certainly looked like Paul and Peter—and the third man undeniably favored Frank. But they were too far away to see in detail, their faces blurred in the glare of the sun. "It must be the next stage of island fever," I said, not able to tear my eyes away from the group. On the breath of the wind, I could almost make out my name, as though the man was Peter, and he was calling out to me.

"Piper," Lorelei stepped forward, "I think that man is calling your name."

My heart started beating a little faster. It couldn't be possible… could it? Peter? On Alu? How could he get here?

I put my hand up to shield my eyes from the sun. The tall one called out once more. It was Peter. It *was* Peter!

"It's a miracle!" I shouted over and over, dropping the pork loaf. Lightheaded and hardly knowing what I was doing, I began running towards him. I don't remember what I said or if I said anything at all. I only remember the feel of his arms around me. The scruff of his unshaved beard, prickly and familiar on my skin. I was crying, and he was crying, and I promised myself that never again, never again, would I allow myself to be parted from him. It was a miracle, an honest to goodness miracle. Help had come, faster than any one of us could have imagined.

When I was finally conscious of myself and our surroundings again and pulled my tear-stained face off of Peter's shoulder, I saw Lorelei standing in front of Paul Sinclair, her mouth wide open.

Frank stood off to the side, watching sadly.

CHAPTER 22

OPERATION RAT-CATCHER

I looked from Peter to Horatio, "So... where is the *Malahini* now?"

"Somewhere in the Pacific, floating around." He shrugged.

I looked at Peter. "So now we are actually homeless... As in, our home is floating around on the ocean, never to be seen again."

"She was a casualty of war." Peter looked out at the ocean solemnly. He was dressed in casual slacks and a white t-shirt, the same as Frank. Horatio, Paul, and Chito were in uniform, though none wore their jackets. It was much too hot. We were all crammed in our tent. Grace remained under the cot, keeping watch on Ansel's tent, where the director had bunked down for the night.

"Don't worry, dear." Edie fanned herself with a palm branch. "I'm sure it was insured."

By the looks on our faces, she instantly realized that the *Malahini* was *not* insured and paused contemplatively before adding, "Well, most likely it would have been deemed an act of God, and you wouldn't have been able to collect anyway."

"Thanks, Edie," I said flatly. "That's a real comfort."

"We," Horatio said, referring to himself and Edie, "joined

General MacArthur on a battleship headed towards Rabaul, but the ship was badly damaged by Japanese planes, and we were forced to stop for repairs. MacArthur decided it would be best to continue towards Rabaul on a sub that was nearby rather than wait for the repair to be completed. That sub happened to be *The Swordfish*. As God's will would have it, the submarine started to have some sort of trouble with one of the turbines."

"Up top we went to fix the turbine." Edie tilted her head to the side. She wore a light white suit fashioned after a men's navy military uniform. The blazer, with side shoulder pads, was slung over her lap, and the silk blouse, a creamy tan sort of color, matched the khaki of the tent. As usual, Edie looked remarkably elegant. Katrine, Grace, and me, all in our shorts and blouses tied up at the waist, looked quite disheveled in comparison. "And that's when *The Swordfish* caught site of the *Malahini* somewhere between Alu and Hawaii."

It was absurd. Unbelievable. Impossible even. And yet, here we were, all together. In the words of Edie, it was providence. Pure providence!

"Why didn't you come straight here? After what Peter and Frank told you?" Katrine asked.

"We practically came straight here." Edie dabbed her brow with a silk handkerchief embroidered with an enormous lobster. "It was torturous! We had to go all the way to Rabaul and drop MacArthur off first." She inhaled dramatically and continued. "Tiny little beds and claustrophobia and men, men, men everywhere all the time! All the while avoiding the enemy and having nothing to do but play cards and try to write—but I've been so distracted!" She wiped a tear from her eye. "When I thought of my beauties, left all alone in such a treacherous... traitorous... with a traitor!"

"We knew with the show on pause, the traitor would have his hands tied," Peter explained. "We couldn't risk warning the authorities without implicating you or blowing your cover. And we didn't want to risk warning Joe. The traitor may know his radio's frequency, and our warning may have done more damage than good in the long run."

"So, how did you get here?" Grace's muffled voice from under the cot sounded confused.

"Horatio made a slight change to the itinerary and added Alu at the last minute." Frank kept his voice very low. "All very hush-hush."

"Do you know who he is?" Horatio asked, referring to the traitor. "Any leads at all?"

"Ansel Thornton." Lorelei glanced at Paul out of the corner of her eye and quickly back at the ground. Much to her chagrin, she still found Paul painfully distracting.

The young man, his arm nearly healed and no longer in a sling, squeezed in beside Frank, Peter, and Chito on my cot, blushed and coughed.

"We found a ring in his tent with a hidden swastika." I paused. "And he's made some pretty rude comments about Jews. He uses all sorts of shameful, degrading names."

Frank frowned. "I knew it! That little shrimp who thinks he can sing and dance! The one who cut me out of the show! A Nazi!" Cynically, he cracked his knuckles. "Talk about perfect casting."

Horatio scratched his beard. "Come now, Frank. We need more than a hidden swastika. Anyone might think we planted it there to frame him and then accuse the girls or us of being the traitors. We need solid proof he's up to no good."

"We are pretty sure he stole our mail which explains why we never heard from Joe. It was only by accident that Becky's letter came through. Thank goodness, she wrote more than 'Oh yes, Joe and I got engaged...'" Katrine rolled her eyes.

Lorelei took over. "And there is a possibility that he was planning to use us to send messages to the enemy. But with the show canceled, we haven't been able to do any message transmitting at all."

Paul smiled. "That was our doing. As we said, we knew if we

shut the show down, we could at least prevent anything bad from happening, even if we couldn't catch the traitor."

Edie shook her head. "All those poor boys deprived of entertainment! Vital information for the war effort silenced! Horatio, something must be done about this!"

"I know, I know, Edie." He looked out at the sea gravely. "So the question remains, how do we catch Ansel in the act without implicating the girls?"

Finally, Chito looked up. "I wonder…"

"Wonder what?" Paul looked at his friend.

Chito's dark eyes flashed, his golden skin luminescent in the bright sun. "We send out a *fake* message. We pretend the USO show is on. How did you normally get the messages you needed to transmit?"

"The captain of the troopship or base is supposed to give us a line or two containing the code." Lorelei went on to explain how she would quickly write a song that would be broadcast during the show.

"That poses a problem." Chito heaved a sigh after she finished. "We need a code to send."

No one spoke. Every face in our little circle—Lorelei, Grace, Katrine, Peter, Frank, Paul, Chito, Horatio, and Edie—contemplated the problem in front of us.

Suddenly, Edie exclaimed, "Why, I have it! The show must go on!"

"What?" Horatio asked.

Her excitement was palpable. "We give the captain of the base a message from Horatio via MacArthur. You have rank enough, don't you, dear, to carry secret orders from MacArthur?"

"Indeed, I've rank enough." His eyes brightened in understanding. "I do believe you are a genius, Edie!"

"It will be a fake message, mind you," she continued, "that the girls are supposed to sing, a *special* broadcast. The message will have no effect on anything or anyone, completely innocuous, see?"

"Then, we make sure Ansel gets the message before us," Katrine caught on. "If the message is changed once we have it, we'll have all the proof we need."

Peter's arm was wrapped around my shoulder, and I felt him squeeze me quickly. "That's got to work! It's just got to work!"

"Keep your voice down," Frank said. "Who knows who might be listening."

"Chito," Paul glanced at the code-talker, "can you write up a fake message?"

"No problem." Chito nodded sharply, his eyes darting left and right.

"Good." Paul sounded pleased and flashed his award-winning trademark smile at Lorelei, who choked on her Coke.

Horatio exhaled. "And Edie and I will take it to the base commander."

"What about us?" Peter asked.

"You and Frank are going to keep an eye on the rat." With a quick glance at his watch, he finished, "I won't rest till this is finished. Everyone, to arms!"

In my pocket, I felt the sharp edge of Ansel's playing card, an eerie reminder of the dangerous game we were playing.

THE NEXT MORNING, Horatio and Edie approached the captain of the base with the fake message from MacArthur, courtesy of Chito. Captain Dana was given express instructions to give the message to Ansel, and a bulletin was immediately put out that the USO show would *finally* put on a performance three days hence. Great excitement and anticipation filled the camp. The men's choir began to practice the 'chicken song,' as they had lovingly dubbed it. Everyone was ecstatic. After months, there would be a break in the monotony. Some entertainment! Some singing and dancing and glitter!

Meanwhile, all ten of us waited to see what Ansel would do. At lunch, the theatrical man talked of the show and new staging and choreography. It all felt rather silly. But we played along. It was like the lights had come back on. Ansel Thornton was back, and he was going to be better than ever, even if was only to a bunch of hick farm boys stuck on an island in the Pacific. He was really excited because he could smell money on Horatio and Edie. And as Horatio said, "show people are always looking for another sucker to back their show." He fawned over them, sidling up to Edie and telling her she had a future in show business. She blushed and vehemently shook her head no. Her show days were over, she sighed wistfully.

"You were on the stage?" Ansel tilted his head to the side.

"I was a great opera star once. Sort of." She cast a smile at Horatio. "My husband too. But actually, I'm a writer."

"Have you ever written musicals? Plays?"

"No. I haven't gotten around to that yet. But you never know. One day, I *might* be inspired."

"One day soon, I hope. Broadway is always looking for fresh young talent." He turned his eyes onto Lorelei, Grace, and Katrine, sitting side by side opposite Horatio, Edie, and himself. The rest of us sat at the table next door and tried to listen to the conversation above the din of the soldiers at supper.

"Fresh young talent," he continued, "like these young ladies." He pulled out a slip of paper and passed it across the table towards Lorelei. "By the way, Captain Dana asked me to give this to you."

She took the note and glanced at it. "Thanks. I appreciate you… passing it on."

Ansel then clapped his hands together, rubbed them vigorously, and said he had to run. New choreography to compose and what-not. The show was only three days away.

As soon as he left, Chito, Paul, and Frank hovered over my cousin's shoulders, looking at the message.

"So?" Horatio and Chito locked eyes. "Do we have him?"

Chito frowned, his large dark eyes clouding over in fear, "No one is supposed to know our code. *Nobody.* This right here," he pointed at the paper, "this is treason. Why, he is telling our men that there are no Japanese on islands where I know for a fact there are Japanese. They could walk right into a trap. He's leading our guys right into the enemy's hands." He pointed at the paper. "This, 'paaki,' means 'houses on water' in Hopi. And this? 'Atsa?' It means eagle. We use it to mean transport planes. These other words are coordinates."

Ominously, we all looked at one another.

My mouth opened, but no words came out.

"Operation rat-catcher, commence!" Horatio's voice was steely with resolve.

And so, in a long line led by Horatio, we marched to headquarters, past the sentry at the door, and right into Captain Dana's small bamboo office.

"COORDINATES!" Captain Dana, the easily excitable type, knocked a glass of water over on his desk and let out a loud, "What in the blazes?"

He was a career soldier. Not overly brilliant but dependable. He could follow orders, knew a good man when he saw one, and was honest. Just under six feet tall, his two-and-a-half decades in the service had kept him fitter than most men his age. But he was rounder around the middle than he used to be, and his hair had begun to thin out.

"I'll tell you what in the blazes." Horatio pointed to Chito and Lorelei. "Tell him everything."

In bits and pieces, they tried to explain the whole mess. And though it was rather jumbled up and not concise, within a few minutes, Captain Dana had the gist of it.

"You mean to tell me," he leaned back in his chair and stared at our ten eager faces and motioned with his envelope opener towards my cousins, "that Ansel Thornton changed the message," he turned his eyes to Chito, "and actually was going to broadcast classified information to the enemy."

We nodded.

"Sergeant Stevens! Get in here!" Captain Dana roared.

A sergeant stepped into the crowded space and saluted sharply.

"Take Mr. Thornton into custody immediately. I've got some questions that must be answered. These folks have leveled quite the accusation against him, and if it happens to be true, we've got ourselves a traitor."

The sergeant who appeared to be no more than 18, opened his eyes widely and gasped out a "Yes, Sir!" before running off to find the director.

We all stood there, no one speaking. I pulled Ansel's card out of my pocket and stared at it, fingering the edge nervously.

"What is that?" Edie asked.

"A Queen of Hearts."

She took it in her hands and shook her head. "No... it's not. It doesn't feel right."

"What do you mean, doesn't feel right?"

"Dear, Piper, I know cards. Sleeping puppy aside, this card is not normal. The weight's all wrong. And the smoothness of the paper. Absolutely bizarre. What are you doing with a trick deck? Not cheating, I hope! I've taught you better than that."

Everyone, including Captain Dana, was staring.

"It's not my card," I explained. "It's from Ansel's deck."

Katrine stepped in. "We were... borrowing it."

By now, Edie had moved beside Captain Dana behind his desk and held the card up to the lamp. With one fingernail, she split the corner, pulling the Queen's face down. Concealed between the back and front of the card was nothing more than a highly detailed aerial photograph of Alu.

"What'd I tell you," Edie said with a self-satisfied smile. "I *know* cards. I'm an expert poker player, remember?"

Captain Dana took the card and examined it closely, his face steadily turning beat red.

At that point, the sergeant returned. By the looks of it, he had been running. "Sir!" he gasped out. "Mr. Thornton is not in his tent. Apparently, he's taken a walk. One of the guys saw him wander off into the woods."

Captain Dana slammed the aerial photograph down with a resounding thud and sprang into action. Within five minutes, he had every off-duty soldier (Peter, Frank, Paul, and Chito included) combing the jungle. They would look under every fallen log, behind every bush, and up every tree! They would find Ansel, he assured Edie, oh yes, they would! And then, they would get to the bottom of this mess. Alu was a small island. He couldn't hide for long!

CHAPTER 23

THE TRAITOR AMONG US

*C*aptain Dana was right. No one could hide for long on Alu, not if 40 men were looking for you, anyway.

As fate would have it, Chito, Paul, Peter, and Frank came across the opening to a cave and discovered, thanks to Chito's good hearing, Ansel Thornton. To their horror, it wasn't just Ansel. He had, somehow, managed to smuggle a radio transmittal device into the cave, probably in boxes marked as costumes and props, and was in the middle of transmitting something (he refused to say what) on the enemy's frequency. Between that, the Nazi ring, the tampered message, stolen mail, *and* the photograph of the island, Ansel would be lucky if he got life in prison. Who knew how much information he had shared with the enemy? It was impossible to tell.

"We found him in a cave, sir," Chito explained, glancing at the traitor.

Ansel Thornton stood, handcuffed, eyes downcast, in the center of Captain Dana's office. He refused to look Captain Dana, or anyone else for that matter, in the eye.

Including the sergeant, there were thirteen of us stuffed into Captain Dana's office, designed to hold four comfortably, six if you pushed, and thirteen, never. (Edie and Horatio sat in the two chairs meant to be across from Captain Dana's desk but now were pushed to the side. The rest of us were crammed up against the walls.) It was hot, crowded, and eerily quiet. In our midst was the worst kind of enemy, the kind that wheedles his way inside, gains your trust, and then turns you over to those who would wish you dead rather than alive.

"How'd you do that?" Captain Dana sat on the edge of his desk, observing the prisoner. "Hear him, I mean?"

"I'm a trained tracker," Chito said. "But to be honest, I heard a strange mechanical clicking coming from inside the cave. Couldn't be no animal that would make a noise like that. It was the radio."

"So, on the live broadcast with the USO show, you could confuse our men, and on your cave-radio, you could transmit straight to the Japanese. I'm giving you a moment to explain yourself." Captain Dana looked at Ansel. "One minute, to be precise."

"What did they promise you?" Horatio asked quietly. "Money?"

"Oh, come now, Admiral." Ansel smiled a slick smile. "Money and much more. The Nazi Party appreciates my art, unlike those Jews who have kept me out of my rightful place as a leader in the theater. It's the communist Jews who are to blame for this war. They are to blame for everything."

"And you would willingly put thousands of my men's lives at risk for the theater?" Captain Dana was stunned.

"No." Ansel looked past us at the wall, an odd, unsettling glow filling his eye. "For *America*."

Holding his head erect, his voice grew resonant and strong. "President Roosevelt and his Jewish communist friends are going to destroy our country," he spat. "Only fascism can win against communism. Hitler is our only salvation!"

"That's enough!" Captain Dana shouted. "You are a traitor and a disgrace to this country and everything we stand for!"

"Me," he laughed, looking back at Captain Dana, "a traitor? Oh no, I am America's greatest patriot! I have risked my life, my art, everything, for my country. *You* are the traitors. *You* are the ones who don't see the light!"

"What are you talking about, Thornton?" Dana demanded.

The director's voice took on a creepy, ethereal tone. "I have seen the light. I know what can be. I have seen a vision of a glorious future!" We watched in horror as Ansel's face contorted. "Heil Hitler!" Then, he threw his right hand out straight in front of him, forgetting he wore handcuffs. As a result, both his arms flew to the sky and hung suspended above his head for a moment as we looked on in shock. After a second passed, with a violent growl, he drew both arms back down and lunged like a madman at the captain.

Frank, Peter, Paul, and the sergeant pulled him back and threw him on the ground. The man writhed and twisted like an insect, laughing and crying simultaneously. "I am the world's greatest actor! I had you fooled. I had you all fooled!"

"Show's over, Ansel. Everyone's curtain falls eventually, and yours just did," Captain Dana growled. Immediately, two more guards entered and took over, firmly lifting him off the ground and holding the director slightly suspended between them.

"You didn't have us all fooled." Grace stepped a bit closer and leveled a steely gaze in his direction.

"I suspected you almost from the beginning," Frank added for good measure. "You stink. Your whole outfit stinks. And your acting stinks more."

"How dare you!" Ansel raged and sputtered. "I am a consummate professional! You know nothing, you stupid, good-for-nothing sailor."

"Good-for-nothing *Jewish* sailor." Frank winked victoriously.

Ansel winced.

Edie sighed. "Don't take it to heart, Ansel. No one can keep up that sort of act forever."

"Get him out of here." Captain Dana turned away and put his hands on his desk. I saw him close his eyes, and when he opened them, he suddenly looked much older.

As Ansel was dragged away, he looked over his shoulder and shouted at his audience in Captain Dana's tiny office, "You Macleay Sisters can't sing a lick *or* dance. And your aunt has no talent whatsoever. She writes like she has a pen between her toes! Long live the Third Reich!"

No one moved or even blinked. From outside the office window, we watched as the guards half-pulled, half-dragged Ansel, still raging, to the brig.

"A pen between her toes?" Edie broke the silence and looked down at her sandaled foot.

"The man's completely insane. Certifiably bonkers." Lorelei shuddered and looked up at Paul, standing beside her.

Paul inhaled and shook his head. "He's not insane. He's greedy. Jealous of those more successful than himself and eaten up by hatred and bias." Paul looked out the door that the guards had dragged Ansel through. "A little flattery by the enemy, a few cheap promises... Judas did as much."

"He won't have to hang himself though." Horatio pulled Edie close. "A military guard will do it for him, most likely."

"He'll never put on a show again, and for that, the free nations of the world will be eternally grateful to all of you. Myself included." Captain Dana was visibly shaken. He shuddered. "I've never seen one before... A Nazi, I mean," he clarified.

Frank shook his head. "I have. Ugly creatures, aren't they?"

"No," Horatio spoke slowly and clearly. "They are deceived. We can be just as easily deceived, if not by the grace of God."

Captain Dana walked back behind his desk and picked up Ansel's infamous playing card. "Custom-made and a gift from his mother, huh?" He was disgusted. "This photograph shows everything. Absolutely everything. It had to come from a Japanese plane." He put the card down flat on the table. "It's essentially a perfect map. If the Japanese wanted to take out all the men and ammunition on Alu, they could."

"If they could." Katrine looked tired. "Wouldn't they have done so already? I mean, they have the photograph."

"I don't think so," Peter answered. "Odds are, they were protecting Ansel. Having an inside man who had access to our frequencies... It's a valuable asset."

"That's it, right there," Captain Dana agreed. "It's the only thing that makes sense."

Peter paced back and forth for a moment, steadily growing more agitated. "How did Ansel learn the code? I've been thinking about it ever since he was captured."

"I think I can answer that," I spoke up. "Ansel once bragged that he had spent months doing 'research' for a show set in the American West. It would have been the perfect cover to learn Navajo or Cherokee or whatever language."

"That's true." Lorelei looked at Peter.

"That accounts for learning the language," Peter answered. "But it doesn't account for the actual code. Chito," Peter leaned forward, "I've got a question for you."

"Yeah? Shoot." His dark eyelashes reflected off his brown eyes.

"You're a code-talker," Peter began.

"Yes, of course."

"And a loyal American."

"Of course!"

Peter pressed, "But do all of your people feel the same way?"

"My people know that the United States government is better than any Nazi tyrant if that's what you're asking." Chito was adamant.

Peter shook his head, trying to explain what he was thinking. "Chito, Ansel had to have had a partner somewhere. Someone who taught him the codes."

Chito leaned back and exhaled in understanding. "Ah, I see the direction of your mind. You think that there is another traitor, one among the code-talkers, who shared our secrets with Ansel."

His brow furrowed. Slowly, he shut his eyes and lowered his

voice. "In truth, there are those among the tribes who still carry much bitterness against the pioneers. There is still bad blood between us and the White Man, who forced our people off our land and onto barren reservations." He opened his eyes and stared into Peter's. "There *are* those who long for revenge against the White Man."

"Those who long for revenge... They might share the code with a Nazi spy to hurt the United States government?" Captain Dana leaned around Horatio so he could see the young man.

"They might." Chito nodded. "It would be an idiotic, stupid thing to do. Regardless of how badly we have been treated by our government, we know how much worse it would be with the Nazis. My people are not Aryans. We would, no doubt, be subjected to slave labor or who knows what else." He laughed angrily. "But a bitter heart bent on revenge will sell his soul to the devil to get satisfaction."

"How poetically spoken, young Chito!" Edie clapped her hands together.

Captain Dana exhaled as though a great weight had taken up permanent residence on his shoulders. "Now, if you would all excuse Admiral Macleay and me, we've an official report to write up." He swallowed. "This has created an enormous mess, and we've got to start cleaning it up."

"What should we do?" Peter asked.

Captain Dana wiped the beads of perspiration off his forehead with a wrinkled handkerchief he had stuffed in his pocket. "How about you all go cool off? Get some coffee."

"That sounds marvelous, mon capitan!" Edie stood up and grabbed my hand. "Coffee with my niece after that adventure is exactly what the doctor ordered."

237

CHAPTER 24

REASSIGNED?

$\mathcal{R}$oughly two hours later, Peter and I sat at one of the long plank tables under the shade of an awning just outside the mess hall, debriefing the events of the afternoon across from Edie, who was staring thoughtfully into her coffee cup. "What a story we will have to tell, darling Piper! Ansel Thornton, traitor to the stars!" Her voice belied an underlying tension. She had been afraid, and her nerves were raw. I could see Katrine and Grace still in line along with Chito. The coffee percolator was taking an absurdly long time.

Edie went on and on. Distractedly, I watched Katrine and Grace. Both had changed clothes and looked much more relaxed than when we'd all been in Captain Dana's office for the 'interrogation,' if you could call it that. Suddenly, my ears perked up. Had she said *Australia*?

"Everyone's going there these days. It's quite the thing. The MacArthur's. All the top British officers. Everyone who's anyone will be there. It's the next location on the list, for Horatio and me at least. You know Horatio. He's wonderful with strategy and such. He's one of the Navy's top advisors."

"Why Australia?" I looked at Peter.

"It's where all the battles in the Pacific are being staged." Peter arched his back and rolled his shoulders forwards a few times.

"The sooner we get to Australia, the sooner we can go back home," she said thoughtfully, then stopped talking and stared past us intently.

"Why, look at that!" A faint smile played about her lips.

Turning my head, I saw Lorelei. She was sitting across from Paul Sinclair at a table a stone's throw away. Paul flexed the bicep that Peter had fixed up and said above the chatter of the crowded mess hall, "Good as new! See?"

Lorelei smiled.

"Really!"

Straining to see, I heard him practically shouting, "Punch it! Punch it hard, right there!" He pointed at the spot where the bullet had gone through.

"No, no," I could make out Lorelei's words, "I'd rather not."

"Come on. Won't hurt a bit."

I caught Lorelei's eye. She shrugged her shoulders. Cautiously, she slowly reached her hand out and gently rapped Paul's arm.

"Not like that," Paul said self-assuredly. "Hard. A solid punch. Show me what you're made of!"

"I don't think it's a very good idea." She looked at the bicep, still flexed. "It hasn't been that long since you were shot. Just a few weeks!"

"The bullet missed the bone! And I won't take no for an answer." Paul reached out and took her hand, bringing it up to his arm rather forcefully. In the process, her hand hit his cup of coffee, and it spilled all over his pants. Surprised, he jumped up and began to wipe at the offending stain with his fingers. Lorelei took her handkerchief from her pocket and passed it to him.

"It's fine." He waved the handkerchief away, "I'm perfectly all right. You keep that."

"Really, Paul," she reached further across the table, "take it."

He put his hand up to signal that he was fine and fortuitously hit *her* coffee cup, flinging the brown liquid all over her white shorts. Her eyes opened very wide, and then, she politely excused herself to go clean up.

Now alone, Paul groaned to himself in embarrassment.

He waited till she had left and then came over, pulled up a chair, and sat down at the end of our table with a huff. "That did not go well, did it?" He glanced at Peter. "I don't know what came over me."

No one spoke.

And just as quickly as he sat down, he stood back up and left.

Katrine and Grace, coffee now in hand, watched him leave and then sat down along with Chito. Katrine was visibly stressed.

"What's the matter you? We caught the bad guy," I said playfully trying to cheer her up.

"I know that." She gingerly sipped her coffee and glanced at Grace, who left her cup untouched. "I was just... Well, I'm not sure what comes next." Nervously, she began to rub the tips of her fingers. "I don't want to keep up this song and dance routine. We've been compromised, you know? I've done this sort of thing before. I know how it works! We can't go on. But I don't want to go back to Palestine. Not without knowing what's happened to my husband." She was on the verge of panic.

Grace put her hand on her older sister's shoulder. "Take a deep breath, Katrine." She motioned with her eyes towards Captain Dana's office. "They are not going to send you back."

"You don't know that," Katrine protested.

Chito's face, clouded by worry, betrayed his inner thoughts. He too was concerned about the future. For a moment, he looked as though he would say something to Katrine, but in the end, said nothing.

It was then that Frank appeared, seemingly out of nowhere, at the foot of the table. "Where have you been?" Peter asked.

"A sergeant found me napping and woke me up to tell me to round up the troops." He rested his hands on the table. "Apparently, our little outfit is wanted by the brass." His eyes scanned the room. "Where's Paul and Lorelei?"

I shrugged.

"Is everything all right?" Edie asked.

"Don't know," Frank answered.

"Looks like we are going to find out what happens next, Katrine." Grace sighed.

ONCE AGAIN, we crammed into Captain Dana's office with the whole gang. Crossing one leg over another in the chair across from the desk, Edie leaned forward in total command. "So, Captain, we are all here. Proceed."

Captain Dana coughed at her boldness and took a moment to gather himself. "Yes, yes." He turned his attention to my cousins. Bluntly, he made his opening statement. "Operation Song-Bird is suspended. You have been compromised."

"I knew it." Katrine braced herself.

"So, you are sending us back to Palestine?" Grace lifted her eyes to the captain's. "Or Hawaii?"

"Not quite so far as all that."

Lorelei frowned. "What do you mean? You are going to have us just be another act on the circuit? Without sending messages?"

"Most definitely not." Horatio shook his head solemnly and repeated, "You have been *compromised*. Who knows what Ansel shared about you, true or otherwise. It would be unwise for you to continue on the road. It would put you and other performers at risk. The Macleay Sisters are officially, and honorably, discharged from the show. Their work will always be greatly appreciated."

"What will we do?" Lorelei shifted her large green eyes to Paul and then back to the two officers behind the desk.

"Your new assignment is not nearly as glamorous as your last gig, but it is still important to the war effort." Captain Dana exhaled.

JESSICA GLASNER

Horatio took over. "There's an opening for Lorelei at the Red Cross in Townsville. She has experience on the front lines as a field nurse that many young nurses will glean from for when they are sent to the front themselves. We are expecting some major battles in the next few months. We need these young ladies ready to face just about anything. And for Grace," Horatio looked at the young woman, leaning against the wall with her arms across her chest like a shield, "there is an open position at a base for a flight instructor."

"RAF?" she asked.

"No. U.S. Army Air Force," Captain Dana answered. "We are in desperate need of qualified pilots to train our fighters. I've already put in a call. The commission is yours."

She blinked once and uttered a quiet, "I see." Then, louder, she asked, "And these are *official* assignments?"

"Unofficially." Captain Dana smiled. "It is your choice to accept or not, but you would be doing a service to your country."

"I don't have a country." Grace's eyes flashed.

"What about me?" Katrine's voice trembled. Her eyes welled up with tears. It was obvious she was very fragile. Her strong exterior throughout the Ansel Thornton episode was melting away to reveal an unstable core.

Horatio looked at her. "Katrine, you are free to travel to Australia or back to Palestine. But I can answer for Edie and myself, we'd love to have you stay with us." He glanced at Lorelei and Grace, adding, "All of you, actually. I've rented a house right in the middle of Townsville." Smiling a sad smile, he settled his gaze once more on Katrine.

"Oh, Horatio!" Edie exclaimed. "What an absolutely brilliant idea. Why, I should have thought of it myself!"

Before Katrine could answer, Edie continued, "I won't take no for an answer. Your sisters are coming, and you are coming. It's all settled."

"Edie, I—"

"I don't see any reason not to go," Lorelei said softly. "And it

242

would be easier to look for Harry from Australia. It's much closer to the Philippines than Jerusalem."

"I would hate to impose," Katrine protested without conviction.

"And how could my adopted daughter ever 'impose!'" Edie put her hand up to stop her from saying anything, "I feel responsible for your well-being. Piper's parents are a world away, your husband is who-knows-where, and you don't have a job or anything substantial to live on. I doubt you would have enough money to get back to Palestine. I would hate for you to get stuck in Honolulu waitressing your way back to the Middle East, though it would provide some great inspiration. Perhaps, we should try that someday, Horatio!"

Katrine looked at Lorelei and lifted her shoulders slightly. "It certainly sounds much better than being alone."

Lorelei nodded.

"You can discuss your vacation plans on your own time," Captain Dana interjected. All business, he turned to Chito and asked earnestly, "Now, Chito, I've got a proposition for you. Would you be open to transfer? Back to the mainland?"

"What for?" Chito's brow furrowed.

"If Ansel did have a partner within the code-talker program, we need an insider to root him out. You have the perfect cover. And we trust you."

Chito nodded once and narrowed his dark eyes. "I will not rest until this man is found."

Paul, uncomfortable, looked from Chito to Captain Dana. "When do we leave?"

"Chito leaves on the next mail plane. There's room for one passenger. We believe it is imperative to get Chito on the ground back home as soon as possible."

Paul paused, raising a questioning stare at the captain and Horatio. "I'm not going too? He's my partner..."

Captain Dana explained, "You would stand out, Major."

Chito agreed, softly telling his friend, "My brother, this is a journey I must take alone."

243

"Paul," Horatio said, "*you* are reassigned to Townsville."

Gulping, Paul managed an awkward, "I am?" as he stole a glance in Lorelei's direction.

"Coding and Translation Department. Horatio tells me you speak pretty passable Japanese and would enjoy the community life in Townsville."

"*I* told him to tell you that, dear Captain." Edie lowered her chin, graciously correcting him. Then, she fluttered her eyelashes in Paul's direction and tilted her head towards Lorelei.

Paul fought a blush creeping up his neck, squared his shoulders, and saluted. "Yes, sir."

"And that just leaves you three." Horatio scratched his beard and pointed vaguely at Peter, Frank, and me.

"Yep," Peter repeated, "just the three of us."

Frank frowned. "I don't want to hang around here for another month just to hitch a ride back to Hawaii."

I looked at Peter and could tell he was thinking the same thing. (For the record, the thought had crossed my mind too).

"Well, just Frank and Peter, actually." Captain Dana looked at me. "We didn't want the press to get wind of what happened with Ansel. It would be terrible for morale." As I nodded understandingly, he continued, "We sent your editor a story that Ansel came down with a bad case of Malaria and no interim director can be found on such short notice. It was Horatio's bright idea to have you reassigned, given that this branch of the show is dissolving, and the battle lines have shifted very close to the eastern coast of Australia."

"I'm off the show?"

"Indeed." He nodded. "You are now *The Honolulu Herald*'s first correspondent on the front in Townsville, thanks to your uncle."

"The front?" I felt my heart rate speed up, amazed that Horatio and Captain Dana had worked all of this out in a few hours.

Edie's eyes brightened. "Horatio! What a stroke of genius!" She turned to face me in her seat. "If you play your cards right, you'll probably get a column!"

"A column?" My heart started racing. "I'm just a photographer."

"Really, Piper." Edie sighed. "You have no confidence in your abilities! You've completely forgotten about those little articles you wrote as the 'Girl Reporter' for *The Scotsman*! And the brilliant work on my last novel!"

I felt my jaw clenching. A paragraph here and there as the 'Girl Reporter' for *The Scotsman*, as reputable as the paper may be, when I was a teenager and editing my aunt's unpublished (and still unfinished) novel was not enough to strike confidence into my soul. If anything, my resume did quite the opposite.

Peter and I shared a secret look. He was thinking deeply, and I wondered if he was praying. Finally, he said, "It's not like we have anything waiting for us back in Honolulu. The *Malahini* and all my school books are at the bottom of the Pacific." Peter looked down into my eyes and put his hand around my shoulder. "I'm game if you are."

What a day it had been. I felt like I was dreaming. When I woke up that morning, I thought I might never leave Alu. I thought we might be falsely accused as traitors. I thought... oh, I thought a lot of things. Here we were, 12 hours later, a Nazi spy behind bars and a new adventure on the horizon. It didn't matter what it would entail. At least we would be together. I was determined never to be separated from Peter again if I could help it.

"I'm game." I breathed, scarcely believing the turn of events.

"All of us, together!" Edie didn't try to mask her exuberance.

"That's the general idea. That is if everyone agrees." Horatio looked at Grace. It was impossible to read her expression.

"Grace," Katrine faltered, "do you want to go?"

After a second, Grace blew a long stream of air out of her lips. "Oh, it doesn't matter to me. I don't care where we go, just as long as we get off this island."

"What about me?" Frank spoke up suddenly. "What am I supposed to do?"

"We wouldn't leave a man behind, Frank," Horatio answered.

"After all you've done to help my adopted daughters out, my home will always be your home."

"I guess it will be better than changing hospital beds or playing the accordion." Frank stuffed his hands in his pockets.

"So, Australia." Peter looked at us. "One for all and all for one?"

"Indeed. The whole affair is settled! We are all going to Australia!" Edie jubilantly stood up, her mission accomplished. "I'm going to get some more coffee!" She turned to Captain Dana. "Unless we're not finished?"

"Oh, we are finished." He pushed back from the desk and crossed his foot over his knee. "You are all free to go. And good luck to you."

With the attitude of a Viking queen leading her warriors to battle, Edie led the charge out of the Captain Dana's office.

Frank, at the rear, muttered as he followed us back outside, "This war has me floating all over the place like a piece of driftwood."

"All of us, Frank," Peter answered. "But at least we are drifting somewhere new."

"And maybe a change of scenery is exactly what we need to stop drifting," I threw over my shoulder.

"That's very deep, Piper."

"I try my best, Frank." I took Peter's arm beside me and yawned uncontrollably. I had never felt so tired in my life. And for the first time in months, I was pretty sure I would sleep in near perfect peace when night fell.

THIRD MOVEMENT

"The course of true love never did run smooth."
-*A Midsummer Night's Dream*[1]

CHAPTER 25

AUSTRALIA BOUND

*K*atrine and I stood on the bow of the boat. It was the first evening on our two-day journey to Townsville. Just one more day of being crammed like sardines in a tin. The speed of the transport ship hovered at a steady 90 miles-per-hour.

"Do you think the light is different on this side of the equator," Katrine asked, looking out at the greenish grey water.

We had turned philosophical of late. It was the natural thing to do. So much time, so little to do—onboard a ship, that is.

Pushing a wisp of her dark hair behind her ear, she suddenly grew more serious. "Piper,"

I looked at her.

"Do you really believe the story in *The Robe?*"

"What do you mean?" I asked. "It's a fictional story..."

"But the heart behind it. I know that both you and Lorelei believe that Yeshua is the Messiah, just as Marcellus comes to believe in the story."

I waited to answer her, knowing that this was a pivotal moment. "I do believe it. With everything in me."

"How can you know, without evidence?"

"I have evidence."

She tilted her head to the side, questioningly. "What kind of evidence?"

"Right here," I patted my chest, "inside my heart."

"That doesn't sound like evidence to me. Not what'd I'd call evidence anyway."

"Isn't peace of mind evidence?" I answered quickly. "You know how Marcellus, the minute he trusted in Yeshua, regained his sanity."

"But I am not mad." She bit her lip. "Only very... sad. I feel like my life in the last year and everything I ever wanted or hoped for has slipped through my fingers."

I took Katrine's hands in mine. "But we rejoice in our sufferings, knowing that suffering produces endurance, and endurance produces character, and character produces hope... A very wise woman told me that when I felt much as you feel now. I have to remind myself of it often enough. I have to tell myself to let go of my burden to God."[2] And there were plenty of burdens to be had these days, I told myself silently.

"I'm not ready to believe the way you do, Piper. I am not ready to let go... I wouldn't know how if I tried."

"It's not so difficult."

From down below, I could make out a great chorus of men's voices singing, *"Don't Sit Under the Apple Tree (With Anyone Else but Me)."*[3]

"Maybe for people like you and Lorelei, but you are not me."

"That's true." I looked down. "But regardless, I do know you shouldn't become bitter over the loss of your dreams. If you use the pain and unknowing to strengthen you and grow you, you won't become small and angry. Your life will be better in the long run." I stopped, thinking of Grace and wishing for the moment that I was talking to her and not Katrine.

Ever since things hadn't worked out with Amos, it was as though her life had stopped. She had no hope for the future. Her passion and zest for life were glaringly absent, and her spark was diminished. The truth was, pain had changed her. And not for the better.

"What I would give to see your mother right now! How I could use a walk with Aunt Rose this very moment." Katrine looked down.

"I'm a poor stand-in," I sighed, "but I'm available if you ever need to talk."

She smiled sadly.

The sound of music from below grew louder. "How about we go below?" I offered. "It sounds like fun."

Shrugging, Katrine turned and followed me back inside and down two flights of metal stairs to where the music was coming from in the hold.

There, in the center of several hundred men, bunks, and hammocks, Edie stood proudly. She wore linen pants and a linen shirt rolled up at the cuffs. She had her hands out and seemed to be directing everyone clapping and singing. By her side, Paul held a borrowed guitar in his hands and strummed skillfully, his deep tenor leading the chorus made of men in uniform, who swayed back and forth, singing with abandon. He had healed quickly once he was under professional care.

Leaning against the wall, Peter waved us over. By his side, Lorelei, Grace, Frank, and Horatio watched the scene, quite amused.

"Frank, get up here," Edie shouted over the ruckus. "We need the accordion."

Frank groaned and stood next to Paul, playing the instrument, without any enthusiasm at all, along with the popular song.

Edie looked up at Horatio, smiling softly and putting her hands up in a sort of mock pantomime, mouthing the words.

Katrine held back. "I don't think I can handle this."

"Sure you can," I answered, pulling her with me through the

crowd. "Katrine, years ago, I tried to protect myself from grief by putting up a wall in my heart. I thought if I blocked out the joy, I would block out the sadness too. But it doesn't work that way. Even now, Katrine, let the joy that is here and now in. I can't promise you that it will keep you from sadness later, but it will make you stronger. Take what joy you can get, Katrine! Who knows what tomorrow will bring?" A tear spilled down her cheek, and she looked at me as if to say she couldn't, even if she tried. With one last squeeze, I encouraged, "I believe there is joy for you now and joy for you later too, Katrine!"

As I made my way next to Peter, he leaned in and whispered, "I mean it now—you are not allowed to sit under any tree, apple or otherwise, without me."

"You don't have to worry about that." I patted his cheek.

"All right boys, all right!" Edie quieted the crowd. "Now, I have something really special for you. Something to add a little spice to this voyage."

The boys whistled and cheered.

"We'll need some space," she motioned for a few boys to step back, "and some volunteers."

Her eyes scanned the crowd, and she pointed at Peter. "Peter, darling, come here. And you too, Frank." She turned to Frank, standing motionless with his accordion still in hand. "I need you to do the background music."

The boys shot each other a look as Peter reluctantly left the safety of the wall.

"And you, Paul." She smiled a funny smile. "No guitar." Questioningly, he handed the guitar to another soldier and waited.

"Lorelei!" Edie shouted. "Where are you?"

"I'm here," she answered nervously.

"I need you. You are going to play Thisbe." Her eyes swept over the space. "That's right, fellow travelers. Welcome to Shakespeare on a Ship! It's like Shakespeare in the Park but more informal, and much less practiced. The boys in the sub loved it to bits, and I know a hold of good Marines could never be outdone by a bunch of Navy boys, eh?"

Horatio grimaced quietly, and mumbled, "blasphemy" as he struck his fist down.

"Dear, I'm speaking of Americans just now," she placated.

Edie passed short handwritten scripts to each of her 'volunteers.'

I could see Lorelei's face turn beet red. "I can't play this part!" she exclaimed.

"Oh, sure you can." Edie ignored her. "You were born for the role. You and Paul make a stunning couple! I may just be an amateur, but I know good casting when I see it. Who agrees that Lorelei should play the part?"

Everyone erupted in agreement and shrill whistles as Lorelei's eyes widened uncomfortably. Edie lowered her voice and whispered, "Lorelei, trust me! I know what I'm doing."

"I know what you're doing." Lorelei groaned. "You're trying to get me and Paul to—"

"No time to chat, dear!" Edie cut her off and faced the crowd, announcing in a proper English accent, "And now, dear fellows, we've no time for the whole of the play, but what follows is composed of the best excerpts from a *Midsummer's Night's Dream*. I give you, a play within a play." She paused for effect. "Pyramus and Thisbe!"

"Wait." Peter stopped her. "I'm playing a wall? Seriously?"

Edie grabbed a blanket from one of the bunks nearest him and passed it to Peter. "Hold it up, like this."

And so began one of the funniest scenes Shakespeare ever penned. The ill-fated Babylonian lovers, forced to meet through a small crack in the talking wall that separates them. In due turn, the wall speaks and gives them advice. It was even funnier because the players had no idea what was coming next in the script (beyond what they had quickly scanned a moment before).

Lorelei spoke haltingly, with Frank playing the accordion softly behind her, "O Wall, full often hast thou heard my moans, for parting my fair Pyramus and me. My cherry lips have often kissed thy stones..."[5]

Leaning into the opposite side of the wall, Paul (playing Pyramus) put his hand to his ear. "I see a voice. Now, will I to the chink, yo spy an I can hear my Thisbe's face. Thisbe?"[6]

"My love thou art, my love, I think?"[7] Lorelei moved closer to the blanket Peter held aloft.

"Oh, kiss me through the hole of this vile wall!"[8] Paul answered, fully enveloped in his role.

Frank abruptly stopped playing the accordion.

"I kiss the wall's hole, not your lips at all.[9] Lorelei quickly pecked the blanket, shooting Grace, Katrine, and me a tortured look, and waited for the audience to stop cheering. Someone in the back called out that Paul should just step over the wall and "Kiss the girl for crying out loud!"

Paul broke out of character and shouted back for the audience to be quiet and then tried to press on. He looked at his script, saw that he had to kiss Lorelei, blushed, and said, "I'm going to skip the next part."

"Thanks," Lorelei added, relieved.

Paul, back in character, flipped the page to his script over and put his hand over his heart. "Thus die I, thus, thus, thus. Now am I dead. Now am I fled. My soul is in the sky. Tongue, lose thy light. Moon, take thy flight."[10]

I stifled a laugh.

Paul collapsed on the floor. As his leg twitched up in the air, signaling the character's death, outrageous laughter erupted from the crowd.

Edie stepped into the center of the ring and motioned for quiet. "And there our scene ends, for, to quote dear Theseus, 'No epilogue, I pray you, for your play needs no excuse. Never excuse —for when the players are all dead, there need none to be blamed."[11]

"And now," she took the guitar back and handed it to Paul, (who was standing again), "I think we would all like to request a reprise. Would you and Lorelei do us the honor?"

"I guess so." Paul smiled, glancing at Lorelei. Once more, but this time much slower, Paul and Lorelei began to sing, *"Don't Sit Under the Apple Tree (With Anyone Else but Me)."*[12] A calm descended on the men, and it seemed everyone was thinking of their sweethearts at home. Lorelei's voice melded beautifully with Paul's confident tenor.

By the third verse, when Paul and Lorelei were promising not to walk down lover's lane, except with each other, Frank had returned to where Peter and I were watching and leaned up beside me.[13] He listened to the song, a frown etched on his brow. He was clearly concerned with what was happening between the singers.

I looked at Lorelei and Paul more closely. Every once in a while they would look at one another before their eyes would dart to the ground or the faces of the soldiers… anywhere but where their eyes might meet.

OUR ARRIVAL IN TOWNSVILLE, the strange city on the north-eastern coast of Australia, came just before the sun rose. Flinders Street, which ran right up the center of the city along the river, was essentially rows and rows of bars and gambling halls with raucous music, swinging doors, and ornate Victorian facades.

If there hadn't been a beach, enormous 1,000-pound crocodiles, kangaroos hopping around the side of the road, and the thick tropical climate, I would have bet you a million dollars that we were in some old ghost town come to life in the American West.

There were even Australian cowboys.

What brought the scene back to the reality of our mission were the 50,000 American and Australian troops. Townsville was *the* major staging point for many of the battles in the South West Pacific. There were multiple bases and over half a dozen airfields.

Horatio had managed to secure a high-set Victorian Queenslander large enough for all of us. Like most Queenslanders, the house was a single story built on stilts to allow drafts to cool the house from underneath because the heat in Townsville was something awful. And then there was the serious issue of termites and other pests. A large veranda wrapped around the whole thing, and it was covered with a corrugated iron roof.

From the room I shared with Peter, we could see Castle Hill, an enormous pink granite monolith that rose out of the earth and dominated the city's skyline.

"We'll climb it one of these days," Peter said that first day as he tested out the mattress. It was a big brass bed covered with an old but clean quilt. The walls had a dark green patterned wallpaper and a dark heavily oiled wooden vanity.

"You think your leg will hold up?" I peeked through the curtain. "It looks pretty steep."

"I'll be able to manage if we go slow. The 5th Australian Division is up there now. They've got a radar station."

I exhaled and sat down next to him, leaning back and looking at the ceiling. The bed wasn't too bad. Maybe a little hard, but after sleeping on a cot for weeks, it was the lap of luxury.

I could hear Frank whistling in the room next door. Lorelei and Grace had the third room, Katrine the fourth, and Horatio and Edie the large master suite.

(While Lorelei and Grace would have been given official housing due to their new assignments at the U.S.A. Army Air Force Base and the Red Cross hospital dormitory, respectively, both young women fit the special housing provision for those with 'family' within three miles of their posts. As such, we *all* moved in with Horatio and Edie: Grace, Lorelei, and Katrine, Peter and me, and Frank. Needless to say, it was a full house.)

There was a quick rap at the door, and Edie poked her head in. "Are you free to go with the girls into town?"

"Go where?" I asked.

"Horatio has invited some very, very important mucky mucks over to the house." Her face froze. "Some generals and admirals and their wives and who knows who else. The kitchen is completely bare, and we need to have something that resembles a dinner party by 1:00 in the afternoon *tomorrow*. And we've no Ferguson or Mr. Yamaguchi to help!" She sighed. "I'm thinking about a Thanksgiving theme. I want turkeys. Three of them. And all the fixings. We've so much to be thankful for!"

"But it's September," I said, slightly confused.

"I don't care what month it is. I want to celebrate Thanksgiving."

"I think that's a great idea, Edie." Peter smiled.

As I sat up, my thin cotton blouse ripped dramatically in the shoulder. "Oh drat!" I huffed. Everything I owned had been worn thin by harsh weather and numerous saltwater washes that had left them barely cleaner than before.

Edie put her hand on her hip and narrowed her eyes at the frayed cloth. "You've got to get some new clothes. And the girls do too. Everything is threadbare. It's completely baffling to me how quickly clothing wears out in this climate."

"I guess we'll see if they have any clothes in town. We can certainly dig up a few skirts and blouses in an afternoon, I should think." I held the blouse together, wondering what I could wear that was still semi-decent. Glancing at Peter, I said, "Mind if I borrow one of your shirts?"

"Go ahead." He looked puzzled.

I grabbed one of his two white button downs and threw it on, rolling up the sleeves past my elbow and tucking in the ample extra fabric into my shorts. "Don't I look like Grace now?"

"Do you want me to go with you?" he asked.

"No." I brushed my hair quickly and glanced in the mirror. "Well, actually, on second thought, maybe you should come. We'll have a lot of packages."

"You probably need Frank too." Edie's brow creased. "Turkeys are heavy, and I don't like the idea my girls wandering around a strange town without chaperones."

"Why don't we stop and pick up Paul too?" Peter began to lace up his shoes. "Sounds like a three-man job."

"Isn't Paul on his base by now?"

"Nah," Peter shook his head, "he doesn't have to report for duty until the day after tomorrow. He's staying at one of those little hotels on Flinders Street for the night before moving onto the base. We'll pick him up on the way."

"What's he going to be doing?" I asked.

"Intelligence work—because he speaks Japanese." He looked up momentarily from his shoe and explained, "You know, listening in on communication, translating documents... time-sensitive stuff."

"Sounds important."

"It is. It's the sort of work that will determine the outcome of the war. Communication is everything these days." He finished tying his other shoe. "Okay, I'm ready. Let's go."

Taking my hand, we walked towards the veranda where Katrine, Grace, and Lorelei sat on the steps, looking up at the tree in the front yard. A little tiny creature that looked almost like a teddy bear clung in the branches, sleeping peacefully.

"Have you ever seen anything like it?" Lorelei asked, her eyes glued to the animal. "A real live koala bear. I never thought in a million years I'd ever see one in person!"

Grace was on her feet now and began walking down the street without looking back. "Wait," I shouted. "I want to get my camera and take a picture!"

But Grace kept moving.

"I guess we're going then." Lorelei tried to laugh the moment away and took off after Grace.

Peter looked at me. "I'll wait if you want to go get your camera."

Nodding, I ran back inside and was back in a flash. Quickly, I snapped the shot of the adorable animal, and we took off after the group, swatting enormous bugs out of the way and marveling at the rough and rugged terrain that met the ocean.

"Where first?" Lorelei asked, turning around.

"We are going to pick Paul up and see the town." Peter grinned.

Lorelei groaned. "Paul Sinclair?"

"Do you know another one?" He laughed to himself and took my hand.

CHAPTER 26

A DATE DOWNUNDER

*K*atrine read the sign in the store window out loud and adjusted the parcel in her hand.

"BUY NOTHING YOU CAN DO WITHOUT. BE A SAVER, NOT A SPENDER."

"Well," she sighed, "I couldn't do without any of these things. And I didn't spend that much. The cost of clothing here is much less than in Palestine, or England for that matter!" Her parcel held the same simple items that Grace, Lorelei, and mine held; two sets of underwear, three new blouses, two skirts, and a new pair of sandals. They were sturdy pieces, not too fashionable but not too expensive either. Rationing for clothing and food in Australia was much more minimal than we were used to. We hadn't seen such prices or abundance since before the war.

Paul, Peter, and Frank had their arms full of parcels and bags. While the butcher had plenty of meat, more than I knew still existed, they did not have any turkey. For one thing, Australians obviously didn't celebrate Thanksgiving. For another, it wasn't

Thanksgiving. I thought we could roast a few chickens instead, but whole chickens were exorbitantly priced, treasured more for their value in producing eggs. Back home, chicken was always the cheaper choice, but here, it was all about beef and lamb. There were steaks two inches high. Frank ordered twelve. The butcher tried to get us to buy the lamb chops. He said they were famous for them. But the boys could not be argued with. They wanted steak. Lots and lots of it.

There was nothing close to pumpkin, canned or fresh. Katrine said she could make a pretty passable custard, so we settled on buying some pre-made biscuits (Australian for plain vanilla wafers) and bananas and hoped for the best. We also got all the basics like flour, sugar, butter, tea, a sack of potatoes, and several cans of green beans. It would by no means be a traditional Thanksgiving, by nature of the date and menu, but it was sort of American. Steak and potatoes, banana pudding. There would be no complaints.

So, there we were, walking in a parade back to the house with 12 enormous steaks. Frank led the charge, followed by Grace and Katrine, Peter and me, and in the rear, Paul and Lorelei.

As the others strolled along, distracted by every new sight and sound, the rear guard was solely focused on trying not to be so uncomfortable.

Paul broke the awkward silence. "Ms. Adleman?"

"Yes?" Lorelei's voice was unnaturally high.

"Can I carry that package for you?"

"Oh…" she exhaled. "Are you sure? You already have quite a few."

"Don't worry about me. I'm strong enough."

At that, he started laughing, and she quickly joined him as the tension broke.

"I…" he paused before starting again. "I wanted to apologize for spilling coffee all over your uniform."

"It's okay. Don't give it another thought."

"Thank you." He gave a short laugh. "Can I be very honest with you for a moment?"

She nodded with questioning apprehension.

"I've been trying to impress you. You're so beautiful, and I was trying too hard . . . I don't think we've started out on the right foot."

Lorelei's face froze. She didn't know how to respond.

They walked in silence a few more feet.

"Ms. Adleman?"

"Yes?"

"Would you allow me to buy you a cup of coffee sometime? Uh, to replace that one I spilled all over you?"

Her heart raced. "I, um... I'm not sure about that."

Paul stopped walking. Determination was written all over his face. "I won't take no for an answer."

She paused and looked off into the distance. "I don't think it would be the best idea."

Suddenly realizing her seriousness, he continued with less confidence, "Why not? I don't smoke, drink, or chew, don't run with those who do." He chuckled at his own joke and then grew quieter.

"What about tea?" He tried his best 'sell it' smile.

Untouched, she responded, "Can I be honest with you?"

"Yes."

"I value the truth very much. It's one of the most important things in my life. I have a rule, Paul. I don't date dishonest men."

"What in the world would make you think I am dishonest?"

He stopped short, and his face reddened as he hoisted his heavy load.

Her minute-long pause seemed to last an hour.

"Is that your real hair, Paul?"

"What? Of course this is my real hair!"

"Exactly!"

I stole a look, knowing they had no idea I could overhear them. Paul seemed desperately confused.

"How does having my real hair make me dishonest?!"

She paused again, then, growing more heated, continued, "I saw your photograph, Paul, on the Dr. Boulder's Bountiful Bald-No-More Balm box."

"You, Mr. Perfectly-good-looks, modeled your beautiful head of hair under the guise that Dr. Boulder's cured you of a baldness you just attested to not suffering from!"

A blush crept up his neck as she kept going.

Barely knowing what was flooding out, she explained, "You are the epitome of false advertising. Your hair lied. And you and your hair are one and the same! All those men out there, buying that balm, thinking it will make them look like you!" She finished abruptly, feeling vindicated, but a bit confused as to whether her logic lined up perfectly or not.

"You've got to be kidding me." He swallowed and appeared to be sick. "Do you know how much I hate being on that box? I was saving up during school. I got paid $50 to sit for a modeling agency. They sold my picture to the Bald-No-More people. I had no say in the whole thing. Believe me, Lorelei, I had no intention of being dishonest."

"Then why did you tell everyone that you were an academic?"

"Because I am one."

She stared at him, not fully believing him.

"What? Do you want to see my diplomas? I've got three. A Bachelors, a Masters, and one and a half PhDs."

"What sort of student at Yale Theological Seminary models?"

"One who needs money! I knew that job would come back to haunt me," he said under his breath. "Trust me, Lorelei, I may not be a lot of things, but I am a man of my word, and I'm not balding. Tug away. Have no fear!"

Lorelei stole a glance at Paul's earnest face and a laugh escaped her lips. "I don't know what to say."

Paul smiled at her. "Look, I'll make you an offer. I won't hold your looks against you if you don't hold mine against me."

"Mr. Sinclair," Lorelei took a package out of his arms, "you have yourself a deal."

He paused, hesitating. "As long as we are being honest... I've been wanting to buy you a cup of coffee for a long time. Ever since I pulled you out of the ocean. I've thought about little else, just between us."

Lorelei was amazed. "Mr. Sinclair, you don't even know me!"

"There's a foolproof remedy for that." He grinned. "You're a nurse, you should know that!"

Lorelei tripped on the curb and caught herself.

"It's just a cup of coffee," Paul spoke gently. "That's it."

"All right, Mr. Sinclair," she replied. "A cup of coffee."

BY NOW, it was nearly 2:00 in the afternoon. The delicious smell of fried fish emanated from the open doors of a pub called "Captain Cook's Hideaway."

Frank's voice called out from in front, "How about some lunch?"

"Sounds good to me!" Peter exclaimed.

"Peter!" I exclaimed. "We can't go in there!"

"Why not?" he said. "It smells good!"

"Yeah!" Frank stopped and turned around. "We're starving!"

"I'm hungry." Katrine looked at me, and Grace nodded.

Something in me hesitated. I knew they were hungry. I was hungry. But something about this place felt... unsafe. Like there might be pirates inside.

Grace took my arm. "Come on. It's fine, I'm sure of it. It *does* smell good."

I tried to shake off the feeling of dread, looking at Peter with a look only he would understand. But he ignored it.

"Piper," Lorelei stepped back, "if you want to go back home, I'll walk with you."

"I'll go with you girls," Paul offered magnanimously.

"No." I shook my head, feeling slightly betrayed by my husband for some reason. "No... I guess it's fine."

And so, we entered the dark bowels of the old wooden structure. As my eyes adjusted to the dim light, I could make out tables of Australian soldiers playing cards and billiards and a sign for 'Pokies,' which I later learned was some sort of lotto. There was a long umber-colored bar where a line of rough looking soldiers were drinking and smoking. I didn't like it one bit.

Peter pointed to a large round table in the corner, and we all maneuvered to our seats and waited as the bartender looked our way and motioned he'd just be a minute.

Peter whispered in my ear, "Kind of adventurous, right? Captain Cook might have been here! Who knows?"

I refused to look at him. It still felt creepy, Captain Cook or no Captain Cook.

"Who's Captain Cook?" Lorelei asked.

"He was a British explorer… the first European to contact this part of Australia and Hawaii," Paul answered.

By now, the bartender, a rotund, balding fellow with a dirty apron, was at the edge of our table.

"We'll take whatever smells so good," Peter said.

"All we've got is fish and chips." The man did not crack a smile.

"Then," Lorelei counted those at the table, "we'll take seven orders."

Without a word, he turned and disappeared behind a curtained doorway.

"Friendly sort." Paul frowned and looked at Lorelei. "Not exactly the sort of place I had in mind for our first date, but I guess it will do."

Suddenly, a soldier who had drunk one too many wobbled out of his chair at the table next to ours and hovered ominously over Frank and Peter. "You sound like *Yanks*," he spat out.

"That's because we *are* Yanks," Frank answered, shooting the man a sideways glance.

"I know all about you," he moaned and pointed at Katrine, Lorelei, Grace, and me. "You come down here with your Yankee cash, and you take our girls away!" He held up his fist under Peter's nose. "It was fellows like you that took away my Mary."

My heart rate skyrocketed, and I felt beads of perspiration form on my forehead. I was afraid to move, but I knew I had to do *something*. "He hasn't done anything of the sort!" I tried to explain. "I'm American too. In fact, I'm his wife!"

He faced me with blurred eyes. "Yeah? And what about them? You aren't going to tell me he's married to them too?"

"No! Of course not!" Katrine stood up and tried to take the young man's arm, exhibiting the take-charge, self-assuredness that only eldest children can. "I'm married to another American. I'm sorry about your Mary, but some things are not meant to be."

The man was teetering precariously, when all of a sudden, he began to tip forward towards Katrine, and in the process, both came down with a thunderous crash. Frank was up on his feet in an instant. "He hit her!"

"No, he didn't." Peter pushed Frank back down as Grace and Lorelei and I helped Katrine up, and Paul leaned over the soldier who appeared to have blacked out. When he stood back up, the soldier's companions were circling up. A rather large one stepped in and decked Paul right on the jaw.

"That's for Mary!" he exclaimed. After that, it was pandemonium. I remember ducking under the table with my cousins, clutching my camera to my chest, watching feet lunging and darting around and hearing the awful sound of fists hitting ribs and the wood of chairs crack and shatter on the bar.

"What are we going to do!" Katrine shouted, panicked.

Grace looked furtively to the left and the right. "Listen," we leaned in, "when I give the signal, grab your men, and we are getting out of this mess. None of these guys know who they are hitting anyway!"

"Whose 'our men?'" Lorelei asked.

Grace pointed, "Lorelei, you take Paul. Katrine, grab take Frank. And Piper, you get Peter. I'll take up the rear."

With that, she grabbed a glass bottle that had rolled under the table, slammed it on the side of a chair and whistled shrilly.

Katrine, Lorelei, and I emerged from the table and looked for our targets in the fist-fighting bedlam. There was Peter! He had a chair in between him and a hulking giant of a man and was trying to fend him off. Mustering all of my courage, I adjusted my camera strap and lunged towards my husband, pulling him towards the door with all the strength in me. The hulk didn't even realize Peter was gone and immediately started attacking the shrimp next to him.

We all stumbled out of Captain Cook's Hideaway at roughly the same time. Peter, struggling for breath, looked at my camera hanging from my neck. "You should have taken a picture, Piper! Don O'Leery would have killed for a shot of *real* Australian-American relations." His shirt was torn, and he had a bright red welt forming on his cheek.

Before I could respond that Australian-American relations would still be on the up and up if he had listened to me and never gone in that awful bar, Katrine exclaimed, "Our groceries! What of Thanksgiving dinner!"

"We've got to go back in." Peter looked determinedly at the door. The sound of the brawl carried out onto the street.

"You are most certainly *not* going back in there." I held him back.

"Paul! No!" Lorelei shouted, but it was too late. Paul had plunged back into the fray. For a tense two minutes, we waited and hoped for the best. And then, triumphantly, Paul emerged with a pile of packages and two sacks of groceries.

He smiled. "I think the steaks made it."

"That's good," Lorelei said, taking several packages, "because it looks like you are going to need one for that eye!"

"Hey, it wouldn't be Thanksgiving without steaks and banana pudding."

Frank groaned and looked at his fist. It was bloody.

"Boy, I'd hate to be the guy who saw the other end of that," Peter said, lugging one of the sacks over his shoulder.

"Yeah… if only it had been a guy. I aimed for that creep with the big nose and wound up hitting the wall. I think my hand is broke."

"Was it your bad hand?" Peter asked.

"Yup." Frank groaned. It hurt fiercely.

"Oh, dear," Lorelei sighed. "Come on, let's go home. We'll get you boys cleaned up."

With that, we trudged back up Flinders Street to the Queenslander. Peter held back.

"Piper," he started, "I'm… I'm sorry. I should have listened to you. You were right about that place. We shouldn't have gone in there."

I held myself very erect. "You shouldn't apologize to me. Frank and Paul are the ones who are hurt!"

"Piper!"

"Peter," I felt my face flush very red, "let's face it. You don't respect me!"

"That's not true," he spoke calmly. "It's just that I was so hungry. I couldn't think of anything else."

I harrumphed and walked faster.

"We need to talk about this!" he called after me. But I pretended I hadn't heard him. If I'd turned around to look at him, I would have seen that my words had hurt him more than any punch from a drunken soldier.

CHAPTER 27

ON FIRST ACQUAINTANCE

eter looked through the doorway to the large Victorian
kitchen where the women of the house were hard at
work preparing Edie's Thanksgiving feast.

"Piper?"

Edie was covered in flour, rolling out one tray of thick flaky
biscuits after another. I stood with Grace over a large bowl peeling
potatoes. Katrine leaned over the old range and whisked eggs, milk,
cornstarch, and sugar together with vigor.

"Piper," he repeated.

Grace elbowed me in the ribs. "Peter's trying to get your
attention."

I knew that. I just wasn't in the mood to answer him. He
wouldn't listen to whatever I had to say, anyway.

Reluctantly, I craned my neck around to face him.

"Paul says the grill is ready for the steaks."

Edie hung her head and lamented, "Two generals and an admiral
at my table, and I'm serving them barbecue."

"What's the matter with barbecue?" Peter was surprised. "Paul says he makes the best grilled steaks in Pasadena. Everyone at USC said they were the best. He used to make them on the beach all the time."

"*Exactly!*" Edie raised the rolling pin above her head. "A beach bonfire does not a Thanksgiving make! I'm always such a traditionalist," she said with passion.

I was about to tell her that having Thanksgiving with steaks in September wasn't exactly traditional, when she exclaimed, "We'll just have to make do I suppose, but I had so wanted Lorelei to make her Beef Wellington or at the very least her steak with Béarnaise sauce. You know, something with a little class!"

At that moment, Lorelei walked in and grabbed the stack of folded napkins off the edge of the counter. She had already set the large oval dining table with the fine porcelain plates painted with intricate designs of red roses and beautiful crystal goblets. The house had been magnificently well stocked by the last officer and his wife, who had recently returned to London on furlough.

"There's no reason I can't still make the Béarnaise sauce if you want." Lorelei smiled. "I have no idea how it will turn out with a grilled steak, mind you, but I doubt it will be that much different from pan searing it. That is, if Paul won't mind."

"Just make it! We need something to add to the meal to make it a little more celebratory." She looked out the window to the backyard where Horatio, Paul (one eye black and blue) and Frank (one hand bandaged) hovered over the makeshift grill.

"I haven't had a steak in months. Believe me, it will be celebratory." Peter looked at me again, and I looked away. How could he talk about steaks? After what had happened yesterday? It was infuriating. We had never fought like this. Never. Not once since we had been married!

"So… where are the steaks?" he asked as Lorelei went to finish setting the table.

"In the icebox." Edie went to work punching out circles of dough with a glass cup and laying them on a tray. "But don't cook them right away. They need to come up to room temperature." Deftly, she swatted a fly away from her face. "In this heat, that will be about two minutes."

"Piper?" Peter said once more. But I ignored him. Everyone could feel the chill in the room.

Edie opened the oven door, and a gust of black smoke puffed out. Coughing, she pushed the tray of biscuits inside. "I don't think anyone has cleaned this oven in ten years." She shoved the door shut with a clang.

I felt her suddenly by my shoulder, her hand pulling mine away from the potatoes.

"Yes?" I asked archly.

Her voice dropped as she said, "I don't know what happened between you and Peter, but it's been going on since you came home yesterday. I don't like how you've been acting. If he's hurt you, forgive him."

"I'm... I'm not ready to."

"God doesn't ask us to forgive when we are ready to. He tells us to do it. Besides, he's sorry."

"How do you know?" I retorted.

"I looked at him."

I pursed my lips together and looked down.

"Trust me, he loves you, and he's sorry, and what you're doing now is most likely worse than whatever he did to you. Don't let your anger cause you to sin, dear. In my humble opinion, it seems you think you may be 'right' in your head, but you're not right in your heart."

Before I could respond, she returned to her biscuit dough. Katrine and Grace pretended they hadn't heard anything.

"Right." Lorelei clapped her hands as she came back into the kitchen. "Béarnaise sauce! I'll need butter. And lots of it!"

~

AT 5:30 p.m. on the dot, the guests arrived, and Edie passed out paper pilgrim's hats and feather headdresses we had painstakingly cut out and glued together the night before. American Admiral Knox brought his wife, an aging, soft-spoken Southern belle. They'd never had children, and, like Horatio and Edie, refused to ever be separated. Both of them were given pilgrim's hats. Edie said that Knox reminded her of William Bradford.

English Admiral Stark came alone. His wife was back in the Cotswolds on her family's estate along with their three children. He was dubbed a pilgrim too and hesitatingly put the paper hat on over his balding head, feeling rather traitorous.

Then, there was General Linton of the U.S. Army Air Force. He was on a tour of the airfields in the Pacific and was joined by his wife, Bee, and their daughter, Dorris. Bee was a rather angular woman who rarely smiled, while her daughter was a wild, vibrant young woman with titian hair and intense green eyes. From the moment they walked in the door, Bee was subtly telling Dorris what to do, and Dorris was flagrantly ignoring her.

"Definitely Pocahontas." Edie passed Dorris a feather headdress.

"I'm pretty sure Pocahontas wasn't at the first Thanksgiving," Dorris took the paper feathers and placed the band around her temple.

"It's the spirit of the holiday." Edie turned to me and placed a pilgrim hat over my hair. "And you can be Catherine Carver, and Peter will be your husband John."

"Don't put your purse there, Dorris!" Bee spoke through tightly clenched teeth.

In response, with a defiant smile, Dorris dropped her purse on the couch. She thought no one saw, but I did. And so did Frank. But while I didn't really appreciate Dorris's disregard for her mother, no matter how tightly laced Bee Linton might be, Frank admired it.

"Now there's a spunky dame." He whistled slowly under his breath, following me back into the kitchen to get another tray of drinks. Dubbed 'Squanto' for the holiday, he had a fan of feathers spread out over his forehead. He pushed the headdress back an inch.

"I think the word 'rude' is more appropriate." I filled a tray with some more fake crab meat canapés and caviar sandwiches piped with cream cheese.

He shook his head as he poured two Cokes into glasses. "Nah, she's spunky. I like spunk in a girl." He paused before asking, "Have you noticed something going on between Paul and Lorelei?"

"Yes." I adjusted the sandwiches and looked up at Frank. He was frowning.

"Yeah… me too. You think he's serious about her?"

"Would it be a problem if he was?"

He shook his head. "I just… you know how much I love Lorelei. And Katrine and Grace and you… all you girls. I'd hate to see someone go and break her heart again."

My voice caught in my throat. "Frank, I'm pretty sure that Joe Miller never broke Lorelei's heart. It was a mutual decision… not to be together."

"She's a choosy lady."

I thought of a way to explain it to the sailor, but I couldn't. He was still in love with her, even though he knew and I knew and everyone knew that Lorelei could never love him back in the way he wanted.

"All right," he hoisted his tray up, "these are ready. Let's go."

Admiral Knox stood by the fireplace (which had no fire in it) and took a drink off of Frank's tray as he passed by. "We have to completely redesign our whole plan of island hopping. We've had way too many losses. We need new weapons. New landing craft. Anything to help speed up the end of this terrible, terrible war."

Admiral Stark, the stately Englishman, nodded gravely. "Indeed, but we've heard that you've begun training new underwater demolition teams? An intriguing idea, really."

"A necessary idea." Horatio took a sandwich and patted my shoulder. "We must be able to maneuver around the islands with greater speed and precision. Underwater demolition teams are one of the most brilliant strokes to ever hit the Americans. It will win the war, believe me!"

"No," General Linton put his glass down firmly on the little side table by the settee he sat on with his wife, "it will be won by the air. By bombs. Or *a* bomb... I'm sure you've heard the rumors of the super-weapon they're developing in New Mexico."

"I have, actually," Katrine said, her voice breaking the momentary silence. Her white pilgrim hat was slightly too big and hung down over her ears.

"From who?" Grace looked at her sister, shocked.

"Dr. Einstein." She stopped abruptly. It was always best not to share how much one knew or where one's information came from with people one did not know or trust.

"You know Einstein?" General Linton blinked several times.

She swallowed. "He's sort of an old family friend..."

Edie shook her head. "A bomb to end all wars? What sort of talk is this? It's absolutely inappropriate. Let's have some nice conversation." She thought a second. "How did you celebrate Thanksgiving last year?" She stopped. "Actually, maybe we shouldn't talk about that. I was with my children and thinking of them makes me tear up."

"Let's see," Mrs. Knox, unhearing, spoke with a heavy southern drawl, "we were with my mother in Charleston. She makes the most amazing sweet potato pie, or rather, her housekeeper Matilda does. And Mrs. Macleay, I just have to say having a Thanksgiving party does a heart real good. It's so unexpected and creative!"

"We'll be having Katrine's banana pudding," Edie said, blushing at the compliment. She took great pride in being 'unexpected and creative.'

"I suppose you're not familiar with American customs and such,

273

being from Germany and all, but usually, dear," Bee Linton spoke down her nose, "we eat sweet potato pie or pumpkin pie." Bee Linton was neither unexpected nor creative. Thanksgiving in September made her uncomfortable and confused.

"Actually," Katrine answered firmly, "I'm quite familiar with your customs. I married an American and have one American adopted parent." She looked at Edie. "There simply was nothing resembling a sweet potato or pumpkin at the grocer's."

"Ah," Bee smiled thinly, "I see."

"Peter and I were at a church potluck feeding the homeless last year," I offered, trying to lighten the tension.

"I was in Cairo," Lorelei said. "Frank and I went to Joe's place. There were all these embassy people there. It was quite exciting. President Roosevelt, Winston Churchill, and Chiang Kai-shek were all in town for the Cairo Conference. The whole city was in a tizzy. And somehow, Joe managed to get a turkey of all things."

Paul's eyebrows raised at the name 'Joe.'

"His father probably sent it to him on ice." Frank sneered.

"You enjoyed it!" Lorelei exclaimed.

Horatio scratched his beard and put his arm around Edie. "The Cairo Conference is what got us here. If the Allies had not agreed to continue to deploy military force until Japan surrenders... Well, here we are, a year later. Still no surrender. The battle continues."

"What about the year before that?" Paul asked. He was totally focused on Lorelei, determined to learn all he could about her.

She paused, a conflicted look on her face. "I... I don't remember. It was either Scotland or Germany." She suddenly remembered. "It was Scotland. And the year before that I was with Rolf... and my parents. Of course, we don't celebrate Thanksgiving in Ger..." Her voice broke abruptly.

"And where are your parents now?" Mrs. Knox said sweetly. "And Rolf? Your...?"

"He was an old friend." Lorelei tried to smile, but she did not like talking about her intimate history with a bunch of strangers, and it showed. "He passed away. So did my parents."

"Oh, I'm terribly sorry!" Mrs. Knox looked at her pityingly. "Was there some sort of an accident?"

"It's not exactly party conversation." Lorelei squirmed.

Edie stepped in and offered, "Mrs. Knox, Horatio and I adopted Lorelei and her sisters after her parents were murdered by the Nazis. We rescued them and spirited them out of Germany."

"How remarkably epic, Mrs. Macleay!" Mrs. Knox said admiringly. "What an adventurous life you must lead!"

Edie fanned herself. "Well, I do try. It's good for my career, of course, to have adventures and such."

Mrs. Knox honed back in on Lorelei. "What was it like? Escaping Germany, that is?"

"Really," Lorelei spoke quietly, "I'd rather not talk of it."

I'd rather not talk of it?

Paul repeated Lorelei's statement in his head, feeling terrible that his innocent question had obviously brought up such unpleasant memories in such a public setting. He could imagine what Lorelei had survived. He knew what was happening in Germany—everyone in the room did. And Lorelei was right, it was not party talk, not at all. Mrs. Knox should have known better than to pry!

Then, he remembered something I had told him at Don's luau, which now seemed such an eternity ago; Lorelei was very sensitive. He was a smart man and quickly put two and two together, concluding that talking about whatever happened in Lorelei's past was too painful for the beautiful young nurse's delicate sensibilities. He understood; he was a soldier. Some things were too difficult to remember or discuss, sometimes forever.

"But we're among friends here," Mrs. Knox pressed. As sweet as the Southern woman was, her curious personality bordered on that of a busybody.

Paul turned abruptly, determined to rescue Lorelei from Mrs. Knox. "And what about you, Dorris?" he asked bypassing Mrs. Knox's question completely.

"What about what?" Dorris looked like a deer in the headlights.

"What did you do for Thanksgiving last year?" He glanced at Lorelei, who smiled a secret smile and mouthed a silent 'thank you' in his direction. Paul nodded subtly, pleased that he had been able to come to the aid of the fair damsel in distress, and shifted his gaze back to Dorris.

"Last year, Mother and Father came to visit me at the base." Dorris shot her mother a look.

"Are you a nurse, dear?" Edie smiled.

"Me?" Dorris laughed huskily. "As if! I'm a WASP."

"A what?" Edie looked confused.

"White Anglo-Saxon Protestant," Frank said bluntly. "I'm a Jew, I can smell them a mile away."

Her father, General Linton, took over, ignoring Frank's comment. "She's a Women's Air-force Service Pilot. I taught her to fly before she could tie her shoes. She was one of the first girls to sign up two years ago."

"Dad helped get the whole program up and running."

Grace, who had been sitting disinterestedly in the corner, suddenly became very interested. "I'm a pilot too," she exclaimed. "I used to fly with the RAF."

"Used to?" Dorris asked.

"The Jewish Paratroopers—my unit—was disbanded after our last mission. I chose not to sign up for another round. I've been working on the ground in Palestine for the last year or so. I'm with the U.S. Army Air Force now."

"No kidding!" Dorris beamed. "Why, you ought to come out with Dad and me to the airfield on Saturday. You should see this new plane we brought over on the carrier. It's as fast as a lightning hellcat and can shoot down those Jap zeros in a heartbeat. I'm going to be training the boys how to use it for a couple of months before going out myself. "

"Saturday?" Grace looked at Dorris admiringly. "I'll be there already. I'm one of the new flight instructors at the base."

"Then we'll be working together! Wait till you see how this plane handles in the air! I can't wait to get out on the front and take down a few Kamikazes for myself."

"But how can you?" Grace was confused. "They don't allow women to fly combat."

"I plan to change all of that, one day." Dorris said confidently.

"Dorris," her father checked her, "don't push this. I pulled a lot of strings to get you on this trip."

I saw Bee shoot her daughter a look, warning her to rein it in. Barely restraining her fury, Dorris turned her blazing green eyes on me. "Your aunt told me you work for *The Honolulu Herald*. You should write a piece on how the U.S. Army Air Force treats their ace pilots. They let them *observe and teach*. Why wouldn't they let their best fighters take down the enemy?" She glanced at Grace. "I've heard it's the same in the RAF. Am I correct?"

Grace nodded.

"But girls like us are going to change things!" She pounded on the side-table, startling Edie and almost knocking the lamp over.

"Like I said, we'll talk about this later." General Linton and his wife shared an exhausted look. I couldn't imagine having a daughter like Dorris. She was a serious handful.

Paul, sensing the need to divert the conversation yet again, smiled and leaned back in his chair. "Last year, my sister and I flew out with my nephew Timmy to my grandfather's ranch. He put on the full works. Three turkeys. A pile of green chili chicken tamales that Jauna makes, she's my grandfather's housekeeper, and pecan pies with pecans from his pecan grove. Nothing like those pecans. Nothing in the world."

"What's a tamale?" Peter asked.

"It's a Mexican dish. Shredded chicken and green chili sauce all

277

wrapped up in corn masa, that's something sort of like cornmeal but better. We drink a lot of coffee." He winked at Lorelei. "Strong coffee."

"I can't even imagine what that tastes like!" Edie smiled pleasantly. "How exotic. Horatio, we really must make it down to Mexico one of these days. Once the war ends."

"Ma'am," Paul bowed, "you would be welcome at the ranch anytime. Anytime at all. My grandfather has a great big piano, and my sister plays. Strictly classical when my grandfather's up, but once he's asleep, she lets it rip with all the top 40s. Not that she's any good, but she can work her way around a piece of music."

"You should hear Lorelei," Edie offered not so subtly.

"You play?" Paul looked at Lorelei. "I mean... not that I'm surprised. You and your sisters are all so musical."

"Does she play!" Edie interjected. "Why, Lorelei is practically a professional."

Lorelei blushed. "Oh dear, I'm nothing near a professional. But... I do love music. It helps me think."

"Me too." Paul smiled. "That's why I picked up guitar. One of my grandfather's ranch hands taught me. The beauty of a guitar is you can take one with you anywhere you go."

"Music helps all of us think, I should think," Mrs. Knox added. "I took lessons as a young girl. Never seemed to stick. I hated practicing."

Grace sniffed. "Lorelei sometimes practices in her sleep. I see her fingers moving on the sheets. Chopin. Always Chopin."

"How do you know I'm playing Chopin in my sleep?" Lorelei exclaimed.

"Lucky guess."

"Classical music is the music of dreams." Paul stared at Lorelei and then looked down as though he had surprised himself.

"And jazz is the poetry of the soul." Edie grinned. "You both impressed all of us at the show with that duet on the ship. It's too bad we don't have a guitar here. We could all stand for a little music."

"Well, ma'am, I actually bought a guitar yesterday."

"Did you happen to bring it?"

"I did." Paul smiled. "What would Thanksgiving be without music?"

CHAPTER 28

AN AUSTRALIAN THANKSGIVING

*H*oratio sat at the head of the table. "Now," he said, his Scottish brogue coming through stronger than ever, "we don't celebrate Thanksgiving in Scotland, but my darling wife is an American, and I believe that anytime to give thanks is the right time, Thanksgiving or otherwise." He nodded at Paul. "And, thankfully, we happen to have a chaplain on board this afternoon. Paul Sinclair, a very brave and fine young man if I ever met one, would you do us the honor of saying grace?"

Paul nodded and stood up. "It would be my honor, sir." He bowed his head and waited a moment before beginning, "Heavenly Father, on this Thanksgiving Day, we come before you humbly and thank you for all you have done and all that you are doing in our midst to reveal your love, your plan, and most importantly, the truth of your Son, Jesus, in our lives. We pray, Lord, that you would bring freedom to the earth from this war, and more importantly, freedom to our souls. May your name be glorified."

As Paul prayed, I looked around the room. Peter reached out and tried to take my hand, but I pushed him away. No matter what Edie had said, I wasn't ready to forgive him yet.

"We thank you for friends, old and new." He looked at Lorelei.

"We pray for our loved ones, those who are sick, those who are wounded, those who are not with us."

A tear slipped down Katrine's cheek, and I saw her finger my necklace still clasped around her neck so many months later.

"We know that you deny no good thing to those who earnestly seek you."

Grace bit her lip and stared angrily at her plate.

"We thank you that we have one another to celebrate and worship with. For the gift of family and love, for the gift of your Son who freely forgave us so we could forgive one another."

My heart pricked, and I saw Horatio lean over and kiss Edie's cheek. "I'm grateful for you, darling," I saw him whisper.

I could feel Peter beside me. I could feel the pain I had caused him in my stubborn refusal to believe him and accept his apology.

Then, I saw Katrine and Grace. Both were so utterly alone. My husband was beside me. It hit me like a load of bricks… Somewhere down the line, I had stopped being thankful for Peter.

He was alive and well, and he loved me, and sure, maybe he didn't always listen to me, but he was trying. And that was the whole point! Certainly, I could try too.

I reached out and took his hand. He grasped it and looked at me, his eyes resting on my penitent glance in his direction. I mouthed 'I'm sorry' as he squeezed it.

A wave of relief washed over me. I had hated that feeling of disconnection. It was awful, one of the most horrible feelings I'd ever had! Why had I waited so long to make things right? Why had I waited so long to forgive him? Once we were alone, I would have to ask him to forgive me, but he would. He always did. Peter was much better at that sort of thing than I ever was. Another wave of thankfulness for my husband, unlike any I'd ever known, washed over me. God had given me a very good man. He didn't want me to ever treat him the way I had ever again. It was wrong.

"We thank you for this abundance. In Jesus' name we pray. Amen."

A chorus of voices rose up with a resounding "Amen!"

"Now, that was a very nice prayer," Mrs. Knox said approvingly. "Very nice indeed."

"Thank you, ma'am." He took a biscuit and began to butter it liberally.

"What an absolutely wonderful steak," Admiral Stark said admiringly. "Perfectly cooked."

Paul smiled. "It's an old family recipe. My grandfather's... Texans know beef."

"So I've heard," the Englishman said with a laugh. "But the sauce, the sauce is certainly not a Texan tradition? Why it tastes like a Béarnaise!"

"*If* steak needed sauce, God would have made it that way . . . *but* it doesn't! I don't put 'Béarnaise' on my steak," Paul said firmly.

Mrs. Knox took a bite and lilted, "If ifs' and buts' were candy and nuts, it would be Christmas every day." She pointed her fork at Paul. "No more excuses, young man, try the sauce."

"You really should try it with the sauce," Admiral Stark insisted.

Paul shook his head. "If it's all the same to you, I'd rather not. Call me stuck in my ways, but there are certain things I simply cannot do and putting sauce on my steak is one of them."

Edie looked at Lorelei. "That's Lorelei's sauce. It's one of her old family recipes."

Lorelei blanched. "If he doesn't want sauce on his steak, let him be, Edie."

"Some things are better together," Edie said in a sing-song voice. "You can't be a lone wolf forever, Paul Sinclair, unlike your steak. Mark my words, you aren't getting any younger."

There was an awkward pause, and then Edie and Mrs. Knox and Bee Linton each dove into their horror stories of traveling with their husbands throughout the Pacific. "The boy who drove the supply truck was dumber than a box o' rocks, bless his heart," Mrs.

Knox laughed gaily. "Dumber than dirt! Blind in one eye and couldn't see out of the other. And things went to hell in a hand-basket from there on!"

"I don't think I understood one word she just said," Katrine said beneath her breath.

"Mrs. Knox is from the South dear," Edie explained quietly, taking a sip of water.

Meanwhile, their husbands spoke of strategy and Japanese battle tactics. Peter, Paul, Lorelei, Grace, and Katrine continued listening to Paul's tales of the cowboys and cattle drives of his youth.

I was too interested in what was happening across the table to care what anyone else was talking about.

I watched as Frank picked at his steak and stared at Paul and Lorelei. Dorris, at his side, leaned in.

"What's the matter with you? Vegetarian?"

Taken by surprise, Frank laughed out loud. "What would make you say that?"

She looked at his untouched steak as she sawed into her own.

"I'm just preoccupied, ma'am."

She flashed him a smile. "With me sitting beside you, right? I have that sort of effect on people."

Frank cracked up even harder.

She put her knife down, touched his arm and said cryptically, "Let me give you a little tip. If a girl's not interested, she's not for you."

"Are you trying to tell me something?" He held his fork midair, frozen.

"You're a smart guy, I think you can figure it out."

Frank's eyes widened, and he gulped.

WITH THE PSEUDO-THANKSGIVING supper nearly over, the conversation dropped off, and everyone waxed nostalgic.

"Can't you imagine the first Thanksgiving?" Edie said, removing her feather headdress and placing it on the table beside her. "All the Pilgrims escaping religious persecution! The Indians helping them survive and the celebration of an abundant fall harvest. So much to be thankful for. I feel like one of them, sort of. In a new land, perilous adventures ahead."

Grace locked eyes with her. "I don't see any similarity to our situation and the pilgrims. And I really don't see much to be thankful for."

Edie, refusing to acknowledge Grace's bad attitude, shook her head. "Well, I suppose it is a thin comparison. Nonetheless, we are having to defend our beliefs and those we love from those who would seek to destroy all we hold dear." She looked at Bee Linton and Mrs. Knox. "Did you know I have ancestors that go all the way back to The Mayflower!"

"I'm a member of the DAR myself." Mrs. Knox smiled.

"I'll tell you something, Grace." Edie leaned into Grace and spoke quietly as the rest of the table continued to converse. "If you see no reason for giving thanks, the fault lies in yourself. When I give thanks, I find my troubles are lessened, my burdens lightened. It reminds me that there is hope for the future and that God has not left me."

"How can you say that? Katrine's husband is in prison or dead. The war drags on and on. We don't have a future to hope for!" Grace glared at Edie as though her hope was offensive.

"You can always find something to be thankful for," Paul agreed with Edie. "Why, here we are, all together—with steak! Now that's something, isn't it?"

"I think you are all acting like children," Grace retorted.

"Jesus tells us to become like little children." Paul smiled at Lorelei. "It makes life a lot more fun, trust me."

"Well, I'm not in the habit of listening to his ideas. And I'm not a child. I'm an adult, and I know how the world works, and I know there is nothing to be thankful for that we don't work for ourselves.

Life is a fight to the top. You have to claw your way up." She put her napkin beside her plate and stood up abruptly. "I think I'd better go fix the dessert. Excuse me." And with that, she slid out of her chair and disappeared into the kitchen.

"Your sister is quite a firecracker, isn't she?" Paul asked Lorelei.

"You have no idea."

"Boys!" Admiral Knox boomed from across the table, taking our attention off of Grace. He pointed a long finger at Frank and Peter. "Horatio here has been telling me of your bravery in battle."

"Thank you, sir!" they responded in unison. I could tell Peter was tempted to salute.

"I heard you both sustained injuries in battle and were honorably discharged from His Royal Majesty's Navy."

Frank and Peter looked at him questioningly.

"I can imagine how hard it must be to stand on the sidelines," he continued. "Horatio's been telling me you boys would like to get back in on the war?"

"Would we!" They looked at one another like they'd been handed the moon. My heart rose up into my throat and threatened to choke me.

"Not combat," Edie checked Admiral Knox. "Remember our agreement!"

"Of course not." Admiral Knox laughed. "I was thinking of something here in Townsville. We need men behind desks as much as behind guns."

"I'm not great at the whole 'desk job' thing." Frank frowned.

Admiral Knox nodded understandingly. "I think we can work something out."

CHAPTER 29

MOVING ON

*T*wo days later, I learned what exactly Admiral Knox had worked out.

Peter looked pretty pleased with himself, saying as he shut the door once they returned from the base, "I'm going to serve as one of the personal secretaries to the main supply officer."

I put down the sock I was darning, "What will you do?"

"I'll spend all day going over lists to furnish the barracks. Blankets. Beds. Towels. Chairs. Chewing tobacco. And food too. We have to make sure the accounts line up and no one is skimming money or selling the supplies on the black market."

"I suppose that's all right."

"All right?" Peter puffed out his chest a little. "It's an important job, kiddo. Supply lines win wars."

"He's right," Horatio agreed. "And you are pretty good with numbers. Knox did a fine job."

"And what about you, Frank?" Edie asked politely, coming in from the kitchen where a crab pie baked in the oven.

Frank, who had looked rather shell-shocked from the moment he had returned, didn't answer.

"He's a pigeoneer," Peter answered for him.

I giggled. "A what?"

"A pigeoneer."

"They put me on bird duty!" Frank shuddered. "Feathers... everywhere!"

"You said you didn't want a desk job," Peter chided him.

"Sure," he agreed, "but now they got me caring for a bunch of chickens."

"Pigeons," Edie corrected him. "There's a big difference, dear."

Frank rolled his eyes.

"Wars are won with pigeon lines," Grace said sarcastically, looking up from the magazine she was reading at the dining room table.

"I don't want to talk about it." With a glum expression, he plopped down next to Grace.

"Actually," Peter said, "it's a very important position. Probably more important than mine."

"Really?" Edie put her hand on her hip and waited for Frank to explain.

"Well, you know all about homing pigeons, right?"

I shook my head no.

"Well," Frank began, "they can find their way home after traveling miles and miles. Because of that, they make great messengers. Apparently, our boys have been using them to carry messages for the last 40 years."

"Haven't they ever heard of a radio?" Grace asked, one eyebrow raised. "This is the 20th century!"

"Yes, of course." He shot her a look. "The birds are for emergencies, in the rare case of radio failure. Flights as long as 1,100 miles have been recorded. They can fly pretty fast too — 60 miles per hour at cruising speed, and 100 miles per hour when they are racing." He blushed, betraying a secret pride in his feathered wards. "I learned all this today."

"I've painted my fair share of the humble 'Columba livia domestica.'" Edie sighed wistfully. "Amazing how a creature can remember its way home after traveling such a distance. You should be proud of your new position, Frank!"

He sighed. "I guess so." He looked around and asked, "Where's Lorelei and Katrine?"

"Katrine's in her room. Lorelei is out."

"What? With that Paul Sinclair I bet!"

"You bet right." Edie shrugged. "With that sort of uncanny betting ability, you might even beat me in a game of poker. Which leads me to my next question, any of you up for a game? Canasta? Hearts?"

"Go Fish, and you have a deal." Frank took his jacket off and began to help my aunt move the foldout card table near the couch.

"Well, I'm thankful we both get to work. It's a blessing from God." Peter smiled at me.

"You want to play?" Frank asked, looking at Peter and me.

"No, no. I think I'm done for the day." Peter motioned for me to follow him into our bedroom. He sat down on the edge of the bed and began to take off his shoes. "What's going on with Katrine?"

I thought back to earlier that afternoon. Katrine had seemed more melancholy than usual, and when I'd asked her what was wrong, she'd told me she realized that even if Harry was okay, he wouldn't know where to find her. I'd told her not to worry about that. Katrine knew where his mother Bertha lived on Delancey Street in New York. She could write to Bertha with her new address, and then, Bertha could tell Harry where Katrine was once Harry contacted Bertha. This had provided some relief to Katrine's worried state of mind, and she'd wondered why she hadn't thought of it herself, racing off to send Bertha a letter. I explained this as I sat down next to Peter and leaned my head on his shoulder.

Looking around the room, a cold little chill came up over me. "This not having a home thing is getting old."

"I know."

"I knew our life together would be different, but I have to be honest, I wasn't expecting this at all."

He pinched my cheek. "I can imagine how difficult I am to live with."

"I didn't mean that." I struggled to put it into words. "It's not you at all! It's just this war. I wonder if I'll ever feel stable or at home ever again. We've been floating along with no real direction for so long."

"Are you trying to tell me you don't enjoy being a war correspondent?"

"Peter, you know as well as I do that taking pictures around Townsville isn't exactly front-page stuff."

He exhaled and became serious. "We've surrendered our lives to God. He's leading us. He's just not telling us where we will end up. This is a 'one step at a time' season. Like the Israelites in the desert after they escaped Egypt. Pillar of fire by night, the cloud by day."

"It feels more like we are stuck in a whirlpool going round and round and round and round."

Peter put his fingers gently on my lips. "Okay, have it your way. We are on Noah's Ark. When it's time, the waters will recede, we'll land on some rock, get out, and start building our home. But for the time being, we have to find our peace *inside*, Piper. We have to learn to be all right, to thrive even, inside the boat. We have to learn to be content."

"Content?" If there was one thing I did *not* feel, it was content.

"He lives inside of us. He promises us his peace." The way he said it made me know he was struggling just like me. "I understand that up here," he pointed to his forehead, "but, I don't know how to really feel it."

"What are you worried about, Peter?"

"The future, same as you." He laid down on his back and looked at the ceiling. "I'm not like the other guys. I'm not a super-spy. I'm not very funny..."

"That's true." I chuckled.

"Hey," he sounded hurt, "I'm trying to share my heart here. That's not always the easiest for me."

"I'm sorry." I backed off. "You're not very funny?"

"All I can really do is carpentry and sail. I just don't know what I'm going to do once this war is over." He sighed. "I'm just not very good at anything important. I'm just not very good at anything."

His insecurity pricked my heart. "You are good at fixing things. Bikes. My watch. Paul's arm."

He sat back up. "You are only saying that because you married me."

I looked into his discouraged eyes, trying to think of what to say.

"And you are good at business. That's why you were in business school!"

He grimaced.

"What's this?" I felt his hesitation. "You don't want to take over Scottish Lobster when Horatio retires?"

He shook his head. "Not really. Just between us, I don't really like lobster… or business."

"You probably need to talk to Horatio about that."

"No. It would break his heart if I didn't take over the business."

I highly doubted that, but at the moment, I knew not to say anything.

"God's got us, Peter."

"I know." He tried to smile. "And I'll take over the business if I have to. I'm just saying, I'd rather be doing something else." A second later, he said slowly, "I see a lot of things I want to change, and I don't know where to start."

"Things like what?"

"Things I never could fix. Nazis murdering Jews, for one thing."

"We can't stop evil in the world, Peter."

"I know." He shook his head. "But the longer this war goes on, the angrier I get. If more people had stood up to Hitler, none of this would have happened. If more people had been brave and just said something!"

"Peter, the Germans elected Hitler. He worked the system and played off of people's fears and emotions."

He shrugged. "Then someone should have changed the system."

I smiled a sad smile and kissed the top of his head. "You are a good man, Peter." With that, I kicked my own shoes off and silently prayed that God would lead my husband exactly where he needed to go. It was obvious he was no lobster salesman.

CHAPTER 30

IN THE MEANTIME

The next month passed without incident. Lorelei fell into her position at the Red Cross, marching to the rhythm of a familiar drum. As a Senior Nurse, she took charge of training young recruits preparing to be sent to the front in the fine art of field medicine. The goal of the medic under hostile fire was simple: stop the bleeding at all costs while keeping the casualty breathing. Considering the 90% of combat deaths occurred from hemorrhaging and airway complications, Lorelei knew that her job could save thousands of lives. She and Paul didn't see each other as much as they would have wished. Although their schedules rarely intersected, they spent their free-time drinking a lot of coffee—together.

Grace, along with Dorris, disappeared on the airfield day in and day out. I had no idea what went into teaching pilots how to fly, and Grace didn't bother to explain.

The first week, Katrine spent her mornings at the War Office petitioning for some sort of information regarding Harry. Finally, the secretary told Katrine to stop coming. There was no news to tell her and most likely there wouldn't be for a while. They would let her know as soon as they heard anything. There were thousands of men like Harry. The Pacific was a floating wasteland of lost men, dead and alive. She'd taken up reading and staring listlessly into space or walking with me through Townsville as I took photographs of American soldiers eating shaved ice on the beach and kangaroos on the side of the road.

Horatio and Captain Dana were right. Our new assignments were not as glamorous as traveling with the show. No false eyelashes. No sequins or grass skirts. No clandestine secret missions. But at least we were all doing something, and that was, well, something. There was plenty to do to keep us busy, if not exactly interested. For instance, Edie, Katrine, and I volunteered several afternoons a week at the Red Cross Club, frying up donuts and serving buckets of coffee to soldiers needing a good time and friendly conversation, though it was Edie who did the conversation while Katrine and I stuck to pouring coffee. The Club, right on the harbor, welcomed the incoming troopships and saw the men off when they were shipped to the field. A donut and coffee at those times seemed the ultimate reminder of what we were fighting for: truth, freedom, and the American (or Australian) way.

And on the days when we had nothing to do, we sat in the big front room of the Queenslander and tried to entertain ourselves with the radio or reading or what have you.

It was on such a Friday that Edie returned from the post office just before lunch; her eyes red and her cheeks moist. She wore a straight brown skirt and crimson silk blouse that made her hair and eyes look that much redder. In her hand was a letter from my mother and a photograph of the children she'd included in the envelope.

Willem and Raffi stared into the lens, pensive and unusually sensitive. Willem held Anna on his back. She was nearly eight years old, playful eyes sparkling and a laugh escaping her lips. Agatha, the baby of the group at three, peddled on a tricycle out in front of the others. Apparently, chickenpox had swept the house. All four children at once. But they all came through unscathed and none the worse for wear. My father had certainly had his hands full. The pesky pox had assaulted the entire children's population of Kingsbarns.

"Your mother says she loves you," Edie said. "She says," she cleared her throat slightly, *"Though the end of this war delays, Agatha darling, wait for it. We will be together again before you know it."* She looked up. "That's just like Rose, isn't it? Taking the Bible and putting it into everyday language."

Katrine, sitting near the window and reading, pushed her dark hair away from her neck momentarily and looked up. "What was in the Bible?"

"I'll need to look it up. Wait a second." A moment later, I returned from my room, pocket Bible in hand. Quickly, I paged through. I was pretty sure it was in Isaiah. No wait, the verse was in Habakkuk. Ah. There it was. "For the revelation awaits an appointed time; it speaks of the end and will not prove false. Though it lingers, wait for it, it will certainly come and will not delay."[14]

"What does it mean? What won't delay?" Katrine asked.

I looked up. "God promised the prophet Habakkuk that the suffering of his people would not last forever. It would end. And at the end, God promises to gather his people to himself. And in the meantime," I spoke to myself more than Katrine, "we have to be... content."

"Too bad God's promises don't come true anymore. At least not quickly enough for me. By the time this war is over, there may be none of us left to keep promises to."

"Tut, tut," Edie scolded softly. "They do come true, whether or not you agree. I'll give you this though, God's timing often feels a little slower than what we would prefer. But he knows best!"

Katrine shook her head. "Edie, we've been here for a month. I'm no closer to finding Harry than I was when I came. I keep hitting wall after wall. That War Office secretary's pitying expressions are becoming unbearable."

"If there is *one* thing I've learned, it is to trust and hope in the timing of God. Wait for it." Edie paused and put her hand to her forehead. "What I need is work! Something to get my mind off of my circumstances."

Looking at me, she added, "Where's that notebook from your birthday? I want to see the notes from the interviews you did on Alu."

Curiously, I opened the bottom desk drawer and gave her the notebook.

Edie began scanning the notes of each of the interviews. "I think you should start with this young man." Her long ring fingernail pointed to a name. "His story is riveting, and he came face to face with a troop of Japanese on Guadalcanal and made it out. Remember, Piper dear, a writer must give her readers hope. The world is a cruel and harsh place. It's hopeless enough as it is."

"What am I starting with?"

"Your future column! For Don! This is perfect material. Don't you see it?"

(I had no lofty aspirations for a column, no matter what Edie imagined I was capable of. But there was no stopping Edie when she had something in her head.)

"I'm not sure all these stories are very hopeful," Katrine commented after listening in.

"Really, Katrine!" Edie glanced up. "You know the rule. 'If you have nothing nice to say then don't say anything at all.'"

Katrine rolled her eyes, and I braced myself.

"These are the stories of survivors. That word, 'survivor' is the very definition of hope! It says, these men are forging ahead after everything they've seen. After eating little handfuls of rice for days on end in Japanese prison camps and marching barefoot in sand, wearing nothing but loincloths, escaping into the jungle only to eat rats and sleep in bark huts. These men prove hope is never wasted. I'm sure it's what kept and keeps many of them alive!"

I stifled a groan as Edie continued her monologue. "And if they can go on after jungle fevers and long separations from loved ones..." She began to carefully rip the pages out of the notebook, "then so can we!"

"Whatever are you doing?" Katrine gasped, horrified. I was too shocked to say anything at all.

"I told you," she took the next section of paper and began to rip, "I'm helping Piper get organized for her new column. I need something to do. We all need something to do. We can't just sit around and wait for this war to end." She looked over the wall pensively. "I know you have raw talent, but you sometimes leave out the essentials. It is absolutely imperative to use adverbs and lots of them. People like them. It makes them feel comforted."

Now, she took the interviews, separated them by name, and pinned them on the wall. "We'll work our way down the list, elaborating where necessary, cutting out the fat. Knowing when to add and when to take away is the mark of a true writer." Looking back towards me, she said, "You have the film of all these young men's portraits in a safe place, don't you?"

Nodding my head yes, I pointed to my camera bag. "All safe and sound." The portraits of the soldiers were, though undeveloped, what I considered to be my best work. They had a grown-up quality, gritty and raw. They were the work of a real wartime photographer. Secretly, I hoped they were good enough to get me a promotion or, at the very least, a raise. I'd been waiting to develop them until I had a proper dark room. A bathroom simply wouldn't cut it this time around.

"Good. We'll develop them as soon as we can and put each man's photograph by the interview. It will inspire emotion as you write. Then, we'll send Don the first batch and propose the project as a weekly serial?" she continued excitedly, "We'll send them along with your first roll of shots from Townsville."

I thought about my first roll. A kangaroo on the side of the road. An Australian soldier hoisting a flag on the beach. A crocodile sunning himself on a rock. As excited as Don was about having me on 'the front,' I worried he would fire me once he realized how boring 'the front' of Townsville was.

"How does that sound?" Edie's voice drew my attention back to the project at hand.

At that moment, Lorelei wandered in and sat down in one of the armchairs near the bookshelf that was filled with silly novels and cheap magazines. Obviously, whoever had stayed in the house before us was not a lover of tasteful literature. She was barefoot, and her hair hung down almost to the waist of her light blue pleated cotton skirt and white blouse. It was very thick and healthy. She'd had the night shift the evening before and had only just woken up.

"Sure is quiet around here." Lorelei scanned the bookshelf. "Is Grace coming back for lunch or staying on the base again?"

"I'm coming back for lunch!" Grace said as the front door slammed shut, and we all looked at her expectantly as she entered the study after loudly dropping her purse on the floor.

"Hi," Lorelei said, barely moving.

"Hi yourself." Grace kicked off her loafers and sat down on top of the desk, her legs swinging back and forth. Grace's collar to her white blouse was turned up just around her neck. Her slacks were fashionably high-waisted, with sailor style buttons on the right and left hip. "I invited Dorris back here for lunch, but she had a date." She looked towards the kitchen.

"Dorris certainly goes out a lot." Lorelei was wary of Dorris. We all were really—and we made no attempt to hide it.

"You have no idea. She is the craziest, wildest girl I've ever met." Grace paused, contemplating whether or not she should say more. "But she's a great pilot. Excellent instincts."

"She and her mother don't seem to get along." Edie frowned. "You should hear Bee go on. Makes my knees shake when I think of my children reaching her age. Motherhood is very difficult."

"Her mother wanted her to be a debutante or something, but Dorris wouldn't have any of it."

"How old is she?" I asked, knowing that Grace looked up to the daring Dorris. The two women had become fast friends and seemed to spend every waking hour together unless Dorris was on a date with another new beau, which was often. They were like two wild horses, straining at the bit.

"She's 29. Just a few years older than me." Grace flexed her hands. She had dark circles under her eyes. I hadn't realized how tired she looked until now.

Edie shook her head. "And she's still single?"

"She couldn't do her job otherwise, and it really is very important! She used to work at Avenger Field in Sweetwater, Texas. It's the only all-female base in the U.S. Army Air Force. She trained the fresh recruits on the new planes. The women pilots fly them to bases and carriers all over the country. They get to test new aircraft and all sorts of things. She loved it." Grace inhaled and looked out the window.

"If she loved it so much, why did she leave?" Edie asked.

"Her parents wanted her away from the base for a while," she said slowly, carefully considering her words. "I'm not sure why. I think there was a boy she was seeing they didn't approve of. Her dad pulled some strings for her to come along on leave and give some instruction on the new plane on the side."

"She was one of the first test pilots to fly this new plane. But now…" Grace grimaced. "Now, they only want her to do classroom instruction. We can't even go up with the pilots, much less fly ourselves. The flyers down here feel superstitious about having a woman in the cockpit."

"That's too bad," Lorelei said.

"We both miss flying."

"I'm sure it relieves her mother to have her safe on the ground." Edie turned back to my notebook.

With a swift motion, Grace jumped off the desk and chuckled, "Dorris said the first month Avenger Field opened, over 100 men pilots made 'emergency' landings at the field. Obviously, some of them were landing with ulterior motives."

"Who's the lucky boy she's out with today?" Edie looked at Grace out of the corner of her eye.

"Frank."

"Frank!" Katrine exclaimed, surprised.

"Yes, Frank." Grace lifted her shoulders a little and tossed her hair behind her back.

Edie tried to smile. "Good for Frank, I guess. She's an interesting girl—even if I don't approve of her attitude."

Lorelei diverted the situation and exclaimed, "Oh! Before I forget, don't expect me to be home tomorrow afternoon."

"Taking an extra shift?" I asked.

Cheeks turning pink, Lorelei explained, "Paul offered to give me a guitar lesson. We've been drinking so much coffee, he said he needs a break."

"Oh?" Edie clapped her hands together, forgetting Grace's and Dorris's attitudes. "I knew it! Oh, congratulations, dear!"

"Congratulations for what?" Lorelei's cheeks went from pink to red.

Edie looked at her with an all-knowing air. "For securing one of the best men on the Australian continent. If I'd known, we would have invited you both to Magnetic Island with us on our double date tomorrow." She looked at me a winked. "It would have been a triple date."

Lorelei nervously twisted her hair away from her neck. "What do you mean *securing*? It's just a guitar lesson, Edie!"

"Yes, and I'm just a piano leg."

We all looked at Edie, completely confused.

"All right, so it's not a completely stable metaphor. You know what I'm talking about!" She stood up and marched to the kitchen. "I'm making sandwiches. Who's hungry?"

CHAPTER 31

DAYTRIPPERS

*P*eter propped himself up on his elbows. "They say, this rock is the westernmost part of the western world. Anything further, and we are officially in the east."

"They really say that?" Facing him, I smiled. It was wonderful being with him like this. "We are on the edge of the world?"

"The edge of the western world." Coke in hand, and Peter beside me, I was happier than I had been in ages. The boat ride over to Magnetic Island had been magical. Not a cloud in the sky and a magnificent swell. And then, we had taken the bus, the only one on the island, to a tiny seafood shack right on the water. After lunch, we had hiked up the fort—which wasn't a fort at all but a rather unusual rock formation—which was where we were now, looking out over the ocean.

"A double date is almost as romantic as a regular date." I sighed as I glanced over at the neighboring picnic blanket Edie and Horatio sat on before looking back at Peter. "Edie was desperate for some fun. I wanted to get her mind off of… things. And you know how rare it is for Horatio and you to actually get a day off—on the same day, that is. I hope you don't mind."

Peter grinned at me in response.

A minute later, I asked, "Why do they call it 'Magnetic Island' anyway?" I balanced my Coke carefully on the rock.

A gentle gust of wind caused my hair to whip about my face. It was deliciously cool and clean.

Peter responded, "The legend is that the island had a curious 'magnetic' effect on Captain Cook's compass as he sailed up the Australian coast in the 1770s." He turned over on his back and stared at the sky.

Behind us, we could hear a handful of fishermen untangling their nets on the shore lined with a few small huts and one tiny resort up the beach. The island had been relegated to vacationers and fishermen.

However, since the start of the war, it had become an important defensive military base. A plane droned overhead, and the sound of diesel engines carrying supplies up the hill to the base rumbled in the distance. It seemed that no matter where you were in the world these days, nowhere was safe from the sounds of war. You couldn't escape it. Anywhere. Not even the edge of the world.

"Peter," I turned over and looked up at the sky beside him, "this has been the most lovely day."

"We didn't really do anything."

"I think that's what made it so nice." With a sigh of content, I continued, "I don't remember the last time I spent nearly a whole day doing nothing, with no worries at all."

The sun beat down, and my state of near-perfect happiness had a drowsy effect.

The next thing I knew, Peter was gently shaking me awake. "It's time to go, Piper. We've got to catch the ferry back to Townsville."

"Why can't we stay here on this rock forever?" I groaned.

"It's just not practical," he chuckled and helped me sit up slowly.

"Where's Edie and Horatio?"

He jerked his head towards the beach. I saw their silhouettes walking in the water up to their calves. I stood up and brushed my hair back with my fingers, slung my camera bag over my shoulder, and carefully followed Peter down the boulders, neither of us speaking until we'd reached the sand.

Then, we took off jogging towards Edie and Horatio. When we reached them, I noticed that Edie had a fresh slew of freckles on her nose. Her dress, a light linen one with big wooden buttons and a squared neckline, was quite becoming. And Horatio, wearing his pants rolled up and a simple white T-shirt, looked so carefree and happy. The two of them, framed by a handful of palm trees and light from the sun, made a stunning scene.

"Stop just there!" I said, quickly grabbing my camera out of the bag and taking the lens cap off. I had to get the frame just right. Hmm... I needed to get further back. I kicked my shoes off and carefully waded in. Camera in one hand, my skirt held up as high as I could without being immodest, I moved back into the water.

"Let me hold the camera bag," Peter offered, but I shooed him off. It would only take a second.

Looking through the lens, I frowned. It still wasn't right. I backed up a bit more and felt the warm water nip at the back of my knees.

"Don't smile, Horatio!" I shouted. "You always look tense when you 'try' to smile. There, that's right. Natural!"

"Piper! Your dress!" Edie shouted. "The tide is coming in!"

"Don't move, Edie!"

"No!" Peter shouted. "Piper, don't go back any further! The water!"

It was too late. Suddenly a wave rushed in all around me. Instinctively, I held the camera and my camera bag aloft. My drenched skirt, clinging to my legs, was rough and uncomfortable.

"I got the shot! That's all that matters!" I shouted, triumphantly slogging my way towards them, realizing suddenly how far out I had gone. The wave rushed back out and met another at my back, spraying foam everywhere.

I saw Peter rushing towards me, his eyes wide. "Piper!"

Before I had time to respond, an enormous wave came up behind me and pushed me down. My camera slipped out of my hands and my mouth filled with water. I tumbled around for a few seconds (that seemed an eternity) and then, rough sand and sharp rocks met my hands. The wave abated, and I pushed myself up on all fours, eyes burning and breath sputtering. Peter's strong hands grabbed my arms and pulled me up. "Are you okay?" he asked, worried.

I leaned on his arm and straightened up. Nodding that I was fine, my eyes frantically searched for my camera. "It's gone!" I moaned. "I can't believe it! This is horrible! Completely horrible! What will I do without my camera!"

Peter and I both began to look in the dark water swirling around us. We both knew it was futile. My camera was lost, forever.

Stomping through the water, feeling utterly dejected and shivering, we met our aunt and uncle.

"You took quite a tumble, my girl." Horatio's accent seemed stronger than ever. "Are you hurt at all?"

I didn't answer him. My hands were on my camera bag, still slung over my shoulder. A terrible, sinking feeling came over me. I had left the bag open... It was supposed to just be a simple, quick shot. The bag had filled with water. All my film from Alu, all my photographs, my prize-winning photographs, had floated out to sea or were soaked with salt water and sand. I hung my head in my hands. "You have to be kidding me," I moaned.

"Look on the bright side," Peter tried to lighten the mood, "it could be you floating out there."

"Peter!"

"I'm sorry, I'm sorry." He put his arm around me. "I know how much work you put into that project."

Edie was squeezing the water out of my skirt. "We'll think of something. Maybe the film you have left is salvageable?" Even as she said it, we both knew it wasn't true. Saltwater, sand, and delicate film do not mix. I turned my bag over and a splash of water hit the ground.

Edie stared at it. "You'll just have to write the story without pictures."

"But the photographs were the whole point!" I tried to hold back tears.

Sitting on the bus driving towards the ferry, my dress full of sand only grew stiffer as it dried. Edie turned around from her seat in front of me. "No doubt, some great creative good is going to come of this."

I frowned. "How can I be creative without my camera?"

"Necessity is the mother of invention." She craned her neck even further around.

Peter patted my hand. "You heard the woman, necessity is the mother of invention."

Rolling my eyes, I brushed dried sand from my neck. It was everywhere. I itched terribly. In my expert opinion, there was only one thing to do.

Mope.

The camera was replaceable; it was true. Peter had already assured me we would buy another as soon as he could find a suitable replacement. But my photographs were lost forever, and that deserved a solid period of mourning. It was depressing. And no matter what Aunt Edie said, I couldn't even vaguely see what sort of invention the loss of my photographs could ever necessitate.

"What is that?" Peter pressed his face up against the dirty window of the old rambling bus. "'State Home for Half-Caste Children?'" He was confused. "What is a half-caste?"

I looked out the window and saw the sign hung above a chain-link fence. Behind the fence were several rough huts, a playground, and a handful of children running around barefoot.

An older man sitting behind us answered, "Don't you Yanks know anything? You've got half-castes in your country. Half-Indian, half white."

"We prefer to call them Americans." Peter smiled thinly.

The old man snickered. "Hasn't always been the case. I've been to America."

"So," Peter narrowed his eyes and looked back at the sign, "is it some sort of orphanage?"

He shook his head. "Nothing of the sort. His Majesty's Royal Government enforces a policy of assimilation. These kids are half-black and half-white." I knew this was Australian for Aborigine and European. "The blacks," he continued, "will die out. They are inferior to whites. The children are taken from their mothers and put into good institutions to breed the black out."[15]

Looking back at the 'institution,' I couldn't make out anything about it that seemed 'good.' It was dirty, almost derelict. I saw a priest on the grounds and wondered if it was a Church institution or a government one.

"*Breed* the black out?" My aunt turned around in her seat, her jaw open in horrified shock.

"Sure. It's better for them to learn the white culture and language." The man's accent was so heavy I had trouble understanding him.

I blinked several times, remembering vaguely what Chito had said not long ago. *"I spent my childhood in a government-run school where they forced me to speak English and punished me for speaking Choctaw."* I wondered if his school was like the one we'd just passed.

Edie's cheeks reddened. "Why, that is the most awful thing I've ever heard!"

The man shrugged. "As I said, you Americans have done the same thing. Why you only stopped a few years ago."

Edie turned back around in her seat. I could feel the tension emanating from her shoulders. "Well, at least we don't do it anymore... I think." She looked at Horatio. "Right dear?"

Horatio frowned.

"You mean those children were taken from their families?" I asked, all thoughts of my camera gone.

The man nodded and mumbled, "Dumb Yanks," and now finished with the conversation, he pulled his hat down over his eyes and leaned back in his seat murmuring, "know nothing about their own country."

Peter looked out the window and shook his head sadly. "The Nazis think the Jews are inferior. I know there are lots of Americans who think people with darker skin are inferior. I mean, look at the South. In some states, they can't drink from the same water fountain. And here? The Aborigines aren't even considered citizens." He swallowed. "And we think we are so much better than the Nazis."

"Peter," Horatio turned around sharply, his tone ominously serious, "we are not systematically murdering anyone with gas. I'm not saying we are not racially prejudiced. Every nation, every people will find something to make them feel superior to some other nation or people. But we are *not* like the Nazis."

"Sure," he answered cynically, his voice imitating the Australian's lilting speech. "We are breeding out the black slowly, letting the natives die out naturally."

"That's enough, Peter!" Horatio was stern. "That's not us, that's the Australian government."

I could tell Peter was not convinced, and neither was I. "I can't believe you!" Peter said angrily. "How can you be so passive?"

Edie sat up straighter, pushing past Peter's accusatory stare at her husband. "I don't care who's government it is. I find this news shocking to my core, and I think we ought to do something about it. Horatio, I want you to bring this up with the Admiralty."

Horatio exhaled a defeated sigh. "Edie, the Admiralty knows. All the higher-ups know. Your government has had similar policies with the Native Americans. Why it was only in 1938 that it became illegal to remove native children from their homes and 'Anglify' them — in the States, that is."

"Is that so?" Edie was aghast. "Only six years ago?"

"How do you know all this, Uncle Horatio?" Peter asked, surprised.

Horatio's voice became pained. "Because I found the whole business so sickening when we arrived in Australia, I did my research. I couldn't believe the talk on the base regarding the Aborigines. I've been at sea for a long time. I had forgotten how cruel and base men on land can be. On the sea, we measure a man for his ability to work hard and make wise decisions, skin color is irrelevant. I've discovered, or rather, been forced to remember, that is not always the case on land." He looked at his nephew. "Oh, believe me, my boy, if I could change it, I would. But it will take the whole country rising up to end the evils going on here. And prayer."

The two men locked eyes. They were not so dissimilar after all. Both saw the problem. Neither had the power on their own to fix it. It was frustrating, painful, and humbling.

"If you ask me," Edie sniffed, "it will take the whole civilized world to rise up and end all this insanity. Nobody likes anybody anymore! Where are the good ol' days when we all got along?"

"Those days never existed, my dear." Horatio patted her leg and smiled sadly. "That is, after the Fall."

"No," she shook her head sadly, "I suppose they never did."

I WAS STILL SLIGHTLY damp and depressed by the time we arrived back at the house. Peter kissed my cheek as we came inside, and Edie said, "How about I run you a bath?"

"I think I'll probably need three or four baths before I get all the sand out of my hair!"

Horatio scratched his chin. "Maybe we ought to hose you off outside first. All that sand could clog the pipes in the old place."

Edie nodded. "I'm afraid he's right."

I turned on my heel and retreated outside to the front yard and went for the garden hose. Turning it on full force, I began to spray my feet and then my neck and face.

"Whatever are you doing, Piper! Showering outdoors nowadays?"

Eyelashes dripping wet, I turned and saw Lorelei.

"No." I shut the hose off. "A killer wave attacked. It took off with my camera and my film, and it nearly took off with me too." I shook my hair and water droplets rolled off. My career as a 'photographer on the front' had ground to a halt before it had even begun. Everything about the last few months had turned out so differently than I had expected. Nothing was working out the way I'd planned.

"Other than that, it was practically perfect." I sat down on the steps leading to the front door, and she sat beside me. "How about you? Have a nice lesson?"

Shyly, she nodded yes. I shifted to see her face head on. There was an indiscernible expression on it. A sort of question in her eyes. Being a photographer had made me a good judge of facial expressions. At least, that's what Edie told me.

"Did more happen than just a music lesson?"

She nodded once more. "To be honest, we talked nearly the whole time. Well, he talked."

"How long?"

"Three hours."

Three hours? That was quite a long time to talk to anybody.

"What did he talk about?"

"Everything. His grandfather's ranch. His mother's garden in Pasadena. His surfing stories from Southern California."

"Interesting." My eyes narrowed.

"To be honest, he's the most brilliant man I've ever met. And he's handsome too, isn't he?" She looked at me searchingly.

"You know the answer to that!"

I saw her hesitate.

"What is it?"

"In all those hours together, in all our coffee dates, he never really asks about my past. It's like he doesn't want to know about my family or what happened. I'll bring it up, and he'll bring up something else."

"Is that a red flag?"

She shrugged and tried to laugh. "I just wish..." she looked at her hands. "I just wish I knew what to do. I don't want to make a mistake. Sometimes, when I'm with him, I can barely think. He makes me laugh so hard... I think he's in love with me."

"Is that so bad?"

"I guess not." She smiled. "He is a good man, Piper. Better than I could have imagined a man to be. But he's moving so fast, and that scares me."

"Why?" I pressed.

"Because," she tried to come up with the words, "because I'm scared to make a mistake because I'm not myself. I'm not thinking clearly."

"Why in the world would you not be thinking clearly?"

"Because," she paused, taking a breath as though bracing herself, "I think I'm falling in love with him too."

SEPTEMBER PASSED TO OCTOBER, and October turned into November. On this side of the equator, the heat increased in full form. Frank, as a civilian, remained in one of the back bedrooms of the Queenslander when he wasn't at the Pigeon coop on duty. Peter logged the number of canned beans and boots and packs of chewing gum that entered and left the base. I served soldiers donuts and coffee nearly every day now that I no longer had a camera. Lorelei's guitar lessons grew longer. Grace was rarely home. Thanksgiving, the real one, came and went with a beach barbecue, much to Edie's chagrin. December was days away, and still, Katrine had no word regarding Harry.

The War Office could not tell Katrine where his location was because, at that moment, they did not know the answer. If they had known, they would have told her news she'd never have wanted to hear: Harry was, hands blistered and back aching, lugging yet another stack of wood, under the watchful eye of the Japanese POW guards.

The plans for escape had been in motion for days. And out of the corner of his eye, he saw Roy sneak out of the line and dart between boxes of supplies. He heard a shrill whistle. It was the signal.

He passed a load of logs to Claude, who worked beside him, sweating like a pig. "You ready, kid?"

The men had taken to wearing a sort of loincloth, their uniforms long since disintegrated due to the climate. Nodding, Claude took Harry's place.

Harry was supposed to meet Roy on his return, take the single stick of dynamite, and hide it in his makeshift shorts. This would be repeated for several days until they had a solid supply.

Once enough dynamite had been gathered, they would blow up the radio tower that was nearing completion near the airfield.

Claude's grip, weakened by fear, faltered, and he dropped the stack of wood with a staggering clash on the rocks below. The guards, startled, dropped their lunch boxes and moved towards them. One began shouting at Claude to pick the wood up. Claude wasn't moving fast enough, and the guard was about to bring his rifle down on Claude's head. Harry didn't know what to do. Terrified they'd notice the dynamite Roy had just smuggled, he stepped in between them and shouted for the guard to leave Claude alone, not thinking of the consequences.

In horror, Roy, from behind a boulder, and Claude, cowering on the ground, watched as Harry put his hands over his head to protect himself from the rifle's impact. But it was too late. With an awful thud, the butt of the rifle collided with Harry's skull, and he lay on the ground, head bleeding.

When Harry awoke, he was in The Hole.

For twenty-one days, he cooked in the tin oven. Miraculously, he did not die, but he was feverish and yellow and was skin and bones by the time of his release.

Major Canning hovered over him in the barrack like a mother hen. "You took one for the team, Harry."

Harry's breathing was labored and slow. "So, have you decided when we blow up the tower?"

Claude and Major Canning glanced at one another. Sadly, the Major shook his head. "Roy got caught, Harry. He's... gone." He didn't have to say he had been murdered. It was stating the obvious. "Two days after they threw you in the hole. We've pushed the plan back... till we can regroup."

Harry sensed the man's defeat.

"How long was I in there?" Harry's eyes fluttered open. He had lost track of time. Day and night blended together in The Hole. Dreams of Katrine and New York, of Palestine, of dogs barking and grains of rice came and went, and sometimes he was sure he was going crazy. He tried to sit up, but dizziness overtook him, and he quit.

"Three weeks."

"Long time, eh, Major?"

Major Canning nodded. Most men didn't make it that long in The Hole.

Claude pulled two pills out of his pocket and stuffed them into Harry's hand. "Got these from a box from the Red Cross. Take em, Harry. I think it's Penicillin."

"They delivered the Red Cross boxes?"

"Nah. I bribed a guy who saved a stash from the last delivery six months ago. I think that's the last of it."

"What'd you bribe him with?"

"Don't ask." Claude pressed something else into Harry's hand. It was Katrine's photograph. "I kept it safe."

"You are a brave kid." Harry stared at the picture. It felt like a dream—when he and Katrine were together. A part of him wondered if it had been a dream. He was so feverish, he struggled to remember what was real and what wasn't.

"You got any water?" Harry asked. His throat burned, and his skin hurt. He felt boils on the backs of his legs.

"I'll try to find you some," Claude said. "We'll get you up and at em' again."

When the young man was out of earshot, Major Canning sat down wearily next to Harry. "That young man owes you his life. Twice over, or so he tells me."

Harry, ill as he was, could sense the Major's sadness.

"Are you all right, sir?"

"I… I am praying to God that we make it out of here alive."

"You are a praying man?" Harry asked.

"I am indeed. And I am convinced that prayer is the only way we are going home, Harry."

CHAPTER 32

THE WEE SMALL HOURS OF THE MORNING

*I*t was 4:30 in the morning when Katrine found me in the kitchen drinking a glass of water. It appeared to have been a restless night for her too. Nervously, she looked out the window. "She's still not home."

"Worried about Grace?" I asked.

She jerked her head up and down. "Ever since Harry disappeared, well, I've had to know where everyone else is at all times. I mean, Lorelei and Grace specifically. Lorelei is in bed, right where she is supposed to be. But Grace is who-knows-where!"

Katrine looked exceptionally tired. Given how often Grace was gone, I supposed she must be exhausted.

"Would you," she looked at me, "wait up with me? I made coffee a half hour ago. It's probably still hot."

"No," I shook my head, putting my empty water glass on the counter. "No coffee for me. But I'm happy to wait up with you if you want."

"I don't want to be alone right now." Anxiously, she moved from the kitchen to the living room, looking out the window once more before sitting down in the armchair beside it. Folding her fingers together and resting her head on her hands, she shut her eyes.

Gently, I eased onto the couch and watched her, wondering what was going through her mind. She was afraid to be alone, that was clear. Whatever plagued her thoughts was more than Grace's absence.

Several moments passed in silence, and I braced myself for what was coming.

"Everything I've ever loved has been taken from me, Piper."

"That's not totally true, Katrine."

"It feels true. I watch Paul waltz in, whisking Lorelei off her feet, even if she won't admit it. Love only lasts so long. And then," she snapped her fingers, "it's gone. Just like that, in the blink of an eye. He's not even Jewish."

Choosing to ignore that last statement, I backed up a bit. "Katrine," I chided her gently, "that's a terrible way to look at the world. A terrible way to look at life!"

"It's my experience, Piper. Things don't work out for the Adlemans. We are destined to live alone. Look at Grace… Look at me… Even Lorelei! Look at us! Running around the world, looking for somewhere safe to just live! God has not seen us. He doesn't care. If he did, he would fix this." She motioned at nothing in particular with her hand. Her eyes were bright with deep anger and bitterness. "All day, every day, doing whatever it is we are doing…" She continued her ramble, saying, "It's all so pointless. We wake up. We eat breakfast. We run errands. I'm so sick of it all! All of this pain I feel — It's so awful I sometimes don't understand why I was born. What's the point of life if all there is hurt and broken dreams?"

I bit my tongue. So this is what had been ruminating in that big brain of hers all these weeks. She was too wrapped up in her pain and loneliness to trust that maybe God was working on her behalf. I watched her, a sinking ship on a stormy sea refusing to steer towards the light of the shore.

Out of nowhere, I heard myself say, "In this world, you will have trouble. But take heart! I have overcome the world."[16]

"What?"

"Those are the words of Jesus, Yeshua - the one Lorelei and I and my parents and Edie and Horatio all believe is the Messiah."

She arched her eyebrow. "I don't see what that has to do with anything."

"Don't you see? With Jesus, we can walk through the worst that the world throws at us and come through it as better people. He tells us not to be surprised by trouble but to let it refine us, to prove our faith. And then, he promises to wipe away every tear from our eyes. He is the God of all comfort in the midst of the worst pain."

"Well, I don't feel his comfort."

"Because you don't know him."

"How can you *know* him?"

"You are a good student, Katrine. I would say… start studying. Learn everything you can about him. You want evidence? It's out there. But it's up to you to find it."

She stared at me, wide-eyed. "Piper, you are a much bolder girl than I took you for. I underestimated you."

The sound of the front door opened, and Grace's quiet steps tiptoed down the hall. At the sight of Katrine and I in the study, she stopped. No one spoke.

Katrine stood up after a second, the air thick with tension. "I've been up all night, laying in bed, staring at the ceiling."

"You didn't have to wait up."

"No? My baby sister out on the streets of Townsville, the literal *end* of the civilized world, with thousands of soldiers prowling around? Out with Dorris, who I wouldn't trust to babysit my pet hamster! Zi iz meshuge!"

"What?" I asked.

"She's crazy! Dorris is crazy!"

"I wasn't out with Dorris," Grace mumbled.

It was then that I realized Grace's eyes were red. She had been crying.

"I mean," she stopped, "I was with Dorris for part the first part of the evening. But my date was boring, and I didn't want to see *Lassie Come Home*."

"Dorris wanted to go see *Lassie Come Home?*"

"No," she sighed, "she wanted to see *Girl Crazy*, some dumb musical about 'college kids in Codyville.' I saw it last year. Both of the films were old reels."[18]

"Sounds riveting," Katrine said through a clenched smile. "So, you didn't see a movie about a dog or singing coeds. What did you see?"

"My date wanted to watch 'The Wolfman.' I made it through the first scene and then slipped out." Grace was unfazed by Katrine's harsh tone. "Look, I... I went to the post office to pick up the mail. You remember how I was supposed to bring back the mail?" She pulled a letter out of the pocket of her light sweater.

Katrine looked at the letter. It was bent and dirtied and looked like it had been through the wringer.

"Who is it from?" I asked carefully, as my speech to tell Grace never to stay out so late again was instantly forgotten.

"Dafna."

I knew that name. Amos's sister.

"She had no idea where we were, so she wrote Becky in Cairo. And Becky forwarded it to me."

I took the letter out of her hands and unfolded it. "It's dated July 1944. We are in *December*." We all knew how unreliable the post was these days. It was not uncommon to get letters months after they had been posted.

My eyes scanned the letter. Dafna, in a square, clear script, wanted Grace to know that Amos had been taken captive by the Germans on the Russian Front. No one had heard anything from him in months. I passed it to Katrine who also read it quickly.

Katrine sat back down slowly as Grace spoke. "So, I read it once.

Then again. And I walked, and I walked, and I walked. I found myself in a bar, and I drank a cup of tea, and I wondered why she had written to me. I wondered if she thought it was my fault—because Amos left for the Russian Front because of me. I wondered a lot."

Grace's face had a strange, faraway look.

"I'm sorry Dafna told you," Katrine said.

"I'm not." Grace took the letter back. "I needed to know. He was my best friend."

"What are you going to do?" Katrine asked, her voice dropping.

Grace shrugged. "I don't know yet. But I will not sit around here and do nothing, I'll tell you that."

Katrine looked as though Grace had slapped her. "Sometimes, that's all anyone can do."

"I am not *anyone*. Look, Katrine, to be honest, it *is* my fault that Amos left. I blame myself for this."

"You can't blame yourself, Grace," I protested.

"I do. And I will fix it, mark my words. I will fix it if I die trying. I will bring Amos back alive."

"You can't do that! You're not even with the RAF anymore. You're upset and talking nonsense. And above that, I forbid you to do or even think anything of the sort!" Katrine's voice trembled.

Undeterred, Grace continued, "He has to know I... Nevermind. Katrine, you don't understand. Besides, I know he would do the same for me."

"You can't do anything!" Katrine was speaking more quickly now. "Amos is somewhere in Europe, probably in some concentration camp!"

"I know that." Grace's voice was level and calm, but her eyes held a strange, concerning tension.

The room began to fill with that early morning pure white light, and I began to feel that lightheaded feeling that comes with staying up all night.

The front door opened and slammed shut as Frank clomped into

317

the house. He marched down the hall and stopped in the opening to the study, stunned to see Katrine, Grace, and me standing there.

He paused, his hair messy, his eyes tired, and in his hand, a birdcage with a pigeon in it.

"No one invited me to the slumber party," he said, yawning. "Where's Lorelei?"

"In bed," Katrine spat. "Where we all should be."

"What is that?" I pointed at the bird.

"It's a bird."

"I can see that! But what is it doing here?"

"*Its* name is Nina," he started, sounding offended, "and she broke her wing last night in a little fight she got into with one of the other feathered recruits. She's been put into solitary confinement."

I noticed that one of Nina's wings was in a splint.

"But why isn't she in solitary at the base?" Katrine pressed as Nina made gentle cooing sounds.

"It's better Nina gets some good TLC from you ladies. She's an older bird." Frank smiled. "I think they were going to put her down. I thought you girls might..." He looked hopefully at Katrine.

"You mean, you brought Nina here permanently?" Katrine's eyes bugged out of her head.

"Frank," I said carefully, "I don't think it's a good idea to keep a bird in the house."

"I'm a good person. I could never leave a wounded bird with the guy on duty. Trust me. He's a redneck with no sensitivity." Frank put Nina's cage on a small stool. "Nina needs you ladies."

"I'm going to bed now. Please, don't wake me till noon," Katrine blurted out, brushing past us. The bird was too much for her to handle. She was finished for the night.

"I should go to sleep too," Grace said. "I have a lot to do tomorrow—I mean, today. I'm going with Dorris back to the airfield in a couple of hours. She's offered to give me a crash course on engine repair."

"Tomorrow evening we are racing some of our top birds. You

are all invited to come and watch—friends and family only," Frank said.

"Can Dorris come?" Grace asked.

He shrugged. "I guess so." (I found his ambivalence towards Dorris unusual given that the two had eaten lunch alone not that long ago. I'd honestly thought they were dating.)

Grace nodded. "She can't stand being at home in the evenings. Her mother and everything…"

"Her mother struck me as a difficult personality, but I'm sure she loves Dorris very much," I said.

"Oh, Dorris doesn't doubt that. It's just a smothering sort of love. Her mother doesn't understand her." She turned around. "I'm sure she'll appreciate a change of scenery. All that dating is getting to her. And me too." She paused. "On second thought, I think I'll take a walk. It's too late to go back to bed. I might as well just stay up."

"But you walked all night!" I exclaimed.

She was already out the door.

"That is one restless girl," Frank said as Nina rustled in her cage. "Kind of like you, right, Nina baby?" He leaned over and looked the pigeon in the eye. "A caged bird is an awful thing, but sometimes it's necessary to heal. You've got to stay put, kiddo."

"Are you okay, Frank?"

He put his hand on the cage, listening as the pigeon cooed. "Did Lorelei and Paul spend the evening together again for another guitar lesson?"

I nodded.

"Frank," I reached out and put my hand on his arm, "Lorelei never told you she loved you. She never led you on."

"I know that. It only made me love her more."

"You deserve someone who will love you back." I hesitated and then added, "Don't waste any more time wanting someone who does not want you back. Life is too short for that, Frank."

He looked at me, surprised. "Don't waste any more time wanting someone who does not want me back?" he repeated to himself. "You are a very bold young woman. Has anyone told you that before?"

"Yes, actually."

"Wise words, though rather heavy for so early in the morning!" Edie exclaimed, her socked feet padding into the study, her terry cloth bathrobe cinched at the waist and auburn hair wrapped tightly in curlers. She looked at me. "You look like you didn't sleep a wink. You too, Frank."

Neither of us answered.

"I think I'm going to go lie down," Frank said. "I've got to be back at the coop by three this afternoon. Big race later today. You're invited."

"Why, thank you, Frank." Edie sounded pleased. She glanced at me. "I smell coffee."

"It's a few hours old."

"How long have you been up?"

"Don't ask."

Her eyes narrowed suspiciously. "Where's Grace?"

"Out walking."

"I see." Her lips turned down into a frown. She looked like she was about to say something. "Shall I make the fresh pot or shall you?"

"You make it." I began to walk back to our room. "I need a power nap."

Nina fluttered in her cage, and Edie whipped around, facing the bird. "What on earth!" she exclaimed, but I didn't stay to explain; I was completely too tired. I had run out of words.

A minute later, I crawled back into bed beside Peter, and he gently stirred. "How'd you sleep, kid?" he whispered sleepily.

"Not well at all... but I'm going to sleep well now!" I answered, crawling back into bed.

I lay there for the next hour, looking at the ceiling, thinking of Grace and Frank, of Lorelei and Paul, and of Katrine. Sleep did not come. And by 8:00 a.m., I was up and dressed and sipping the new pot of coffee Edie had made, talking of Christmas shopping.

It was so strange that it was already December. It simply did not feel like Christmas on this side of the equator. It was much too hot. Too humid. Too tropical. Even growing up in San Francisco, Christmas had a chill in the air and a solid dose of rain. But nothing was the way it should be. Everything was just 'off' since the war began. And it felt like it would never be normal again.

CHAPTER 33

RACING PIGEONS AND DONUTS

*D*orris squinted into the pigeon loft, a special coop for the drafted birds of the U.S. Army stationed in Townsville, Australia. "So, they are just like regular pigeons?"

"Regular pigeons!" Frank was horrified. "I mean, these girls are the athletes of the sky! Specially bred and trained." He reached in and pulled out a gentle sleek bird. "Look how muscular she is and well-proportioned. Sure, she may come from the same family, the Columba livia or Rock Dove, as those pathetic run-of-the-mill pigeons down at the fountain, but they are altogether a better bird. These will live for twenty years. Those other birds might last three or four. It's all in the breeding, see?"

"They look the same," Dorris challenged.

"Well, they aren't." He put the bird back, and we stood aside as he came out of the loft. "I've been studying."

"I can imagine." She looked at him squarely. "They don't seem to mind when you hold them."

"Pigeons like people. They are actually pretty social."

Edie adjusted her straw hat and slipped her arm around Grace's waist, as though she was afraid the girl would bolt at any moment. "And to think, they mate for life!"

"They do. Not like some people." Frank's expression was emotionless.

Peter and I peered into the loft. It was not terribly large, not much bigger than a garden shed. But it was large enough for the fifty birds in the program.

"So, how do you get them to race?" Peter cleared his throat.

"It's pretty simple. These birds have been here since they were six weeks old. They've been trained together, and it's in their genes to come back to their home. They have an amazing sense of direction. We take them somewhere, release them, and they fly home."

"How do you tell them apart?" Paul asked. Much to Frank's disappointment, Paul had gotten yet another afternoon off.

"They wear a little rubber ring with a number on it. Whichever one makes it back first wins. We also time each of the birds so we know which ones are the strongest, fastest fliers."

"This should to be interesting." Dorris elbowed Grace playfully. Grace tried to look interested, but she was obviously distracted.

Frank checked his watch. "We ought to be going. How about you all go get in the jeep with Horatio? Peter, Piper and I will follow with the birds. We'll all meet up at the base on the top of Castle Rock."

THE DRIVE UP CASTLE ROCK, the enormous pink granite mountain rising out of the earth in the center of town, was breathtaking. Surrounded by eight cooing pigeons in their cages, Peter couldn't help but laugh. "Well, this certainly beats walking."

"I thought you *wanted* to hike up this monolith," I protested, remembering his words upon first laying his eyes on the mountain.

"I take it back." Peter looked down over the edge of the mountain.

As we wound our way up the steep switchbacks, Frank switched on the radio. Immediately, a newscaster with a heavy Australian accent broke into the gentle birds' songs.

"One week ago on December 16, 1944, German forces launched a massive offensive campaign through the Ardennes region of Belgium, France, and Luxembourg. They have completely encircled and destroyed four Allied armies, and there are rumors that the Allies are willing to negotiate a peace treaty favoring the Axis."

Peter and I shared a pained look.

"American forces have suffered more than others, and the casualty list is higher than any other operation during the war. Between 63,000 and 98,000 men are killed, missing, wounded in action, or captured."[20]

"How can they know?" I exclaimed. "I mean, so soon! It's only been a week!"

Frank slammed his hand on the steering wheel, barely containing his rage.

"We'll counter-attack," Peter said firmly. "We will. You mark my words. We will. We are Americans."

The radio announcer continued, "Disagreements between the Allied forces have caused delays in a clear response. German Panzer units…"

Frank shut off the radio, and we drove up the rest of the mountain in silence.

We did not speak of the news as we prepared the small flock of birds for the race. But by the looks on Edie, Horatio, Grace, Lorelei, and Katrine's faces, they too had listened to the radio on the drive over. I wanted to scream and cry. I wanted it all to end. I was infinitely finished with death. How could it go on and on? It was absurd. And the absurdity of it all was frustratingly infuriating.

One by one, we released the graceful birds off the granite rock at a set time and watched them soar back to their coop, where another birdkeeper waited to catch them and clock their arrivals. But the excitement of the race was lost.

It was Edie who was humming under her breath, "His eye is on the sparrow." I knew she was thinking of all our boys in the Ardennes forest, and she was reminding herself that God saw them, just as he saw our pigeons soaring over the Townsville skyline in a magnificent sunset.

"Well," Frank said, rubbing his hands together, "that's it. The show's over."

Dorris tried to smile. "Maybe we could all go to dinner? I know a great place right on the water. It's called Longboards. They make a great hamburger."

"That sounds good to me." Peter nodded.

"I could go for a hamburger," Lorelei agreed.

"Nothing like a riveting pigeon race to wake up the metabolism." Edie took Horatio's hand. "Don't you think, so dear."

Paul paused and took Lorelei's hand and whispered quietly as the group made their way back to the car, "I have the night off, Lorelei. I was wondering... Maybe I could take you out. You know, something nicer than a hamburger."

Horatio, just ahead of them and accidentally overhearing, stopped dead in his tracks. "What's this?" He turned on his heel and looked up at Paul. "You are asking Lorelei out... to dinner?"

Paul smiled innocently and shrugged nonchalantly.

"But you haven't asked my permission," he stated bluntly, rolling his brogue 'r's' especially long as he stared menacingly at Paul.

Lorelei stepped in. "Horatio, I don't think it's necessary. *Really—*"

He put his hand out and stopped her. "Lorelei, you are my pseudo-adopted daughter. If a man wants to ask you out, he must go through me."

"Sir," Paul looked at Lorelei, "Lorelei is 28 years old. And just between us, we've been going out for quite some time now."

"Is that true?" Horatio's eyes widened in shock.

Edie rolled her eyes. "Where have you been for the last two months?"

"Oh, I don't know. Fighting a war. Kicking the Japanese back to where they came from? And apparently, this young man's been gallivanting about in the bush with my daughter!"

"Oh my." Edie fanned herself and smiled. "I had no idea you were such a protective father, Horatio! I like this side of you!"

Horatio shrugged to Edie. "Just practicing for the young ones." Then, back in character, he continued to Paul, nearly shouting, "I think I deserve an apology, young man."

"I'm sorry?" Paul had no idea what he was apologizing for.

"And…" Horatio waved his hand for Paul to continue.

"And…?" Paul looked at Lorelei for a clue. She looked nervous.

"And dinner is a lot more serious than coffee," Horatio hinted.

"May I have your permission," Paul said solemnly, "to take your sort-of daughter to dinner?"

"I'm not sure."

Edie slapped his arm. "Horatio!"

Horatio frowned. "Oh, Edie, I'm just teasing the young lad. Well, I already know you're an upstanding citizen and a true Christian. I can't think of any reason off the top of my head to say no." He looked at Lorelei. "Unless you don't want to go."

"I want to go." She smiled up at Paul.

Horatio waited, enjoying the moment. "Have a lovely time, dear."

"I'm planning on it."

Paul offered his arm to Lorelei. She nodded, and arm in arm they began descending the switchbacks down the mountain.

Watching them, Edie exclaimed, "My my my, that young man reminds me of Horatio when he was young. He could be your twin! It reminds me of our old courting days, doesn't it you, darling?"

Horatio nodded in agreement. "I definitely see the resemblance."

"Don't you think so dear?" Edie called to me.

"Think what?"

"That Paul looks like Horatio!"

I looked at Paul's back. Well… if Uncle Horatio was a foot taller, clean-shaven, had more hair and a tan, and a stronger jawline… there *might* be a resemblance, I thought.

"So," Dorris clapped her hands together, "how about that hamburger?"

"You all go ahead," Katrine said. "I'm not very hungry. I'll meet you at home. I'd like a walk myself. I need some time to think."

THOUGH THE WEATHER made it feel nowhere close to the holidays, Christmas *was* just around the corner. And despite the heat, I woke up early the next morning with a subtle desire for the familiar of Christmas's past. I could make my mother's Linzer cookies with spiced jam. She always made them this time of year. The problem was, I couldn't remember how many cloves she used. Or maybe, Katrine and I could make an almond-filled stolen. That was always a crowd favorite.

I glanced at my watch. It was 6:30 in the morning. Coffee cup in hand, I was ready for a pleasant moment of quiet spent reading my pocket Bible in the living room. But my pocket Bible was nowhere to be found.

"Where is it?" I huffed under my breath, glancing around the room. I was sure I had left it there the morning before. Out of the corner of my eye, I saw the menorah we'd made of tinfoil and wooden beads. Hanukkah this year fell right over Christmas, and we had, of course, gone to great trouble to honor both holidays in our house. But it was difficult to feel celebratory. All our thoughts and prayers were directed towards our boys on the other side of the world.

"There it is," I thought relieved. It sat beside the menorah and underneath a stack of books and papers scattered on the desk.

As I moved to push the clutter aside, the writing on a page from the open notebook covering the Bible caught my eye.

WHO IS THIS JESUS?

"What's this?" I whispered to myself, picking up the page and scanning it.

It was Katrine's writing.

> *FINDINGS: OBVIOUSLY, THERE IS ARCHEOLOGICAL EVIDENCE FOR THE EXISTENCE OF A JEWISH RABBI NAMED YESHUA WHO WAS BORN IN THE FIRST CENTURY... THE EYEWITNESS ACCOUNTS, THE SOURCES OUTSIDE OF CHRISTIAN SCRIPTURES... THERE IS NO DOUBT THAT YESHUA EXISTED. THE QUESTION AT HAND: WHO WAS HE, AND WHY IS HE SO IMPORTANT? AND WHY DO LORELEI AND PIPER FEEL SO STRONGLY ABOUT HIM THE WAY THAT THEY DO?*

My heart started beating in my chest. Katrine had taken my challenge! And she was doing it the only way she knew how, through research. There must have been 20 library books stacked beside the desk on the floor. The notes on the page were detailed, her handwriting small and even. I assumed she had been up half the night. Carefully, I continued to read.

> *THE GOSPELS ARE CLEAR THAT JESUS WAS CONVINCED HE WAS THE SON OF GOD. BUT DID HE MATCH MESSIANIC PROPHECY?*

Below that, on one side, she had begun a numbered list.

> *1. A DESCENDANT OF ABRAHAM? (GENESIS 12:1-3)*
> *2. THE TRIBE OF JUDAH? (GENESIS 49:10)*
> *3. THE HOUSE OF DAVID? (2 SAMUEL 7:12-16)*
> *4. BORN IN BETHLEHEM? (MICAH 5:2)*
> *5. CARRIED TO EGYPT? (HOSEA 11:1)*
> *6. BORN OF A VIRGIN? (ISAIAH 7:14)*

The list went on and on for several more pages. At the bottom of the list, she had written in a hand that was not as firm or as straight as before, the last lines underlined:

THE FIRST CHRISTIANS WERE JEWS... YESHUA, **JESUS**, DID NOT COME TO START A NEW RELIGION.

I felt nervous, as though I had stumbled onto something not meant for my eyes. The books, the papers. I could feel her internal struggle, her mind's restless wandering to find the truth. She would never find it on her own. But I knew God's promise, "Seek, and you will find; knock, and it will be open to you."[19]

Silently, I extricated my Bible and sat down behind the desk, still looking at Katrine's research, praying God would lead Katrine on her journey. If Katrine was looking, she would find him. If she was knocking, he would open the door. As I prayed, my thoughts turned to the day ahead.

My notebook full of notes from the soldiers waited to be edited and expanded and cajoled into some sort of cohesive whole. The task seemed daunting, and I geared up for a morning of frustration. The pain of losing my camera and film still stung. No suitable replacement had been found and I was resigned to do without until we returned home. Where that was and when that would be was up for grabs.

And then, there was the Christmas shopping to be done. I had been assigned Grace via my aunt's Secret Santa plan. That would, possibly, take even more work than my attempt to become a journalist.

Grace was not the easiest of my cousins to shop for. In the past, she had always been fashionable, more so than I. But now (for the most part) the new Grace stuck to trousers or shorts and blouses rolled up to the elbow. All frill and fun was gone, replaced with a sort of strict, militaristic harshness. I thought of perfume or maybe a new lipstick. But that sort of thing was so personal. A woman needed to pick out her own lipstick. Nylons were too expensive. Edie suggested a book, but Grace wasn't much of a reader.

However, it *was* in the bookstore I found it—a beautiful leather journal. It was not dissimilar from the journal my mother had given me long ago when I'd first arrived at Edie's lighthouse the summer of '39. The paper felt handmade. I purchased it and a box of brand-new colored pencils. The pages, unlined, were perfect for writing or sketching. She had so much locked up inside of her... If she couldn't share with me or her sisters, maybe she could share within the safety of a blank page.

"What do you think?" I asked, holding it up for Lorelei, who was staring off into space.

"What did you say?" The fog cleared, and she looked at me.

"What do you think? For Grace?" I tilted the journal to the side.

"I have no idea what Grace would like these days." Absentmindedly, she backed into a stack of books on a table. They crashed to the floor and, startled, she knelt down to pick them up.

"Here," I set the journal down, "let me help you."

She smiled and one by one; we re-stacked the books.

"What's going on, Lorelei? You've been acting awfully funny all morning. Did the date last night go badly?"

She shook her head, an indiscernible expression on her face. "Not badly..."

"What then?"

She put another book on the stack and whispered, "Oh, Piper, he asked me to marry him."

"He didn't!" I exclaimed.

Loudly, she shushed me and motioned for me to come closer. "Keep your voice down, please!"

I leaned in, whispering, "What did you say?"

"I couldn't answer him. I... I didn't know what to say!"

"You didn't!"

She nodded. "I'm just not sure yet! Piper, this is not just something you rush into! You knew Peter for years before you married him! You knew his family, his friends. . . his life. Paul is still a mystery to me. Everything about him and his life is foreign and strange. I feel I barely know him! And he barely knows me!"

"Marriage is always a risk, Lorelei, and you can never fully know a person enough to safeguard against that risk. It takes time. The more you talk, the more you will learn about each other," I offered.

She nodded. "We *do* talk, just not about the things I think we should talk about—like the war or my family or, oh, I don't know. He doesn't ask the right questions... Sometimes it seems like he doesn't want to. It makes me nervous."

"Sometimes you have to help people out. If there are things about you that you think Paul needs to know, you need to just tell him."

She raised one eyebrow. "I need him to ask, Piper. I need him to know to ask on his own. What if everything in my life, all these hard years, is too much for him to handle? If that's true, how could we be together if he doesn't want all of me?"

I shook my head. I knew from experience that you could never expect men to know what you were thinking, even if it seemed obvious.

"But surely, you understand what I am feeling, Piper? I can't say yes now, not without *knowing* if it's the right thing."

At that moment, Edie bounded around the corner. "All right, ladies! Tempus fugit! We've still four more shops to hit before closing time."

Lorelei looked at me, silently pleading for me to keep what she'd just told me in confidence. She walked around in a daze behind Edie and me the rest of the afternoon. Later, once we made it home and began stringing popcorn, listening to Christmas music, frying up donuts, and trying our best to act festive, Lorelei sat with her bowl of popcorn and string, barely moving, not saying a word.

"How absolutely international we are," Edie said, munching on her donut. "Christmas and Hanukkah together."

"It's not a bad fit really," Katrine said thoughtfully, "Yeshua celebrated Hanukkah, and we are celebrating his birthday, even if he might not have been born on Christmas..."

I looked at Katrine surprised.

To my astonishment, she continued sharing her recent research in her usual confident, 'teacherly' fashion. "You know," she said, "Jesus wasn't a Christian at all. He was a good Jew. I never realized that." Her tone was serious.

Grace, not hearing what Katrine had said, began a list of complaints. "No dreidel, no latkes, no cheesecake. It doesn't feel like Hanukkah at all. And these donuts are oily."

"Don't disparage the donuts." Horatio poured another mug of eggnog. "They may be a little 'oily,' but the jelly in the middle is excellent. Eight nights of donuts," Horatio patted his stomach, "on top of whatever is coming on Christmas Eve tomorrow at the party and Christmas and New Year's. The children won't recognize us when we get back home, darling Edie!"

"More than likely we won't recognize them." Edie frowned. "Imagine how much they've grown, dear." Her face fell. "The presents we sent them won't make it in time most likely."

"Happy thoughts, love, only happy thoughts." Horatio brought her a mug filled to the brim with eggnog.

Lorelei smiled and said softly, "Eating oil-based foods is one way we remember what God did on the first Hanukkah after the Maccabees rebelled against the Seleucid Empire. Once they got the temple back and purified it, they needed pure olive oil for the lamps. But they couldn't find any, except for one bowl that was sealed with the signet ring of the High Priest, all the way from the days of Samuel. That's how they knew it was pure. There was only enough oil for one day, but God made it last eight whole days, long enough to find other pure oil for the lamps." She took another donut.

"Only the Jews could think of such a way to remember." Frank smiled, "My mother made great donuts."

"Our boys need that same oil in the Ardennes right now if they will survive the Germans, much less defeat them. If things keep going the way they are..." Peter trailed off. The Nazis, as usual, were proving a formidable enemy. He looked up. "Well, all I can say is we need a miracle."

"A Hanukkah miracle." Lorelei picked up the popcorn garland and began to wrap it around the small potted palm tree that was standing in for a Douglas fir.

"A Christmas miracle." Edie nodded.

"God doesn't perform miracles anymore." Grace stood up. "If you want something done, do it yourself."

"That a girl." Frank winked at her from across the room where he sat at a small card table playing solitaire. "My sentiments exactly."

My heart dropped, but no words came to mind to refute their doubts. But I knew. I *knew*. God was performing miracles every day, all around us. Miracles had marked every stage of our journey; the boys' survival of the storm in the Malahini, Paul's rescue, the submarine pickup, catching Ansel Thornton, being together now, the list went on and on in my mind. Grace and Frank just couldn't see them or didn't want to.

CHAPTER 34

CHRISTMAS EVE

The officer's Christmas party at the base was a black-tie affair. Admittedly, it was not quite as gilded and glittering as it might have been before the war, but everyone tried to make it as festive as possible with what they had. My dress, a white taffeta with pink polka dots and a big bow on the waist, had a small little tear right where the sweetheart neckline met the left puff sleeve.

"There's nothing I can do about it." I groaned, looking at myself in the mirror.

"Never say never," Peter said, his clear blue eyes flashing playfully. "How about an early Christmas present?"

I stopped and turned towards him. "Oh, Peter! You didn't! I have nothing for you! We were supposed to do Secret Santa, remember?"

"Don't tell a man when he can buy his wife a gift," he said slyly as I noticed he held something behind his back.

"But I didn't get you anything, and now it's too late to go shopping." I felt terribly disappointed and awful. How could I have not bought Peter anything?

He came over and kissed my cheek. "It's okay."

"What is it?" I peeked behind his back, and he darted to the left.

"Well," I huffed playfully, "are you going to give it to me or not?"

"For a kiss."

"You have a deal."

From behind his back, Peter pulled out a beautiful white orchid.

"A corsage?"

"I think if we pin it over that rip, no one will be the wiser."

"For that," I smiled, "you might get two kisses."

"That's all I could want for Christmas." He pulled me close. "But you already know that, don't you?"

Horatio's voice boomed through the house, "Time to go everyone! The party starts at seven-thirty, sharp."

"The captain is back." Peter stifled a laugh.

"Admiral," I corrected him and straightened his tie. "So, is Paul going to take Lorelei? Or is she coming with us?"

"He's meeting us there. Said he had to pick something up on the way."

He put his hand out and bowed. "My lady, can I take you to the ball?"

"Why, sir," I fluttered my eyelashes, "I thought you'd never ask!"

THE U.S. NAVY won the coin toss of who would host this year's Christmas party. As such, the Officer's Lounge, a dark cozy bar set a block back from the harbor in a hotel where many of the unmarried American naval officers had set up shop for the duration of the war, was filled with the upper crust of the armed forces based in Townsville. They decorated the room with dozens of green and red paper garlands. Officers from the U.S. Army and Air Force were present as well. Australia's hot summer weather added an interesting touch to the otherwise traditional Christmas party. While Bing Crosby crooned Christmas carols from a phonograph, the officers mingled, drinking iced cranberry wassail, munching on popcorn, filling plates with ambrosia salad (made of mayonnaise, marshmallows, and canned pineapple) and chomping on barbecued lamb chops.

Horatio beelined for General Linton, Admiral Stark and Admiral Knox, all of whom sat at a small table eating salted peanuts.

Mrs. Knox waved at us from across the room from behind a large bowl of punch which she was dishing out into little crystal cups along with Bee. "My oh my," Edie said, taking my arm and pulling me closer to the punch bowl, "have you ever seen punch that color green?" Lorelei and Katrine stepped in behind us while Grace went in search of Dorris.

"Food coloring," Katrine answered. "Has to be."

"And with all those maraschino cherries floating in it," we reached Mrs. Knox and Bee, "it's like Christmas in a cup, isn't it?"

"It's about the only thing that feels like Christmas in this sweat-house." Mrs. Knox dabbed at her brow with a delicate linen hand-kerchief with a flouncy "K" embroidered on the corner with dozens of tiny pink roses.

"You look frazzled, Mrs. Knox," I said, taking a cup of the bright green beverage. I nodded to Mrs. Linton. "Thanks for manning the punch bowl."

Bee didn't crack a smile and just kept pouring. She was brewing over something.

"I've been running around like a chicken with my head cut off." She sighed. "And praying for Patton's Third Army to relieve Bastogne."

"Indeed, aren't we all?" Edie put her hand over her heart.

"But I love parties, especially Christmas parties." Mrs. Knox continued and then added to Lorelei as she pushed a cup into her hands and looked past her to Katrine, "Looks like your sister isn't having a very good time." The eldest Adleman looked completely depressed, like a balloon whose air had been taken out of it. She didn't even attempt to smile.

A loud burst of laughter from the middle of the room took our attention. It was Dorris. Grace was by her side.

Bee stepped out from behind the table and huffed. "I've got to talk to that girl!"

"If you haven't made a lady of her by now," Edie smiled, "I doubt you have much of a chance. Besides, a little laughter is good for the soul. Let the girl be, Bee." But Mrs. Linton would not be stopped. She pushed her way through the young men and pulled her daughter aside for a talking to.

"Well," Edie tilted her head to the side, "I won't say she doesn't have her hands full. I was lively like that when I was a young flit of a thing."

"I don't envy Bee," Mrs. Knox confided. "That girl will never fit into the debutante box, but Bee will probably try to push her into one until the day she dies."

"She has adventure in her blood." Edie nodded. "Like a character I once wrote about in a novel. Her name was Esmerelda Viola Splat."

"Oh?" Mrs. Knox asked. "I didn't know you wrote? What's the book called?"

"It wasn't published." Edie frowned. "Actually, I never finished it."

"Edie is a very fine writer," I said.

"What do you write?" She looked at Edie.

"Nothing at the moment. Can't seem to write a thing these days. Too many unfinished stories around me to settle down and just pick one."

"That must be very difficult for you," Mrs. Knox said with as much sympathy as she could muster.

"Oh, it is… But I'm helping Piper put together a little project she began recently. It is a sweeping exposé of life on the front. Sweeping," Edie said again.

"It is?" I asked. Bee had Dorris in a corner and was pointing her long bony finger repeatedly in her face. Dorris rolled her eyes and brushed past her mother, making a straight trajectory for the punch table.

"I'll take a glass of that," she said, acknowledging me, Edie, Lorelei, and Katrine. She was flushed. Whatever her mother had said, though she tried to hide it, had hurt.

"You have quite a lot of admirers, Miss Dorris." Mrs. Knox gave her a cup filled to the brim.

"They don't mean a thing to me." She cast a quick glance at Frank across the room sitting at a table with Peter. "I've got my sights set on something better. And when I see something I want, I go and get it." With that, she turned on her heel and re-joined Grace and a small circle of pilots from the base.

My mouth opened slightly in shock. She was brazen. No wonder her mother was always on edge. But one couldn't help but sort of like her.

"Decisiveness is admirable in a young woman," Edie affirmed, oblivious to the fact that Dorris's sights were set directly on Frank. Her eyes stopped on the dessert table where a hundred mini-Pavlovas—little meringues topped with fruit and cream—waited to be enjoyed. "Doesn't it strike you as odd that Australia's national dessert is named after a *Russian* ballerina?"

Mrs. Knox's eyes narrowed, not leaving Dorris. "That girl's as tough as a pine nut and not old enough to know that her wants won't hurt her."

"What?" Katrine asked holding her green punch warily out in front of her.

"It's something we say in the South. She's strong and determined but not mature enough to have good judgment. Girls like that tend to learn the hard way."

Out of the corner of my eye, I saw Dorris motion to Frank across the room. He pointed to himself, surprised she was singling him out. Then, she pushed her way out of the circle and sat down next to him and Peter.

Mrs. Knox stifled a laugh. "Why, she's sitting as close to him as a cat's breath!"

"I think I ought to go join them," I said, excusing myself. "Frank might need help." By the looks of things, he'd broken out into a sweat. Katrine followed me to the table while Lorelei hung back, leaning against the wall and watching the door for Paul, who still had not arrived.

A moment later Katrine and I were both listening as Dorris explained with great animation how that very night, the 2nd Armored Division would attempt to cut off the 2nd Panzer Division at the Meuse. Patton's Third Army, in the south of the forest, was battling to relieve Bastogne. It seemed the outcome of the war hung in the balance.

Dorris appeared to be speaking to one person only, even though Peter, Katrine, and I were all right there sitting at the table.

"So," I offered cheerily. "How about this green punch?"

It was as though we were invisible. Dorris kept right on going.

Peter looked at Katrine and me, "Well, the three of us can talk." Awkwardly, he held up his glass. "Sort of neon, don't you think?"

"It tastes like watered down cough syrup." Katrine's nose wrinkled.

We all watched Dorris. She was still talking and Frank was still listening, pinned down by her penetrating gaze. Then, out of nowhere, Dorris stood up from the table and left abruptly.

Peter scooted his chair closer to Frank. "Where'd she go?

"To find some music we could dance to."

"Did you ask her to dance?" I asked.

"Nah, she asked me."

I leaned towards him. "You know," I kept my voice low, "I think she likes you."

He blushed. "Yeah, I was sort of getting the same idea."

"Oh boy," Peter looked at the redhead across the room. "How's it feel to be on the other side? The hunter is now the hunted."

"The question is, how do you feel about her?" I asked. But before he could answer, Dorris was back, and the music had picked up. Frank stood up, shrugged, and was led by the young woman to the dance floor. Peter looked at me with a half-smile. "I know it's neither of our 'thing' really, but… you want to join them?" He held out his hand, and I took it.

"Sure," I said. "Why not?"

He glanced at Katrine, "Are you okay here by yourself?"

"My dancing days are over. You two go on. I'll save our table and *not* drink this." She shook her head and looked disdainfully at her drink.

With that, Peter and I took our places near Dorris and Frank, who were already dancing away. Neither were particularly graceful, and both seemed to be much more interested in looking at each other than in moving their feet in rhythm.

"Listen, Frank," Dorris enunciated clearly and loudly enough for me to hear, "I am going to lay all my cards on the table. I'm not going to be in town that much longer."

"Is that so?" Frank swayed to the music and gently twirled near Peter and I. Frank had learned a step or two since the last time I'd seen him dance.

"Yes." Dorris looked up at him. "I've never given any guy a chance like I'm about to give you."

Frank swallowed and stopped dancing.

"Oh, don't worry, kid," she giggled, "I'm not proposing. I'm asking you to—" She leaned in and started whispering in his ear.

I tried to nudge Peter closer so I could hear, but he wasn't getting the hint.

"Me?" Frank's eyes opened wide. "Why me!"

"Because," she patted his face, "you happen to be smart, not too bad-looking… and available. And I don't think you want to spend one more hour in the harbor than me. What do you say, sailor?"

Frank's brow furrowed and he stopped moving. Then, he said firmly, "I've got to think about it," and he started dancing again.

"Well, don't take too much time to decide. I'll move on to

someone else if you aren't up for the challenge." She laughed confidently. "But I think you are up for the challenge."

~

TWO HOURS LATER, Lorelei still stood alone against the back wall, looking upset.

The party was in full swing, and everyone was well into dessert. Everyone spoke of nothing except Bastogne. Would Patton's third army make it in time? What an awful Christmas it must be for those men in the Argonne, I thought. So hopeless a situation in the midst of the season of hope. Such darkness at a time to celebrate the coming of light into the world.

As Lorelei moved towards the back exit of the club, I pulled Peter off the dance floor and skirted around the other pairs, asking quietly once I had reached her, "You okay?"

Her brow furrowed, and she bit her lip. Pushing the door open, we stepped out into the back alley. "It's so noisy in there, I can barely think."

"Where's Paul?" I asked, sensing intuitively that there was something else going on.

She shook her head to the side and stared at her feet. "I don't know where Paul is. He was supposed to meet us here."

"Maybe he got held up on the base?" I wondered.

She dropped her voice and said, "It's always felt easier when it came to men for me. Before Paul, I knew what to expect. I was in control. Paul's so different. He's so strong, and he knows his mind. He's so single-minded in everything he does. He's made up his mind about me, but I haven't about him, and I don't enjoy feeling put into a corner when it comes to making big decisions!"

"You need to tell him this."

"I know!"

I waited, wondering what else she would say.

Her shoulders caved in, and she looked straight ahead. "Sometimes, I think Paul is so perfect, so handsome, so kind… Why certainly no man can actually be that wonderful! What if it's all a lie, and he's the wrong one? How can I *know*?"

"Remember, Lorelei, you can't ever know in a way that keeps all mistakes at bay," I said. "People are people. We all make mistakes."

"But you knew enough with Peter to feel secure about your decision."

I paused. She was right. Never had I for one moment doubted that Peter was my one and only.

"I'm terrified I'll make the wrong decision," Lorelei continued. "I've prayed and prayed, and I have gotten no direction at all. I feel like I am floundering around in the dark. Before I moved to Egypt, I opened my heart to whatever God might have for me. I thought that might be if I'm honest, marriage. I waited and waited, but nothing really happened. I don't want to do something foolish just because I don't know what to do next. My mind is spinning!"

"Then," I answered carefully, "what is your heart saying?"

"I'm afraid to listen to it. You know as well as I that God must lead our hearts, and I've determined to let him, so I haven't let my heart lead me. I haven't gotten one sign, not one dream! Nothing at all. It feels like God is silent on this subject." For a brief second, a flash of fear passed behind her eyes. She paused before adding, "Then again, 'Besser a hon in hand eider an odler in himmel.'"

Glancing at me, she explained: "It's an old Jewish proverb that means 'Better a hen in the hand than an eagle in the sky.'"

"Lorelei," I swallowed, "you have to include your heart in this discussion. God cares about your feelings. If you love Paul, you need to be honest with yourself about it. There is no fear in love, remember?" I thought of 1 John 4:18. *There is no fear in love, but perfect love casts out all fear.*

"What if God is not calling us to be together?" She bit her lip nervously.

"What if he is?"

It was as though she hadn't heard me. "And we come from such different backgrounds! He's all-American. I'm a German-Jewish girl who has found her true home in Palestine..."

"You both love Jesus," I answered. "Background doesn't matter anymore, you know that."

"Of course, I know that! But some people, even in America, don't take kindly to Jews. What if his family doesn't accept me? What if he... Well, what if he doesn't accept that part of me? No matter what, I'll always be Jewish." Her voice caught, and she tried to gather herself. "I don't know if he is consciously avoiding the subject or just doesn't care."

"I'm sure he cares, Lorelei. But some men have trouble catching on when you try to subtly tell them you want to talk about certain things. You might have to be more clear."

She shrugged my advice off.

"I wish I could hear what God is saying. If he'd just tell me what to do..." Then, as if on second thought, she added, "But he isn't even here. Maybe he's not as serious as I thought, and all this stress is for nothing. Maybe he didn't really mean it when he asked me to marry him last night. He's late. Maybe he's too late. Maybe *we're* too late."

"But God never is late, Lorelei. Besides, has he ever been late before? Maybe something is wrong?"

She shook her head no, irrationally upset. "You'd think he'd at least call!" She swallowed nervously and adjusted the waistband to her dress. "What do you do, Piper, when you're waiting on God, and he is not showing you the direction to go?"

"Sometimes," I tried to explain, "when I don't hear God speak, I go back to what I know is true and go from there. Maybe God's waiting on you?"

Lorelei shook her head. "I want what God wants."

"And what do you think he wants?"

"I don't know, Piper," she answered with an agonized expression as her eyes watered for just a moment. "I just don't know. I don't want to make a mistake!"

I rubbed her shoulder as I stood by her side. I felt terrible for her and all the anxiety she was facing, but I also knew that if she let the fear of making a mistake decide for her, it could cause her to do just that—make a mistake. I prayed silently, "Lord, let your love cast out the fear in her heart!"

BACK INSIDE, Edie waved us down. She was working her way through a large bowl of peanuts at an empty table and offered us some that had already been shelled.

"Well, Lorelei," Edie looked at her, "the mystery deepens. What great drama!"

"What are you talking about?" Lorelei glanced at the shells and sat down across from her.

"Paul's not here."

"You noticed too?" Lorelei looked at me, dejected.

"My dear, not only am I your adopted mother, but I am also a writer. Of course I noticed." She popped a peanut into her mouth. "Besides, it's not like you could just fall in love at first sight with a perfect man, get married, and live happily ever after. There's no arc."

At this point, I too had sat down.

"An arc?" Lorelei looked perplexed.

"Yes. Every good story has to have one. It's like math. You introduce your main characters, the action rises, you reach a climax, the action falls, everyone's problems are resolved. You are a musician, dear, it's like ending a song on the wrong note. It leaves everyone feeling like it isn't finished."

It was getting a little too serious for Lorelei. "Well, I'm not entirely sure Paul and I have an arc to reach, Edie. And I also wouldn't say I've fallen in love at first sight. Please, don't presume that just because he is a fairly good-looking and nice young man with a certain charisma, that we are more to each other than, well, than what we are."

"Dear," Edie protested, "what exactly are you to each other? And admit it, he's a little more than fairly good-looking. I'd say he is *insanely* handsome and nearly perfect on every level."

"Yes, all right," she consented, but her voice remained flat.

Edie looked at her triumphantly.

"But at this moment we are just, well . . . we are not even together at this moment because he's not even here like he said he'd be! So there, he's not perfect. I know better than to think they made men *that* good-looking and perfect."

"No," Edie shook her head, "I heartily disagree. Think of Horatio."

As I sat observing, I did think for a moment of Horatio, thick-waisted and short, with an even shorter temper that rivaled any Atlantic storm. But to Edie, he was the picture of masculine perfection. The thought made me laugh, and I choked on a peanut. Lorelei jumped up and began to pat my back.

Unfazed, Edie continued, "I am a great judge of character. And Paul is one." She looked up and batted her eyelashes. "I mean, not that he *is* a character, though he certainly can take over a room with that smile, but that he *has* character. Great character."

"He didn't show up here tonight," Lorelei said sullenly.

At that moment, Peter came up. "Lorelei, Paul just phoned and said he got held up. He can't come tonight. He is so sorry. He knows you were expecting him."

Edie lowered her chin knowingly. "Don't let it sway you, my dear. When you find a man," she swept some peanut shells onto the floor, "as near to perfection as Horatio is, you hold on to him, and you never let him go."

Lorelei was silent.

"Like ships in the night, dear," Edie looked out at an imaginary horizon. "Like ships in the night."

CHAPTER 35

A CHRISTMAS MIRACLE

*E*die held up a bright blue robe with a mandarin collar. "Horatio! It's silk!"

"You bet it is." He smiled. "All the way from China... Which really isn't that far, if we are being honest. I thought you might enjoy wearing it about the house instead of that terry bathrobe while you're working."

She bounced up off the floor where she sat near the potted palm dripping with popcorn and paper chains and tried it on over her cotton pajamas.

We were all still in our pajamas, sipping coffee and munching on a coffee cake sweetened with dates and pineapple that Katrine and I had made early that morning.

"Not that I'm doing that much work these days." She sighed.

One by one, we opened our gifts from our Secret Santas. Lorelei had given Katrine a new pair of sandals. Grace had given Lorelei a new set of kid leather gloves the color of fresh cream. Katrine gave Horatio a smart new bowtie. Frank gave Peter a Remington Electric Shaver. Peter gave Frank a new fishing rod and a can of bait.

The only one left was me, but there were no presents left under the tree. Edie disappeared for a moment and then returned, a large canvas in her hands. Slowly, she turned it around, revealing a rather fetching scene of three young women doing the hula and another taking their picture. It felt vaguely familiar. And then it hit me. "That's the photograph I took of the girls on Hawaii for *The Honolulu Herald*!"

"Yes." Edie beamed. "I've been painting it in secret in my closet in the middle of the night. Except, you weren't in the picture, and I wanted to capture forever the four of you doing what you do best!"

"The hula?" Grace smirked. In her hands, she held the journal I'd given her and the pencils. She hadn't said much of whether she liked them or not.

Horatio nodded. "I'm rather relieved she's finished."

"I love it." I took the painting and held it up. "Why, I'll treasure it always."

"It's different from your usual, Edie," Peter stood next to me. "It's so bright, and there's not one bird."

"Yes," Horatio folded his hands over his belly, "I'm rather proud of it myself. She's improved."

"I painted this out of creative overflow, not writer's block. The process is very different," Edie explained.

"Of course," Peter agreed, looking at me and hiding a smile.

Edie took the painting out of my hands and leaned it up against the wall, studying it from a few paces back.

"This is the most unusual Christmas of my life." She took her coffee cup back up from where she'd left it on the floor. "My children are millions of miles away. This war seems to go on indefinitely. I hope to God it ends soon. I want to go home. I just want to go back home! Nothing feels right anymore." She suddenly burst into tears.

"Oh come now, Edie dear." Horatio stood up, his face etched with concern. It was obvious how much he adored her and how much her hurt pained him. He wrapped her up in his big bear-like arms as we looked on, no one knowing what to do. "It will end. All things come to an end. We will go home, I don't know when, but we will. Hold on. Be a good soldier. Chin up, Edie!"

"There's one more for Piper." Peter smiled and took a medium-sized box out from behind his back.

"Peter!" I exclaimed. "You didn't! I told you, no more presents!"

"Just one. Flowers don't count, and as I said, you can't keep a man from buying his wife a present."

Lifting the lid from the box, I gasped. A beautiful new Leica. My lips turned to a smile and lovingly, I lifted the camera out and examined it. "You didn't!"

"Oh, but I did." Peter winked. "And there are a couple of rolls of film too."

At that moment, a sharp knocking against the window caught our attention. It was Paul, his fist tapping against the glass and his muffled voice asking if we could let him in.

In an instant, Peter was up and opening the window. Paul hoisted himself through the window, much to our shock, and before anyone could even say 'Merry Christmas,' he was standing in front of Lorelei.

"Young man," Horatio raised one dark eyebrow, "in case you haven't noticed, we have a front door."

"I know." Paul was breathless.

"Where were you last night?" Lorelei frowned.

"I got held up in Toowoomba."

"Toowoomba?" Horatio exclaimed. "What were you doing there, you young fool? That's over 1,000 miles away."

"I can't say I know the distance, but it was a 14-hour train trip. And a 3-hour bus ride. And to answer your question, I was picking up Lorelei's Christmas present." He pulled out a folded piece of music from his pocket. "I looked all over Townsville, but they really had nothing that suited."

He turned back to the open window, reached down, and pulled up his guitar. "It's a song. I have to play it for you. You'll have to put up with my singing, okay?" He blushed.

"I thought you stood me up." She smiled an awkward, half-afraid smile.

"Just listen to the song," he said seriously.

"Did you write it?" Lorelei asked.

"You know I can't write music." His fingers strummed the first chord and stopped abruptly, his voice shaking just a hair. "I changed the words just a little."

Once more, he played the first chord. And then, he began to sing.

> *"Oh, I like you in the morn morn morn morn morning*
> *And when the day day day day day ends*
>
> *I'll be your roo roo roo roo rooster*
> *If you'll be my chick chick chick chick chicken!"*

She stared at him, rooted to her spot on the floor.

With that, Paul slid down to one knee and held out a small velvet box. Lorelei looked so nervous she might pass out.

Inside the box, on a silk cushion, lay a ring. Slipping it on her finger, he said, "Lorelei Adleman, will you marry me?"

She looked at it and bit her lip. It was beautiful. A perfect diamond set with two small emeralds on the side of a thin, graceful gold band.

"I didn't have the ring before. I thought you must have not taken me seriously."

"You were right."

"So?"

She shook her head, instantly forgetting everyone else in the room. "But Paul, do you think it will work?"

"How could it not work?"

I glanced over at Edie. She had tears streaming down her face. (Emotional scenes did that to her.)

"Paul, I'm just not sure this is the right time. We've been moving so quickly."

Horatio leaned over and whispered in Lorelei's ear, "For the record, he asked my permission. And I gave it."

"Life is short." Paul got down on his knee. "Please say yes, Lorelei."

Her eyes darted around the room. "I... uh... oh my. I guess I will."

And then, after Paul had swept her up in his arms and kissed her, she blushed and looked at the ring and around the room once more. He was swept up in the moment's drama. He didn't notice Lorelei's conflicted expression or her trembling hands. He only knew that he had won his prize — the woman he adored. And in that moment of victory, he forgot all about her feelings. With all of his charm, he began to work the room. He and Edie immediately began wedding plans, and Lorelei sat down on the couch, a stunned expression on her face.

Katrine moved towards her sister and lightly kissed her cheek. "Mazel tov, dear. I hope you and Paul will be very happy."

"Thank you." Lorelei tried to smile.

"Yes," Frank said slowly, reaching out to shake Paul's hand. "Mazel tov. Good luck to you both."

Edie clasped her hands together and threw her head back. "Why, isn't this the most wonderful Christmas we've ever had?"

By then, we had all erupted into excited chatter, and hardly anyone noticed that Frank quietly excused himself and slipped out of the house. But I noticed and so did Grace.

"Where is Frank going?" I asked her as we watched him cross the front lawn and walk towards Flinders through the open window.

"He said something about a meeting with Dorris. He said he had decided about something that she needed to know about as soon as possible."

"It's Christmas." My jaw dropped. "Whatever could he need to discuss with that little tart?"

"I'm not at liberty to discuss it. Air Force stuff."

"What does Frank have to do with planes?" I asked suspiciously. He was a sailor, not a pilot. And he wasn't even technically on active duty. I mean, the guy took care of pigeons. "Seriously?"

"As I said, I'm not at liberty to discuss it."

"Oh."

Grace had become increasingly difficult and frustrating to talk to of late. I turned on my heel and joined everyone else huddled around Paul and Lorelei.

Horatio had his head bowed and began to pray, "Heavenly Father, we thank thee this Christmas morn your son was born. We ask you to bless the union of Lorelei and Paul..." As he continued to pray, my thoughts turned to Frank and to Amos and to Harry and to how strange life was.

"Piper!" Edie's voice was jubilant. "You must take a photograph, dear! We must commemorate this moment."

Lifting the camera to my eye, I focused the lens and told everyone to smile.

Click.

"How's it feel?" Peter asked.

"Strange and new," I chuckled, "like everything else these days."

"IT SEEMS RATHER SUDDEN, doesn't it? I mean, we've really only just started seeing each other, you know. Marriage is such a big step. So permanent," Lorelei confided to me and Grace the next day. "There's still so much we haven't talked about."

"Why wait?" Edie sipped her tea. "You can talk after you're married."

"Why wait?" Katrine horrified, stared at Edie. "Lorelei and Paul have just barely met! She has every right to wait as long as she wants."

"But when you know, you *know*." Edie's tone was decisive.

"Just like you knew?" I stifled a laugh.

Lorelei, barely above a whisper, said, "The problem is, I'm not sure I know. Sometimes Paul can just take over a room. He is very charismatic. He can't help it. He's like a movie star. I think he brought the ring and asked in front of everyone so I had to give him an answer."

"Maybe that wasn't such a bad thing," Edie answered. "You have a tendency to drag your feet, Lorelei. You went out with Joe for over a year knowing nothing would come of it."

"Joe and I were always just friends," Lorelei said firmly. "I knew he was all wrong — for a husband, that is. I think Paul *may* be the right one. I just don't *know*."

Edie pointed her long fingernail in our direction. "I knew the moment I laid my eyes on Horatio that he was the man for me."

"Then why did you wait 20 years to marry him?" I asked.

"That is something I haven't figured out yet, dear." She flushed. "I'm choosing not to live in regret of the past, but there is no reason for Lorelei to make the same mistake I did. You are getting married," she turned to Lorelei, "and you are getting married this spring with a *real* wedding!"

Edie brushed back her red hair with her fingers. "The only things we need to discuss right now are the details, like whether you want a beach wedding or a garden wedding. Morning or sunset? And the color scheme. How do you feel about fuchsia and lemon? There are simply a million things to decide."

Looking down, I stifled another smile. Edie had not made one of those decisions for her own wedding. Horatio had planned the whole thing.

Lorelei protested, "I just want a simple ceremony. And only the family. I don't really have any friends in Townsville. Not really."

"It doesn't matter." Edie put her hand on her hip. "Horatio is an Admiral, and everyone knows you are his adopted daughter. Certain members of the brass would feel quite offended if they weren't invited. He did our wedding, and everyone back in Maine said it was *the* event of the year. I've learned everything about event-planning from him."

"You are starting to sound like Bee Linton." Grace laughed with a hint of cynicism.

Edie shook her head and turned the page of the dress catalog she was looking through. "None of that, young lady. I'm *nothing* like Bee Linton. I just know we have a family name to uphold. The Macleays do things right the first time around."

Lorelei couldn't argue anymore. "Well, I give you full control of the planning then. The only thing I'm requesting is that you don't go overboard."

"I'll do my best," Edie said magnanimously. "So, raspberry or lemon filling?"

"For the cake?"

"No, for the Petit Fours."

"Petit fours?" Lorelei laughed, slightly overwhelmed.

"Never you mind," Edie said. "Leave it to us. Don't worry about a thing! Just tell me, raspberry or lemon?"

"Chocolate," she answered. "That's the one thing I feel certain about in the whole affair."

I held up a photograph of a bride in the last issue of *Vogue*. "Look at this one." I pointed, and Katrine, Grace, Lorelei, and my aunt peered at the dress. It had slim long sleeves, and a gathered bust. "The back has buttons up it, and there are ecru lace inserts on each side."

"I like the ruched shoulders," Katrine said.

"And the trained skirt would be so elegant on your tall frame. I think it's perfect!" Edie clasped her hands together. Even Grace had to agree that the dress was lovely.

"But... it's made of silk. How are we going to find that much white silk these days? It's not like we have a bunch of old night-gowns lying around this old place." I said.

Edie shrugged. "Horatio was able to find that silk robe for my Christmas present."

353

"And he probably paid thirty-five dollars for it. This dress would take thirty times that much material. And we don't have enough clothing rations between us to pay for that sort of thing. Why we wouldn't be able to buy anything but new underwear for a year!" I added, suddenly sorry I'd found such a perfect, or rather, perfectly unattainable, dress.

Grace tapped the photograph. "I think I might have an idea, but I need to talk to Dorris."

"Dorris?"

"She has a... a supplier."

"For wedding dresses?" Edie was agape.

"For just about anything. She is rather resourceful."

"I noticed." Lorelei cocked one eyebrow.

"Do you think her supplier could help us out?" Katrine asked.

"Can't lose a thing by asking."

"Do you think," Lorelei paused, "that Horatio would walk me down the aisle? You know, given that my father is... well, unable to." She'd never been able to bring herself to say that he was dead.

"I'd be honored to, my dear," Horatio said with gusto as he burst into the room. It always seemed like Horatio was bursting into places. "In fact, Edie already suggested the idea to me last night."

"Is that so?" Lorelei laughed.

"I was born blessed with the gift of foresight." Edie bowed slightly. "I have a feeling that 1945 will be a much better year than 1944. Your engagement is a fresh wind in my sails!" She looked up at her husband. "Isn't a little early for you to be home?"

Horatio put his hand behind Edie's chair. "This morning, Patton's Third Army was able to relieve Bastogne. The siege in the Argonne is over. We've won. Heavy losses, yes, but we've won. The tide has officially turned. It is now just a matter of time. I wanted to tell you the good news in person."

"A matter of time?" Edie rose out of her chair, facing Horatio. "What do you mean?"

"I mean, the war on the Western Front will soon draw to a close.

The Axis has lost its hold. We have the advantage. And we have right on our side. Right always wins in the end."

I realized I was standing now too. "What excellent news!" I started to jump up and down.

"Whoa there, lass." He laughed. "It's not over yet. Oh dear, no. But your aunt is right. The tide has turned. I also believe that 1945 will be a much better year than 1944, God-willing."

Edie wrapped her arms around her husband. "Do you think, I mean, will we get to go home soon?"

He shook his head no. "That I can't say. The job is far from done. We've got the Eastern Front right on our doorstep, and the Japanese have given no indication of stepping down yet."

"So, we are still here indefinitely?" Katrine bit her lip.

"It's not over till it's over," he answered.

Grace tapped her fingers impatiently on the table. Her eyes had a faraway look in them, and when they met mine, she quickly looked away, as though she was afraid I might be able to read whatever troubled thoughts were plaguing her.

CHAPTER 36

A NEW YEAR

*T*he front door slammed shut, and Grace clomped in. Her hands were full with a large lumpy package wrapped in brown paper.

"Still reading that silly book!" she exclaimed, seeing *The Robe* in Katrine's hands.

"Re-reading," Katrine corrected her. Then, to herself, she added surprisedly, "For the fifth time."

Edie held up the sweater she was knitting. One sleeve was nearly three times as long as the other. "I don't think Anna will fit into this by the time I get it to her."

"Not unless one arm has grown faster than the other." Lorelei chuckled. "But children tend to grow at the same rate. Their body parts, I mean."

Exasperated, Edie threw her needles down and looked back at Grace. "So, did Dorris come through?"

Grace ripped the paper open triumphantly. "Did she ever!" Her hands grabbed hold of something white and shook out an enormous piece of material.

"Why," Lorelei touched the fabric, "it's silk!"

"Parachute silk," Grace clarified. "The supplier knows a few of the boys in the parachute unit."

"Not too shabby," Edie said. "A little trimming here and there, and it should serve nicely! Though, I don't think I should help with the actual sewing. We *could* recruit Mrs. Knox in that department. She strikes me as an excellent seamstress. If only your mother Rose were here. Now, there is a woman who can handle a needle!"

I sighed. It was true. My mother had done a beautiful job on my dress. But she wasn't here, so Mrs. Knox would have to do.

"And you musn't forget Grace," Lorelei said squeezing her sister's hand. "You are a genius with alterations. Such an eye for line and shape!"

Grace shuffled her feet awkwardly. "Well, yes. But I will be pretty busy over the next few weeks. It might be good to ask Mrs. Knox... just in case I can't finish it."

"Busy doing what?" Edie's eyes narrowed, instantly suspicious.

"Oh, you know... things."

"I don't have any idea what sort of things you could possibly be talking of. So, why don't you share with the crowd?"

"I'm very busy with all the pilot training," Grace answered too quickly and glanced at the clock. "I've got to run. I'm meeting Frank and Dorris for a soda and sandwich downtown." And with that, she ran out, the front door slamming behind her.

"A soda and a sandwich?" Edie shook her head, and she frowned. "And we weren't even invited."

Katrine shrugged and looked back down at the book in her lap. "That group has become rather exclusive."

Edie moved away from the parachute and sat back down behind her desk. "Piper, this last interview, the one about Finley O'Donald? Unbelievable."

I remembered Finley. He was one of the Marines who'd stormed the beaches of Saipan, the Japanese island with an air base that was crucial for the U.S. to attain in order to launch the new B-29s. The battle, long and brutal, had taken place around Mount

Tapochau. Its nickname was Death Valley and Purple Heart Ridge.[21]

Finley was one of many who'd received a purple heart. He was also one of the 800 African-American Marines in combat. He was given the task of unloading and delivering food and ammunition to those under fire on the beach. A rogue bullet from a Japanese sniper went right through his thigh.

"He had a witty sense of humor." I smiled and quoted, imitating Finley's slow, steady, rhythmic speech. "The general says to the private, 'Have you come here to die?' And the private says to the general, 'Sir, I came here yester-*die*.'"

"That's awful." Katrine shut the book and stood up.

"I thought it was sort of funny," I said. "Well, I laughed when he said it."

"Listen to this one." Edie read down on the page, "Hitler visits the front and talks to a soldier. Hitler asks, 'Friend, when you are in the front line under artillery fire, what do you wish for?' The soldier replies, 'That you, my Fuhrer, stand next to me!'"

Lorelei burst out laughing… and even Katrine cracked a smile.

"He spent the whole interview telling jokes. And telling stories of growing up as a sharecropper." My stomach grumbled again. "He didn't remember much of the battle though. He was shot after unloading one box. When he woke up, he was on the boat to Alu. We met him about two months later."

"Do you think he is still there?"

"I guess so," I replied. "His wound was not that terrible as far as wounds go. He told me he would much rather be on Alu unloading and loading supplies than back home. He hated picking cotton."

We didn't speak for a while, each of us lost in our thoughts.

"How about we eat outside today?" Edie began to fan herself with the stack of papers. "It's hot as blazes in here. Nothing like January at all. It feels like July!"

Nina cooed, her beak clutching at the bars of the cage. "Looks like Nina is hungry too." For an elderly bird, she was still pretty spry.

"Oh!" Lorelei blurted. "I forgot to pick up more birdseed yesterday. We're out."

"I'll run and pick some up," I said. "I could use a walk."

"I'll make lunch." Edie looked at me. "It will be ready by the time you come back." And then she added, "And as long as you're out, Piper, could you pick up some beef tongue for dinner. It's on sale today."

"Beef tongue." I grimaced.

"It's good for you. Lots of iron," Edie said primly. "We all need our strength, don't we?"

"And these are due back at the library." Katrine pointed to two books on the edge of the couch.

I picked them up, glancing at the titles: *Sketches of Jewish Social Life in the Days of Christ* and *The Life and Times of Jesus the Messiah*, both by Alfred Edersheim. "Alfred Edersheim?"

"A highly respected Biblical scholar," she explained.

"Were they informative for your research?" Edie asked pleasantly.

"I would say they… raised more questions than provided answers."

"In my experience," Edie continued, "when you can't find the answer, it's usually because you already know it. You just have to face it and accept it, even if it's not the answer you want."

At that Lorelei paled and walked out of the room.

THE BUTCHER WAS RIGHT NEXT to the drugstore on Flinders street, and I decided I might as well check on Grace, Dorris, and Frank. But when I peered in the window through the 'O' in a painted sign that said "Prescriptions and Cosmetics," holding a sack of birdseed under one arm and a package of beef tongue in the other, I couldn't see anyone at the lunch counter.

For a moment, I wondered if Grace had lied. But then, I felt someone tapping my shoulder. Above the 'O' and next to the curly 'P,' I could make out Frank's reflection.

"Spying?" he asked.

I turned around. "Something like that."

As though sensing the real purpose of my errand, he took the birdseed out of my hand and explained, "Dorris and Grace had some business back on the base. You just missed them."

"I see."

He began to walk with me back towards home, a few blocks away.

"You and Dorris have been seeing a lot of each other," I prodded.

"Piper—" he started and then stopped. "It's not what you think."

"What do you think I think?" I asked, adjusting the package of tongue. It felt oddly lumpy.

"I think you think Dorris and I have something going on. And I know she was showing interest in me, romantically speaking, but that was just a show. She needs my help with something. Piper, I'm telling you this because I can trust you not to say anything, scout's honor?"

"Scout's honor?" My voice rose. I had absolutely no idea where this was going.

"Dorris is more than a pilot." His voice dropped to a whisper as he said, "She's a member of the O.S.S."

The O.S.S.? The Office of Strategic Services? Why that was the wartime intelligence agency!

"Are you trying to tell me that Dorris is a spy?"

"Keep your voice down. No. She's not a spy, exactly. But she's got a lot more on her plate than teaching rookies how to fly if you get my meaning." He began walking again.

"Why does she need you?" I asked. *"What* does she need you for?"

He didn't answer.

"I guess you can't answer that?"

"Correct."

"Is Grace in on the secret?"

Frank kept on walking, ignoring the question. A terrible sinking feeling washed over me. "Does Dorris' mother know?"

He shook his head no. "Her father knows though. It's one of the reasons Dorris is here. They've been waiting for word from. . . someone. And now they have it." He grabbed my hand. "Piper, things are going to change. I want you to know that I love you and Peter and your cousins... and Edie and Horatio more than I've ever loved anyone in my life, except for my mother. I just want you to know that."

"Are you leaving, Frank?"

He nodded. "But you didn't hear that from me."

"All right," I swallowed, not knowing what to say.

"As you said, it's time for me to move on." He tried to smile.

"I think you are wrong about Dorris. I think she really likes you."

"I think Dorris knows how to get what she wants." He took the tongue, and together, we ascended the steps of the house. Before I opened the door, he gave the packages back to me.

"You aren't coming in?"

"I've got pigeon duty tonight." He looked past me into the house. "Tell the others... tell Lorelei... tell them, oh, tell them anything." Unable to finish, he leaned over and awkwardly kissed my cheek. "Bye, Piper."

"Frank?" I called after him. But he was already gone. He didn't turn around or wave. He just kept walking.

I AWOKE in the still of the night. I didn't know what woke me, but something just felt wrong. There was a strange creaking in the hall, and then, a distinct pad of footsteps. Another, deeper creak followed.

"Peter!" I whispered fiercely. He didn't move. I shook him and said his name again, this time louder. But it was as though he was drugged. Ugh.

As silent as a mouse, I slipped out of bed and creeped out of our room. Furtively, I searched the hallway. No one was there. Then I saw it, the light coming from the kitchen.

I pushed the kitchen door open and saw, to my surprise, Grace. She was fully dressed, pouring herself a glass of milk. Her suitcase leaned against one of the kitchen table chairs, upon which sat Nina in her cage.

She looked at me and put the milk down.

"You're leaving too?" I felt my hand tremble. "With Nina?"

Wordlessly, she nodded.

"Where?"

She didn't say.

It hit me then. "Frank's not at the pigeon coop, is he?"

"No. He's not."

"Grace." I paused. "Tell me where you are going. Your sisters... Edie... What's going on! You can't leave. You can't!"

"I'm not going on Frank and Dorris's mission."

"You aren't?"

"No. I'm not. I don't have the authority to tell you this, but under the circumstances . . ." She paused. "Look, Piper, I'm just hitching a ride. I'm... I'm going back to Europe."

It felt like a blow to my stomach. "Europe? Where are Frank and Dorris going?"

"China first, then Europe."

"You are going to Europe via China?"

"It's the only way right now. I have to get to Amos. I have to find him. I have to make things right."

"Grace," I reached out and took her hand, "the war will end soon! Horatio said so. Just wait it out. Please don't go. If you are captured, you could be tortured, or worse!"

"You think I don't know that, Piper! What do you think has

happened to Amos? If he is even still alive. I know it's my fault, don't you see? If I had only—"

"And for another thing," I was on a roll, "how exactly are you supposed to get back to Europe via China?"

She looked at me seriously, contemplating how much she should share.

"I won't allow you to leave unless you tell me what is going on," I spoke boldly, grabbing onto her wrist with more force than I intended. "I'll wake up the whole house!"

Grace glanced at my hand, unmoving.

"Maybe you should sit down."

Slowly, I lowered myself into a chair, still not letting go of her wrist.

"There's a land route between Burma and India. Captain Brooke Dolan and Major Ilia Tolstoy, who happens to be Leo Tolstoy's grandson, found it a year and a half ago. That's actually the reason Dorris and Frank are going. Dorris has to find something important that Brooke and Ilia left with the Dalai Lama and bring it to Chiang Kai-shek's army in China before the Communists find it." She paused and looked at me straight in the eyes. "You understand that this is totally confidential, right? I shouldn't be telling you this!"

"Oh, Grace! What are you talking about? The Dalai Lama is eight years old!" I cocked my eyebrow. "And just between us, this sounds like a bunch of hogwash."

"It doesn't really matter how it sounds to you. It is what it is."

"You really want me to believe that Dorris and Frank are going to Tibet to get something Tolstoy's grandson left with the Dalai Lama? It sounds like a big fat fib, Grace Adleman."

"A year and a half ago, the Japanese blocked off the Burma Road. It's the most important passage we have to supply China with ammunition from India, you know, to fight the Japanese. We tried sending planes to the Himalayas, but the weather is pretty bad up there. Too many of our pilots were crashing into the side of the mountains."

"So what?"

"So... Captain Brooke Dolan and Major Illia Tolstoy, an explorer, set out to discover a new land route between China and India. They had to pass through Tibet, and as such, sought the permission of the Dalai Lama."

"And they left his mysterious 'thing' with this child?"

Her face expressed that that was exactly what she wanted me to believe. In fact, I was pretty sure that was exactly what she believed too. It wasn't a joke. She was telling me the truth.

"Dorris has offered to let me tag along. Once I'm in India, it's just a series of train journeys until I reach Holland."

"Holland?"

"My sources say that Amos was last reported to be in a prison camp in Holland. Camp Amersfoort."

"Grace, you're Jewish! This is the most foolish thing I've ever heard. I'm going to go get Edie and Horatio. They will talk some sense into you!"

She held me back, locking me in a stronger grip than I had just held her. "You can't stop me, Piper. I'm leaving. If I don't go with Frank and Dorris, I'll find another way. But I'm going. My mind is made up. I will never be able to live with myself until I find him. Or die trying."

I glanced again at the suitcase leaning against the wall, feeling very cold suddenly.

Seeing my gaze, she softened her grip. "I packed the journal you gave me."

"Planning to catch up on your writing?"

"I've never been much of a writer. But I thought it would remind me of . . . us." She looked around the kitchen. "I have to go."

"Frank and Dorris are leaving *tonight*." She wouldn't meet my penetrating stare. "Lorelei has Paul now, and Katrine is strong. Stronger than she seems. They will both be okay." Quickly, she pulled a paper folded in half out of her pocket and passed it to me.

"I was going to leave this for everyone. You'll give it to them when they wake up?"

"You aren't going to say goodbye to everyone?"

"I'd lose my nerve." She kissed my cheek. "Tell my sisters I love them."

"They'd rather hear it from you. This will be very difficult for them. What about Lorelei's wedding?" I heard the words come out of my mouth but was not exactly sure of what I was saying.

In one hand, she grabbed her suitcase and in the other, the handle to Nina's cage.

"I'll write you as soon as I can. I promise."

"Grace?" I called. But she'd left, leaving the front door wide open. A breeze swept through the house, and the light of a full moon cast long, lonely shadows on the worn wood floor.

FOURTH MOVEMENT

"Love can transpose to form and dignity.
Love looks not with the eyes, but with the mind,
And therefore is winged Cupid painted blind.
Nor hath Love's mind of any judgment taste;
Wings and no eyes figure unheedy haste."
    -*A Midsummer Night's Dream*[1]

CHAPTER 37

FEBRUARY

Katrine found me in the kitchen several hours later, nervously pacing back and forth. She didn't even stop to ask why I was awake. Or why I was pacing. No, she was completely preoccupied.

"Oh, Piper," she said, walking into the dim light of the kitchen, "I just had the most awful dream."

I stopped walking and leaned against the counter, wondering if I should tell her that Grace and Frank—even Nina—had flown the coop. Before I could decide, she plunged in.

"I dreamt about Harry. He was burning up with a fever somewhere in a jungle. I kept trying to get to him, but all these barriers kept getting in my way. Barbed wire, mountains, rivers. He was calling out for me, and every time I tried to call out to him, my voice got stuck in my throat. He couldn't hear me. He was... dying." Her face looked very white. "There were all these Roman soldiers keeping me from him."

"I think you've been reading too much of *The Robe*."

It was as though she did not hear me. "The Roman soldiers took my arms and dragged me away, and they threw me into the prison below the Colosseum."

I pulled out a chair and sat down. She wouldn't stop talking.

"And then, I woke up in the dream. You know, a dream within a dream. And for some reason, I had to tell Grace something. I don't remember what. I went to wake her, and she was gone."

A terrible sinking feeling filled my stomach. "Katrine…"

"I looked all over the house, all over Townsville. *Everywhere.*"

She saw the look on my face and paused.

"Piper?"

I couldn't speak.

"What's happened?"

My mouth felt like it was filled with balls of cotton. "She's gone, Katrine. She's left."

"What do you mean, she's left?" Her fingers gripped the side of the table.

"She's left to find Amos."

Katrine looked completely deflated. "But it's certain death. How can she? Whatever does she mean to do?"

"Redeem herself, I think."

Katrine made a dash to the door. "I've got to stop her!"

I was faster and caught her arm, exclaiming, "Katrine! She's long gone by now! No doubt they are already over Papua New Guinea."

Katrine sunk down to the floor and began to sob. "At the end, Piper, who will be left? My parents? Harry? Now, Grace? My sisters are all I have left. Oh, Piper, they are all I have left."

I bent down and held her. "Katrine, oh, Katrine. That's not true. You have me and Edie and Horatio. And my parents. You have lots of family!" I said, running my fingers through her hair. "It will be all right. It is, it will be all right."

Her tears streamed down her face. "How can you know that? Nothing is all right. It won't ever be all right again."

"I don't believe that."

She wrapped her fingers around the necklace and ripped it off her neck, breaking the clasp. "Take it back." She thrust it into my hands.

And so, we sat in the kitchen another few moments until Katrine stood up abruptly and told me she was going for a walk and would be back when she could think. She didn't know when that would be.

"But you aren't wearing any shoes!" I called out after her. But it was too late. Like Grace, she was gone. That said, I was pretty sure *she* would come back. Her feet were quite sensitive.

In her wake, I looked down at my necklace, the words in Hebrew naming The Hope, *Ha Tikvah*, looking back at me, etched in gold. The clasp twisted and mangled. How it must have hurt when she yanked it off like that.

What a tragic night this was turning out to be.

When the rest of the house finally awoke, I broke the news about Grace. It was received much as I expected. Her note, brief and to the point said that she was going to find Amos via the China route. Horatio roared and then quieted down when he realized that it was no use, and it was too late to be angry at her, anyway. She was already long gone and was probably somewhere deep in the sky over the East Indies. Peter, distressed, mentioned how Frank had been talking about China a lot. He had thought nothing about it until now. Edie, shocked, responded, "I hope she packed her long underwear. It gets very, *very* cold in Tibet." But I could tell she was quite upset. She started pacing right alongside me and didn't touch her coffee.

Grace's abrupt departure removed the usual joy and anticipation felt before a wedding. Paul, reluctantly, agreed to wait to set a date after Lorelei burst into tears and exclaimed that she couldn't get married without Grace by her side as a bridesmaid. I could tell he was confused and hurt by her forcefulness to delay the event. It was obvious that there was something deeper going on in Lorelei's heart than the pain caused by Grace's disappearance. But Paul didn't ask what it was, and Lorelei only went on and on about how insensitive

Grace was and how her little sister had lost the common sense God gave her.

To make matters worse, the waters of the Pacific Front were heating up. Something was coming. Something big. We could feel it in the air.

Over the next few weeks, Peter put in countless extra hours checking lists of guns and ammunition. Horatio was at HQ day and night. Paul disappeared into the bowels of the translation bunker, hour after hour spent bent over a line of wireless transceivers, listening for messages from Japan. Messages arrived in strange groupings of apparently disconnected letters and encrypted texts. Decrypting the messages was exhausting and risky. Incorrect information could cost lives. As one of the top translators, he could barely spare more than three or four minutes for a stressed bite of a sandwich and two meaningless sentences with Lorelei, asking how she was and how things were at the Red Cross.

Life went on, as did the war, and we had to go on with it, with or without Grace, with or without a wedding. But it was a strange, tense sort of life. Everyone was on edge, and that was putting it lightly.

ULTIMATELY, however, it was Katrine who took Grace's departure the hardest. She felt abandoned on a deeper level by what Grace had done then any of us. Her world had fallen apart with Harry's disappearance, and the last little thing she felt she could control, the simple daily life she clung to with her sisters, was crumbling, and she was crumbling with it.

She disappeared into her room for a week, only leaving to go to the library and come back with yet another stack of books. Barely eating, barely sleeping. And then, one afternoon, she found me in the study as I was editing my notes from the interviews with the soldiers on Alu, yet again. It was difficult putting words on the page in my attempt to fill out their stories as Edie had instructed, much more difficult than I expected—and I expected it to be difficult.

"Piper?"

"Yes?"

Her voice was steady. "I'm ready. I've had enough."

"Enough of what?"

"I want what you all have."

I looked up from my notes, confused. "What we all have?"

"Lorelei has it too, ever since she became a Christian. Now, I'm not spiritual like her, not nearly as deep. But if what she believes is the same as what you believe, I'm ready to believe it too."

"It *is* the same." I set the manuscript down and prayed God would help me find the right words. "But, it's not an 'it.' It's a who."

"You are talking about Yeshua, I know."

I nodded, somehow sensing that the less I said, the better.

"You told me once that 'without faith, it is impossible to please God because anyone who comes to him must believe that he exists and that he rewards those who earnestly seek him.'"[2]

I waited.

"I've done my research, just like you challenged me to. I'm convinced by everything I've read that Yeshua did in fact exist — historically, that is."

"That's a start." I looked at her, trying to prepare myself for whatever was coming.

She grew excited. "Did you know that Yeshua fulfilled over three hundred prophesies written in the Hebrew Scriptures about the Messiah? Prophecies written over 1000 years by numerous different authors. How did he do that!" she exclaimed. "It's incredible. Unbelievable."

"He did it because he *is* the Messiah, the Son of God," I explained.

"But Piper, to believe that, I also have to believe in God — in Elohim." She looked down. "My relationship with religion has always been academic. Between everything I learned at the University, everything I've seen with the war... I've found it very difficult to believe in God at all. Much less the idea that Yeshua is the Messiah!"

I didn't move. She was somewhere else, speaking half to herself, half to no one in particular. "His bones weren't broken, they cast lots for his garments... sold for 30 pieces of silver..."

I remembered her numbered list. She had been painstakingly fact-checking one prophecy at a time.

"It's not a coincidence, is it?" Her eyes met mine, penetrating deep into my soul. "He alone matches the description of the Messiah in Scripture. *He* certainly was convinced he was the Son of God."

"It doesn't matter what he believed about himself, does it? What matters is what is true."

"He was either wrong, and everyone around him was wrong," her eyes darted around the room nervously, "and every Christian since has been wrong... or he really is the Son of God."

She looked up, afraid. "And the resurrection?"

"Look at my mother, Katrine." I rested my eyes on her face, speaking gently. "I believe God healed her body. If medical miracles like that can happen, why couldn't God raise his Son from the dead?"

"I," she hesitated, "I have thought of this too. And I am convinced that Yeshua really was who he said he was. I am convinced that the God of the Bible is who he says he is. I am convinced by the evidence that God exists and that Yeshua is the promised Son of God." Her voice caught for a moment. "But it's not enough, is it? To just believe? I don't know where to go from here, Piper. I feel stuck. I don't know how to... believe the way you do!"

Seriously, I took her hand, inwardly wishing my mother was here, or Peter, at least! But I knew the Holy Spirit was with me.

"You want what Lorelei and I have?"

Nodding, her eyes began to water.

A peace washed over me, and I felt the answer go straight from my heart out of my mouth. "Then you are right, it is not enough just to believe that Yeshua is who he says he is."

"What must I do?" Her voice was tinged with urgency. You could hear a pin drop.

"Paul, a great Jewish rabbi, wrote that 'if you confess with your mouth, 'Jesus is Lord,' and believe in your heart that God raised him from the dead, you will be saved.'[3] When he uses the word 'Lord,' it means living under his lordship. In other words, it means giving him control of your life and using your life as a service for his will to be done, instead of our own."

Managing a slight laugh, she shook her head. "I'd much rather he have control than me. I can tell you I've not exactly been doing a stellar job."

"It's actually not that hard." I smiled.

"But how do you do it?"

All those days in Sunday school came rushing back. "Confess that you are a sinner and allow him to heal you where you are wounded. Learn to listen and follow his voice. He still speaks today, you know."

"Can he really do all of that?" She was like a little girl, unlearning all she relied on that had proved false in the long run. All the self-reliance. All the answers and rationalizations. Everything she'd relied on because she didn't know he wanted to help her.

I nodded. "You've read *The Robe*. You know what happened to Miriam."

"Yeshua gave her back her song?"

"He'll give you back your song." I paused then added, "If you trust him with your life, that is."

"Would you, oh, Piper." Her eyes filled with tears. "Would you pray with me?"

"It would be my honor."

I knelt by the chair where she sat and took her hands in mine. She hung her head and said, barely above a whisper, "Dear God, it's me, Katrine. I've come here to tell you I am convinced that Yeshua is your son, that he is the Messiah." Her voice cracked. "What I'm trying to say is, that… that I trust you are who you say you are, and I will serve you the rest of my life."

A deep sense of wonder and peace enveloped us, and when Katrine looked up, it was as though she had been touched with a supernatural light. It flowed out of her eyes and rested wherever she looked.

That's when I stood up and pulled Katrine with me into my room. "I have something for you," I said. "If you want faith, Katrine, it doesn't come by wanting or emotions or warm fuzzy feelings. If you base your faith on those things, at the first sign of trouble, you'll doubt."

I pressed my necklace back into her hands, along with my old pocket Bible. "Faith comes by hearing and hearing by the Word of God. Read God's Word, Katrine, and your faith will grow."

Her hands fingered the necklace. "I think I'm starting to understand the true meaning of hope, Piper. It's him. It's Yeshua, isn't it?"

I nodded, feeling almost as awestruck as she at the turn of events.

"The clasp is fixed!" she exclaimed.

"Miracles happen." I grinned. "That, and I happen to have a rather handy husband."

"Girls!" Edie's voice rang out as the front door opened. "We're back! I kidnapped Lorelei on her way home from the Red Cross and brought her to Mrs. Knox's for her first dress fitting. You will be absolutely floored with what Mrs. Knox did with the parachute. Lorelei looks like a dream in it." She paused and then continued, now talking only to Lorelei, "Don't look at me like that. I know you think a wedding dress is premature, given the fact that you postponed the wedding indefinitely, but we'll only be with a seamstress like Mrs. Knox every once in a blue moon. I made the appointment with her several weeks ago, and I wasn't about to break it because of a little hiccup with the date of the wedding. You'll thank me for this later, Lorelei!"

Smiling with a secret shared joy, we stepped back into the hall, looking towards the front door.

Lorelei, visibly tense, repeated what was quickly becoming a broken record, "I feel uncomfortable with all of this. You know we haven't set a date yet. I want to wait for Grace to return before we settle on anything."

Lorelei paused, sensing something important had happened in her absence. "What's going on?"

"Something wonderful." Katrine stood up and kissed her cheek. "Something wonderful. I... I met someone. A certain friend of yours."

Lorelei looked at me questioningly and followed us into the study, leaving Edie to shut the front door.

"I met Yeshua, Lorelei. I... I believe."

Lorelei threw her arms around Katrine, her face a mixture of wonder and joy. "You don't know how long I've prayed for this day." Her eyes opened wide in amazement. "How did this happen?"

"He spoke peace to my heart and truth to my mind." Katrine's eyes glistened.

Just as Katrine was about to explain what she had discovered through her research and how the immense burden of fear had lifted from her shoulders the moment she accepted the truth, or rather, believed the truth, my aunt burst in, humming cheerfully. "I do hope Horatio practiced the wedding march on his violin." Edie smiled and then said, "How do you feel about a small operatic piece called 'Oh Promise Me'?" Before we could answer, she jumped right in, soaring to unnaturally high notes of the classic song that seemed to have been sung at every wedding for the last 50 years.

We stopped and stared, stunned. "Well, Edie," Lorelei tried not to laugh, "if it's in your heart to sing, I'm sure Paul and I would love it."

"The gift of music," she said magnanimously, "is the best gift one can give. And maybe I can come up with something to sing for the engagement party."

"Isn't it rather unconventional to throw an engagement party without a wedding date set? You remember, Paul and I have postponed the date until the summer," Lorelei asked. "You know, to give Grace ample time to return." She looked down. "And me more time to..."

"Don't start with that again," Edie scolded. "You will not deny me the pleasure of throwing you a party, even if you postpone your wedding until the end of the war!"

I stepped closer to Lorelei, pulling her back into the hallway. "More time to what, Lorelei?"

She raised her eyes to mine, her voice barely above a whisper. "More time to know if I am supposed to marry Paul."

A sick feeling filled my stomach. "Why did you say 'yes' when he asked you to marry him?"

She blinked. "He asked me in front of everyone," she choked out. "I felt pressured."

"But he loves you," I said.

"I feel like we are rushing things!"

"You haven't even set a date. How rushed is that?"

"Piper, I feel like he doesn't *know* me."

"Lorelei, you can only know a person so much before you are married. Then, you spend the rest of your life learning about one another. That's the way it works."

"I have to *know*! Don't you understand?"

The situation reminded me so much of Edie and Horatio. Only, Lorelei's reasons for dragging her feet to matrimony were greyer. She had been through such trauma. Only recently had she found some sort of stability in knowing Yeshua. But it was impossible to know how things would go with Paul, and so, Lorelei was stalling. If she couldn't know how things would turn out, she refused to move forward. Ultimately, holding out for Grace's return was a cover-up for Lorelei's fear of making a mistake. It differed from Edie's excuse for postponing marriage, but it was equally tragic.

"Timing is never perfect," I put my hand on my hip, "trust me.

Something, somewhere, will always be wrong. You two need to talk. You really have to."

"Paul's been so busy lately. Something's up at the base. I think they are planning some sort of operation."

"It's not fair to either of you to keep on going like this. You have to find time to communicate."

"I know," she said. "I know."

CHAPTER 38

THE ENGAGEMENT PARTY

*T*wo weeks later, as I helped button up Lorelei's creamy white suit for the engagement party, I asked, "Have you talked yet?" The gathered waist and straight skirt showed off her slim figure. In any photograph, I would have bet money she really was engaged. But in person, given the pained look on her face in the mirror's reflection, I doubted it.

Nervously, she shook her head. "He's practically been living underground at the base with his radio. I've barely seen him for more than 10 minutes at a time. He's been completely exhausted." She faltered as she said, "I told him we need to talk, and he promised me we would, once everything calms down. But I think he's brushing me off. He doesn't want to hear what I have to say."

"And it hasn't calmed down, has it?" I buttoned the last button, and she turned around to face me.

"Conveniently, for him." Her green eyes watered. "And now here we are, having an engagement party."

It was true. Edie's engagement party for the couple (whose wedding was indefinitely postponed) was in full swing, and I prepared Lorelei to make her grand entrance.

"Are you ready?" I asked slowly.

She jerked her head up and down and put on her best fake smile. "I guess so."

Again, going off of a photograph alone, anyone would have believed the party was a hit. Everyone was there, all the officers and their wives and Lorelei's friends from the Red Cross. Edie was in full-on hostess mode, wearing a long red dress and her pearl necklace. She'd brought in a classical string ensemble and ordered a miniature wedding cake. It was the pinnacle of wartime elegance, restrained yet generous. Classy yet fun. Paul and Lorelei were the picture of soon-to-be conjugal happiness.

But one cannot go off of looks alone. Over olive canapés and punch, Lorelei tried to get Paul's attention and pull him outside several times, but Paul waved her off. They could talk later once their guests left. Her face fell momentarily, and then she wandered through the crowd, trying (unsuccessfully) to mingle. I saw Paul staring at her through the rest of the party.

Admiral Stark, the Englishman whose family was back in England, and Horatio were both in the study, talking in hushed tones over the battle that had been raging for the past month to retake the island of Corregidor.

We all knew something was coming to a head.

The moment Paul and Lorelei had waited for was coming. The clock was quickly ticking towards the showdown. And it came abruptly, almost as soon as the last guests had left.

Katrine walked into the kitchen with a stack of dirty dishes threatening to topple over in her arms. She sighed as she contemplated where to put them. It seemed all the counter space was already taken with more dirty dishes. She gave up and set down the stack on the floor.

I groaned. "I think we will be doing dishes for the rest of our lives."

Peter waltzed in, another stack of dirty plates in hand, and exclaimed, "Have no fear, lady fair. This is the last of the lot." Gently, he pushed me out of the way and took over. "My turn. You sit and eat another tomato sandwich."

"My hero." I passed him the sponge and sat down next to my aunt and Katrine. "I barely ate anything at the reception." I bit into the sandwich and swallowed it down.

"That makes two of us," Edie agreed, reaching out for one of the remaining olive canapés. "Too busy schmoozing and making sure everyone else was eating. Hostess's curse!" She rubbed her calf muscle. "Remind me to hire a wedding planner when Anna gets married, won't you, dear?"

Katrine sipped a cup of cold tea thoughtfully. "It was a very pretty party though."

"Yes," I nodded, "beautiful." Even as I said it, I realized how tired we were. The conversation seemed to be going in circles.

"Edie!" Horatio bellowed from the living room.

"Yes!" she shouted back.

"Anymore of the chocolate cake?"

Pushing herself up from the table, she muttered "Duty calls," cut two slices from the last of the groom's cake, and put them on paper napkins. "We are out of dishes," she said, looking at the kitchen dejectedly.

"Here," I took the cake, "you eat your cheddar scone. I'll play delivery girl."

"You are a good woman, Piper," Edie said with thankful solemnity. "A very good woman."

Just as I made my way into the living room, the telephone rang. I put the cake down on the table beneath the phone and answered it.

"Is General Stark and Admiral Macleay at home?" A young male voice said from the other end of the line.

"Which one do you need?" Out of the corner of my eye, I saw Paul lead Lorelei into the hall. The two were whispering, and Lorelei looked rather stressed.

"Please tell both that they are to report to their headquarters immediately."

Heart pounding in my chest, I turned my attention back to the man on the line, asking, "Is everything all right?"

"Yes, ma'am. Oh yes. We've recaptured Corregidor. Five-thousand Japanese troops dead. One-thousand casualties."

I nearly dropped the phone. Corregidor! Three years earlier, the Japanese had taken the island in the Manila Bay. Now that we once more had the island, we would no doubt be able to retake Manila and then the Philippines. That meant we had gained the upper hand in the Pacific. For the first time in the war, the Allies were winning on both fronts.[4]

"Horatio!" I shouted. "Edie, Peter! Katrine! General Stark! We've got Corregidor. It's ours!"

"Ah." General Stark stood up as everyone rushed in. "Excellent. Excellent. I imagine we'll be needed at our respective posts, old boy." He shook Horatio's hand. "I'm in charge of refueling lines. It will be a long night." As if on second thought, he turned to me. "Lovely party, ma'am. Thank you."

"I'm right behind you, Stark," Horatio said, rubbing his hands together. "You go on ahead. I need to discuss some things with my family now if you don't mind."

"Right then." He nodded. "I'm off."

By the time General Stark had left, we were all in the hall in a huddle around the telephone. Horatio's eyes had an intense brightness. "Now that we have Corregidor, we will push on to Manila. They have appointed me to oversee one of the destroyers headed towards the Bay. We leave tonight."

Suddenly, it all became clear. No wonder Paul had been so busy at the base, and Peter had been spending extra hours at his desk. This was why Horatio had practically moved into HQ; an operation like this took weeks to organize and prepare for.

"Tonight?" Edie's voice rose very high. "Horatio! How can you say that? What are you talking about?"

He looked at her.

"You've been planning this for quite some time, haven't you?"

Slowly, Horatio nodded.

"But why didn't you confide in me!?"

"Edie, I plan battles every day. You know that!"

"Oh poppycock!" She huffed.

"It's the final push, Edie. We have to finish strong. No giving up now. No slowing down."

"Am I going with you?" Edie asked slowly, knowing full well what the answer was before she asked it.

Horatio rubbed his chin. "I can't ask you to come, Edie. It will be very dangerous."

"But if I volunteer?"

He didn't speak.

"You can't make me stay here!" Edie nearly shouted. "We took vows, remember. We promised we would be together through thick and thin. It's why I'm here and not in Scotland with our children. Our children we waited 20 years to have!"

"I, oh, Edie." Horatio looked away. "You can't come. Not this time. It's much too dangerous."

Peter pulled Edie close. "Edie, you understand, don't you?"

"I won't pretend I don't. I *do*. But this is all very distressing," she said, beginning to cry.

"Don't cry, Edie," Horatio said. "I promise I'll send for you as soon as we have Manila." She began to cry harder. "I don't want to remember you crying. I want to remember you smiling and cheerful. My Philipa Edith Gordan-Macleay."

"Well," she sniffed, "you can't always get what you want, can you? So, you'll just have to be content to remember me like this. Eyes red with grief, puffy and tired from worrying over you, my darling, darling husband." In moments like this, Edie could not help but press into the drama. It was not in her nature to restrain the moment in any great story 'arc.'

Katrine reached out and grabbed Horatio's arm. "You'll look for him, won't you?"

"Yes, Katrine. The minute we get into Manila, I'll look high and low for your husband. Have no fear of that."

Edie reached up and caressed his beard. "Farewell, sweet playfellow… Love's stories written in love's richest books. To fan the moonbeams from his sleeping eyes."[5]

Horatio smiled. "And yet, to say the truth, reason and love keep little company together nowadays."[6]

I realized they were quoting *a Midsummer's Night's Dream*.

"Lord, what fools these mortals be!"[7] Edie bit her lip.

"The course of true love never did run smooth, dear, dear wife."[8]

"Promise me, oh darling, Horatio, promise me this is not the end of our story."

"You should know better than anyone, Edie, that the play has only just begun."

Suddenly, the sound of raised voices in the hall drew all of our attention from Edie and Horatio to Lorelei and Paul. The scene shifted from a semi-comedic goodbye to a full-on tragedy. Not quite Shakespearean in proportion, true, but perhaps more dramatic because it was real, and it was happening right there in front of everyone.

"I just don't understand why you want to postpone… again!" Paul clenched his fist.

"It's not that." Lorelei's tone was tightly controlled. "We can't postpone what we don't have a date for."

"I want to marry you, Lorelei, and I would marry you today if I could. Not next summer, no matter what I might have said. Who knows when Grace is coming back. She may not come back at all! How can we let her decisions affect *our* future!"

I saw Paul's face. It was steadily growing redder.

"I just want to wait until things are more settled before diving into a whole new life! You know, make sure that Katrine and Grace are all right."

"You are repeating yourself, Lorelei. We've been through this a million times!"

"Paul!"

"You need to trust God with your sisters," he said firmly. "Trust me, Lorelei, you will calm down the minute we are married and settled back in California. You'll see."

The air hung still.

"California? We didn't talk about that." Lorelei froze. "Married and living in California?"

"Well…" He paused before saying, "I always assumed we would move to California." Studying her face, Paul frowned. "What's this really about, Lorelei?"

"We have to talk about these things! You can't just go and say we'll live in California!"

"We are talking about it!"

"No," she was growing angry, "*we* aren't talking about it. *We* never really talk! *You* are talking about it."

"That's not true."

"You've been avoiding me. Admit it!"

"Oh, come on!" His California blue eyes flashed. "There's a war on if you haven't noticed? I've been doing my job!" She stiffened as he continued angrily, "And don't talk about me avoiding you. *You* are the one who wants to postpone our wedding."

The cat was out of the bag. Paul's deep hurt and confusion rose to the surface for all to see. "Lorelei, all I want is to set a date. That's all."

"All I want is for you to listen to me for once," Lorelei spoke rapidly. "But you can't! You only do what you want to do. You only hear what you want to hear!" All the frustration of weeks of words unspoken that needed to be spoken were coming out fast and furiously, threatening to do more damage than not.

"What are you talking about?"

"You can't do anything for me. You can't wait for just a few months. Just like you couldn't even try my Béarnaise sauce."

"Are you seriously still angry at me for not trying your sauce? I can't help it I like my steak the way I like it. Plain and simple."

I felt Peter by my side and looked up at him, wide-eyed. "Hey you two," Peter tried to stop them, "maybe you should take a time-out and regroup. It always helps Piper and me..." But they were so focused that they had completely lost track that they had an audience and were speaking without thinking.

"You aren't interested in who I am," she threw out.

"Lorelei," Paul was bewildered, "I'm in love with you. Of course, I'm interested in you."

"Then why don't you ever ask me... about *me*? About what *I* want?"

"Let's be honest, Lorelei. You aren't waiting for Grace. You are waiting for some voice in your head to tell you I'm not a mistake, and our life together will be perfect. Well, let me tell you something. Some things you can't know. Some things you only find out by diving in headfirst." Paul was almost shouting.

"That's not fair, Paul!"

"But it's the truth, isn't it? You can't trust me. You can't trust *us*." Paul's eyes slowly softened from anger to something else. Something like defeat and sadness.

"You and I both know this isn't about that at all! This is about the fact that you won't listen to me!" Lorelei replied.

"I'm hearing you loud and clear. Look, Lorelei, I know you aren't sure about marrying me. I'm a smart guy. This isn't my first rodeo. I *am* sure about you. Surer than I've ever been about anything in my life."

"Paul. I just think we should wait... until..." she trailed off.

"Until the cows come home?"

"What?" She stopped, confused.

"It's an American expression."

"You're comparing me to a cow?"

"No! Of course not!"

"You just said 'until the cows come home.'"

"It was a miscommunication." Paul was frustrated.

Lorelei swallowed, and her eyes welled up. "That's why this isn't working."

They stopped and stared at one another for a painfully long second. Finally, Paul inhaled. "If that's how you feel, why did you agree to marry me at all?"

"You asked me in front of everyone. How was I supposed to say no?"

Silence fell.

The explosion came as a shock, as much to them as to us—the innocent bystanders. Paul stepped back as though someone had struck him. "I love your family. I wanted everyone to be a part of our moment." His eyes watered, and he hastily brushed away a tear before it could fall. "Sometimes, Lorelei Adleman, God does not tell us everything we want to know. Sometimes he leaves the choice up to us. I chose you. I risked loving you. But I couldn't help it. You made me jump headfirst the first day we met. I guess I lost my head a bit when I lost my heart. But I'm beginning to find it again."

Slowly, she pulled Paul's ring off her finger and held it out in her palm. "I don't think it would be fair for me to keep this."

"I never really had you, did I?" Paul stared at the ring for a moment and then slowly took it back. Stoically, he walked down the hall and out the front door.

Lorelei's slim figure in her new white dress disappeared down the hall in the other direction. I could hear her sobbing a minute later through the closed door. Something had gone terribly wrong, and we all knew it.

A second later, she came back, the wedding dress in hand, and threw it in the wastebasket (or rather, on top of the wastebasket—it was too big to fit inside of it) stone-faced. Once more, she turned on her heel and went back to her room.

"I..." Horatio cleared his throat awkwardly, "I guess I better go pack."

Edie nodded and wordlessly went to the dress and shook it out. "I'll hold on to this." She looked at me and sighed sadly. "God, help her not make the same mistake I did." But we all knew it was already too late.

CHAPTER 39

WHAT'S DONE IS DONE

*M*arch 3rd, three days after the disastrous end to Paul and Lorelei's engagement, Horatio made good on his promise, sending word that Edie was free to join him for the next few weeks. Given the high-drama of their parting, Edie's departure was remarkably anti-climactic, seeing as their separation had only lasted a couple of days. Manila, the capital of the Philippines, was in Allied hands and declared free of the Japanese. Edie boarded the first flight to land in Manila, along with Colonel and Mrs. Linton, promising to do everything in her power to find Harry.

Her last words were to Lorelei. She took both her hands in her own and said simply, "Darling girl, don't let fear keep you from what you know is right."

Lorelei pretended she didn't know what Edie was talking about, but Edie refused to buy it. "Sometimes, you don't need a sign because you already know in your heart what you must do. Don't be a fool like I was… waiting for 20 years because I wanted to live my life, my way. And then there is poor Grace. She missed the fact that she and Amos would be better together, even for the war effort, than alone. Both of us were dreadfully wrong. I know it's in our family history, like a disease or something, to delay like this. But it can stop with you. Go back to him. Make it right." She reached out and took her hand. "Talk to him."

"We are past talking." Lorelei frowned. "We've said everything there is to say."

"I highly doubt that." Edie let go of her hand. "There is more to Paul than meets the eye. There's more to you too."

"Edie, 'Ois kale, weiter a moid.'"

"Translation, dear." Edie put her hand on her hip.

"'The marriage negotiations are broken off.'"

"An old Jewish saying?"

"Something like that."

"Well, dear girl, here's a saying of my own. 'A good man is hard to find. It doesn't matter if the world is falling apart—if you find one, you hold on to him.'" Then she boarded the plane and soared off into the wild blue yonder, leaving Lorelei speechless.

The day she arrived, March 4, the government of Finland declared war on Nazi Germany. She wrote and told us how Manila was filled, ironically, with Jewish refugees. Thousands of Jews denied entry to America and the UK, found refuge in Shanghai in China, Sousa in the Dominican Republic, and Manila in the Philippines. But those in Manila had no idea that they had only replaced one front for another. The city was a pile of rubble.

It was like a wave was picking up speed to crash on the shore—the enormous tidal wave called, 'The End.'

Everything was moving so quickly, it was difficult to keep up. On March 5, Allied troops marched on Cologne. Rumors spread that the Germans, desperate for men, began conscripting boys as young as 16. The next day, the U.S. Army Air Force secured the island of Iwo Jima. The battle was prolonged and terrible, leaving thousands dead on both sides. But in the end, we won.

March gave way to April. April made room for May. Life went marching on if you could call it that.

Grace did not write. Lorelei threw herself into work at the Red Cross. There was an unspoken rule that we were not to bring up Paul or what had happened. It was as though he had never entered our lives.

But it was all an act. He had existed, and he had left a mark. Paul added a dose of joy and strength to our family circle, and his absence was keenly felt by everyone. We all missed his genuine cheerfulness and winsome personality. Lorelei felt it the most, but next in line came Peter. In Paul, my husband had found a faithful friend and a trusted brother.

"He wasn't avoiding, Lorelei," Peter said as we spoke quietly in our room, getting ready for bed. "He was avoiding further rejection. Most men do. As he said, he never really had her."

I brushed my hair and slathered cold cream over my hands and up to my elbows. For the umpteenth time, we privately tried to figure out what had gone wrong.

"He confided in me he's not doing well." Peter huffed.

(At the exact same time, on the other side of the world, the Allies crossed the Rhine River and advanced into central Germany.)

"Though I could have figured that out myself. He threw the engagement ring into the harbor." He finished buttoning up his pajamas.

"Oh no," I groaned, sliding under the sheets. The two friends still saw each other on the base when they could. After everything they had been through, they would be friends for life.

"I watched him do it. I've never seen a guy so angry. Said he'd never love again." Peter laid down beside me, and we both stared up at the ceiling. "He really loved her," Peter said. "Still loves her, obviously. Even with the ring in the harbor, he can't stop talking about her. She's all he talks about. All he does is ask me questions about Lorelei."

I shook my head, feeling the rough sheet on my cheek. "They both said things they didn't mean. I wish they would just talk about it. You know, get it all out on the table."

"Do you think she loves him," I asked, after a second.

"She loves him," he said firmly. "Though she may not admit it, she hasn't smiled once since they broke up. Not really. She's pretending to be relieved, but I know she's not."

I thought back to that time on the porch after I'd lost all my film and my camera. Lorelei had come close to expressing she was falling in love with Paul. But she had been so conflicted, so terrified that her heart might lead her down the wrong path that she never would fully give into it. Paul was right. Even now, he hadn't really lost her because he'd never really had her.

"One way or another," Peter continued, "they need to talk about what happened. They both love God, and it's not right for believers to leave it this messy. Forgiveness has to be a part of this, whether or not they end up together."

IT WAS right after the Red Army had entered Austria and captured Danzig, just as the other Allies took Frankfurt. At dinner, out of nowhere, Lorelei told us she had written Dr. Herring in Palestine.

"As soon as I can work out my passage, I'll be back on the lake." Lorelei put on a brave face. The kibbutz was struggling and needed help. Arab rebels working for the Mufti in Jerusalem were doing everything they could to terrorize the small community of teenagers, slashing their tractor tires at night, blocking their trucks of dates from making it to market with sniper fire. The tension in Palestine was increasing. It was not an easy time to be a Jew in the world. It was not an easy time to be in Palestine. But it was a place Lorelei could help, and helping always made her feel better, and she felt perhaps God wanted her there again.

"Really, I'm glad Paul and I ended our relationship," she confided to us. "I'm needed in Palestine. He is too self-centered to really care about me, just like I always worried he was. He's fine without me. I'm obviously just fine without him."

Obviously, I thought.

Grimacing, Peter mumbled, "That's a bunch of hogwash."

"He didn't care about me," Lorelei shot back, "or he would have tried to get to know me and what I want harder than he did."

"Harder than he did?" Peter hadn't slept well the night before and was grumpy. Whenever that happened, a certain filter seemed to disappear, and he would say whatever idiotic thing, no matter how true, that came into his head. "I see Paul a couple of times a week. All he can do is talk about you. He asks about you, every part of you! He wants to know how you are doing, what you've been up to. He asks about your parents and where you grew up. He can't stop asking about you."

"Sounds like he is more interested in me now that I'm gone than when I was with him."

"You don't get it, do you? He loves you! Maybe he needs to work on his communication skills, but who doesn't?"

A flicker of confusion crossed her features. "Why didn't he ask me those things himself?"

"Why don't *you* ask him why?"

"Peter, don't you understand? I tried talking! Paul was always busy, or he wouldn't ask the right questions, or he'd change the subject!"

"That's an exaggeration, Lorelei. There is a war on. It's been a little crazy. Some guys need a little help. You have to tell them what they need to know!" He raised his voice. "You can't expect him to do all the work. That's not fair. It's setting him up for failure!"

In response, Lorelei shot him a stony look and walked into her room.

"Peter!" I chided him, sliding out of my chair and following her. "Give it a rest, Peter. Can't you see she's hurting!" I threw over my shoulder.

I found her, sitting on the edge of her bed.

"You think I made the wrong decision, like Peter, don't you?"

"Only you can answer that." I sat beside her cautiously. "But for the record, I don't think Paul handled this whole thing the way he should have either."

Peter knocked on the door softly and stuck his head in. "Lorelei, I… I have to apologize. Paul is my friend. You know, it gets complicated when two people you like a whole lot are fighting. It's not like I'm choosing sides or anything. I really want the best for you both, and I think it goes without saying that we all thought you were the best for each other. You didn't deserve my anger. I'm upset about a lot, and I took it out on you."

She looked down resolutely. "I forgive you, Peter. And anyway, what's done is done. It can't be undone. We can't unsay what was said."

I glanced at Peter. It was nearly the same thing Paul had said.

"You can make it right. You can talk to him and make peace—with yourself and with him."

"No." Her voice tightened. "If he wants to talk, he knows where to find me."

Squaring her shoulders, Lorelei stood up, abruptly changing the subject. "How about we try that mock apple pie recipe, Piper?" She tried to smile. "Now that I'm single, I can do whatever I want! All my time is my own. We could go swimming or shopping after we make the pie? What do you say?"

Mock apple pie, I repeated to myself. Just like this mock charade that everything was all right.

CHAPTER 40

NEXT YEAR IN JERUSALEM

*W*e made the mock apple pie with a filling of Ritz crackers, water, sugar, cinnamon, and a lemon rind. Apples were few and far between in Townsville these days. But for some strange reason, there was an abundance of Ritz crackers.

Katrine had been dubious of trying it out, sure it wouldn't taste anything like apple pie, but I was in the mood for something that felt like home. If I didn't have a home to go home to, and no prospect of one, the least I could do was make something that would remind me of the feeling of home. Plus, apple pie was one of Peter's favorites, and Lorelei loved apple strudel.

In the background, the radio droned on and on about how General Eisenhower had just demanded the Germans to surrender.

I cut a slice. It looked remarkably like an apple pie. Excitedly, I took a big mouthful and then spit it out.

The filling, a strange gelatinous sickly sweet paste, was revolting.

Katrine bore it better than I but refrained from taking a second bite. "Well girls," she glanced at Lorelei, "it looks like we've wasted two cups of sugar."

Lorelei held up her slice and examined it, lamenting, "It smells so much better than it tastes."

"Katrine!" Peter called out as the front door slammed shut. He had just returned from work. "I've got a letter for you. It's from Edie!" He came into the kitchen and gave her the letter with one hand and reached out to try the pie with the other, commenting that it smelled good.

"Try at your own risk," I warned him as Katrine tore the letter open and began to read so quickly her words blurred together.

"Dearest Katrine," she began.

Peter loudly stuffed another bite of pie in his mouth and stopped chewing as Lorelei shot him a look to be quiet.

"What?" He shrugged sheepishly, his mouth full. "It's a good pie."

"Please, Peter!" I groaned. "Be sensitive!"

He swallowed and motioned for Katrine to keep reading.

"I won't say what I have to write will be easy for you to hear. They already are saying the Battle of Manila is one of the worst of the war. The city, once considered one of the finest in the world, is decimated. 150,000 Filipino civilians died in the battle. They say that only the destruction of Warsaw rivals it. The silk shoots from our parachutists still blow in the trees. But in between the bombed-out buildings, signs of normal life are returning. The USO show arrived. I saw dear Bob Hope. His troupe touched down a few days ago. You should have seen the turnout! And the relief. You know what they say, if the USO show has arrived, the war has left. At least, it has for Corregidor and Manila. But that's not the case at Okinawa. More than one brave soldier has confided to me they think they are going to their deaths. Over half a million of our boys are being shipped out. They expect an 80% casualty rate. They are so afraid. I am so afraid! I could tangibly feel their fear. And what could I do but offer hollow words of comfort? Horatio says this is the last stop in the island-hopping scheme. Once we have it, we have a clear shot to Japan. Nothing else will stand in our way.

However, Horatio expects that the battle for the island will last for months."

Katrine stopped and tried to gather herself as Lorelei came up behind her and began to read over her shoulder. "Horatio and I are staying on the ship. All the decent buildings have been blown up... So there you have it, all my news, except that which is the most important. Horatio and I have not been able to find out anything about Harry at all. He could be in the jungle or in a Japanese camp elsewhere in the islands. I pray that he is not in Japan working as a slave in a mine. But take heart, the 8th Ranger Battalion, with the help of Filipino guerrillas, were able to push past the Japanese and fight their way into the Bataan Death March Prison.[9] They found 513 prisoners who were still alive. We expected Harry to be in this group, as all of our sources pointed to Harry being at that camp... if he survived."

"Could Harry have been one of them?" I asked hopefully.

Katrine shook her head, her hand trembling. "It says here that none among the survivors were named Harry Stenetsky."

"That doesn't mean he didn't make it," Peter said firmly. "He might have escaped and still be hiding in the jungle."

"It's true," Lorelei added. "He might have escaped."

"Yes," Katrine said, a faraway look in her eye, "he might have. Or he could be working as a slave in some iron mine in Japan."

"CLAUDE!" Harry wiped sweat from his brow and vigorously shook the young man's hand. "We made it. We made it! What'd I tell you?"

The two men smiled at one another and continued crawling through the underbrush of the jungle. It had all happened quickly. They had gathered rations for two weeks and had swiped canteens for water from sleeping Japanese guards. Then, under the cover of darkness, they'd slipped through a hole in the barbed wire fence. Major Canning, a month before, had been put into The Hole. By now, the men had assumed that their fearless leader was never coming back out. The Japanese soldiers treated the POWs with unyielding savagery. Whether it was because of fear or brainwashing, Harry didn't know. All he was sure of was that he had to escape now before he was too weak to try.

"Are you okay, Harry?" Claude whispered and passed him the canteen, stopping once more to rest.

"Yeah, just need to catch my breath." Water from the canteen dribbled down his chin.

"Maybe we should stay here tonight?" Claude's eyes darted from tree to tree. "Seems quiet."

Nodding, Harry leaned back against a tree trunk. He was exhausted and shivering.

"What are we going to do next?"

"We'll make a raft and sail to China," Harry said.

"Can we do that?"

"I think so, given the location of this island and the trade winds."

Both men tired quickly, but the adrenaline of the escape kept their minds alert.

"I wonder what's happening with the war." Claude sighed.

They were a pitiful sight with their bare feet and clothes in tatters. However, they were too exhausted to feel the fear that any normal person would experience in such dangerous circumstances. Harry reached in what was left of his pocket and then remembered that Katrine's photograph had long since disintegrated in the humidity.

"You have any idea what today is?" Harry asked.

Claude shrugged.

"Well, I'm pretty sure it's sometime in April." Harry groaned as he said, "Ma Nish Ta Nah…"

"Ma what?" Claude's eyes, which had closed, fluttered open.

"Ma Nish Ta Nah… The four questions for Passover. I have this feeling that it's Passover."

"Passover? Are you Jewish, Harry?"

Harry nodded. "Yup."

"I didn't know that. I never met a Jew before."

Harry laughed. He continued, thinking about the holiday, "Not sure I ever really bought it though. I mean, a whole sea parting?"

"It's not so crazy. God parted the sea for us tonight, Harry. We slipped right out from under the eyes of the Japanese."

"Whatever you say, Claude."

"Why is this night different than every other night?" he asked himself the refrain from the Seder. *"Why is this night different than every other night, ol' Harry boy?" Because you're alive, and you're free for the first time in a long time.*

"What do you do for Passover?"

"What do you mean, 'what do I do?'"

"Well, for Easter, my family always makes a ham, and we go to church, and we have an Easter egg hunt."

"Right… Well, for starters, we don't make a ham. You gotta clean the house of all chametz, or leaven, for the Seder service." His brain hurt trying to think about the 101 other things that had to happen in order to make a Passover, and he gave up after a minute. Instead, he simply stated, "We always say, 'Next year in Jerusalem.'"

"Why?"

"Because it's home, that's why. Mark my words, Claude. I'm going home, and you're going home. Next year this time, we are both going to be home. That's what Passover is all about, God setting us free to go home."

"Sounds like my sort of holiday. Happy Passover, Harry."

"Pesach Semeach, kid."

With nowhere further to go that night, both men stretched out on the jungle floor and shut their eyes, waiting for sleep to come. Harry had no idea when he actually did fall asleep, or for how long, but when he awoke, it was with a sharp jab to his ribs and Claude's hand clasped over his mouth. "I hear something," Claude whispered intensely.

In the brush, a stone's throw away, he could make out the

sounds of Japanese boots clomping through the jungle and indiscernible shouts. It was quite the commotion. "They're combing the jungle." He swallowed hard. "They're almost here. They must have discovered the hole in the fence."

Harry took Claude's hand away, "Listen Claude, I want you to run that way," he looked to the west, "and I'll run east."

"Separate?"

"We don't stand a chance if we stay together. They would track us in a matter of hours. If we separate, there are two trails. We'll meet up on the beach, okay."

"Right, okay." Claude's voice trembled. Both knew they would, most likely, never meet on the beach. Or ever again. "I—Oh, what's the use. Thanks for everything, Harry."

"Likewise, kid."

They were both up on their haunches now, like sprinters preparing for a race. "Ready?" Harry looked at the young man beside him. It was too dark to see his face.

With as much speed as he could muster, Harry plunged into the brush. Leaves and sharp branches and vines stung his face. The sound of the Japanese grew dimmer and dimmer. And then, horribly, he heard a shot ring out. One called out, "*Amerikahito wa kite imasu!*"

"Amerikahito wa kite imasu?" Harry repeated to himself. His Japanese was slim, picked up in the camp out of necessity. *The Americans are coming?* What in the world? Harry thought he must be going crazy. Hearing things. He had to be.

The Americans weren't coming. It was the Japanese coming, he reasoned. *They were coming after him.*

There were more shouts, this time coming straight towards him. "Over here!" A voice rang out in English. "I heard a shot, Captain!"

Harry froze. Was it possible? Were there Americans on the island?

The voices came closer. They were definitely American voices. To Harry, at that moment, it was the sweetest sound on earth. And

399

it was immediately drowned out by machine gun fire and more shouts in Japanese. Somehow, he and Claude had walked right out of the camp and straight into the middle of a battle. The Americans had made it. They had broken through!

"Guys!" Harry started shouting like a madman. "Hello! Hello! Help! Help me!"

"Hello!" A voice shouted back. "Who's there?"

"Harry Stenetsky! I'm an escaped POW!" He could make out the bright flashlights of the oncoming American soldiers and began moving towards the lights.

"Don't move, soldier!" the voice responded. "This whole jungle is mined. Wait for us to come to you."

Harry called back out, "There is a troop of Japanese soldiers in the brush, probably half a mile or so back."

A shot rang out, and a bullet whizzed over Harry's head. Harry, instinctively, dove towards the ground. *Whew*, he thought, *that was close*.

"Looks like they are closer than that Harry Stenetsky." The soldier laughed.

Somewhere to the left, a mine exploded, sending branches and roots every which way, along with a burst of fire. In that split second, Harry could see. He was on the edge of an open field.

On all fours, Harry inched forward. He'd rather risk a mine than a bullet in the back. Japanese shouts and more shots followed on both sides. Harry was caught in the crossfire.

"Over here, Harry!" the voice called out. "Follow the sound of my voice!"

Just go in a straight line, Harry told himself. *Just get to that voice*. As though in slow motion, he took off. And then, his foot caught on a root. He felt himself falling and put his hands out to catch himself, but it was too late. He was coming down too fast and too hard. With a thud, he felt a sharp pain on the side of his head as it collided with a rock. Then, everything went black.

When he came to again, he was on a stretcher inside a tent in broad daylight.

On a scratchy radio, he heard a British Newscaster's voice blaring: "Buchenwald concentration camp and Bergen-Belson concentration camp were liberated by American and British forces while the Soviets conquered Vienna. In the Pacific, the American invasion of Okinawa began in full force while American bombers firebomb Tokyo. The fight is on. It is Japan's last stand. Wait, this just in. Wait… Wait… American President Franklin D. Roosevelt has died suddenly. Harry Truman has been sworn in as the new President of the United States."

Harry felt intense confusion. Roosevelt was dead? And why couldn't he lift his head up? The room spun around and around.

"That Harry Truman has huge shoes to fill," a soldier on the cot beside Harry said. As he spoke, it sounded muffled and slow. Harry turned his head and saw the speaker. He had a bandage over his eye.

"Franklin managed the Great Depression, and he's carried us through this war with his courage and wisdom." The soldier shook his head. "He held out until the end, almost. Kind of like all of us."

Like all of us? Harry shut his eyes. *Am I dead too?*

"Hey, soldier." A pretty blond nurse smiled down at him. "Look who's awake."

He tried to speak, but his mouth felt dry. He wondered what soldier the nurse was talking to. A doctor in a dirty white coat stood at the foot of his bed, "This one goes too. Get him on the convoy to the *Comfort*." He winked at Harry. "You're going home, kid. You're going home."

Home? Harry's eyes fluttered open. Where was that?

He couldn't remember.

CHAPTER 41

APRIL SHOWERS

*O*n May 8th, Europe erupted in a mass celebration. It was Victory Day in Europe, or V.E. Day as it was lovingly dubbed. All over the world, there were enormous parades and parties.

In the last week, Benito Mussolini, the Italian dictator, and his mistress had been captured while trying to escape northern Italy under heavy disguise. The next day, the Americans liberated Dachau, the camp of horrors where thousands of people, Jews, those with handicaps, and countless others deemed 'undesirable' by the Nazis, met a perilous end. Two days after that, Hitler and his wife Eva Braun shot themselves. It had been quite a month. Hitler, Mussolini, and Roosevelt... dead.

Roosevelt's passing, like a chime on a grandfather clock, signaled that time was out. The Allies moved in, determined to choke out whatever life was left in the Axis Powers in the West. German forces retreated from Finland. The Allies encircled the last of the German armies in Italy, ending the Italian war. Concentration camp after concentration camp was liberated, along with news footage revealing the survivor's emaciated bodies, more dead than alive. The world stood by, horrified. Finally, the nightmares of the past few years were broadcast in the light of day. But for many, the broadcast was too late.

But the night *was* ending. And along with it, the nightmare of war, at least in Europe.

In the Pacific, we were still right in the thick of it. We cheered ourselves with the thought that maybe now we'd get the best supplies and more men, now that everything was wrapped up in Europe.

And so, as those in Paris, London, and Rome took to the streets and celebrated as they had never celebrated before, Peter and I led the charge to a smaller celebration at Longboards, with Katrine and Lorelei in tow. And as we walked, we discussed the contents of Edie's telegram delivered early that morning.

Horatio was being sent back to Honolulu, along with a few others. Okinawa had become a black hole in the Pacific. Too many of our boys were coming back in pine boxes if they came back at all. That was why Horatio was being recalled to Honolulu—to help decide on how to end the war quickly and keep as many of our boys alive as possible.

WE ARE ALL GOING BACK TO HAWAII STOP
SECURED MAY 9. ROSE AND NATHAN EN
ROUTE WITH CHILDREN. LOVE EDIE.

"Hawaii!" I exhaled happily. "I guess we better get packing." I started walking again, feeling a deep and tangible sense of relief at the prospect of returning to Hawaii, equal only to the wonderful excitement I felt about seeing my parents soon.

"May 9? That's tomorrow!" Peter rubbed his forehead. "How am I supposed to explain that to the base commander?"

"You are a civilian. You can just quit, can't you?"

"But they need me," Peter argued. "I'm finally doing *something!*"

"Peter," I looked him in the eye, "I've been taking pictures of kangaroos, and you count cans of beans. I think we can find occupations of equal value back in Hawaii." I adjusted the strap of my camera bag.

"Ouch." Peter shot me a hurt look, though I knew that he knew I was right.

Trying to soften my words, I grabbed his hand. "Besides, we haven't seen my parents in so long. This may be our last chance in who knows when to be together again!"

Katrine was also reluctant to leave. "But... what about Harry?"

I looked behind me. "I know you've been waiting for Harry. But I can tell you, Katrine, it's a madhouse. Edie said it will take months for everyone to get organized. You will do as well waiting in Hawaii as here."

She swallowed. "I can't leave until..." Her conflicted emotions rose to the surface. "The war office still hasn't told me anything. It's been months! How can I leave when I don't know where he is yet?"

Suddenly, the sound of a loud siren began to blare across the street. "It's an air-raid!" Katrine exclaimed. Instinctively, I reached for my camera and took the lens cap off as we looked around wildly for a shelter. If this was the real thing, it might be my only chance to actually be a war-correspondent after all this time had passed. My heart raced with anticipation. *This is your chance!* It thumped. *This is your chance!*

We dashed across the street and towards one of 15 concrete bunkers constructed to protect the citizens of Townsville from Japanese aircraft. Dozens were racing for the large bunker. Just as we made it inside, the drone of three enemy planes roared overhead. I paused at the top of the concrete stairs and aimed my camera towards the sky, snapping a shot of a red plane that was flying very low, seemingly right towards me. And then the thud of bombs began to hit the street.[10]

The moment the first bomb hit, I forgot all about getting 'the shot.' My hands were shaking too much to focus the lens. It was really happening. It was really happening! Peter pulled me down the stairs. It sounded like they had hit the harbor. The sound was terrible. Low thuds. Crashes. Screams. Deafening roars. In the midst of the war's end in Europe, the mortally wounded Japanese army was audacious enough to keep at it and bomb our little city.

The Japanese were starving. They were low on supplies. Low on men. They had no hope of winning. It was unbelievable.

"What are they doing here?" a young woman cried out.

Another blast caused the shelter to tremor like an earthquake back in California.

We had to get out of here! I panicked.

The war was ending, and we had come too far to meet our deaths at the end of a Japanese air-raid! I clutched my camera, palms clammy, rivets of sweat running down my back.

As though he could read my thoughts, Peter suddenly grasped my hand. "We're safe. We can't get hurt down here."

"First air-raid, dear?" a kindly old woman asked, the single bulb swinging overhead casting dark shadows in the crowded shelter. I nodded. Out of the corner of my eye, I saw Katrine and Lorelei clinging to one another.

"Used to be more common at the start of the war. In '42 we had more than our fair share of Jap bombings. That's why they dug these shelters. These planes must have broken through the lines. Last-ditch effort."

No one spoke for several minutes. The drone of the planes and the sound of explosions faded. We waited in the dim light for the all-clear siren to sound, wondering what sort of scene was waiting outside. As the seconds ticked by, the intensity slowly diminished, and my breathing evened out. The old woman spoke up again, her voice strangely cheery. "You heard about the latest? Japan's bizarre high-altitude balloon bombs made it to Bly, Oregon and blew up a small church group having a picnic two weeks ago. That's in America."

I nodded. Just what I needed, more bad news. But it was true. For the last year, the Japanese had launched thousands of these pilotless bombs. All of them had floated across the Western United States and Canada. One even made to Michigan. But none had caused any casualties or even any real damage, except for one that brought down a power line and caused a temporary power outage.[11]

That is, until now.

I felt done. Done on a very deep level. "Do they really think they can win? With balloons?" I exploded.

"Emperor Hirohito thinks his forces can deliver a final devastating blow to the Allies to save face and negotiate a surrender that is easier to accept... and not so, well, what they would consider humiliating," Peter said, looking up at the swinging lamp. What Peter said was true. By now, I knew about the Japanese's fundamental belief that to surrender was a dishonor of the worst kind. As such, many Japanese soldiers would rather fight to the death than raise a white flag.

I steadied myself and tried to remember what was happening. Right, it was V.E. Day. The war was over in Europe. The war was *over*. Except, it wasn't. We were in a bomb shelter while Japanese planes dropped bombs on our heads.

Another bomb hit near the shelter. Its impact shook the earth and caused dust to fall all around us. I buried my face in Peter's chest. "I want to go home, Peter! Can't we please go home."

Peter brushed his hands across my hair, whispering in my ear, "Yes, Piper. We'll go home. I'm taking you home."

WHEN THE ALL-CLEAR signal finally sounded, and we stumbled back outside, our eyes blinking in the bright sun, we saw, several blocks away, a large plume of smoke. It was coming from Paul's base.

Lorelei immediately took off running towards the smoke.

"Wait!" I called out. But it was too late. She was gone.

It was pure pandemonium. Several buildings had been hit, and a row of jeeps and convoy trucks were burning. The ground smoked, and fire crews fought back the blazes that spread through the city.

No one seemed to notice as we ran past the guardhouse and the gate mangled by the bombing. All the attention was on fighting the fires. Sirens and smoke loomed in every direction. Lorelei tore through the center of the base, working her way around the rubble as though she was running for her life.

"Where is Paul Sinclair?" Lorelei called out to a soldier jogging in the opposite direction.

"Get out of here, you idiot dame!" the marine shouted, pulling another hose towards a burning truck. "You want to get yourself killed?"

"I'm looking for Paul Sinclair! Have you seen him?" she shouted over the din.

The man didn't answer. I could feel the heat of the fire on my face, and my throat filled with smoke. Katrine and I both grabbed Lorelei's arms and began to pull her backward. Behind me, I saw Peter. He looked at the burning base and rubbed his hands through his hair.

"Where is he?" Lorelei cried out.

The sirens of fire engines and men yelling droned in the distance. The air smelled acrid and sharp.

"Help!" a man's voice from under a collapsed wall called out.

Peter, Lorelei, Katrine, and I jolted towards the wall. The lower half of the man's body was trapped beneath the concrete. "We can lift it," Peter shouted. "On the count of three!" He gripped his hands on the wall. "One, two, three!"

Peter and Katrine heaved and raised the cement block a few inches. But it was enough for Lorelei and me to pull the man out. Lorelei went into field-nurse mode. "Sir, sir!" She held the man's face in her hands. "Look me in the eye." The man's eyes fluttered back in his head, and he passed out.

"He's lost consciousness." She ripped the edge of her skirt, creating a long thin piece of linen. Quickly, she wrapped it around the man's leg that was bleeding profusely, creating a makeshift tourniquet. "We have to stop the bleeding."

Peter's eyes scanned the row of broken buildings. "There will be more men trapped. We've got work to do."

"Where are they taking the wounded?" I asked, frantically looking at Peter.

"Oh, God," Lorelei plead, "please let him be okay!"

"Ma'am," a sentry called out, "only certified personnel are allowed on the base. It's too dangerous for women!"

"I'm with the press." I held up my camera, my voice sounding strange and far away. The moment didn't feel real.

"I'm one of the head nurses at the Red Cross." Lorelei fished a badge out of her purse. "You need us here!"

Katrine remained silent.

"I'm a civilian volunteer." Peter gently picked up the man we'd just rescued. "Private, where are we taking the wounded? Where's the infirmary?"

The sentry was very young, 19 at most. His light brown hair was grey with ash, and his eyes yellow and red from the smoke. "They hit the infirmary hard. The doctor on duty is dead. A few of the nurses too. We are lining up the wounded on the dining tables." He looked at Lorelei.

"All right," she said, beginning to lift the man's upper body. "Peter, please?" she asked. Instinctively, he lifted him from her arms and brought him to the makeshift infirmary.

Lorelei looked around at all the mayhem, imagining the worst. "I have to find Paul!" she said, about to dash off.

Katrine stopped her. "Lorelei, there are a lot of men who need us right now. Paul will turn up."

Lorelei was frantic. "Oh, Katrine! What if he's hurt? Or worse!"

Katrine jerked her sister's shoulders. "Listen to me, Lorelei Adleman. You must go where you are needed the most right now! For such a time as this, my sister." Unconsciously, Katrine slipped into Yiddish, *"Now, gay ga zinta hate."*

They were old and beloved words used to wish the ones you loved the most a safe journey—*Now, go in good health.*

Lorelei's jaw clenched as she put her worst fears about Paul aside and listened to her sister. She nodded, placing her hand on Katrine's cheek. "Yes, *mein sheifale*—my dearest—yes."

WITH NO OFFICIAL MEDICAL LEADERSHIP, Lorelei stepped in. Within an hour, she had organized the fleet of Red Cross nurses, who worked side by side with the Army Nurse Corp, treating burns and crushed limbs, carefully transferring the worst cases to the hospital in town. With an uncanny calm, she comforted the dying and administered shot after shot of morphine.

The fires kept burning. Ammunition, gasoline, and who knows what else took a long time to burn out. Some of them would last for days.

We worked for hours and hours. After months of complaining of not having enough to report on, I was inundated with the exhausting task of commemorating the tragedies of the present. It was a lot for a single newsagent to handle alone. But like Lorelei, I focused on the task at hand and took pictures of the wounded and the burning buildings. A whole roll. Katrine brought canteens of drinking water to the men fighting the fires and searching the rubble for survivors. And Peter put his first aid skills to work, right alongside Lorelei and the nurses. Still, there was no sign of Paul.

I caught sight of Katrine, filling another slew of canteens at a hose beside the mess hall, and motioned for her to join me for a break inside where the air was slightly better.

Exhaustion was quickly overtaking us. My arms felt like lead, and my heart was pounding. I had to sit down. Inside, the initial pandemonium had diminished. The Red Cross had created a sense of order, despite the upheaval all around us. There was a system in place. One by one, nurses checked wounds and blood pressure. The urgency had calmed. At the moment, all efforts were directed towards stabilizing the wounded.

I leaned against the wall like a rag doll, near collapse. Katrine followed suit. "We'll rest here for two minutes and then start again? Deal?" I said.

"Deal," she answered, shutting her eyes. When she opened them, she looked in wonder at Lorelei across the room. At the moment, she was carefully snipping away a young officer's tattered shirt from a burned shoulder. "Lorelei is so calm, cool, and collected in a crisis." She laughed mirthlessly.

"I was just thinking the same thing of Peter." I watched him on the opposite side of the enormous room as Lorelei. Gently, he lifted a man off a stretcher and onto a table. With tender love and care, he looked every man in the eye and told them it would be all right. They would make it.

"Not me." Katrine kept on talking, her voice hoarse from the smoke. "I tend to pass out. Lorelei's been like that since she was a little girl, but since she met Yeshua, the gift has grown. Look at her!"

"She's an amazing woman," I agreed.

"I know," a man's voice answered. Katrine and I both looked up. Looking down from the door of the mess hall turned emergency infirmary was none other than Paul Sinclair. He was covered in debris, and his shirt was torn. But other than that, he appeared unharmed.

Lorelei looked up from across the room. The two locked eyes, unmoving.

He started to move toward her, but a nurse stopped him at the door. "Medical personnel only soldier."

His eyes didn't move from where she worked.

"Where have you been?" I asked.

"I was in the bunker when the bombs fell. The entry collapsed. They just dug us out." He shook his head, his eyes still on Lorelei."

"Out of the way, soldier!" an orderly called, carrying the front end of a stretcher.

"Sorry." Paul tripped slightly and stepped out of the way. His eyes again went to where Lorelei, who had turned her attention back to the case at hand, stood working.

"I was hoping we could talk," Paul stuffed his hands in his pocket, "but it looks like she's got her hands full."

Katrine put her hand on Paul's shoulder. "She wants to talk too. I... I think that's all she's wanted for a long time."

Paul kept his steady, serious gaze on Lorelei but whispered, "Really?" He looked surprised by what I'd said.

"You should know, we are leaving tomorrow—if all this mess calms down enough to leave. We're going back to Honolulu."

"Lorelei too?"

"Yes, but she has a ticket back to Palestine. She's returning to the kibbutz."

At that moment, a focused young secretary with a terrible gash on her cheek carrying a clipboard clambered through the door of the mess hall. At first, she was taken aback by the turmoil of the scene in front of her. There must have been 40 men stretched out on tables or slumped in folding chairs. Nurses hovered over them, their only barrier between life and death.

"Miss Wood?" Paul took the young woman's arm and steadied her. "Are you okay?"

"Sinclair," she ignored the question, "I was sent to find you."

"You need to get that scrape cleaned up," he said.

She shook her head. "This will wait. All the translators and coders are being sent back into the bunker. They need you on your radio."

Paul looked at Lorelei, who, holding a needle mid-stitch, looked up and caught his eyes for only a moment and then returned her attention to the patient. His brow furrowed with conflicted emotion. He looked once more, wishing to say so much, able to say nothing at all. Reluctantly, he followed the young woman back into the chaos leading to the bunker. Lorelei could not break her concentration, and by the time she could look again, he was gone.

A tear slid down her cheek. *He was alive.* Then, she dried her cheek with the back of her hand and returned to mending the poor wounded soldier lying on the stretcher.

CHAPTER 42

THE LAST COFFEE

*W*e worked by Lorelei's side until late that night before
returning to the Queenslander for a fitful four hours
of sleep. My hair smelled of smoke, and Peter's palms were raw
from lifting rough blocks of concrete.

At six in the morning, Lorelei rushed back to the base with a
thermos of coffee. Most of the wounded had already been transferred to the city hospital. She was on the base for an altogether
different reason than nursing. She had to see Paul.

She wore a high-waisted dark green skirt and a slightly lighter
green cashmere sleeveless sweater that showed off her long tan
arms. She'd had no time to wash her hair and had quickly brushed it
back into a bun.

She stood out on the base, a bright green burst of life amidst
clean-up crews working to clear the rubble. Most of the fires had
cooled. Leftover glowing embers smoked by the shells of bombed-
out jeeps. The air was still grey and ashy.

When she asked for Paul Sinclair, they directed her to the
bunker. They told her to wait outside while a sergeant went to find

him. She waited, leaning against the wall to the cement entrance looking out over the damage. The Japanese had hit them very hard. It was a destruction zone.

Five minutes passed, and Paul emerged. The two stood looking at one another, exhausted.

Paul finally said, "I heard there was a Red Cross Nurse who had a message for me."

Lorelei didn't speak.

"What's the message, nurse?" he asked, wary of her using the Red Cross as a cover.

"I... I didn't know what else to say to get you here." She looked at his face. Dirt was creased in the stress lines across his forehead. He hadn't changed from the day before. "Did you get any rest last night?"

He shrugged and tried to smile, still on guard and defensive. "If you could call a 20-minute catnap a rest, sure."

Not giving up, she continued, fingering the strap to her messenger bag. "Can I buy you a coffee, soldier? That is, if you can take a break."

"I've only got 15 minutes, but..." he eyed her cautiously, "but I don't want any of the weak stuff the Red Cross is serving up." His voice was tired.

"I know." Lorelei smiled and tapped her bag. "That's why I brought a thermos of my own coffee. It's so strong and black it will keep you going the rest of the day. It's Arab-style coffee. I think you'll like it."

Softening slightly, he tried to smile. "Sure. Some Arab-style coffee sounds great." A truck roared past them, and they both moved out of the way. "Okay then." He looked behind him. "Follow me. I know a quiet spot where we can talk."

"I would like that," Lorelei said.

"So would I," Paul replied hesitantly.

On a secluded bench along the peripheral fence of the base

under the shade of an enormous curtain fig tree, Paul and Lorelei poured tin mugs of steaming, spicy coffee. Neither spoke. Neither knew where to start.

Finally, Paul put his mug down and looked at Lorelei, "I was hoping to see you before you left."

"You knew I was leaving?"

"I did. Katrine told me yesterday. When do you head out?"

"This evening."

"I'm leaving myself, actually."

"Oh really?" Her eyes met his. "Where are they sending you?"

"Confidential... But I leave in a week."

"I see." Lorelei looked as nervous as she felt. She inhaled, attempting to steady her breath. "I know we only have little time." Shutting her eyes, she gathered her strength. "When those planes came and the bombs started to fall, I could think of only one thing. If you were injured, or worse, I couldn't live with myself given the way things ended. I said a lot that day that I regret, things that aren't true about you. Paul, I am deeply sorry."

He looked at his hands wrapped around the mug. "Well. . . we both said things that didn't reflect the truth that day." He paused and then said, "But, you know, you *were* right about one thing."

"Right about what?" Lorelei faced him questioningly. Being near him again made her heart beat irregularly. She tried to control her breathing.

"I've been thinking a lot about what you said the day of our engagement party. You said I was avoiding you, that I didn't want to talk." He looked down. "You see, I could feel you pulling away. It terrified me that you didn't love me the way I love you. So, in order to not hear what I didn't want to hear, I didn't stop to listen." Paul's shoulders dropped slightly. "I guess my fears were right, but fear never gives good advice. It just prolonged our situation... and pain. At least, my pain."

"Maybe that was true, Paul. I felt like we didn't know each other well enough to get engaged, much less get married." She spoke honestly, more honestly than she had spoken with Paul ever before.

"I've told you pretty much everything there is to know about me. I'm an open book."

"I know that." Lorelei stopped. Her nerves faded away as the thoughts that had plagued her with fear and doubt for months came to the surface. "But you know next to nothing about me."

Paul's brow furrowed in consternation. "It's not my fault I don't know what happened. *You* never told me anything about your past, Lorelei."

"I was waiting for you to ask the right questions," Lorelei insisted. "You never asked them. I thought you didn't want to know. I thought—Well, I thought you didn't want to know more about me because... because I'm Jewish."

"Oh, Lorelei." Peter exhaled heavily, deeply burdened by this revelation. "You really thought that?"

Her big green eyes looked up into his kind, tired blue ones. "I was afraid you didn't want to know or accept that part of me, like so many others in my past and even my present, Paul."

This information stunned Paul Sinclair. He blinked once, then twice, and then said: "I didn't press those issues because I know how sensitive you are. It was one of the first things your family told me about you. You've been through so much, more than anyone ought to go through in a lifetime. I didn't want to inflict any more pain by asking you to re-live those memories until you were good and ready." He looked into her eyes. "Lorelei, I was trying to *protect* you."

She bit her lip. "I thought you knew I wanted you to ask, and just... weren't asking."

"Most people don't read minds, Lorelei. You have to help them out. Especially guys like me. I won't try to pretend I fully understand everything you've been through—escaping Germany, your life in Palestine, or even your connection with your people as a Jew."

"But I know this." He continued, "You are the most wonderful, beautiful, kind woman I've ever met. And I didn't want to marry anyone else. And I wanted to marry all of you—the Jewish part especially, because that is part of what makes you so unique and wonderful and sharp. Lorelei Adleman, when I met you, I realized I never wanted to live life alone again. Besides, as followers of Jesus, we are part of the same body, 'in Him,' remember?" He paused, attempting to read her expression.

"Really?" She looked up, almost not believing her ears.

He chuckled sadly. "From day one, communication was not our strong point, was it? Talk about misread messages. We need a master code to decipher what the other is saying!" Then, looking at his lap, he quietly spoke as if to himself, "Who knows, maybe with practice, we would have finally learned how to understand one another."

"You really weren't asking about me because you wanted to protect me?" Her eyelids fluttered in amazement.

She looked down and gripped the side of the bench and considered their actions for the last few months. Between her expectations and judgments and Paul's unsuccessful method to protect his own heart (and Lorelei's), a beautiful friendship had been pushed off a cliff. If they had done what they were meant to do, to share one another's burdens and care for one another in love, they would never be having this conversation. All of this avoiding the truth and skirting around hard questions and not speaking up when something was wrong had ruined something wonderful.

He nodded. "Lorelei," he took her hand, "I've told you a hundred times or more how I feel about you. But you would have needed an enigma machine to discover what I was trying to tell you!"

Lorelei froze. "A what?"

He caught himself. "You didn't hear about the enigma from me. Got it?"

She shrugged. "I honestly do not understand what you are talking about. Is it a part of your work?"

He nodded and stared straight ahead. Neither spoke.

"What are you doing here, Lorelei?" Paul finally asked.

"I... I wanted to say goodbye. I didn't want any hard feelings between us."

He stood up and looked at her with deep hopelessness that he himself had never felt more acutely. He handed her the mug back. "Thanks for the coffee." Regaining his composure, he checked his watch and ran his fingers through his thick blonde hair, "I've got to report back at the bunker. There were several other attacks on a few nearby islands last night. It's been crazy."

"God bless you, Paul, wherever he leads," Lorelei whispered.

"Wherever he leads, Lorelei Adleman." He extended his hand, his voice caught in his throat. "I won't ever forget you."

He pivoted and walked steadily towards the bunker so she could not see the tears he was just barely holding back. Several minutes later, just as he opened the door to the coding building, about to plunge back inside, he heard Lorelei's voice calling out about 30 yards behind him.

"Paul! Paul!"

He turned around. She stood behind him, one arm raised in goodbye. She looked very waif-like and alone. Her dark green skirt blew about her legs, and her blond hair swept back from her face, made her appear almost childlike. A plane roared overhead. American—routine surveillance. She opened her lips and mouthed something to him, but the engine drowned her words.

He stopped and held on to the side of the bunker, watching her lips moving, wondering if she had said the words he longed to hear —that she loved him back. Just then, someone from inside the bunker yelled, "Major Sinclair! Incoming message. It's go time!"

Paul didn't move.

The voice from below called out again, "Major! What are you doing up there?"

Lorelei shouted out once more, but still, he couldn't hear her. His eyes lingered on her face a moment longer before he tore himself away and disappeared down the steep steps to his radio. She had no idea if he had heard her or not. In shock, she turned to return home, holding back tears that equaled the strength of Paul's. She had a lot of packing to do. She was going back to Palestine, and she was going alone.

CHAPTER 43

OPERATION SONGBIRD

*W*hen Lorelei returned, she joined Peter and me at the breakfast table. By the looks of it, she had been crying. Neither of us had slept much. The air had been too full of smoke. And our nerves were on edge. Now, we had only a few hours to pack up the house before we caught the boat back to Honolulu later that day.

"Katrine's still asleep?" Lorelei sat down, and I poured her a cup of coffee and nodded.

"You were up early." Peter took a bite of toast.

"I made a mistake." Lorelei looked very sad and very beautiful. "It just wasn't the mistake I expected to make." A sad laugh escaped her lips.

"What are you talking about, Lorelei?" I asked, suddenly afraid.

"I know it now. I know more than I've ever known before. I love him. I love him with everything in me. It's different than with Rolf. Different than with anyone I've ever met." Her eyes met mine, watering. "It's funny. Now that I *am* sure, it's too late. Our timing was never very good. It seems like Paul and I have always been out of sync."

Peter looked up from his scrambled eggs. "Are you sure about that? Why don't you just tell him how you feel?"

She raised her shoulders, "I tried! But he didn't hear me. There was a plane and. . . Oh! What's the use? It's too late now."

"You *do* love Paul," I said. "Quite a lot."

"I didn't really know it until yesterday when I realized I might never see him again." She braced herself and kept on talking, though her words were directed more to herself than to Peter or me. "He was right when he said I wasn't sure. I wasn't. The world's changed too fast, and I haven't been able to keep up. But you know something? It will keep going with or without me. I can't stop it. Can't slow it down. I can't save Grace or help Katrine find Harry. Nothing will ever be 'perfect.' Not really, that is. Something will always be wrong, somewhere. And if I keep waiting to live my life until I think everything's perfect, until I feel sure I won't make a mistake, I'll never start living. God wants me to trust him better than I have the last few months. That is his will more than who or when I'll get married!" She tried to laugh. "He wants me to trust that he is leading me, that he is *still* leading me." She swallowed. "And he makes all things new, even when we mess up. That's the main lesson, isn't it?"

"Indeed," Peter smiled, "that *is* the main lesson."

I poured myself a third cup of coffee and looked up as Katrine shuffled into the kitchen in her cotton nightdress and collapsed beside Peter, unaware of the frank confession that was gracing our morning's breakfast conversation.

"I just had the most vivid dream." Katrine pushed her wild curls away from her face. "I don't know where we were, but Grace had seen Harry, and he was all right. And she was all right too. She told me that everything would be... all right." Katrine shivered. "But it was just a dream, wasn't it? My subconscious telling me it's okay to go back to Honolulu, don't you think?"

"God sometimes speaks in dreams, Katrine," Lorelei said distractedly. "Not always when we ask for them though. Sometimes he makes us step out in faith and believe he is leading us even in the dark." She paused, speaking to herself. "He was right in front of me all this time..."

Katrine shook her head. She did not understand what Lorelei was talking about. "All of this 'taking things by faith' doesn't come naturally. As I've said before, I like hard facts." She shrugged. "Any more toast? Nothing like an air raid to make you starving." She looked up, noticing Lorelei's red-rimmed eyes for the first time. "Are you okay, Lorelei?"

Before Lorelei could answer, a small 'tap tap tap' on the glass of the window above the sink caught our attention.

I looked towards the window. "Do you hear that?"

Peter nodded. "Probably just a branch from the Azalea bush hitting the glass."

"It's not windy." I stepped closer as the tapping continued.

There on the edge of the window, sat a pigeon tapping its beak against the glass. "It's a bird! I think it's trying to get into the house."

Lorelei jumped up and looked at the pigeon through the window beside me. "It's Nina!"

I scarcely believed it. How could Nina be at our house? Katrine moved between us and lifted the glass and reached out, taking the bird gently in her hands.

"It can't be Nina." I looked at the bird. "How could she have flown so far?"

"Remember what Frank said? They can fly thousands of miles!" Peter gazed in awe at the pigeon.

"Why didn't Nina go back to her roost?" Katrine asked.

I shrugged. "Maybe she thinks this is her roost now. She lived here for quite a while."

"But Nina was wounded." I couldn't take my eyes off the pigeon.

"Looks like she is all better now." Lorelei reached out and took the bird from Katrine. "Look!" She carefully examined the bird's ankle. "It's wearing a bracelet."

"Didn't Frank say that messenger pigeons carry messages in little bracelets?" Katrine's eyes grew bright.

Carefully, Lorelei removed the bracelet and unwound a tiny piece of paper that was rolled up incredibly tightly. "I think we'll need a magnifying glass to read it," she said, moving towards the study and switching on a lamp, all of us right behind her.

Peter carefully took Nina out of her hands as she peered over the message. "It says," she said haltingly, *"Arrived in China..."* She bit her lip. *"Pressing On. Am all right."*

"Does it say anything else?" I prodded.

Lorelei nodded. *"Sorry missed wedding."*

"Her grammar is atrocious." Katrine shook her head. "But I suppose she tried to fit as much as she could on this itsy bitsy piece of paper."

Katrine nervously began to tap her fingers on the desk. "Don't you see?" Her voice grew excited.

"See what?" Lorelei asked, looking up.

Exasperated, Katrine slammed her hand down on the desk. "Don't you get it! I dreamt that Grace was all right. And look, she sent us a message to tell us she *was* all right. God spoke to me! He sent me a message through a dream! Harry will be all right too. I know it!"

Lorelei and I shared a strained glance, and then Lorelei said carefully, "This message could be two months old. I'm assuming it took Nina a very long time to fly all the way from China to Townsville."

"Not that long, actually," I remembered what Frank had told me. "They fly roughly 80 miles an hour. China is 5,000 miles away or so..."

"How do you know that?" Katrine asked.

"I looked it up when I heard where Grace was headed."

Katrine picked up my birthday fountain pen on the desk and scratched out some figures on a scrap of paper. "That's 64 hours of travel, give or take. So..." she looked up, "if Nina was flying 12 hours a day, it would take her 5 days, right?"

We nodded.

"One way or another, this message is not over two weeks old," Katrine said decisively. "Grace is all right. And Harry *will* be all right too."

~

KATRINE, Lorelei, Peter, and I boarded the troopship bound for Honolulu several hours later.

(By now, Horatio and Edie were well ahead of us on a different ship that had left from Manila. They would be there to meet us when we arrived.)

A small 'stateroom' had been secured for the four of us, equipped with two bunk beds. There were roughly 10 such staterooms reserved for civilians near the deck. The rest of the passengers slept in the enormous cavern of the ship outfitted with 7,000 bunks. It was much larger than the one the girls and I had traveled in from Honolulu to Alu.

The last 48 hours caught up with me almost the instant Peter put a key into the door of our assigned berth.

We each had a suitcase in hand, and a porter had previously delivered three trunks full of books and knick-knacks Edie and Horatio had collected in Townsville. These knick-knacks included a pair of crocodile boots for Horatio and a matching purse for Edie, some fine opal earrings — Australia was famous for opals. She also packed kangaroo leather coats of varying lengths for the whole family, Akubra hats for Willem and Raffi, and tubs of emu oil, a bright yellow fatty substance collected from the skin of the emu bird and eschewed to be a miracle balm for a myriad of skin disorders by the Aborigines.

Katrine brushed past Peter and surveyed the tiny room. The U.S. Armed Forces had stripped it bare of its previous lush furnishings.

They had removed even the washroom to make room for more 'civilian' compartments. There was no porthole and little-to-no ventilation. But there were mattresses on the bunks and a communal washroom at the end of the deck, and it would take us home. That was enough.

"That's not ours," Katrine said, eyeing a guitar case leaning against the trunks. "It must have been delivered to the wrong room."

"Well, at least the trunks made it." I sighed, shuffling around the space between the trunks and the bunks and sat down, putting Nina's cage on the ground. My bones hurt with tiredness. It was official, yesterday had been one of the most stressful days of my life. It was as though every ounce of reserve energy I had was gone.

Peter held the door open and waited for Lorelei to enter. Her eyes rested on the guitar case. She stopped and caught her breath. "That looks like—" she paused and reached down to read the luggage tag attached to the case's handle. "It has my name on it." Her fingers dropped the tag as if it were hot.

Katrine was instantly by her side, reading the tag. "PROPERTY OF LORELEI ADLEMAN. WHEREVER HE LEADS."

"What does that mean?" Katrine asked.

She took the case and laid it down on the bunk, clicking it open. Carefully, she lifted the top. There, on the instrument, lay a single sheet of music. *"Don't Sit Under the Apple Tree (With Anyone Else but Me)."*[12]

"Something tells me," Lorelei whispered, "we haven't seen the last of Paul Sinclar, Katrine."

The ship's horn sounded, and the vessel began to pull away from the dock.

Lorelei immediately found the communications deck and sent a single message to the shore, via the ship's wireless radio, in the dots and dashes of Morse code:

"If you'll be my roo roo roo roo rooster, I'll be your chick chick chick chick chicken!"

Her message was received and met with a single-word reply:

"Cockadoodledoo."

Lorelei stood up, thanked the radio operator, and shut her eyes in relief. Even though she had no idea where he was or when they would see each other again, she knew that in God's mercy, one day, they would be together again. And that was all that mattered.

She had sent the most important message of her life, and it had been received. The tide had turned. The battle—her inner battle for love—was won, no matter what might lay ahead. Operation Songbird was accomplished.

CHAPTER 44

BACK ON AMERICAN SOIL

*P*eter yelled as we pushed through the fray of those on the pier. "John! We're over here!"

John Yamaguchi smiled an enormous grin and waved as he caught sight of Peter. He looked exactly as I remembered him. "Good to see you kids made it home in one piece." He heartily shook Peter's hand and then mine. "Edie and Horatio are somewhere back there. Edie's been so excited she hasn't sat still for two minutes put together." He smiled and added, "I brought the Woody. I assumed you would need it for all the luggage." His eyes searched the crowd. "Where are the others?"

I looked back at Katrine and Lorelei. They were a few steps behind us, struggling with their suitcases in the press of the crowd. John jumped forward and took their bags. "Is this everyone? Where's the other boy, Frank? And your sister? There were three of you if I remember correctly."

"Dear John," Katrine exhaled, "they went one way, and we went another."

Behind John, I saw Edie and Horatio coming up the pier, waving. She wore a bright pink hat as wide as her shoulders and an enormous smile. As we neared them, Edie exclaimed, "Here we all are, back in Hawaii. Back on good ol' American soil! Isn't it just wonderful!" Her sing-song voice carried over the noise of the pier. "You look wonderful, Piper."

"So do you, Edie." I pecked her cheek.

"Oh, this old thing?" She swirled around, enjoying the hat. "I thought it was rather loud, but it made me smile." She began walking. "Now, it's no Scotland. And Scotland has taken over my heart, so to speak. There will only ever be one home for me, and it's my castle in Kingsbarns. But, Hawaii is a lot closer," she sighed, "to my heathered hills and jagged cliffs than Australia, and for that, I am eternally grateful."

"How was the trip?" John asked Peter, taking hold of a trunk.

"Crowded," Peter sighed. "They filled up the hold with wounded boys from the *Comfort*."

"The *Comfort*?"

"Yes. A Kamikaze ran right into the hospital ship a couple of days ago. A lot of doctors and nurses died, not to mention those already wounded. We picked up as many of the survivors that we could."

"That makes sense." John picked up the pace. "I was wondering why there was a line of ambulances in the parking lot. Must be to transfer them to the hospital."

A half-hour later, John pulled up to the white plantation house. Founder sat on the porch, barking loudly to welcome us. It hadn't changed, not one bit. Just like John. Lush palms, bright tropical flowers, the gentle mountain slope up behind it, the magnificent Pacific Ocean just beyond. It was so soft and peaceful.

Australia had been tropical too, but it differed from Hawaii with its man-eating crocodiles and enormous jellyfish. Here, everything was... soft. Even the sand. I was tempted to curl up on the beach and sleep, forever.

"Mr. Yamaguchi kept the house up beautifully, and your dog is still alive," Edie said as Founder bounded down the stairs and jumped up on Peter first before throwing all her weight against me. "Missed me?" I knelt down and pressed my face into her soft fur. I looked up at John and said, "Thanks for taking such good care of her, John."

John smiled and set the bags down on the porch. "I'm assuming you are all tired. I've got a casserole ready to go in the oven whenever you are hungry. But I'll leave you alone tonight unless you need me."

"Thanks, John." Horatio patted the kind old man's back. "I think we'll manage just fine."

"All right then." He waved and walked briskly down the road.

"I'm going to take a walk." Edie took off her hat and threw it on one of the rockers. "My legs feel shorter and stumpier than ever. I haven't been keeping up with my usual routine. I'm all lumps and flab." I noticed her auburn hair had grown several inches and was nearly past her shoulders.

Katrine, a solid 5 inches shorter than Edie, laughed. "No one has ever accused you of being short or stumpy, Edith Macleay! Statuesque is more like it."

Edie tilted her head to the side, basking in the compliment she knew to be true. "Do you girls want to come?"

Lorelei shook her head no and smiled. "My flight back to San Francisco leaves early tomorrow morning. I'd like to get a little rest." Then, raising Paul's guitar slightly in her right hand, she said, "And I've got some practicing to do."

"Of course you do, dear. You'll want to show Paul all your skills the next time you see him. Maybe you'll be nearly a professional!"

"I hope not!" Grimacing, she hoisted the guitar case to the other hand and pushed through the screen door, throwing behind her, "Because it will take me a very long time to learn to play as a professional, and I'm hoping we'll be reunited much sooner than that."

"But of course, dear." Edie nodded. Turning to me, she said, "I'm so happy to hear they worked everything out. To a certain extent, that is. I won't say I wasn't hoping they might elope or something wonderfully exciting."

My stomach grumbled. The food on the ship had not exactly been palatable. It felt like I hadn't eaten in four days.

"What did John make for dinner?" I asked as the three of us stepped off the porch and moved towards the path leading to the beach.

"Chipped beef with noodles and an eggless chocolate sponge," Edie replied.

I wrinkled my nose. I hated chipped beef. One could always fill up on chocolate cake, I supposed. But eggless?

Edie kept talking as we walked side by side, explaining that John had used the egg rations to buy us some coffee. "I would always choose coffee over omelets, you know. He remembers so much, though we were with him for such a short time! Such a wonderful man."

"Will a sponge work without eggs?" I asked.

"Oh yes." Edie nodded. "Certain cakes stand up quite well without the use of eggs. I've learned from experience. Back in Scotland, eggs were not just a rare commodity. It was starting to feel like they'd gone extinct, like the dinosaurs or something."

We reached the sand and kicked off our shoes, going to the water's edge.

All three of us were quiet.

"I'm tempted to dive in," Edie said, dipping her toes in the warm water.

She inhaled and shut her eyes. The sun rested on her freckles and bounced off her hair.

"I want to wash away the things I saw." She sighed and opened her eyes. "It won't work though. I tried, on Manila. I swam every day, and the water did nothing. There was always another terrible story to hear once I got back to the ship." She hoisted up her skirt and waded in to her knees. "On Okinawa, the Japanese forced the civilians, gentle farmers and their wives and children, to retreat with them into the mountain caves. If they refused to go..." She hung her head. "It's savage really. Senseless savagery! And I think of Agatha, Anna, Willem, and Raffi safe with your parents, Piper, and I don't know what I feel."

She turned around and looked at us. I could see what she felt plain as day. It was a mixture of exhaustion, relief, and deep, deep sadness—what we all felt.

"I could have been born on Okinawa," she said pensively. "I could be in some cave right now with a bunch of soldiers who prefer death to surrender. My children starving, my husband... But I'm not. I'm here in Hawaii, and my children are being brought to me safe and sound on an ocean liner by my dear brother and his wife. And he's a doctor to boot, so I don't even have the luxury of worrying about their health. It's a strange world we live in, isn't it?"

Katrine and I stood still, watching the waves lap at our toes. The battle on Okinawa continued at a snail's pace as our men tried to take the island one yard at a time. Even as we spoke, it went on. General Nimitz was growing frustrated, Horatio had said, and feared that our ships had become sitting ducks just waiting for another kamikaze pilot to slam his plane into the side of our fleet.

"It feels like it won't ever end." Katrine was sullen.

"It will," Edie said firmly. "It has to. All wars end, eventually." She waded back through the water and stood by Katrine's shoulder.

"And in the meantime?"

"We all have to use our time as wisely as we can, I guess. For myself, I won't deny that that has been exceptionally difficult." She looked at me as if to say, 'No, the new novel isn't working out so don't ask.' And then, she blurted out, "I've started a brand new series; *Ostriches and Flamingos*. I think once the children are here, I'll get my writer's focus back."

"*Ostriches and Flamingos?*" Katrine raised one eyebrow.

"I know, I know." Edie waved the comment away like a pesky fly. She shrugged. "Have you girls thought about what you will do?"

"I'm going to stop by *The Honolulu Herald* tomorrow and drop off the photographs from the bombing. Don's been waiting for some action shots for a long time," I said after a second.

"That's a fine idea," Edie approved.

"Do you think," Katrine asked, "that I could get a job there?"

Katrine wanted a job? I looked at her questioningly. "As what?"

"Oh, I don't know." She tilted her pretty face to the sun. "I'm good at research. I could be a fact checker or something. Or a proofreader. I need to make some money. I need to do something while I'm waiting, just like you said, Edie." A heavy sigh escaped her lips.

"That was a loaded sigh, Katrine Adleman." Edie slipped her arm over my cousin's shoulder. "Spill."

"Spill?"

Edie smiled. "Tell me what is on your mind."

"I've been thinking," she squinted in the bright light, "if Harry is alive, he would have written me. I thought we would have heard *something* by now. But we haven't. If he *was* in that group that was liberated... Well, there is no reasonable explanation for why he hasn't contacted me... or the war office, that is." She didn't need to say it, but we all knew what she was thinking. The odds were not in Harry's favor, not at all.

"What if I was wrong," she looked at me, "and I didn't hear from God after all?"

"What if?" Edie repeated. "We've all thought we heard from God and been wrong before. We just have to pick up and keep going, plodding forward the best we can, trusting that God loves us and has a plan for us. All the while not stopping, listening or believing that he speaks, and we can hear him."

Katrine nervously rubbed her fingernails. "I don't know if I can do that."

"Katrine," Edie looked down, "I've been around the block a few times more than you have. I've been disappointed by God more than once because I thought one thing when he thought another."

"What's that supposed to mean?"

"Just because things are not going the way you thought they would, doesn't mean that God is not trustworthy. It just means he works in mysterious ways. But if you give him your disappointments, he'll use them to grow you and strengthen you."

"And if I don't?"

"Dear," Edie looked out at the ocean, "we both know how that story will end. The question is, did you give your life to God because you thought he would give you what you want? Or because he is worthy of being made Lord of your life?"

Katrine looked stunned. "Edie! I gave him my life because I truly believe that Yeshua is the Son of God. I know he won't always give me what I want. I'm not a child, even if I am new to the faith."

"Good." Edie patted her arm. "Then stop doubting what you know to be true."

"What I feel to be true," Katrine intoned, "in my heart doesn't line up with what I see in front of me. *How* can Harry be alive?"

"You feel in your heart that he is alive?" Edie pressed.

"I… do. But it feels like a misguided hope right now. It would be a miracle if he lived. I feel foolish for even daring to hope."

"Then be a fool. Don't give up hope until you are sure, absolutely sure, that you are wrong. What have you to lose, Katrine?"

"But it hurts to keep hoping, Edie, only to be constantly met by disappointment at every turn. I don't know how much longer I can keep this up!"

"You can keep it up until God tells you to let it go. But it seems he hasn't told you to let it go yet. So you just go on acting foolishly in the world's eyes."

Katrine's eyes opened wide in surprise.

"I could treat you with kid-gloves, Katrine, but there's no time anymore. There's still a war on. We either trust God right now, or we don't. I'm telling you the truth, and I will keep telling you the truth whether or not you like it. Until you know for sure what has happened to Harry, don't give yourself the luxury of mourning his loss. It'd be a waste of time and energy."

Edith could be very blunt at times. And at the moment, it almost appeared she was treating Katrine's pain without an ounce of understanding or sympathy. But that would be incorrect. To Edie, the kindest gift she could give Katrine was the *truth*, unfiltered and frank.

"You really think so?" Katrine swallowed, looking at Edie with a troubled expression.

"I do. I promise you, your story will not end in tragedy. No matter what happens. If Harry makes it, you will be all right. If he doesn't, you will *still* be all right. You have Jesus. You have hope for the future, no matter what the world throws at you. It's just a matter of perspective, you know. It's a question of whether you will still love him, even when you are in pain and confused and feel lost. If you choose to do so, then even in the darkest night," she put her palm gently on Katrine's cheek, "you will be able to see the stars. But that is a choice only you can make."

"A choice only I can make?"

"Yes." She paused. "To keep loving God and believing he is worthy of praise even when you don't understand what's going on around you."

A strange heaviness descended on the beach as Katrine let Edie's words sift through her troubled thoughts.

Katrine had come to a major decision, almost as serious as the day she came to know Yeshua. The question at hand *now* was not if he was the Messiah but whether she would love him and follow him when the future looked bleak.

Katrine's voice caught in her throat. Her eyes welled up, and she embraced Edie, holding her tightly. She didn't want to run from God. She knew what it felt like to be on the other side of the chasm. Fear, death, and darkness were on that side. She never wanted to go back there again. She longed to run towards him. She wanted to see the stars. "Oh God," she whispered. "I will keep loving you."

And as the older woman held the younger, a deep peace settled into Katrine's spirit.

No matter what happened, whether Harry was alive or dead, God would never leave her or forsake her. Despite whatever loss might come her way she knew, the battle was won. What happened on earth was momentary and fleeting. What waited for her in eternity eclipsed all pain with a glory she had never tasted, but knew beyond any doubt existed.

I watched them, not moving, almost afraid to breathe. It was a riveting moment that came and left like a dove swooping in and landing for a brief second before taking off in flight once more.

Katrine's shining eyes met mine and then looked towards my aunt. "I am very grateful for you, Edith. How I shall miss you when the day comes and we must part."

The tide rushed in, drenching us to our knees. We scrambled up towards the dry sand, laughing a little. "Don't speak of such things!" Edith laughed, wringing her skirt out. "We may be together a while yet... given the way this war's been going."

"Katrine!" Peter shouted from the edge of the lawn that met the path to the beach. "Katrine!" He waved a paper in the air. "John said these arrived yesterday." He walked as quickly as he could down to meet us and passed two letters into my cousin's hands.

"Both for me?" she asked, taking them. The first was a telegram. It said, "IN HOLLAND. SAFE. G. SEND MAIL TO 48 SURI-NAMESTRAAT." It was dated from the end of March and had been forwarded from Australia. It must have arrived just after we'd left, and, thanks to airmail, made it to Hawaii before we did.

"Well, even if she skimps on words, it's good to know that Grace is safe and sound—at least enough to receive mail." Edie frowned as Katrine tore the second letter open.

"We need to write her right away," I said, "so she knows where we are. Paul can't check our postbox."

"Where is Paul?" Edie asked, surprised.

"He is being re-stationed. He didn't say where... it's confidential." I answered.

I thought over Grace's words and wondered if she was being

honest. She'd written before VE Day, when Holland was still Nazi-occupied! I tried to comfort myself with the thought that if she was safe enough to send that telegram a few months ago; she was probably safe now.

When I looked back at Katrine, she'd already read the second letter. Her face had turned white, and her hand rose over her mouth. "It's from the war office! It says that Harry's name was on a list of POWs who were liberated and being transported back to the States." Her hand shook. "Oh no. He was going to be transported on the *Comfort*—that hospital ship that was torpedoed!"

Peter reached out and steadied Katrine as she wobbled. "Are you okay?"

"Come, Piper!" she nearly shouted. "We have to get to the military hospital." She grabbed my hand and began to run towards the house. "He might be one of the survivors *we* picked up on our way over! Remember, they were from the *Comfort*!"

CHAPTER 45

WAITING

*T*he young nurse looked at the list and then back up at Lorelei, Edie, and me, standing nervously behind Katrine.

(Peter and Horatio had dropped us off at the hospital's entrance and went to park the Woody.)

"I see his name on the original list for those aboard the U.S.S. *Comfort*, but the survivors are still being organized." She paused. "Some don't have their dog tags anymore... We don't know the names of all the men who were brought on shore. Some are *still* being transported here. It will take hours to unload all of them. And even once we get them all settled, it could be several days before they are classified."

"Several days?" Katrine's face paled.

"Mrs. Stenetsky," the nurse put the clipboard down, "I promise you, the moment I learn anything of your husband, I'll call you personally. I understand what you are going through. My husband is on Sugar Hill right now on Okinawa. However, hospital policy will not allow you to be here until we are certain he is. I am terribly sorry, but I can't let you wait here. You understand, don't you?"

Her face completely stoic, Katrine nodded and thanked her before turning and leaving the waiting room with us on her heels. Outside, Horatio and Peter made their way up the walk to the hospital.

"No news yet, I take it."

She shook her head. "I'm afraid not."

Horatio took Katrine's arm and steered her towards the Woody.

Peter stepped in beside me and whispered, "What now?"

"The nurse said she'd call the minute she learns anything. It's all rather chaotic at the moment."

"Understandably." Peter opened the door, and I slid in beside him in the backseat. No one spoke the whole way home.

Once we arrived, the chipped beef and noodle casserole had burned beyond salvaging, and we all picked at our food. Not that chipped beef needed to be burned to make it inedible. Edie sliced extra-large slices of the eggless sponge, and I made a pot of coffee (extra strong) and we all settled in for a long night.

As expected, Katrine set up shop by the telephone and waited, looking straight ahead.

At midnight, the call finally came in. "Yes?" Katrine barely breathed. "This is Katrine Stenetsky."

A female voice hummed out of the receiver as the operator put the hospital through. I stepped in closer, ear to ear with Katrine, so I could hear.

"Mrs. Stenetsky, this is Nurse Janice Hopkins. We spoke earlier this afternoon." The woman paused before saying, "I am sorry to tell you, your husband's name was not among those who came in today."

Katrine didn't move.

"Mrs. Stenetsky?" Janice spoke directly into the phone. "Are you there?"

"Yes," Katrine whispered, afraid to move.

"However, there *is* a man without tags who fits your husband's description. But he's—" Katrine dropped the phone before Janice could finish.

"Piper, drive me to the hospital!"

UPON OUR ENTRANCE, Katrine sped through the lobby. "Where is he?" she demanded, slamming her hands down on the counter of the front desk where a young male orderly looked up in confusion.

"Who?"

"My husband!"

"Who's your husband?" His eyes narrowed.

"Harry Stenetsky! Janice called me and said to come and that she'd found my husband."

"Janice? Oh, you mean Mrs. Hopkins. She just got off duty. She didn't tell me anything about anyone coming. It's the middle of the night, lady! Not visiting hours."

At that moment, Janice, no longer in her uniform, came ambling down the hall, her hair down, wearing slacks and a light sweater. She looked exhausted. When she saw Katrine, she stopped. "Oh, Mrs. Stenetsky... you came." Her tone was carefully controlled, and I wondered what in the world was going on.

"Take me to him!" Katrine exclaimed.

"I don't know if that's a good idea." Janice pulled Katrine aside. "The man with your husband's description is—Oh my, this is difficult. I tried to tell you on the phone, but I believe we got disconnected."

"Don't keep me from him another minute!" Katrine demanded.

Janet inhaled and exhaled. "This is against protocol. I could lose my job." Then, she turned back around and walked up the hall. Wordlessly, we followed.

The hall's linoleum floor gleamed under the bright lights swinging overhead. Nurses and doctors and orderlies rushed back and forth. It smelled strongly of antiseptic.

Janice stopped outside a door marked #314. Katrine was about to push her way in when Janice grabbed her wrist. "Mrs. Stenetsky, if this man is your husband, he will not be the way you remember him. I would be doing you a disservice to tell you otherwise."

Katrine looked down at the nurse's hand on her wrist angrily. The nurse let go, and Katrine pushed her way into the room. Lorelei and I followed at a safe distance. Immediately, a wave of nausea swept over me. Two rows of 20 hospital beds on each side of the room were lined up neatly. Several nurses hovered over broken bodies, each of which seemed merely a skeletal frame.

Suddenly, I felt terrified. More terrified than I had ever been in my life. I'd never seen human beings look like the ones in front of me. "Oh God," I prayed, but that was all I could think to say. Nothing more would come.

Katrine's eyes wildly swept over the forms of the POWs in the beds. Then, she froze and reached out for my hand. I felt Janice come behind us. "Bed 11." She pointed with her eyes, and Katrine took a few steps forward towards the bed. "It... can't be him!" she whispered.

There, in the bed, an unnaturally thin man lay on his back, staring listlessly at the ceiling. His head was shaved. Katrine stepped closer to the man and leaned over him. "Harry?" she said. "Harry!" Her voice rose.

The man on the bed did not move. His eyelids did not flutter. I wondered if this shell of a man could be Harry, the strong and dashing man Katrine had fallen in love with. The brilliant, funny man-about-town. The tireless agent for the Jewish Agency. Could this man be him? If it *was* him, he was unrecognizable.

It had to be another man, I thought, hanging back. This had to be a mistake, a huge terrible mistake. There was no way that this was Harry. No way in a million years.

"He hasn't spoken since he came in," Janice explained.

Katrine moved closer. Carefully, she knelt down and turned the soldier's face towards hers. Suddenly, with a gasp, she realized that the man in her arms *was* her husband.

"Harry! It's me. It's Katrine!" From behind her, I saw the man's big beautiful blue eyes stare past her at nothing, a glass wall separating him from the world. "Oh God," Katrine cried out, cradling the head in her arms. She broke into sobs. "Oh, Harry, what have they done to you? What have they done!"

"He doesn't know who you are, Mrs. Stenetsky." Janice put her arm on Katrine's shoulder.

"That's not true!" Katrine nearly screamed. She looked back into the man's eyes. "Harry! Harry! It's me. It's your wife. It's Katrine." She buried her face in his neck. "It's Katrine, Harry, I'm here."

Janice, Lorelei, and I were rooted where we stood, watching the awful scene play out before us. I saw Janice wipe a tear out of her eye. Harry, once so strong and handsome, lay listless and still, unaware of the woman whose tears bathed his face. In between her sobs, I heard Katrine cry out, "Oh God, please. Bring him back. Bring him back!"

The earth seemed to stand still as Katrine's sobs penetrated the quiet of the ward.

The blue eyes blinked once or twice and suddenly focused on Katrine's hair sweeping over his face. He reached out his bony hand and touched the ends of her mane. The hand moved to her back and patted it gently, and a rough, gravelly voice whispered, "There now. Don't cry, ma'am. Nothing to cry over."

The nurse raised one eyebrow and smiled slowly. "Well, I'll be... He can speak."

~

THE NEXT DAY, after a cold lunch at the hospital, Peter and I left to drop Lorelei off at the airport for her flight back to San Francisco on Pan Am's Boeing 314. Horatio would have come, but he was in top-secret meetings from sun up to sun down nearly every day. The end of the war was at hand. You could smell it in the air.

Lorelei's plane left at 4:00 in the afternoon and arrived in California a very long 21 hours later, where she would catch a train all the way to New York and board an ocean liner bound for London. From there, it was a matter of catching a smattering of trains, planes, and smaller ships back to Palestine. She pressed a small slip of paper into my hands as she left with the address of Kibbutz Kinneret written on it, asking me to give it to Paul, if I discovered where he was before she did.

"I will," I answered as I pulled her close, not knowing the next time I would see her. "I'll write to Grace as well, now that we have her address."

"Thanks." She inhaled. "God knows when we'll all be together again, but I'm a firm believer that what God brings together, no man can separate." She patted her heart. "In here... we'll be together again. I know it."

I smiled, looking into her beautiful face. Her green eyes, full of hope. "And when things calm down, you and Peter ought to come. Everyone should see the Holy Land at some point in their lives."

"We would love that, Lorelei. And you always have a home with us, wherever we wind up," Peter added.

"And take care of Katrine and Harry for me." She sniffed. Then, she wistfully looked out at the ocean behind the runway, and before we knew it, she was gone, and we were on our way back home.

When we finally returned to the plantation house, we found Edie in the living room on one of the plush couches in the midst of writing a letter. Katrine, she informed us, was still at the hospital.

In the background, the emotionless voice of a reporter on the evening's news-broadcast said, *"And today, a victory parade was held in Moscow as Marshal Georgy Zhukov on a white charger led the procession and 200 Nazi banners were dragged through the mud in Red Square before being tossed on Lenin's tomb..."*

I could smell Mr. Yamaguchi's meat and potato patties (the

potato was added to the meat to extend it) in the skillet. It was nearly time for dinner. It had been an exhausting few days, I thought as I sat down next to Edie and slipped my shoes off my feet. Peter stood in the center of the room, listening to the radio for a moment more. Frowning, he stepped towards it and switched it off. A welcome silence filled the room, and I shut my eyes.

"Dear Grace." Edie scanned the page, reading over what she had written. "It was awful. All his beautiful curls, gone! And his arms are skinnier than mine. He looked right through Katrine, as though she wasn't there. Even when he spoke, I'm not sure he really knew who Katrine was."

I opened my eyes and slightly turned my face towards Edie. I was too tired to move.

"That's rather dramatic," Peter said, listening. "You don't want to scare her. Katrine just wanted you to tell her what's happening."

"And that is *exactly* what I am doing." Satisfied with her narrative, she folded the letter and slipped it in the envelope and loudly licked the back of a stamp. "I also told her that Lorelei is going back to the kibbutz without a ring on her finger." She shook her head. "Nothing has turned out the way I thought it would. But then, nothing ever does."

I looked at her questioningly. "I wanted nothing more than for Katrine to find Harry. She did, and he doesn't even remember her. And then, I wanted Lorelei to find love. She did and now look? No wedding, no engagement, nothing! She and Paul will be stuck in some sort of limbo until this war is over."

It was getting dark, and I stood up to turn on a lamp. As I did, I saw the Woody drive up. Horatio was back from the base. When he got out of the car, his shoulders slumped forward a little, as though he were so tired he couldn't hold himself up straight. He looked at the house and suddenly drew himself up, calling on some inner-strength to will his feet up the stairs, across the porch, and through the front door.

"Poor boy has shock-induced amnesia," Edie continued,

explaining it to us in an expert tone. Peter rolled his eyes, and Edie pointed the letter at him accusingly. "You weren't with me and Katrine at the doctor's this morning. Amnesia happens when you hit your head really hard but can also be caused by psychological trauma. Like Harry, when something so distressing happens, the mind chooses to forget," she insisted.

"So why doesn't he remember us? And Katrine? We aren't traumatic."

"The mind is a very complex organism," she sighed.

Peter shot me a look.

"Dear," Edie sighed looking at Peter, "was your father a doctor?"

He shook his head no.

"Is your brother a doctor?"

"Edie," he said with a groan.

"No. But my father and brother are, so don't argue with me. I know what I'm talking about, much more than you. I come from a medical family."

"But not a psychologist's family!"

"Well, that's true, but I have a brain, and I've had one a solid 20 years longer than you, give or take, so I know a little more about how people think than you do." Edie looked down her nose at Peter. "For all we know, Harry might have hit his head too. The doctor said there is evidence of a serious bruise on his skull."

"If he hit his head," Peter blinked, "then we know it wasn't psychological."

"I personally—" Edie stopped momentarily to blot the ink, "— think it is a mixture of the bruise *and* the brutality he suffered."

Horatio pushed open the screen door and Edie turned to him.

"We are just discussing Harry's case," she said as I fluffed a pillow on the back of Horatio's favorite chair, one made of bent bamboo with bright tropical print cushions. He sat down gratefully and unbuttoned his collar, exhaling in relief. Then, he leaned forward and hollered, "Mr. Yamaguchi!"

John immediately came out of the kitchen, wiping his hands on a dishtowel.

"Coffee, please! And make it strong."

John nodded and disappeared.

"Hard day?" Edie asked.

"Everyone's reeling over Simon's death. It was a big blow." He meant General Simon Bolivar Buckner Jr. who had been killed in action a few days before on Okinawa.

"Douglas (as in MacArthur), is appointing Joseph Stillwell as the new commander of the U.S. Tenth Army."

"Do you think he is a good choice?" Peter asked as John returned with Horatio's drink, which he took and held lightly in his hands.

"I don't know the man personally, but he has a good reputation."

Edie's eyes narrowed. "That's not all. What's really going on? Has something else happened?"

"We are putting together a plan for a ground invasion of Japan." Horatio shook his head and shut his eyes wearily. "It looks like this whole mess will keep on going... for another year at least."

"Another year?" I exclaimed.

"I'm 'fraid so." Horatio grimaced. "God help us. God help all those poor soldiers out there. Ours and theirs."

KATRINE ARRIVED after we finished dinner, and as Mr. Yamaguchi was clearing the dishes. Peter immediately stood up and pulled out a chair. She sat down gracefully.

We all looked at her expectantly, waiting. "So," Edie pressed, "what's the latest?"

Katrine had dark circles under her eyes. "The latest is that they still won't let me stay with him in the ward overnight."

Mr. Yamaguchi brought Katrine a steaming cup of coffee, which she took with both hands. "Thank you, John. You're very kind."

"I can heat some leftovers for you, Ms. Katrine."

She shook her head no. "One nurse brought me a cheese sandwich from the hospital cafeteria a few hours ago. I'm fine."

"Just thought I'd ask."

"Thanks again." She sipped her coffee as John pulled up a chair for himself, and we all leaned in.

"Well," she paused, "there are no medications to treat amnesia."

"Oh, my poor girl." Horatio took her hand. "I'm so sorry!"

"But that doesn't mean there is no hope," she continued. "The doctor said that in many cases the condition just 'fixes' itself."

"You mean," Peter asked, "Harry might just wake up one day and remember who he is?"

"He might." Katrine tried to smile. "It's happened before."

Mr. Yamaguchi cleared his throat, "If you don't mind, I'd like to pray for your husband."

"I think we should all pray for him," Edie agreed. "Lead us, John."

John nodded and bowed his head, his kind, steady voice speaking out into the stillness, "Father, we know that we live by faith and not by sight. We know that your Word says that you are close to the brokenhearted, and you save those who are crushed in spirit. We call upon your name to draw Harry close to you and to bind up the wounds in his heart and mind, and those in his body. For this reason, you were broken and bruised. For this reason, you died and rose again, that we might have life, even after such dark days. We declare that you will wipe every tear from our eyes and that in you, there is no more death or mourning or crying or pain. We trust you, and we cast our cares upon you, and we thank you now for carrying Harry. In your name we pray, Amen."

When I looked up, both Edie and Katrine's eyes glistened with tears.

THAT NIGHT, Peter and I lay in bed at the house talking until the wee hours of the morning. We didn't have enough money to buy another sailboat to replace the *Malahini*. Don O'Leery would happily keep me on at *The Honolulu Herald,* but Peter wasn't sure he could find employment so easily. We had to decide what in the world to do with ourselves, and we needed to decide soon.

"What about going back to school?" I asked. "Have you thought about it?"

"It's hard to think about studying when there's a war on." Propped up on one elbow, Peter's face hovered just above mine, and we spoke in low whispers of what Horatio had confided in him earlier that afternoon. "I don't know how I'd concentrate. They think an invasion of the mainland in Japan will be too costly. That's why we've been launching so many fire-bomb strikes." He hadn't shaved in a few days, and the moonlight made his scruffy beard look like fine threads of silver.

"It hasn't seemed to do anything," I said, thinking of how tumultuous the day had been.

He nodded. "You've heard of the ultra top-secret Manhattan Project."

Of course I had. The secret weapon that was being worked on in the desert somewhere in the middle of nowhere. We all pretended not to know about it, but given Horatio's position and Katrine and Harry's friendship with Albert Einstein, we knew more than most.

His whisper grew even quieter. "Horatio said that we've done it. The bomb is finished. We did it before the Germans!"

"Are we... going to use it?" I shuddered.

"I don't know. I think they will try to get the Japanese to surrender. It's a part of their religion, almost, to never surrender. Most of them would rather die. It's a Samurai thing, fighting to the death and all. They think it will give them eternal life."

"I don't enjoy talking about this." I fluffed my pillow. "It's not exactly the sort of talk conducive to sleep."

With that, Peter and I lay there, staring at the ceiling, feeling strange and uncomfortable until, finally, sleep overcame us. I dreamt of bombs and the *Malahini* floating out on the ocean, abandoned; the mast broken and the sails ripped to shreds. It was a restless dream that had no end, just like the war.

CHAPTER 46

JULY

I finished typing and pulled the final page from the typewriter, laying it proudly on top of the stack of pages I'd already finished over the last week. It still needed to be edited by another set of eyes, just to check for any glaring inconsistencies or embarrassing typos, but on the whole, I was pleased. My 'office,' if you could call it that, was comprised of a card table in the living room pushed up against the couch. The full view of the Pacific Ocean through the window in front of me had proven a serious distraction. Nevertheless, I had finished it. I had a manuscript. A slim manuscript. Very slim… But it was still a manuscript, and it was all my work. I had taken the story of every single soldier I'd interviewed on Alu, every one of them, and written them down, filling out the gaps and trimming the fat, just as Edie had instructed me to. All that time hadn't all gone to waste after all. Now the question at hand was, would Don want to publish it? Would anyone want to publish it?

Katrine blew into the living room, looking trim and professional. "I'm ready to go, Piper."

Standing up and smoothing out my skirt, I nodded. "Just let me get my hat." A moment later, my fingers deftly pinned the little hat, a soft grey felt one, over my pin-curls. There was a small mirror on the wall, just beside the wall clock. It was 11:00 in the morning. Catching sight of my reflection, I licked my fingers and smoothed back a stray hair. On closer inspection, I realized it wasn't a stray hair.

"Oh no!" I exclaimed.

"What's the matter?" Katrine asked, concerned.

"I have a wrinkle!"

"No, you don't," Katrine said decidedly.

"Oh yes, I do. Look, right there across the middle of my forehead!"

"It's all in your imagination."

"It isn't!" I turned around and stomped my foot. "It's all the stress of this war. I'm aging before my time."

"If that's the truth, I'd be as wrinkly as a prune." Katrine's eyes twinkled. "All you need is some cold cream. You'll see, it will be gone in a few days."

I grimaced. Youth was so fleeting! "I've been putting cold cream on my face every night since I was 16! It's not working."

Katrine grabbed my arm and pulled me outside. "Come on! I don't want to be late. I need this job. Besides, as the good book promises, 'charm is deceptive and beauty fades.'"

"Mr. O'Leery," I said, pulling up a chair in the newspaperman's office, "you remember my cousin, Mrs. Katrine Stenetsky."

He reached out and shook her hand vigorously. "Of course, but I think the last time we met, you were a Macleay."

I had given Katrine strict instructions to let me do all the talking. Donald O'Leery was a shrewd negotiator.

"Actually, I was a Stenetsky then too," she mumbled.

"Okay," he frowned and gave me a quick glance, "Mrs. Whoever-you-are, I'll put it to you straight. I don't have any positions open for singers. Especially singers who are missing two-thirds of their act."

"Mr. O'Leery," Katrine looked at him firmly, "I'm not really a singer. I was, up until last year, working on my Ph.D. in Biblical Archeology."

"I definitely have no open positions for people who spend all day looking at chipped pots that are so old no one wants to use them."

"Of course you don't!" Katrine laughed. "I want to apply to be a proofreader. As an academic, I have a great eye for detail. And I speak four languages fluently, Hebrew, English, German, and Yiddish."

I shot her a look, trying to communicate our prior agreement that I do all the talking.

Don shook his head. "I've already got three very good proof-readers."

"Please, Don," I stepped in, "give her the job. Her husband's over at Bradley Sanitarium. Certainly, you could always use another proofreader."

"I need the work," Katrine stated bluntly. "Just until he's well enough to leave."

"Bradley, huh?" He kept his eyes on Katrine. "What's the matter with him?"

"He was a POW in the Philippines... He's recovering."

"A POW, eh?" O'Leery's eyes lit up. "He must be some hero."

"Yes." Katrine nodded.

"We owe those boys just about everything." O'Leery instantly became sympathetic. I could see the wheels in his brain spinning, and a greedy smile played at his lips. "I would hate for it to be said that I refused to help one of our heroes. I'll hire you, part-time, mind you, on one condition."

"And that is?" I asked suspiciously.

"You get me an exclusive on your husband's experience."

"Don!" I exclaimed. "That's practically blackmail."

"Tough times, kid. You've been gone a while."

"Long enough for you to lose all sense of human dignity?" My mouth dropped open. "What will Horatio say!"

He paused and backed up, reddening. "Oh, Piper, you know I would never take advantage of your cousin's situation. Never in a million years. I only meant, if her husband feels up to it."

"Sure you did." I lifted one eyebrow suspiciously. I knew Don could sink pretty low to get a story, but this was unprecedented.

He ignored me and addressed Katrine as though I wasn't there. "I'll give you 46 dollars and 50 cents a week. I expect perfection. Only Sundays off. You start tomorrow."

"Give her 50 dollars a week, and you have a deal," I interjected.

"A deal it is." He reached out and shook her hand.

"Have I just been hired?" Katrine asked, surprised.

"Yes. And I'm already regretting it. Now, you two get out of my office. Show her the ropes, will you, kid?"

Nodding, I decided now was as good a moment as any to ask about the interviews. "Don?"

He paused.

"I was wondering. What would you pay for a series of soldiers' firsthand accounts of their experiences in the Pacific?"

"Firsthand?"

"I have a collection I've been working on based on interviews we did while we were on Alu. I've got just about 40 of them."

His eyes popped open. "You've got 40?"

I nodded.

"Pictures?"

"No."

He paused. "That poses a problem. Pictures sell papers."

"Good stories sell papers," I retorted.

"Well, I'd have to see them. I don't know if you can write."

"But if I can?"

"I'll give you 50 bucks a story."

I did a quick calculation. With nearly 40 stories, that was two thousand dollars!

Hungrily, he leaned in. "But only if they're good."

"They are," I answered more confidently than I felt. "I just need to run a final edit on the collection."

"I'll take a look."

I stood up and reached out to shake his hand, "You have a deal." Then I added, "Any more assignments this week? Besides covering the 4th of July ceremony downtown?"

"That should keep you busy, don't you think? I expect pictures of all the preparations of the floats and the beauty queens. They will crown 'Miss Surf and Sand.'"

I must have looked as exasperated as I felt. Who actually cared about 'Miss Surf and Sand'? It felt like a waste of time.

Out in the hall, Katrine heaved a sigh of relief.

"Come on." I led Katrine to the proofreading room.

"That was a trial by fire."

"I think he likes you." I laughed.

"You would never know it." Katrine looked about *The Honolulu Herald*'s buzzing office with renewed interest. I grabbed her hand. "It's not forever, Katrine. It's temporary."

"I know," she said, trying to brave. "I was just telling myself that very thing."

We continued walking, and she turned and asked, "Has Peter found a job yet?"

"It's difficult to move forward with the future of the whole world so uncertain."

"I understand exactly how he feels," she sighed, "but here we are." She peeked into the proofreading room.

"Yep," I groaned, "here we are. Right back where we started. Except, not at all really. We are all so different."

"My thoughts exactly."

~

I SPENT the next few days shooting floats covered in red, white, and blue bunting and teenagers in evening dresses as Katrine dove into proofreading and editing for the syndicated gossip columnist Norma Davies. The woman was spending three months on vacation at a resort on the island. She made a living—and had more readers than most correspondents from the front—telling salacious stories of Hollywood starlets' personal lives, gleaned from people who had promised someone to keep something secret. Katrine disdained her, but at least she was getting a paycheck.

It was frustrating, mind-numbing work for both of us, but not nearly as frustrating as Peter's ongoing search for a job.

I'd just returned from the last shoot before the parade and quickly freshened up and choked down a peanut butter sandwich. On my way back out, I met Edie on the porch. She had her feet up and was reading my manuscript.

"What do you think?" I asked nervously.

"I told you," she set the stack aside, "I'll give you my honest, critical feedback when I've *finished* it."

"Don's getting impatient."

"Don will just have to wait." She smiled.

I sat down with a huff, which she ignored.

"Peter still hasn't found a job?"

I shook my head no and looked down. All these questions about 'what Peter was going to do' were getting embarrassing.

At that moment, the man in question opened the screen door and stepped outside. "Just about time to leave for the parade, right?"

"We have got a few more minutes," I answered.

Edie looked at Peter out of the corner of her eye. "I hope the children will adjust to the heat after so much time in Scotland." She rubbed her hands together. "Just another two days! I can barely contain myself!"

"When do you plan to go back?" Peter asked.

"We are here till the Japanese finally call it a day. They'll quit before the Macleays do, I guess. Though just between us, dear, I wish Horatio might call it a day a little sooner." It was plain that Edie was tired and just wanted to go back to her normal life in the castle, waking up to the fog coming in from the sea, her brisk walks across the moors and heather, mornings of cream and porridge, and afternoons in her garden.

"Is Katrine going with you to the parade? Shouldn't she be here by now?"

I shook my head no and grabbed my camera bag. "She's finishing her shift at *The Herald* and will go straight to Bradley to be with Harry. We are meeting her there to watch the fireworks. The front lawn has a great view of the hill."

"HOW WAS THE PARADE?" Katrine asked, leading Peter and me to the lawn at Bradley where the staff had set out a BBQ, and soldiers sat in small groups or on lawn chairs. Bradley Sanitarium was a somber place.

"Uneventful," I answered. "Only three floats. But the turnout was okay. I got a couple of good shots."

"And the new camera?"

"I'm breaking it in, by and by." My eyes swept over the scene. After Townsville and Alu, taking pictures of floats and pageants seemed remarkably boring. I kept telling myself that I was helping Peter and I save up... I was trying very hard not to complain and to be content. But it was difficult.

"Edie was in her element riding in that convertible. She wore a bright red suit." Peter laughed.

"I wish I could have seen it. Where are they?"

"They went back home after the parade," he answered.

"Now," Katrine leaned in, "don't act shocked when you see him. He knows I'm his wife, even if he doesn't really remember me. He knows he's supposed to, so he tries. I told him you were coming."

"What do we do?" I asked, suddenly nervous.

"Just talk about old times." She picked up the pace. "They said anything might spark his memory coming back. A sound. A smell. A word."

There, at the end of the lawn, a man who looked vaguely like Harry sat in a wheelchair.

"Why's he in a wheelchair?" Peter asked. Katrine looked back but kept walking. "He lost nearly 70 pounds. There are scars all over his back from a severe beating. Some of them haven't fully healed yet. They think he's had dysentery, malaria, and survived the kamikaze attack on the Comfort, which left a nasty break in his shoulder."

"Wow," Peter said.

"Harry was always marvelously strong. It's a miracle he can sit up at all. Yesterday we even took a few steps around the garden. And he's gained seven pounds." She swallowed. "All in all, I'm very optimistic."

"You just need to spark the right memory?" I said.

"No. I don't," she said, her eyes dazzling. "I never could. But God can. However, I do plan on being here when it happens."

"Have you thought about what you will do if that doesn't happen?"

"We'll just have to get to know one another all over again. He fell in love with me once." Her eyes teared up. "I only hope he'll give me another chance."

Shock must have registered on my face.

"I'm not afraid, Piper," Katrine said with such confidence that I fully believed her.

She pulled forward and waved at Harry. "Hiya, soldier." Her voice was cheerful. "Look who I brought! Peter and Piper, remember them?"

He looked at us and shook his head slowly from side to side, offering an unconvincing, "Sure, sure. They look sort of familiar. From the hospital, right?"

"Um." Katrine stood there a moment. "How about I go get us some weenies? You'll help me, won't you, Peter?"

Suddenly, Harry and I were alone.

Harry looked at me and smiled a strange smile. "This is awkward, isn't it?"

I nodded, not knowing where to look. Thankfully, my eyes found a young man sitting under the tree on a folding chair. He was strumming a guitar softly, singing the song of the season, *"Don't Sit Under the Apple Tree (With Anyone Else but Me)."*[13]

"I have to keep telling myself that I'm not dreaming," Harry said. I looked back at him. His eyes were glued on Katrine's back. "I have trouble knowing what's real and what's not these days. Like her…"

"Katrine?" I sat down on the grass beside him.

"I know I'm married to her. I saw the pictures she showed me. There's a ring on her finger… But I'm struggling to believe anyone that gorgeous would ever fall in love with me."

I laughed out loud. "Well, you can take it from me. She did. Hook, line, and sinker." For a moment, that old sparkle glittered in his clear eyes behind his glasses. "Do you remember anything at all?"

He nodded slowly. "Vague pictures, impressions really. I couldn't remember my name a few days ago."

"And now?"

"Well," he looked confused, "I know my name is Harry Stenetsky because everybody's told me that. But that's not the same as remembering, is it?"

"Do you remember Palestine? Or Europe?" I stopped. "Or Rose? She's my mother. You went to high school with her."

"Sorry, kid. Doesn't ring a bell."

"Don't worry about it," I said, much more cheerfully than I felt.

Harry shifted in his chair and faced me. "Seriously though—that woman married me?"

"It was definitely a mutual decision." I sighed. Then, leaning in, I added, "You think she's pretty?"

"Pretty? I think she's the prettiest woman I've ever seen. I just wish I could remember her! The worst part is," he gripped the side of the chair, "how I don't even know how much I've lost. And I can't help but wonder what she and I had. I'll never get it back. I can't ask her to stay with me. Not now."

"Why not?" I asked, surprised. "She loves you."

He shook his head, not believing it could be true. "Look at me. I'm a shell. A gaunt, hollowed-out shell of a man I can't remember."

"Harry," I put my hand upon his knee, "my husband came back from the war a couple of years ago. His leg got shot up pretty bad. It took him a long time to heal... and longer for his inside to heal than his outside, if that makes sense."

"You have no idea how much it makes sense." He looked down at me. "How'd he do it?"

"We prayed a lot."

"You pray?"

I nodded.

"Maybe..." he faltered. "Maybe you could pray for me. For Katrine and me, that is."

My eyes welled up with tears, and I turned away so he wouldn't see me cry. And then, I prayed that God would touch this hero in the same way he had touched my husband.

By then, Peter and Katrine had returned with paper plates stacked with weenies and baked beans. It was then I noticed how tense things were between Katrine and Harry. They spoke to one another haltingly, barely meeting one another's gaze, and seemed afraid to touch one another.

"Should be quite a show," Peter said. "I think it should start any minute."

"I hope nobody cracks up." Harry laughed, "I heard some of these guys have shell-shock."

We all looked at him worriedly and then realized he was telling a joke. He put his hands up. "Sorry. Sorry. I know, we are in a mental hospital. It's not funny. I can't have shell shock. I don't remember any shells."

Katrine burst out laughing, more from nerves than from Harry's sense of humor. "You never could tell a joke," she said.

"I couldn't?" He laughed with her. And then, they both fell silent and stared straight ahead.

A moment later, there was a burst of color. Blue and red and white sparkles boomed above us, one after another, in a brilliant show of explosive freedom. We watched, our necks craning backward. It was odd watching the show in daylight, but the curfew demanded it. I leaned into Peter and felt his arm wrap around me. I wished it was darker.

And then, from behind me, I heard Harry say, "Katrine?"

I turned and watched as Katrine asked, "Is it too much? I can bring you inside if it's too close to a bomb or something."

"Nah. It's nothing like that. I told you, I don't remember any explosions. I just, uh, wanted to ask you something." His words came out in starts and stops.

"Yes?"

"I have a memory, I think." He looked at me. "Maybe it's your prayers, kid... I feel goose pimply."

Her voice became excited. "You do?"

"Yeah." He stopped. "Please don't think I'm being fresh or anything, ma'am, but would you kiss me? I know I don't really know you, and you don't know me, at least not really... But for the sake of clinical research and—"

Before he could go on, Katrine dove in, her lips touching his. When she moved back, I could see tears streaming down his cheeks. "I've kissed you before, haven't I? With fireworks."

"Yes! Yes, Harry! Our first kiss *was* on the Fourth of July." She nodded, her voice coming out barely above a whisper. "But I hear fireworks every time you kiss me, Harry."

"I remember." Harry looked up at the sky and then back into Katrine's eyes. "I remember that kiss... I still can't believe you married me though."

"You better believe it, buster," she said, leaning in and kissing him again. "I'd marry you again if you asked me."

"I'll have to work up the courage. You are a little out of my league."

"Oh, Harry." She smiled. "Your memory is definitely coming back!"

He reddened. "So... will you marry me?"

"I already did."

"Again?"

Katrine's eyes didn't leave his face. "It would be my honor."

And then, out of nowhere, it was as though the whole of Bradley exploded in the chorus along with the guitarist, singing, *"Don't Sit Under the Apple Tree (With Anyone Else but Me)."*[14]

Harry rubbed his hand over his cropped hair and swallowed. It was all coming back. He remembered growing up in New York. He remembered his mother Bertha and his father Israel. He remembered the Jewish Agency and countless secret missions. He remembered Katrine riding a camel somewhere in the desert. And then, he remembered the Philippines. "I remember, Katrine. I remember... everything."

I closed my eyes and savored the moment. For the first time in... oh, I couldn't remember how long, I felt something in my heart. I was almost afraid to really believe it was there. But it was. It really was. It was quite the real thing too. Real joy. For the moment. For Harry. For Katrine. Even for myself. And in only one day more, it would be nearly complete. My parents would arrive and everything would be back to normal. Almost.

But as soon as the feeling came, I suppressed it. It was too soon to allow myself to breathe yet. I wasn't ready.

"Everything?" Katrine asked, her eyes riveted to his face.

A flicker of pain crossed Harry's features, and he closed his eyes. "Everything," he repeated.

CHAPTER 47

HOMECOMING

*T*wo things can happen when you see someone who is one of the most important people in your life, and you haven't seen them for ages and ages. You either say nothing at all because there is simply too much to say. Or, you try to say it all at once, which is impossible, but it is the route I chose when my mother arrived.

Almost as soon as I was able to pull mother away from all the others, about two hours after they had arrived from the ship with the Woody full of children and trunks and a dog, I began to talk. I talked and I talked as though my mouth had forgotten how to shut. I had just finished with the tale of Harry's miraculous recovery and had plunged into my job with *The Honolulu Herald*. We must have walked three miles up the beach and were now on the way back.

"'Operation Downfall is planned to begin this November, and President Truman is calling for five million troops to invade Kyushu." I looked at her, catching the new flecks of grey in her hair. Her smile was softer, wiser even. I continued, "Mother, this war is never going to end... and I'm going to be taking pictures of pageants and generals and parades for the rest of my life."

"Is that such a bad thing?"

I shrugged. "No. But it's not what I thought God would do with my life. And I never thought this is what God would do with Peter."

"And what is God doing with Peter?"

"Nothing! He's not lazy, you know Peter. He's looking for a job, but nothing seems like the right fit and all the jobs he is qualified for are taken on the island. It feels like God is silent and we are left waiting, trying to fill the time…"

She stopped walking and turned to me. It was such a relief to be near her again. To share the burdens on my heart the way I'd longed to for months, years actually. Having her right beside me, feeling her warmth, knowing what the slightest change in her expression meant.

"Oh, Agatha," she gently touched my cheek with her hand, "if God is silent, then you know what to do."

"What?"

"Go back to the last thing he told you to do and do it."

Oh yes. I laughed mirthlessly. To be honest, I was too tired to remember the last thing God had asked me to do. "And maybe," she added, "It's not you who needs to ask that question. It's Peter. The war's been going on a long time. We all have battle fatigue."

"What are you saying, Mother?"

"Maybe," she spoke slowly, "Peter needs to finish what he started. Sometimes God won't let us move on until we… well, until we finish."

"You mean, going back to school?"

She nodded. "I do. I know it may not be Peter's favorite way to spend his time, but sometimes we have to do things we don't like, or else we won't be prepared for what God is calling us to do in the future."

She had a point. Hand in hand, we kept walking down the beach. "And while we're on the subject, have you thought about it?"

"Thought about what?"

"You will have to decide what *you* are going to do too. No matter what you may say, this war will end, and it will end soon."

"Well," I floundered, "I guess I'm going to keep working for Don."

"But you just told me you were bored with photographing beauty pageants and parades."

"Well, after all the excitement the last few months… it feels sort of bland going back to the mundane day-to-day stuff." I shook my head. "I guess I don't care about parades like I used to. But it pays the bills. And I'm not complaining… much. I'm *trying* to be content."

"In my opinion," she breathed, "you never really cared about that sort of thing. But as long as we are on the topic, what *do* you care about these days?" She looked into my eyes penetratingly.

"Important things. A lot has been happening in the world. People need to know what is going on. What I'm doing now seems sort of frivolous. But a job is a job, and I *am* grateful for it."

"You aren't stuck, Agatha."

"I'm not stuck?"

"You can do something new too, like Peter."

I looked at her questioningly.

"We have to adjust to the season we *are* in *now*, dear. We can never return to the season we *were* in. Maybe," she inhaled, "your season with *The Honolulu Herald* is over and done with? Maybe you need to ask God what's next?"

"But what else could I do?" I exclaimed.

"I don't know." She laughed. "But you are a very bright and very brave girl! If you are open to learning new skills, God will use all the experiences you picked up over the last few years to change the world. If you let him." She paused and then said, "And just between us, I am pretty sure God is not calling you to photograph beauty pageants and parades for the rest of your life."

"You've been talking to Edie, haven't you?" I laughed.

She shook her head. "No. I've been talking to *you*. As your mother, there is nothing I want more in the world than to see you

463

right in the middle of God's plan. For Peter, that might mean finishing school. For you, it might mean starting something new."

With that, she faced forward and once more began to walk. I waited a moment, her words stuck in my mind. Starting something new? What a thought that was! It was almost too much to think about. I ran to catch up with her, taking her hand once more.

She looked over and smiled. "I can't tell you how happy I am to see you, my darling girl!"

"Are you all right?" I started, suddenly embarrassed I hadn't asked before. "You and dad?"

"I suppose so, all things considered. It's been months since Victory Day, but we still are under strict rations. In fact, in some cases, it's gotten worse. Twenty-five percent less bacon. Less soap. Less cooking fat. I don't remember the last time I saw a good steak, you know, a *great* steak. So many new territories are under British control, and so many people have to be fed." She sighed. "And it's not like all the young men have come marching home. They haven't. Many British troops remain mobilized to help with post-war reconstruction. There are so many refugees…"

"I was so sure things would go back to normal," she continued, which was not what I had expected to hear.

"But I suppose it's impossible for things to go back to the way they were." The soft sand gave way beneath our feet. "We've learned to do without so much. I've learned to do without so much. Your father too."

I waited, knowing she wasn't finished.

"I've been without my own home, my own furniture, for years now. I didn't know how much it mattered to me until it was gone. Your father's entire profession changed. From a full-time doctor with a brilliant little clinic to life in a provincial Scottish village. Everything he used to define himself with is gone. We have one thing left, our faith in God. All the other props we used to lean on for security don't exist anymore. God used this war to take them away, to see what we are really made of."

"But you came out better for it!" I exclaimed suddenly. "I feel like I came out... smaller." It was the only word I could think of to describe how I felt. "I want to believe I've grown, become more like Christ, more giving, more loving, less selfish. But all I can think of is how uncomfortable I am and how all I want is to be comfortable again."

My mother smiled and spoke slowly, "You have more gold in you than you can see. We should never judge our own growth, I think."

"Do you think I've grown?"

"I think you have grown more than you or I will ever understand."

I felt a tear come down my face. "Are you sure?"

"Positive." She inhaled.

The sound of two dogs barking along the beach drew our attention back towards the direction of the house. "You were brave to come all this way with P.H.L., the twins, Anna, and the baby."

"We could not have done it without Ferguson. But I left the monkey at home with one of the neighbor's children. Everyone has their limit."

The butler immediately came into view, as if on cue. In his hands, Horatio's collie and Founder, on leashes, pulled the poor man mercilessly toward us. "Ms. Piper! Ms. Rose!" he called out, looking remarkably out of place, in his perfectly pressed uniform and bowler hat.

"Fergie," I laughed, "I think we will have to get you more suitable clothes for the tropics."

He struggled to slow the dogs down and shouted out "Sit!" with more force than intended. The dogs both instantly obeyed, and Ferguson wiped his brow with the back of his hand. "I am certain, ma'am, that those brash Hawaiian print shirts and khaki shorts would not suit my complexion."

I reached out and grasped the butler's arm. "It really is good to see you, Ferguson."

"And you, Ms. Piper."

Looking at my mother, he continued, "Willem and Raffi have begun to build the chuppah, on the front lawn." As I walked around the side of the house, I saw the beautiful prayer shawl canopy, traditional to Jewish weddings, standing as the focal point of the ceremony site.

"I thought it would be a proper job for them," he continued. Both boys, nearly 13, had shot up since I'd last seen them. Now nearly as tall as me, they spoke English with an odd Scottish twist peppered with English idioms and American slang. They were the fruit of being raised by my parents, Ferguson, and Edie and Horatio. Willem was a brilliant youth. Armed with a telescope, he could tell you the name of 100 stars and constellations. His brother was more of a class-clown type. Edie thought Raffi would be a world-class stand-up comedian one day. It was hard to believe that, if not for the Kindertransport in 1939, the twins and Anna, wouldn't be alive today. News that all three had lost their parents to Nazi brutality dismissed all thoughts of reuniting the children with their parents, and Edie and Horatio were in the process of legally adopting the trio. This time, however, it was with official documents—unlike the forged ones they used when they'd 'adopted' Katrine, Lorelei, and Grace.

"They are studying for their Bar Mitzvahs," my mother told me as we once more began to walk towards the beach. "We've hired a Hebrew tutor, a wonderful old character who lectures at St. Andrews, Benjamin Kain." My mother's eyes sparkled thinking of him. "We want the boys to know who they are and where they come from. I... I wish we'd done the same with you growing up."

I stopped. "I had a wonderful childhood, Mother. You did a great job raising me."

"I know that." My mother paused. "But I didn't teach you about who you are, about who I am. I didn't understand how important it was until now. I want you to start learning, Piper. Don't forget," she put her hand on my arm, "don't you ever forget, that your mother is Jewish."

My mother was different than I remembered her. Stronger. Deeper. Richer. Her eyes held, simultaneously, a sense of sadness and a new hope that had not been there before the war.

"It means something, Piper. It means something," she said slowly.

She looked at me so intensely; I had to look down. It was something about how she said it—it took my breath away and made me afraid. I had never really thought about her being Jewish or my being half-Jewish other than just that. You know, just a fact. I was an American girl. That's all. Nothing more, nothing less. Until that moment, it had been enough.

CHAPTER 48

I DO... AGAIN

The vow-renewal for Katrine and Harry was all Edie's idea. With Mother and Father and the children present, and Harry getting stronger by the minute, why, it was too marvelous an opportunity to pass up. And so, on a bright Tuesday morning after my parents and the children arrived, we helped prepare the bride for her groom.

"Normally," Edie said matter-of-factly, "I don't stand for vow-renewal ceremonies. You make a promise, and you keep it. But I would say your case is definitely the exception to the rule. And besides, I'd rather not have all those ideas I had for Lorelei's wedding go to waste. Not to mention this lovely dress."

Edie spoke with her mouth half-closed, a pin precariously gripped in her teeth. She pulled the waist in and moved on to the hem as my mother, on the opposite side of Katrine, began to pin like a madwoman.

"I knew it was a bad idea to throw this dress away," Edie continued. "Of course, I had no idea you would be the first one to wear it, Katrine. I thought Paul and Lorelei would kiss and makeup and that would be that."

I sat on the bed, with little Agatha—named after me—sitting on my left and Anna on my right, as I thought about what Edie said and watched them skillfully finish the alterations.

Agatha, Edie and Horatio's only biological child, had Edie's freckles and green eyes and Horatio's dark hair. She was a quiet, pensive child, watching everything with her big eyes opened wide. How different she was then her adopted big sister who sat on my right. Eight-year-old Anna's golden curls had darkened to a light brown, and she talked about everything, all the time, teaching 'little' Agatha everything she knew about life, which, in her mind, being four years older, was a considerable amount. The gregarious Jewish child had trouble keeping quiet. But at the moment, she was as silent as a church mouse, entranced with Katrine, the bride, and utterly consumed with her important role as a junior bridesmaid and doing her best to play the part well.

Still stuck on Lorelei and Paul, Edie continued, "They should have listened to me and let bygones be bygones." Edie shook her head; there was a part of the hem that wasn't straight.

"Come now, Edie." My mother reached out and secured an enormous white orchid in Katrine's hair. "Let's not talk of others while they're not with us." The flower almost seemed to glow against her black locks, done up in a mass of curls right on the top of her head.

My mother turned her attention to Katrine. "Now, you won't be able to get too into the music when you're dancing. This dress is pinned together, and I don't want one popping free and stabbing you or Harry, got it?"

Katrine laughed. "I don't think we'll be doing much dancing at the wedding. Harry needs to get his land-legs back, and that might take a while."

It had taken about an hour to temporarily fit Lorelei's salvaged gown to Katrine's significantly shorter frame. But though it wasn't perfect, it was beautiful. And Harry couldn't care less. At the moment only one thing mattered: they both still wanted to be married to each other, for better or worse.

"You know," Katrine looked at herself in the mirror, "Jews don't take wedding vows… not like in a Christian wedding."

Edie stood up, groaning a little and putting her hand on her back. "What do they do?"

"The wedding reflects a sacred union of two people, blessed by God and their community," Katrine explained, as she blotted her lipstick.

"I think that's very beautiful."

"Isn't it? But I didn't even have that. In a way, this is my first wedding." Katrine turned around and faced us. "At the consulate in Palestine, we signed a piece of a paper and said some simple vows, and that was about it. No ceremony, no dress. It feels like this is the right timing." She grabbed my mother's hand. "Everything would be perfect if only Harry knew Yeshua. Every time I try to tell him, to show him why I believe the way I do, it's like talking to a stone wall. He's never been that into religion, but he says as long as I'm happy, he's happy."

"Give him time," my mother said. "Every man's journey is his own."

~

WE HAD the ceremony on the front lawn at sunset. Katrine emerged from the house where Harry waited on the porch. Together, hand in hand, they walked down the steps, slowly for Harry's sake, and across the lawn. Under the chuppah Willem and Raffi had made, Horatio stood in for an officiant, in his full dress uniform.

"It's good to see you up on your feet, Harry." Horatio beamed. "We," he looked me, my mother and father, Peter, Edie, and the children, "are all rejoicing in this moment, as I'm sure you both are."

Katrine and Harry gazed into each other's eyes.

Horatio pulled a piece of paper out of his back pocket and opened it up with a slight bashfulness. "I prepared a little something. I've been practicing in secret." He winked at Edie and began to read, his Scottish brogue tripping over the unfamiliar Hebrew words. *"B'rukhim ha'baim b'shem Adonay reyim ahuvim. Mi adir al hakol mi barukh al hakol mi gadol al hakol hu y'varekh et ha'reyim ha'ahuvim."* He looked back up. For all of you who don't speak Hebrew, that means, "Blessed in God's name are these beloved companions who come before us. He who is powerful above all, who is great above all, who is supreme above all, may he bless these beloved companions."[15]

Edie, duly impressed with Horatio's recitation, exclaimed, "Amen!"

Katrine, her voice so low I could barely hear it above the sound of the distant waves, turned to Harry. "May God who blessed our fathers Abraham, Isaac, and Jacob, and our mothers Sarah, Rebecca, Rachel, and Leah, bless our marriage. May the love that binds us be strong and lasting, and let our hearts be filled with patience and understanding for one another."[16]

Harry nodded. "And may our home continue to be a sanctuary built on devotion to God, Torah, and Israel. May we be blessed with a long life together filled with good health, good fortune, adventure and peace, as our love and friendship continues to deepen through the years."[17]

My mother stepped forward and put one hand on Katrine's shoulder and another on Harry's. A tear slipped down her cheek. "May God who blessed our ancestors bless my sister's daughter, Katrine and her husband, Harry. Bless them with children and grandchildren and great-grandchildren. May God continue to watch over them and protect them from any sorrow and distress."[18]

She stepped away, and Horatio clasped his hands together. "Well, kids. I think you ought to kiss and re-seal the deal."

Harry gently took Katrine in his arms and kissed her. We all cheered, and the twins snickered, while Anna blushed. I snapped a photograph with my new camera and prayed that someday soon, Harry and Katrine would have a home to put it in.

On the porch, John had set out a lovely little wedding cake and fresh lemonade. We sat on the wooden banister, the steps, the porch rocking chairs, and seats from inside the house we pulled outside. Harry was worn out but happy.

It was after the toasts, after we'd laughed and reminisced and the children were all out on the lawn with Edie, playing croquet with the new set she'd bought in town on a whim, that Harry turned to Katrine and asked, "So... when are you going to tell me more about this new near brother-in-law of mine? He must be quite a mensch to win Lorelei's heart."

"A *mensch?*" Horatio asked, unfamiliar with the Yiddish word.

Harry thought for a second. "A mensch? Let's see... A mensch is an all-around good guy. The kind of guy you want for a friend. The best kind of man."

Katrine paused and said thoughtfully, "Well, Paul Sinclair *is* quite a man. Tall and handsome and as strong-willed as a bull. An American, like you. I can't imagine anyone not liking him. He'll make a great brother-in-law."

Harry said, "I remember you mentioned his involvement with decoding, so I know not to ask what he's up to now... but what did he do before the war?"

"He did a lot of things." Peter smiled. "In 1939, when his sister's husband died at Pearl Harbor, Paul dropped out of seminary and joined the army."

"An aspiring rabbi?" He chuckled.

"No." Katrine shook her head. Haltingly, she said, "He's a Christian, like me."

Harry looked at Katrine searchingly. That his Jewish wife insisted on a Jewish ceremony but believed as the Christians did—that Jesus, or Yeshua as she called him, was the Jewish Messiah come to save mankind—was difficult for him to reconcile.

He couldn't deny that his wife differed from how he remembered her—now that he mostly could remember. She was kinder, gentler, less anxious, and more forgiving. In fact, her newly found inner confidence was something he envied, and he wondered if it was because of her new faith. The same held true for Lorelei, come to think of it. The Adleman sisters, at least these two, were not the Adleman sisters he had left behind.

"So, Lorelei is marrying a Gentile?"

"Watch it," my *very* Gentile father said playfully, winking at my mother.

"He's a good man, Harry. You'll like him," Peter replied.

"You Christians are turning out to be a different bunch than I thought. They are not all like you." He glanced at my father. "A lot of 'Christians' in Germany turned their backs on us."

"Fear drives people to do a lot of horrible things," my father answered. "But it's no excuse." He paused and then added, "But, I would go so far as to say that if they helped or fought with the Nazis, I doubt the sincerity of their faith. Not everyone is who they say they are. On the other hand, there are countless other Christians who gave their lives to stand up against the Nazis. They showed what it really means to be a Christian, displaying the greatest kind of love—when one man lays down his life to save another. The same love Jesus showed us."

At that moment, Edie eased herself up the stairs. "It's getting too dark to play." In the twilight, the first star twinkled. Willem came up the stairs two at a time behind Edie. He paused and looked up at the sky.

"We'll be able to see Lyra in a moment." He smiled and pointed. "Just there."

"Really? What else will we be able to see?" I asked, peering upwards.

"Virgo, Corvus, Antila. we could see a dozen constellations if we stay up all night."

Horatio leaned back, proudly. "This one will make a great navigator. He knows the sky like the back of his hand. You're going to be a sailor, aren't you, my boy!"

Raffi, now beside his brother, guffawed. "He wants to sail in space."

"Space?" Peter smiled.

Willem nodded. "We'll be able to sail to the stars someday. I've read about it! With rockets!"

We all looked up into the sky, imagining a rocket carrying a man into the darkness.

"You never know. One day," Peter shrugged, "a man might sail to the stars. Probably about the same time men stop treating one another like animals."

Willem was adamant. "Oh no, Peter. We'll reach it long before that."

Raffi playfully punched his brother's arm. "He reads too much!"

"No, Raffi. Your brother Willem is correct." Horatio shook his head. "The Germans launched a rocket last June that went into space briefly. It's just a matter of time before one might carry a man into those uncharted waters."

A matter of time, I thought. Just a matter of time—like everything else.

CHAPTER 49

THE END

*T*he end came quickly and suddenly.

Roughly two weeks later, Horatio returned from an urgent meeting. He coughed into his hand and glanced at Edie, who had just begun to knit a new sweater in faith of returning to Scotland at some point in her life.

It was after dinner, nearly nine in the evening. Peter and my father, in the middle of a chess game, pushed the board out of the way and stood up. My mother came in, her hair still damp from the bath. Katrine, Harry, and I were sitting near Edie, doing nothing in particular. There was something in the air; a tense anticipation ever since Horatio had been called out. It was impossible to ignore. It also made it impossible to do anything productive.

"Where are the boys?" Horatio asked, meaning Willem and Raffi.

"In their room." Edie put the sweater down.

"I suppose it's just as well." He sighed and unbuttoned the top of his shirt, slinging his jacket over the arm of the couch. "Anna and Agatha are asleep, I take it?"

She nodded.

"So," my father said, "what is it? Good news or bad?"

The fan whirred overhead.

"Nathan," Horatio shook his head grimly, "I barely know…"

He looked down, as though trying to find the right words. "I've just been notified that we, the United States, Great Britain, and China, will call for the unconditional surrender of Japan in *two days*. Chiang Kai-shek, Winston Churchill, and President Truman will warn Japan that if they do not surrender, they will suffer dire repercussions."

No one spoke for a moment as the news sunk in.

"Dire repercussions?" Peter asked finally, one eyebrow raised.

"Prompt and utter destruction," Horatio answered slowly.

"What's it mean?" My mother looked at my father, her voice fraught with concern.

Horatio shut his eyes and rubbed his forehead, "We can only hope, my dear, that the Japanese 'follow the path of reason,' as our leaders have urged them, and lay down their weapons. If they do, we've promised to help them create a responsible government, to not enslave them or do any of the reprehensible things they have done to so many."

"How long will they have to decide?"

Horatio opened his eyes. "I don't know."

Ten days after the Allies issued their ultimatum to Japan, on August 6, 1945, the U.S. dropped an atomic bomb on Hiroshima.

Three days later, another was dropped on Nagasaki.

Both cities were, for all intents and purposes, leveled; 140,000 people instantly incinerated.

Japan surrendered.

IN THE WAKE of the unthinkable destruction and loss of human life, President Truman said that the use of such weapons was necessary to prevent what he believed would be an even more tremendous loss of life if the scheduled land invasion of Japan was carried out.

No one asked how many would have died if the bombs had not been dropped, and the war had continued on. No one had the courage.

Mr. Yamaguchi, when the news hit the radio, sunk to his knees and cried out for mercy for his people. My mother and Edie sunk down beside him. The elderly gentleman cried right there in front of all of us, and then, he excused himself and went home to comfort his wife; she had cousins in Nagasaki.

IT WAS A HORRIFIC, tragic end. But it was an end... Though no one could talk about it. What could we say? It was too unspeakable. Too confusing. No one could unravel the mess of the last six years. All we could do was try to pick up the pieces that were left and try to rebuild what had been destroyed, just like everyone else.

My parents booked passage on a ship headed to San Francisco. They had not been back to the house I'd been born in for nearly six years.

"And what about us?" Harry asked Katrine.

"I want to go home too."

"Where is that?"

"As long as I'm with you, Harry, I'm at home."

He smiled and squeezed her hand. "I know. But we have to live somewhere."

She paused, looked down and then back up. "Palestine."

"Really?" His eyes opened wide. "That 'back-water swamp'?" He imitated her voice playfully as he remembered one of their first conversations.

"It's our home, Harry. Nowhere else on earth will ever be home for me. Nowhere."

"You have no idea how happy that makes me," He sighed. "So... how about we go home?"

Horatio and Edie had the same idea and, along with Harry and Katrine, booked tickets on the same boat as my parents. Neither Katrine, Horatio, or my mother were keen on flying in those days. From San Francisco, they would travel by train back to New York, and from there, board ships bound for Scotland and Palestine, respectively.

Peter and I had no idea what to do or where to go. Everything was over, and we had no idea where to begin.

"It's a letter from Grace," Katrine shouted excitedly a week later, the morning they were all due to ship out, waving the envelope above her head and running down the lane to the house. The suitcases were neatly stacked on the porch, and we were waiting for Harry to bring the Woody from around the back and drive us to the dock. "Why," she said breathlessly, "if I hadn't checked the post one last time, we'd have missed it."

"What's it say?" I asked, standing close to her. Shoulder to shoulder, she opened the letter and began to read.

My mother asked, coming down the steps, "When's it dated?" She had on her white gloves and a traveling hat.

"Let's see," Katrine peered at the top, "June. So over two months ago. *Dear Katrine,*" she began, "*I found Amos.*"

"Praise God." My mother exhaled.

"*He's been living with a Dutch couple who worked with the resistance. I've volunteered with the Red Cross and still have connections with the Jewish Agency. I've begun working with them to get the Jews left in Europe to Palestine, What's left of them, that is. But it is difficult work, lonely work. I miss you and Lorelei very much.*"

My mother and I locked eyes.

"There are over 850,000 refugees in Europe living in displaced persons camps. Many of them were in concentration camps prior to the war's end. Over 11 million people have lost their homes. It feels like all the world is one big mass of people not knowing what to do or where to go."

And Peter and I were two of them, I thought.

"What else does she say about Amos?" my mother asked growing worried.

Katrine kept reading. *"Amos is different. He says that he believes Yeshua is the Messiah now, just like Lorelei. I don't know what to make of it!"*

Katrine looked up, tears in her eyes. "Amos? A believer?"

"Keep reading," my mother prodded.

"Anyway, I'm writing to tell you I am safe. And something else as well . . ." Katrine gasped and sunk down to the steps as her eyes scanned the next line.

I grabbed the letter and kept reading. *"There is a possibility that Mother and Father are alive."*

"Judith and Chaim might be alive?" My mother looked wildly around and shouted for my father, "Nathan! Nathan!"

Stunned, I continued, *"When I was scouring the survivor's lists looking for Amos's name, I discovered the names of Judith and Chaim Adleman. It looks like they somehow might have made it to Free France and joined the resistance. But I've nothing else to go on. No leads at all. It is as though they disappeared into thin air, like so many thousands of others."*

My father pushed through the screen door. "What is it? What's the matter?"

Peter stepped outside, the last suitcase in his hand.

"Judith and Chaim might be alive, Peter," I said slowly.

He blinked once or twice in amazement. "And Grace?"

"She's all right," Katrine said firmly. "She's... going to be all right." Her eyes met mine. "The minute we get back to Palestine, we can start making inquiries about my parents. The Jewish Agency will help us find them. I'm sure of it! They have connections all over Europe!"

At that moment, the Woody emerged from around the back of the house and stopped. Harry jumped out, the spring returning to his step and the color to his cheeks. He was still thin, but there was no doubt about it, he was getting stronger. "Let's load 'em up! Got to get to the dock."

Katrine grasped my hand and looked out at the Pacific, tearing up.

"Are you okay, Katrine?"

She swallowed, nodding. "Az dos harts iz ful, geyen di oygn iber."

Harry, understanding, translated for me. "When the heart is full, the eyes overflow." For the first time in her whole life, Katrine's heart was full. And it showed in her glistening eyes.

CHAPTER 50

A NEW BEGINNING

*A*nd before I knew it, we were at the pier, saying our goodbyes.

I wasn't ready. Not for any of it. I'd been waiting and waiting for the end, and now it was here.

And I wasn't ready. Was it good? Was it bad? I didn't know. And Peter and I were still at a complete loss at what to do or where to go. Funny how life works, isn't it? I felt disoriented and strangely empty. We'd been fighting for so long. I wondered what one does when one stops fighting...

"I've convinced him to retire from the Navy. And he wants to sell Scottish Lobster. In fact, he's already found a buyer for the company." Edie shrugged and adjusted her purse strap, and the sea breeze blew a stray hair across her freckled nose.

Out of the corner of my eye, I saw Horatio and my mother and father in a deep discussion with Peter.

"He's already discussed it with Peter." Edie smiled. "And in the meantime, I want him to be a full-time father for a while..." She patted her stomach subconsciously. "Imagine, starting over at Horatio's age."

"Oh, Edie, you're not?"

"Maybe I am, maybe I'm not. It's too early to tell." She blushed and quickly changed the subject. "He has some new business ventures to try out. He wants to sail the seven seas and all the adventurous things you can't do when there's a war or you're tied down with a business. It's a brand-new world now. It's time to reawaken old passions and discover the new journey God is calling us all on. He is calling all of us on new journeys, Piper dear."

"That's quite poetic." I smiled.

"I know." She pulled me even further aside and pushed a stack of papers into my hands. "I finished reading it."

"My manuscript?" I took it. Typed neatly on the front were the words: *MY WAR: THE REAL STORY FROM THE ONES WHO LIVED IT.*

"What's this?" I asked.

"The title. Every story needs a title."

It was definitely an 'Edie title.'

"But it is supposed to be a serial for the paper."

Her eyes stared into mine. "You asked for my honest feedback?"

A sick feeling entered my gut. But it was true; I *had* asked.

"It's not finished. It's missing something."

"What do you mean? All the interviews are included! It's just the sort of thing Don wants for a serial. I know it's good enough for the paper. I've read what he's been printing."

"I know." She said solemnly. "And yes, it is good enough for Don but not good enough for my protégé." She gently touched my cheek. "You have more talent than I knew, and I knew you were talented!"

"Then, you think I *shouldn't* let Don print it as a serial?"

She nodded.

"But this was all your idea!" I was growing increasingly frustrated and confused.

"Sometimes my first ideas are not my best." She shrugged her shoulders just an ounce.

"So… what's your *new* idea?" I cocked one eyebrow.

"There is potential here, Piper, for something really great. Something to be proud of. Something much more lasting than a few newspaper articles people will read once and throw away with the week's trash. But only if you tell the whole truth... Only if you leave nothing out."

"What do you mean?"

"You left out the most important character, Piper dear."

"Who?"

"Yourself."

My jaw dropped slightly.

"*You're* the one missing, Piper. Only you can tell your story the way it really happened. Without your voice, it's just a collection of other people's disjointed memories. You're as much a part of this," she pressed the manuscript into my hand, "as Horatio and I, as each one of your cousins."

"But it's supposed to be a collection of the soldier's memories! To tell about the war..."

"We were there too, Piper. Maybe not on the front like these boys. We were on a different front. But that does not mean it is not important. Tell the story, our story, right alongside theirs. Then you'll have something that matters. You'll have something *true*."

"But you are the storyteller, Edie!"

"Not this time." She paused. "And to be honest, there was a time when I thought I might write this one, but my inspiration has dwindled. My creativity has led me down another path. I'm thinking something dramatic and historic, set in 18th century Scotland on the moors." Her eyes took on a faraway look. Then, the moment vanished, and she steadied her eyes on my face. "It's your turn, Piper. You must pick up the baton!"

The ship's horn blasted, warning all the passengers it was time to board. She drew me in for a final embrace and then held me back, examining me at arm's length.

"Too much has happened," I protested again. "I could never get it all down."

"Don't let that head of yours get in the way of your talent. You are my niece, remember? You take after me," she shouted as she walked up the gangplank with Horatio. "There's a novelist in there, darling! Or rather, a biographer. That stack in your hands is the start of a book. A real, true, book!"

I swallowed down a pit of fear in my throat, and my mother and father came and wrapped me in their arms.

"What were you saying to Peter?" I asked.

"Let him tell you," my mother whispered.

"Nathan! Rose!" Horatio shouted. "It's time to go!"

"We'll send a wire once we get to San Francisco," my father smiled.

"Back to where we started." My mother laughed one last time. "Almost."

We watched them as they stood on the bow and waved. The boat slowly left the pier and carried them away, leaving Peter and me all alone.

The wind blew.

A gull called.

A shiver of loneliness and apprehension and a lot of other feelings I couldn't put my finger on caused my shoulders to tremble. I wanted to cry, but the tears didn't come.

Peter took my hand and stared straight ahead. I wondered if he felt the same way I did.

I don't know how long we stood there, but finally, when the boat was past the breakers and steadily growing smaller on the horizon, Peter looked down at me and stared for a moment. I could see it—he felt it too.

"How would you feel, Piper, if we did the same?"

"You mean… go back to Maine?"

"Not quite." Peter smiled. "Where we started is not the right phrase. Maybe, from where we left off?"

I stopped, stunned.

With a decidedly firm grip, he continued, "I'm going back to Boston. I'm going to finish my degree."

"But I thought... you didn't want to go back to what you were doing before?"

"If you aren't hearing God speak, you go back to the last thing he told you to do and finish it." He looked out at the sea. "Sometimes a fresh start means to start fresh in an old place. I'm going to go back to school, but I'm not going to study business."

"You're not?" I asked, wondering what was coming next.

"Nope. I'm going to go to law school."

"Law school?" My jaw dropped slightly. "Peter, this is a little left field, isn't it?"

"Something clicked when we were on Magnetic Island, and I saw those Aborigine Kids behind the fence and then again when you said that someone should have worked to change the system in Germany."

I looked at him questioningly.

"I can't change the system in Australia. I'm not Australian. It's too late to change the system in Germany. But there are parts of our system in America that have to be changed. If it's true that Native Americans were forced to speak English and taken from their homes and put into boarding schools just six years ago, what more is going on that we know nothing about? What else aren't they telling us? And don't even get me started on the Jim Crow laws in the South. We've seen what happens when things get out of hand and nobody stands up to the oppressor. Piper," he looked at me, "I'm going to learn how to change the system." His big beautiful blue eyes stared into mine.

"So, you're going to go to law school? To change... laws?"

He shrugged. "It seems like a good place to start, don't you think?"

At the moment, I wasn't sure what to think. But the idea of being back on the mainland was highly appealing.

"It won't be as exciting as living on a sailboat, catching spies and

485

traitors, and surviving enemy attacks. But... it will mean a house. Or at least an apartment."

Boston was sounding better every second.

He tried to smile and shrugged. "How about it?"

"Why not?" I offered.

"Classes, homework, writing papers, going to games." He took my hand, and we began to walk back towards the parking lot. "Could be fun, in a peaceful sort of way. It takes a lot of guts to go back to where you began... to finish what you started. But," he looked into my eyes, "I'm up for the challenge, if you are."

"To be honest," I said slowly, "an apartment with a key and a front door and my very own coffee pot and a dog-bed for Founder sounds like a paradise."

And as we walked back to the parking lot, I wondered what life would be like. Normal, everyday life without fear. Or curfews. Or sirens.

It would be wonderful.

"More like paradise than this?" He motioned towards the sea and the palm trees and the beautiful tropical flowers lining the parking lot.

I didn't need to answer.

"You don't think we'll be bored, do you?" he asked as we reached the Woody, and he opened the door on the passenger side. Sliding in, I put the manuscript on my lap.

"Maybe," I answered thoughtfully. "To start, it could take some time to get back into the swing of life without constantly having to be on the alert. It will be like waking up from a dream. A very long dream."

"*A Midsummer's Night's Dream.*" He smiled. "Certainly was hot enough these past few months."

"Funny."

He shut the door firmly, and I began to unroll my window as Peter got in the driver's seat and revved up the engine.

At that moment, two beautiful doves swooped down in front of the windshield. Their sleek, grey and tan bodies gently rode the soft island breeze. I could hear their birdsong through the open window.

Peter gripped the steering wheel and began to drive. Neither of us spoke for several minutes. Then, as we rounded a bend, he asked, "What do you think you'll do in Boston?"

"Boston," I said, tasting the word again. "*Boston.*"

"What do you think?" he repeated, glancing my direction before refocusing his eyes on the road.

"I think, we'll need to buy some sweaters. And probably a coat or two." Our little apartment was already decorated in my mind. We'd buy a desk for Peter and one for me and hang Edie's painting of the girls above the fireplace. It would be beautiful. Perfect. Small. Cozy… ours.

"I mean, what you are going to do there?"

"I, uh… I don't know," I answered suddenly. My 'manuscript' (if you could call it that) weighed heavily on my lap.

"There's always a job for good photographers, Piper. You won't have any trouble finding work." The road evened out, and we pulled onto the straight stretch before the plantation house.

"I know that." I looked back out the window as the house came into view. "I'm not sure I want to only do photography anymore though."

"Is that so?" He looked over at me, surprised.

Slowly, I nodded. "A photograph alone was enough for the last season. But, this new season needs something more." I spoke as I processed. "Maybe it is time to put some words to these pictures of mine. *My own* words. I want people to know the truth about what is happening out there." I waved vaguely to the world beyond. "I want to tell people the truth so they don't believe lies… Peter, I want to do something important. Something that *matters.*"

"Why don't you write a book?" He looked at me and smiled. "I already have the title, *She Was Content.*"

"You're kidding, aren't you?"

"Yes," he laughed, "I'm kidding... but only about the title. After everything we've been through, you probably have ten books inside you. You have a story, Piper. *We* have a story."

He pulled up to the side of the house and parked, taking the key out of the ignition. "Who knows, maybe you could take a few classes for yourself. Like some journalism classes, maybe." He chuckled and looked back at me. "Imagine that, Piper, me and you, back in school—together. We could be regular coeds."

I played along. "You could even give me your class ring to wear."

"No letterman jacket though. My sports days are over. Don't forget, I'm an old married man now."

"You are 25-years-old, Peter. I wouldn't exactly say that's an old man."

He shook his head, as though he couldn't believe it. "I think we are going to make a good team someday. I'll fight for the oppressed, and you can tell the world about it!"

"We already are a good team." I smiled and leaned over and kissed his cheek. But as I did, his words stuck. Come to think of it, we really might make a good team... a better team than I ever imagined. And I wondered if this was all a part of God's plan, and he had been leading us to this point all along.

Somehow, I just knew it was.

That's when I saw it, an enormous rainbow that seemed to frame the plantation house. I had never seen a rainbow so bright. "Look, Peter!" I pointed out the windshield. "A rainbow!"

Like a curtain between the acts of a play, it fell across the sky, separating the past from the present, and the present from the future. Like Noah, I felt God's promise that our future would be good and filled with joy rest on my heart like a seal. The war was over. We were stepping into his plan, his good and perfect plan that had not changed from the beginning of time.

And as I got out of the car, I felt my feet touch solid earth for the first time since I had first set foot on the *Grey Goose* six years before. The old season was over.

The scene was finished, to be sure, but the story was far from done.

Yes, the play had only just begun. And the next act promised to be much better than the first because that is the way it works when God is the writer.

~

So, there you have it, Samuel. Perhaps not as it happened, exactly. But as well as I could tell it.

As of writing this, your father is working as a clerk in a small firm downtown. When he is not in class or at the office, he is watching you so I can go to class. I'm nearly finished with my first semester! Only seven more to go and your mother will have a Bachelor of Arts in Journalism. If you want to tell people the truth, you have to learn how to tell them so they will hear it.

The rest of the family is carrying on. Amos and Grace are still in Europe. And yes, they are married, but it's a long story. Another book, if I'm honest.

Paul and Lorelei are not married. She is back in the British Mandate of Palestine, along with Harry and Katrine. No one knows where Paul is, but he sent Lorelei word that he will join her in Palestine before the year is out. They are still in love and definitely engaged. That is, I think they are engaged. Lorelei's ring is still at the bottom of the Townsville Harbor.

No one has heard from Frank or Dorris since they parted ways with Grace. Even though the war is over, the world is still topsy turvy, and there are many who have yet to find a place to call home.

Peter and I will not stay in Boston forever. But it is home for now, and a 'home for now' is something I will be forever grateful for. Sometimes God speaks in dreams. Sometimes in visions. He always speaks through his Word. But his leading? Usually, it is through the still, small voice.

If you spread your sails in sweet surrender, his wind will blow you exactly where you are supposed to go. When we steer against his current on the waves of doubt and fear, we will wind up beached, broken, or drowned. Let go of control and trust his leading. Though the journey may be longer than you expected, you will reach a safe harbor. He will lead you home.

And when you are mature enough to understand, you will grasp how your mother struggled and stretched to describe in words what only a life can fully portray. Hopefully, when you are old and grey, you will remember that your mother might not have been a great writer as far as writers go, but at least she had a story to tell, and she told it, and she told the truth. It is my prayer and greatest hope that it will inspire you to treasure your own story, whatever it turns out to be, and not discount it as some do. And perhaps, one day, Samuel, you will write yours as well.

ENDNOTES

Part 1 (First Movement)

1. Shakespeare, W. *A Midsummer Night's Dream*. ACT 2. SCENE 1. Retrieved June 22, 2019. http://shakespeare.mit.edu/midsummer/full.html.

2. War Bonds were issued during WWII as a way to remove cash from circulation, reduce inflation, and help finance the war effort.

3. Andrews, Evan. "How 'Tokyo Rose' Became WWII's Most Notorious Propagandist." *History.com*, A&E Television Networks, Retrieved June 22, 2019, www.history.com/news/how-tokyo-rose-became-wwiis-most-notorious-propagandist.

4. Ibid.

5."Forbidden Photos Reveal What Life In Hawaii Was Like After Pearl Harbor." *HuffPost*. Retrieved June 22, 2019. https://www.

huffpost.com/entry/hawaii-pearl-harbor-attacks-photographs_n_58462170e4b055b313990dad.

6. Herreria, Carla. "A Look Back at Hawaiian Airlines is Vintage Travel at its Best." *HuffPost.* Retrieved June 22, 2019. https://www.huffpost.com/entry/hawaiian-airlines-history_n_55ac801ce4b0d2ded39f4b65.

7. "Battle of El Alamein." *History.com.* Retrieved June 22, 2019. https://www.history.com/topics/world-war-ii/battle-of-el-alamein.

8. Berlin, Irving. "This Is The Army Mr. Jones." 1943. Berlin Irving Music Corp.

9. Arlen, Harold, and Koheler, Ted. "Stormy Weather." 1943. BMG Rights Management, S.A. Music.

10. Porter, Cole and Fletcher, Robert. *"Don't Fence Me In."* 1934.

11. "Hannah Senesh (1921 - 1944)." *Jewish Virtual Library.* Retrieved May 25, 2019. https://www.jewishvirtuallibrary.org/hannah-senesh.

12. "Jewish Proverbs: MA Weekly Newsletter - CHEMOT Jan 21 2017 23 TEVET 5777." *Maghenabraham.com.* Retrieved May 25, 2019. https://www.maghenabraham.com/?post_id=166233.

13. Vatikiotis, J.Y. "Palestine Railways and Ports, The Mandate Years." *British Empire.co.uk.* Retrieved June 22, 2019. https://www.britishempire.co.uk/article/palestinerailwaysandports.htm.

14.Johnson, Willie. "Stalin Wasn't Stalin." Performed by the Golden Gate Quartet. Recorded March 5, 1943. *History on the Net.com.* Retrieved June 22, 2019. https://www.historyonthenet.com/

authentichistory/1939-1945/3-music/08-Axis-Allies/
19430305_Stalin_Wasnt_Stallin-Golden_Gate_Quartet.html

15. Hans Hofmann was a German-American Abstract Expression-ist. He is regarded as one of the most influential artists and art teachers of the 21st century.

16. Holy Bible, New Living Translation, Romans 15:13.

17."American POWs remember life in Japanese prison camp." May 24, 2007. *Reuters.com*. Retrieved June 22, 2019. https://www.reuters.com/article/us-china-pows/american-pows-remember-life-in-japanese-prison-camp-idUSPEK37053320070525

18. "Guests of the Third Right: Americans POWs in Europe." *Guests of the Right.com*. Retrieved June 22, 2019.https://guestsofthethirdreich.org/home/

19. Entertainers Bob Hope and Myrna Loy were both known for their tireless work with the USO. To this day, they are beloved by Veterans who still remember their onstage antics that brought levity and joy to tired soldiers all over the Pacific.

Part 2 (Second Movement)

1. Shakespeare, W. *A Midsummer Night's Dream*. ACT 1. SCENE 1. Retrieved June 22, 2019. http://shakespeare.mit.edu/midsummer/full.html.

2. "The Pacific Strategy, 1941-1944." July 10, 2017. *National WW2 Musuem.org*. Retrieved June 22, 2019. https://www.nationalww2museum.org/war/articles/pacific-strategy-1941-1944.

3. "Pearl Harbor." March 13, 2019. *History.com.* Retrieved June 22, 2019. https://www.history.com/topics/world-war-ii/pearl-harbor.

4. "Code Talking: Intelligence and Bravery." *American Indian.si.edu.* Retrieved June 22, 2019. https://americanindian.si.edu/education/codetalkers/html/chapter4.html

5. "Battle of Guadalcanal." August 21, 2018. *History.com.* Retrieved June 22, 2019. https://css.history.com/topics/world-war-ii/battle-of-guadalcanal

6. Holy Bible, Psalm 14:1

7. Holy Bible, King James Version, Jonah 2:7.

8.Putz, Catherine. "An Indigenous Perspective on World War II's Solomon Islands Campaign." February 07, 2018. *The Diplomat.com.* Retrieved June 22, 2019. https://thediplomat.com/2018/02/an-indigenous-perspective-on-world-war-iis-solomon-islands-campaign/

9. "Malaria in World War II." *Army Heritage.org.* Retrieved June 22, 2019. https://www.armyheritage.org/75-information/soldier-stories/292-malaria-in-world-war-ii

10. Douglas, Lloyd C. *The Robe.* Magdalen Press. iBooks. Retrieved June 22, 2019.

11. Douglas, Lloyd C. *The Robe.* Magdalen Press. iBooks. Retrieved June 22, 2019.

12. Douglas, Lloyd C. *The Robe.* Magdalen Press. iBooks. Retrieved June 22, 2019.

Part 3 (Third Movement)

1. Shakespeare, W. *A Midsummer Night's Dream*. ACT 1. SCENE 1. Retrieved June 22, 2019. http://shakespeare.mit.edu/midsummer/full.html.

2. Holy Bible, Romans 5:3-4

3. Brown, Lew; Tobias, Charles; Stept, Sam. "Don't Sit Under the Apple Tree (With Anyone Else but Me)." 1944. Sony/ATV Publishing. Memory Lane Music Group.

4. Ibid.

5. Shakespeare, W. *A Midsummer Night's Dream*. ACT 5. SCENE 1. Retrieved June 22, 2019. http://shakespeare.mit.edu/midsummer/full.html.

6. Ibid.

7. Ibid.

8. Ibid.

9. Ibid.

10. Ibid.

11. Ibid.

12. Brown, Lew; Tobias, Charles; Stept, Sam. "Don't Sit Under the Apple Tree (With Anyone Else but Me)." 1944. Sony/ATV Publishing. Memory Lane Music Group.

13. Ibid.

14. Holy Bible, Habakkuk 2:3.

15. "The Stolen Generations: The Forcible Removal of Indigenous Children from their Families." *Australians Together.org.au*. Retrieved June 22, 2019. https://australianstogether.org.au/discover/australian-history/stolen-generations
In the United States, Canada, and Australia, indigenous children were forcibly removed from their families and placed into boarding schools, foster care, or adopted out in order to remove them from their native culture under racist legislation that viewed indigenous culture as inferior to white culture. In the United States, this practice ended in 1948. In Australia, the practice ended in 1970. Children removed from their families are known as the Lost Generations.

16. Holy Bible, John 16:33.

17. "Lassie Come Home." Dir. Fred M. WIlcox. Written by Hugo Butler and Eric Knight. 1943. *IMBD.com*. Retrieved June 22, 2019. https://www.imdb.com/title/tt0036098/

18. "Girl Crazy." Dir. Norman Taurog and Busby Berkely. Written by Fred. F. Finklehoffe. 1943.*IMBD.com*. Retrieved June 22, 2019. https://www.imdb.com/title/tt0035942/?ref_=fn_al_tt_1

19. "Battle of the Bulge." June 7, 2019. *History.com*. Retrieved June 22, 2019. https://www.history.com/this-day-in-history/battle-of-the-bulge

20. Holy Bible, English Standard Version, Matthew 7:7.

22. "Battle of Saipan." August 21, 2018. *History.com.* Retrieved June 22, 2019. https://www.history.com/topics/world-war-ii/battle-of-saipan

Part 4 (Fourth Movement)

1.Shakespeare, W. *A Midsummer Night's Dream.* ACT 1. SCENE 1. Retrieved June 22, 2019. http://shakespeare.mit.edu/midsummer/full.html.

2. Holy Bible, New International Version, Hebrews 11:6.

3. Holy Bible, New International Version, Romans 10:9.

4. Bluhm, Raymond K. "Battle of Corregidor: World War II." *Brittanica.com.* Retrieved June 22, 2019. https://www.britannica.com/event/Battle-of-Corregidor

5. Shakespeare, W. *A Midsummer Night's Dream.* ACT 3. SCENE 1. Retrieved June 22, 2019. http://shakespeare.mit.edu/midsummer/full.html.

6. Ibid.

7. Shakespeare, W. *A Midsummer Night's Dream.* ACT 3. SCENE 2. Retrieved June 22, 2019. http://shakespeare.mit.edu/midsummer/full.html.

8. Shakespeare, W. *A Midsummer Night's Dream.* ACT 1. SCENE 1. Retrieved June 22, 2019. http://shakespeare.mit.edu/midsummer/full.html.

9. "Battle of Manila in World War II." *Facts and Details.com.* Retrieved June 22, 2019. http://factsanddetails.com/asian/ca67/sub428/entry-5337.html

10. The raid on Townsville occured in 1942, not 1945.

11. Klein, Christopher. "Attack of Japan's Killer WWII Balloons, 70 Years Ago." August 29, 2018. *History.com.* Retrieved June 22, 2019.   https://www.history.com/news/attack-of-japans-killer-wwii-balloons-70-years-ago

12. Brown, Lew; Tobias, Charles; Stept, Sam. "Don't Sit Under the Apple Tree (With Anyone Else but Me)." 1944. Sony/ATV Publishing. Memory Lane Music Group.

13. Ibid.

14. Ibid.

15. Adapted from Septimus, Renee, S. "Renewing the Marital Promise: Reyim Ahuvim." *RitualWell.* Adaptation. Retrieved June 22, 2019.   https://ritualwell.org/ritual/renewing-marital-promise-reyim-ahuvim

16. Ibid.

17. Ibid.

18. Ibid.

BIBLIOGRAPHY

"American POWs remember life in Japanese prison camp." *Reuters.com*, May 24, 2007.https://www.reuters.com/article/us-china-pows/american-pows-remember-life-in-japanese-prison-camp-idUSPEK37053320070525 Retrieved June 22, 2019.

Andrews, Evan. "How 'Tokyo Rose' Became WWII's Most Notorious Propagandist." *History.com*, A&E Television Networks. www.history.com/news/how-tokyo-rose-became-wwiis-most-notorious-propagandist. Retrieved June 22, 2019.

Arlen, Harold, and Koheler, Ted. "Stormy Weather." 1943. BMG Rights Management, S.A. Music.

"Battle of El Alamein." *History.com*. https://www.history.com/topics/world-war-ii/battle-of-el-alamein. Retrieved June 22, 2019.

"Battle of Guadalcanal." August 21, 2018. *History.com*. https://css.history.com/topics/world-war-ii/battle-of-guadalcanal. Retrieved June 22, 2019.

"Battle of the Bulge." *History.com*, June 7, 2019. https://www.history.com/this-day-in-history/battle-of-the-bulge. Retrieved June 22, 2019.

"Battle of Manila in World War II." *Facts and Details.com*. http://factsanddetails.com/asian/ca67/sub428/entry-5337.html. Retrieved June 22, 2019.

"Battle of Saipan." *History.com*, August 21, 2018.https://www.history.com/topics/world-war-ii/battle-of-saipan. Retrieved June 22, 2019.

Berlin, Irving. "This Is The Army Mr. Jones." 1943. Berlin Irving Music Corp.

Bluhm, Raymond K. "Battle of Corregidor: World War II." *Brittanica.com*. https://www.britannica.com/event/Battle-of-Corregidor. Retrieved June 22, 2019.

Brown, Lew; Tobias, Charles; Stept, Sam. "Don't Sit Under the Apple Tree (With Anyone Else but Me)." 1944. Sony/ATV Publishing. Memory Lane Music Group.

"Code Talking: Intelligence and Bravery." *American Indian.si.edu*. https://americanindian.si.edu/education/codetalkers/html/chapter4.html. Retrieved June 22, 2019.

Douglas, Lloyd C. *The Robe*. Magdalen Press. iBooks. Retrieved June 22, 2019.

"Forbidden Photos Reveal What Life In Hawaii Was Like After Pearl Harbor." *HuffPost*. https://www.huffpost.com/entry/hawaii-pearl-harbor-attacks-photographs_n_58462170e4b055b313990dad. Retrieved June 22, 2019.

"Girl Crazy." Dir. Norman Taurog and Busby Berkely. Written by Fred. F. Finklehoffe. 1943.*IMBD.com*. https://www.imdb.com/title/tt0035942/?ref_=fn_al_tt_1. Retrieved June 22, 2019.

"Guests of the Third Right: Americans POWs in Europe." *Guests of the Right.com*. https://guestsofthethirdreich.org/home/. Retrieved June 22, 2019.

"Hannah Senesh (1921 - 1944)." *Jewish Virtual Library*. https://www.jewishvirtuallibrary.org/hannah-senesh. Retrieved May 25, 2019.

Herreria, Carla. "A Look Back at Hawaiian Airlines is Vintage Travel at its Best." *HuffPost*. https://www.huffpost.com/entry/hawaiian-airlines-history_n_55ac801ce4b0d2ded39f4b65. Retrieved June 22, 2019.

"Jewish Proverbs: MA Weekly Newsletter - CHEMOT Jan 21 2017 23 TEVET 5777." *Maghenabraham.com*. https://www.maghenabraham.com/?post_id=166233. Retrieved May 25, 2019.

Johnson, Willie. "Stalin Wasn't Stalin." Performed by the Golden Gate Quartet. Recorded March 5, 1943. *History on the Net.com*. https://www.historyonthenet.com/authentichistory/1939-1945/3-music/08-Axis-Allies/19430305_Stalin_Wasnt_Stallin-Golden_Gate_Quartet.html. Retrieved June 22, 2019.

Klein, Christopher. "Attack of Japan's Killer WWII Balloons, 70 Years Ago." *History.com*, August 29, 2018. https://www.history.com/news/attack-of-japans-killer-wwii-balloons-70-years-ago. Retrieved June 22, 2019.

"Lassie Come Home." Dir. Fred M. WIlcox. Written by Hugo Butler and Eric Knight. 1943. *IMBD.com*. https://www.imdb.com/title/tt0036098/. Retrieved June 22, 2019.

"Malaria in World War II." *Army Heritage.org.* My Book. Retrieved June 22, 2019.

"Pearl Harbor." *History.com,* March 13, 2019. https://www.history.com/topics/world-war-ii/pearl-harbor. Retrieved June 22, 2019.

Porter, Cole and Fletcher, Robert. *"Don't Fence Me In."* 1934.

Putz, Catherine. "An Indigenous Perspective on World War II's Solomon Islands Campaign." *The Diplomat.com,* February 07, 2018. https://thediplomat.com/2018/02/an-indigenous-perspective-on-world-war-iis-solomon-islands-campaign/. Retrieved June 22, 2019.

Septimus, Renee, S. "Renewing the Marital Promise: Reyim Ahuvim." *RitualWell.* Adaptation. https://ritualwell.org/ritual/renewing-marital-promise-reyim-ahuvim. Retrieved June 22, 2019.

Shakespeare, W. *A Midsummer Night's Dream.* http://shakespeare.mit.edu/midsummer/full.html. Retrieved June 22, 2019.

"The Pacific Strategy, 1941-1944." July 10, 2017. *National WW2 Musuem.org.* https://www.nationalww2museum.org/war/articles/pacific-strategy-1941-1944. Retrieved June 22, 2019.

"The Stolen Generations: The Forcible Removal of Indgenous Children from their Families." *Australians Together.org.au.* https://australianstogether.org.au/discover/australian-history/stolen-generations. Retrieved June 22, 2019.

Vatikiotis, J.Y. "Palestine Railways and Ports, The Mandate Years." *British Empire.co.uk.* https://www.britishempire.co.uk/article/palestinerailwaysandports.htm. Retrieved June 22, 2019.

FAITH-BASED HISTORICAL FICTION FOR THE TWEEN, TEEN, AND FUN-LOVING ADULT!

*The
Seabirds*

TRILOGY

MEET THE GREY GOOSE GANG AND SET OUT ON THE WWII ADVENTURE OF A LIFETIME THAT WILL CHALLENGE, INSPIRE, AND ENCOURAGE READERS!

CURIOUS ABOUT PIPER'S FIRST JOB AS THE GIRL REPORTER? NOW'S YOUR CHANCE TO FIND OUT WITH THESE BELOVED NANCY DREW STYLE MYSTERIES SET BETWEEN VOYAGE OF THE SANDPIPER AND FLIGHT OF THE SEAHAWKS!

**GIRL
REPORTER**

THE
COLUMBA
DIARIES

PICKING UP WHERE THE SEABIRDS TRILOGY LEFT OFF, THE COLUMBA DIARIES FOLLOWS THE GREY GOOSE GANG ON NEW ADVENTURES SORTING THROUGH THE AFTERMATH OF THE HOLOCAUST AS THE WORLD SPINS TOWARDS THE COLD WAR.

The Seabirds Companion Curriculum

To Order Visit Amazon.com and Hopehousepress.co

The Seabirds Trilogy World War II Companion Curriculum is a 36 week comprehensive high school level history, social studies, spiritual growth, and college research writing prep curriculum. Your student will learn about the greatest conflict in human history through story, the testimony of those who survived, and award-winning films and documentaries. Along the way, they will sharpen their critical-thinking skills, grow spiritually, and learn how to write a college level historical research paper. Students will dive deep into the years leading up to the war and the war itself by experiencing it through those who lived it. Included are articles by authors like C.S. Lewis and Emile Zola, tutorials and clips of specific events during the war, music by Mendelssohn and the Andrew Sisters, original recordings by Roosevelt and Churchill, and memoirs by Corrie ten Boom and other heroes.

ABOUT THE AUTHOR

Jessica Glasner is an author and screenwriter. Young and old alike agree that her lively characters, colorful settings, and laugh-out-loud vignettes display the goodness of God in the darkest moments of the past. Known for instilling hope, faith, and godly values through page-turning stories inspiring tears and laughter, her books are those that are read over and over.

For more adventures with Piper and the gang, check out Jessica Glasner's other stories on Amazon and Barnes and Noble.com.

facebook.com/jesskateglasner

instagram.com/jesskateglasner

Made in the USA
Columbia, SC
28 November 2021

49863319R00307